WARRIOR FROM AVALON

Copyright © 2020 Henry Michael Kincaid

All rights reserved. No part of this publication may be reproduced, or transmitted in any form or by any means, including photocopying, recording, or other electronic or mechanical methods, without the prior written permission of the publisher, except in the case of brief quotations embodied in critical reviews and certain other noncommercial uses permitted by copyright law. For permission requests, write to the publisher addressed "Attention: Permissions Coordinator," at the address below

ISBN: 978-1-7355229-1-3 Paperback
ISBN: 978-1-7355229-0-6 Hardback
ISBN: 978-1-7355229-3-7 Ebook

Library of Congress Control Number: TXu 2-219-577

Any references to historical events, real people, or real places are used fictitiously. Names, characters, and places are products of the author's imagination

Front cover image by Michael Corvin
Book design by Henry Michael Kincaid and Michael Corvin

Printed by Lulu.com in the United States of America

First printing edition 2020.

Henry Michael Kincaid
P.O. Box 331
Holly Springs, Ga 30142

www.warriorfromavalon.com

1

WARRIOR FROM AVALON

*The angel of the LORD appeared to him and said to him,
"The LORD is with you, O valiant warrior."*
  - Judges 6:12

WARRIOR FROM AVALON
By Henry Michael Kincaid

PROLOGUE

The Dark ages were not always shrouded in mystery. Once it was the age of peace and prosperity. Long before, superior beings ruled the world of man. These beings became known as the Olympians. Mankind viewed them as gods and waged wars in their names, fighting to appease their superior rulers in attempts to gain their favors and blessings. For the longest time, this was simply a way of life. However, when the most powerful of the Olympians, Zeus, found himself in love with a mortal woman, Alcmene, he decided to bring the rule of the gods to an end.

Out of sympathy and pity for humanity, Zeus could see the error in their ways and wanted to leave the world of man with the chance to mature on their own. The other gods agreed out of respect and stood aside as promised. Never again would they tamper in human affairs. For a brief time, the world saw a glimpse of true peace. Unfortunately, it did not last long. Hades, the god of the Underworld, hated humanity and told Zeus that they were meant to be ruled. He felt that man was insignificant and destructive in their ways. Hades felt it was only a matter of time before they showed their true nature, but Zeus was adamant in his decision. Hades' fury with the other gods and his disgust for mankind led him to unleash his forces on the world with no concern for the consequences.

The Olympians warned Hades to end his quest, but their words fell on deaf ears. Zeus forbade the others to interfere with Hades, hoping he would come to his senses, but he was determined. With the Olympians ignoring the cries of man, Hades pressed onwards. He felt nothing could stop him and his Ash demons from destroying everything. Hope seemed to be lost until a single brave knight made a vow to Zeus. If he would destroy the beast that plagued the world, he would return any favor Zeus asked of him. Zeus accepted the vow of the knight and told him that he would not destroy his own brother, but instead imprison him, and lock him away far from the reaches of man.

The knight reluctantly agreed, but it was the only choice and a bargain was sealed. Zeus and the other Olympians used what power and influence they could to hide all evidence of Hades' atrocities from the rest of the world, but unfortunately it was too late. The damage had already been done as the corruption of man had begun. They soon began to fight over land and power. Chaos had been unleashed upon the world as Hades had left his mark, bringing about the beginning of the age of death, the age of destruction, and the age of darkness.

CHAPTER ONE

  Sir Bedivere paced back and forth in front of his tent. He saw a vast army before him as he looked across the field only a couple of miles away. They had been camped out for the day with nothing to do but glare back and forth at each other, wondering which side would attack first. Sir Bedivere stopped in his tracks as Arthur walked up behind him.

  "Relax." Arthur spoke. "No one over there wants to spill your blood any more than you want to spill theirs."

  "Arthur, where have you been?" Bedivere asked. "The men are getting nervous."

  "I needed some time to clear my head."

  "What's happening then, why are we here?"

  "I plan to meet with Mordred, unarmed, and alone." A look of shock washed over Bediveres' face.

  "Forgive me my King, but that is a bit…. reckless don't you think?"

  "If we want to negotiate peace with him, we have to show him that we have no intention to fight him."

  "Why must we do it this way? Mordred isn't exactly known for his patience or honor."

  "I'm well aware of his character."

  "What if he attacks you? We should at least be ready."

  "No man here is to draw a weapon for any reason. If Mordred sees anyone with a sword in hand it could jeopardize everything we've fought for."

  "I don't like this. You're putting your trust in a man whose mission in life has been to kill you. He will not miss an opportunity to…"

  "Have faith my friend." Arthur interrupted. "Now if things do happen to go wrong while I'm down there give the order to attack and have no mercy. Until then you will not draw your swords. Is that understood?"

"I understand Sir, but…"

"Your concerns are noted and appreciated." Arthur interrupted again. "Now, have you seen Merlin?"

"He said he was going for a walk and that he'd return soon."

"I'd like you to go and find him please. I'd seek his council before we begin."

"Yes sir."

Sir Bedivere turned and ran in search of Merlin as Arthur continued to gaze across the wide-open field at the army of men on the other side. He had an uneasy feeling in his stomach, one that he couldn't explain. He had seen many battles in his lifetime, but this one had a different feeling all together. Arthur knew what lay ahead for him, but he wasn't about to give up all hope just yet.

"Dear God above." He said silently. "I dare not question your intentions, but if there is no other way to resolve this conflict then I ask that you show mercy to the brave men on both sides of this ridiculous war. May they all forgive me for my actions that led them here and may they each find peace beyond this world."

Meanwhile in the forest miles away, Merlin walked along a narrow path up a slope. He had the appearance of a man of at least fifty years of age, but he was thousands of years older than that. He sported a long white beard that reached passed his chest and his clothing was slightly worn with tares on the sleeves. As he reached the top of a hill, he stopped to check his surroundings. He could see nothing but the wooded forest around him, but he knew better than to believe he was alone.

"Have you been following me my dear?" Merlin asked.

Then a beautiful young woman appeared out of thin air as she stepped toward Merlin, yet she remained transparent as if she were only there in a spirit form. Her name was Nimue, Merlin's apprentice, and closest friend for many years. Nimue was also known by another name, the Lady of the Lake. It was a nickname given to her by the Queens of Avalon. Nimue always enjoyed being around water and even had Merlin help her build a home under one of her favorite lakes. Occasionally she could even be found dancing atop the water as if she were standing on solid ground.

"Why would I need to follow you when I already knew where you would be?" She asked playfully.

"That is very true." He said with a smile.

Merlin stepped toward her with an outstretched hand as she extended hers and yet their fingers simply passed through one another. Then they began walking through the forest side by side.

"I should have known you would want to be here for my send-off." Merlin said. "Well, I mean in your own way of course."

"It will be a long time before we see each other again." Nimue responded. "I wanted to be here in whatever form I could."

"It's the thought that counts. I assume everything has gone according to plan?"

"So far. Everything is in motion, just as it is meant to be."

"There are no do-overs. We only get one chance at this."

"I assure you Merlin. We've planned everything to the finest detail. There is nothing more we can do here now. It's time you rest and let me do my part."

"Very well."

"It has been an honor."

"The honor is mine my dear."

After walking a short distance, they stopped at a large tree with a wide trunk.

"I have always loved our walks together." Merlin said. "I will miss them."

"As will I."

Merlin stared at the trunk of the tree as if he were waiting for something to happen.

"If only there was another way…"

"Merlin, this is the moment we have been preparing for, there is nothing more we can do here now but I promise, Arthur will be cared for along with the other."

A crack of pure light began to move up and down the trunk of the tree. Merlin stared at the light as if he were slightly afraid, but he wasn't surprised by it at all and rather expected it.

"I know that this is necessary, I only wish we had more time." Merlin said.

"As do I." Nimue responded. "You know as well as I do this is how it has to be done. They are going to need your help, and this is the only way I can ensure you survive long enough."

"I suppose I could use the beauty sleep." He said with a chuckle.

The trunk opened all the way as Merlin stepped toward it. Nothing could be seen in the interior aside from the light shining brightly. Nimue watched Merlin as he stepped completely inside the trunk of the tree and turned to face her.

"It's on your shoulders now." He said. "Keep them hidden. Keep them safe. The world will need them both if it is to survive what's coming."

"I will my friend." She nodded.

"Goodbye my dear." He said as the trunk of the tree closed tightly sealing him inside. Nimue lifted her hand as if to press it against the tree and a tear rolled down her cheek.

WARRIOR FROM AVALON

"Goodbye Merlin. May the time go quickly for us both." She said as she dropped her hand and walked away fading out of sight once again.

Back at the campsite Arthur sat on his horse wearing his armor as Sir Bedivere ran toward him. Lancelot, Arthurs' closest friend and greatest knight stood next to him.

"I couldn't find Merlin." Sir Bedivere said jogging up behind them.

"Then he's already gone." Arthur muttered under his breath. "I don't have a choice then. It's time."

"What shall we do?" Lancelot asked.

"Keep things calm until I return. Remember to keep your swords sheathed or this will all be for nothing."

Arthurs' horse moved forward down the hill as Sir Bedivere stepped back toward Lancelot. Across the field Mordred, who was also in full armor, rode down the hill as well. As they moved closer to one another the horses slowed to a stop until they were only a few feet from each other.

"I see that you came down here alone." Mordred spoke.

"As I promised." Arthur replied.

"Unarmed?"

"You know I am, as part of our agreement."

"I have to admit, this isn't an intelligent move for you. Given our history, I'm surprised you'd trust me."

"My actions are proof that I do not wish violence on you. I'm a man of my word. Question is what are your intentions?"

"Speak your terms Arthur."

"I want peace."

"Why should peace interest me?"

"I'm tired of the fighting Mordred. We've both seen too much bloodshed in our own lifetimes. The stain left by

Hades came at a high cost. This hatred between us needs to end. Too many people have suffered from our rivalry long enough already."

"I could care less about your losses and even less about the people. I want what is owed to me!"

"What's owed to you?" Arthur asked rhetorically.

"I was born to be King!" Mordred responded. "It is my birthright and you stole it from me!"

"I stole nothing from you."

"Surrender your land and Kingship to me and consider this rivalry buried and your life spared."

"There's more to being a King than just title."

"It is power. Do you not understand how it feels to hold yourself so high above all others?"

"A true King isn't served by the people but serves. A true King fights for his kingdom and will die to protect its citizens, namely from unjust dictators like yourself."

"You speak of peace, yet you insult me?"

"You insult the very air you breathe. You think yourself above all others, that you're better than anyone else by being who you are."

"I was born to be better. To rule overall. It was my destiny!"

"Destiny is just the destination itself, but the path we take to get there is our choice. I will not allow you to continue to kill just to satisfy your lust for power."

"You think you can stop me?"

"We have all suffered a great loss because of Hades and his army. We have to do better now so that the world doesn't fall any further into chaos." Arthur froze for a moment as an image of Guinevere entered his mind. "We have already lost too much." Arthur said fighting back his emotions. "We have to at least try to come to terms or this was truly all for nothing."

Back on the hill Sir Bedivere and Lancelot watched with caution as the two Kings talked down below.

WARRIOR FROM AVALON

"How do you think it's going?" Sir Bedivere asked.

"In circles." Lancelot answered.

Just a few feet away a large man sat with his back against a barrel. He scratched at his thick beard as he glanced down at his ankle and noticed something moving. The large man's eyes widened at the sudden movement after it let out a soft hiss revealing itself to be a snake. He winced in fear as the snake slowly began to crawl up his leg. Sir Bedivere glanced over to see the man reaching for a sword that had been lying beside him in its sheath.

"NO!" Sir Bedivere screamed.

It was too late; the man had grabbed the sword and made a mighty roar as he cut the snakes head off before he realized what he had just done. On the field below Mordred spotted the glare as the sunlight reflected off the sword. Arthur turned to see what had caught Mordred's attention. The only words that he could muster from his mouth were…

"Oh bugger."

Mordred bumped his horse into Arthurs', knocking both the horse and Arthur to the ground. Arthurs' horse stood without its rider and galloped away.

"You tried to distract me is that it?"

"It's just a simple mistake!" Arthur pleaded. "We still have time Mordred! No one has to die here today!"

"I'll have your head hanging at the entrance to your own kingdom. Everyone will know how you failed before their new King!"

"This is our last chance Mordred! Our destinies will be forged on this battlefield."

Mordred wasn't listening anymore. He shouted to his men an attack order and they charged toward the opposing enemy. Arthur ran from Mordred who pursued him while on horseback. Sir Bedivere ran through the camp screaming at the top of his lungs.

"Prepare for combat!"

WARRIOR FROM AVALON

Lancelot had grabbed Arthurs' sword and rushed to get it to him as fast as possible. Mordred drew a sword he had hidden behind him and swung at Arthur who immediately dropped down to dodge the strike. Arthur then rolled out of the way as Mordred attempted to trample him with his horse.

Arthur leapt to his feet as Lancelot gave Excalibur a strong toss. He caught the sword effortlessly and immediately unsheathed it. His knights ran down the hill charging toward the enemy directly ahead. The battle intensified as men from both sides dropped dead one right after the other.

Arthur guarded himself with his sword as a man attempted to stab him. He shoved the blade of Excalibur into the soldiers' chest and quickly pulled it back out again to guard against another. Mordred swung his sword left and right until he finally jumped down from his horse laughing with bloodlust as he killed every man who dare came close to him. Arthur slashed and stabbed at men all around him. Just as an enemy soldier was about to stab him in the back, he was stabbed instead from a sword that seemed to have come out of nowhere.

Arthur watched as the man fell to the ground with the blade of the sword protruding from his chest. Lancelot reached down and pulled the sword out holding it up to defend against any other that came along.

"Thank you, Lancelot." Arthur said. "I almost missed that one."

"No thanks necessary old friend. I'll not let you die before me." Lancelot shouted back with a smile.

The two men put their backs together as they fought off the enemy soldiers, rushing at them wave after wave. The sun sank below the ocean beside them as the battle between both armies lasted through the evening and long into the night. Mordred didn't have a drop of his own blood on him as he continued to kill Arthurs' knights one by one.

WARRIOR FROM AVALON

Finally, Arthur and Lancelot found themselves outnumbered ten to two.

Across the field only thirty yards away Sir Bedivere killed one last soldier in his proximity. He turned to see Arthur and Lancelot fighting every man around them and raced to them as fast as he could. Lancelot stabbed one man in front of him and then used the enemy's sword to stab the man behind him. Arthur slashed another and then another until he and Lancelot were the only two men left standing amongst the dead.

Both men were exhausted and took as much air into their lungs as they could hold. Arthur and Lancelot turned to one another; swords still stretched out. They gazed upon the countless bodies that lay before them. Arthurs' eyes were full of sweat and tears. His emotions were scattered like the dead before him. So much loss, and yet he felt hope that maybe this wasn't his time after all. Just maybe, there would be another way.

"Arthur!" Sir Bedivere called out.

Arthur and Lancelot searched for the voice that called to them.

"It's Sir Bedivere!" Lancelot shouted with joy. "Arthur, he's alive."

"Only for a moment!" Mordred spoke appearing out of nowhere as he quickly shoved the blade of his sword into Lancelot's back.

"NO!" Arthur screamed as he slammed his fist into Mordred's face sending him to the ground.

"Lancelot!" Arthur cried out reaching down to his fallen comrade. "Don't you dare!"

Mordred returned to his feet and laughed at the dying man in Arthurs' arms.

"Fool." Mordred said. "Did you really believe peace was possible Arthur? Did you honestly think the two of us could co-exist at all? My agenda was war from the beginning. It's always been my greatest purpose in life to take everything you ever had or destroy it. Hades may be gone, but he left a void that must be filled, and I will not allow someone as weak as you to rule what was always meant to be mine."

Arthur ignored the words of Mordred as he turned his attention to Lancelot.

"You finish it." Lancelot spoke as blood erupted from his mouth.

"Lancelot, I'm so sorry for this. Please forgive me."

"Dying in your service has been the greatest honor I could have had. No forgiveness needed."

"It was my honor, Sir Lancelot."

"No worries, you will be joining him again." Mordred said.

Arthur watched as the life faded from Lancelot's eyes. His rapid breathing began to slow and in his final moment, he looked to Arthur one last time.

"End him."

Arthur gently lay Lancelot's head on the ground and stood tall glaring in anger at Mordred. He held Excalibur tight in his hand and guarded himself as Mordred began to attack furiously. Sir Bedivere was only feet away when Arthur shouted out to him.

"Stay back!"

Mordred struck swiftly but Arthur managed to block every swing. The fight between the two men lasted for an entire hour until both men were pouring with sweat and could barely lift their own swords. Arthur shoved Mordred with as much force as he could muster, sending him face-first into the dirt. Just as he was about to shove his sword down into Mordred's back, he turned and threw dirt into Arthurs' eyes. Arthur stumbled backward as Mordred quickly jumped to his feet and slammed his sword downwards as hard as he could into the top of Arthurs' helmet, sending a sharp piece of metal into his skull.

WARRIOR FROM AVALON

The pain was incredible, and Arthur was barely able to stand. Mordred then shoved his sword into Arthurs' stomach knocking him off balance even further causing him to stumble backward until he finally fell to his knees. Mordred looked down at Arthur, feeling an overwhelming sense of pride. Their eyes met for a moment until Arthur could hold himself up no longer and fell forward into the mud and blood.

"Don't worry about your Kingdom. I'll rule it with pride...Brother."

Mordred turned away and returned his sword to its sheath. It took all the strength he had to stand on his own, but just as he had walked a few feet away he paused in his stride. He suddenly felt the sharpest pain he had ever felt in his upper back.

"It didn't have to be this way!" Arthur struggled to say as he jammed the blade against Mordred's back again. Mordred fell to the ground in shock. The moment felt like forever to Arthur as he struggled not only from the enormous pain he was in physically, but with the thought of taking the life of his own Brother. It was something he had known was inevitable and could not be avoided. Arthur held Excalibur tightly and shoved it into Mordred's back once more with force, twisting it, ensuring that he would not be getting back up ever again.

"God have mercy on your soul, and mine." He said softly pulling his sword from Mordred's lifeless body. Arthur used every ounce of strength he could muster to stand to his feet.

Sir Bedivere hadn't been far away during the entire fight. He had to restrain himself on multiple occasions not to interfere. He grabbed Arthurs' arm and helped him move away from the battlefield. They walked silently through a wooded area toward a cliff. Arthur pointed to a path leading down to a sandy beach overlooking the ocean. Sir

Bedivere helped Arthur sit down where he could rest in the sand.

"Arthur, what can I do?" Sir Bedivere asked. "How do I help you?"

"I'm not going to last long here." Arthur said blinking rapidly as his vision began to fail him.

"What are you talking about? I thought it was impossible to…."

"I have to ask you one last request." Arthur interrupted.

"I don't understand. What do you need?"

"Take Excalibur to the nearest lake." Arthur said as he handed Bedivere the sword.

"What am I to do with it?"

"Throw it in."

"Arthur, why?"

"Listen to me. Excalibur will be protected until the time comes when it can be reclaimed. Until then, it cannot fall into the hands of any other."

"But Arthur."

"Do it Bedivere! This is important. Trust me as you always have."

"Of course, my King, I will do as you ask."

"Go now. Quickly."

"I'll be back for you soon." Sir Bedivere said as he jumped to his feet and moved away from the beach.

Arthur watched as his last Knight moved far away until he was no longer in sight.

"I'm afraid I won't be here my friend." He said softly as he looked out toward the ocean.

The wind blew gently against Arthurs' face drawing his attention toward the rising sun. In the distant horizon he could see white sales on a large ship. Using every bit of strength he had left, Arthur stood up and made his way to the water until he stood waste deep. As the ship grew closer, he could see three giant female figures at least ten feet in height, all dressed in white with gold headbands standing on the deck. Each one was transparent, being there only in a spirit form.

"The time has come Sir Arthur." A feminine voice whispered lightly into Arthurs' ear. He could suddenly feel himself being lifted from the water. As the ship approached, he was elevated from the ocean and gently placed on the deck before the three women. From a distance, standing at the edge of the cliff above Nimue watched as Arthur and the ship moved away from the beach. Right before her eyes the ship began to fade into the morning sunlight.

"Peace be upon you now King Arthur." Nimue said. "Go rest and prepare. This battle was nothing compared to the war that is yet to come."

Once the ship and its occupants had completely disappeared Nimue herself turned away and vanished into the wind.

CHAPTER TWO

Parker Wallace woke to find his alarm clock blinking 12:00 a.m. repeatedly. He quickly reached for the watch he had lying on a milk-crate that also doubled as his nightstand. His watch read 8:20 a.m.

"Oh crap." He said as he scrambled out of bed. "I'm gonna be late!"

He quickly dressed in his casual clothing, which consisted of a pair of blue jeans and a gray t-shirt then tossed his security uniform into a duffel bag. After checking his small apartment for anything he might have forgotten he headed for the door.

"Keys!" He reminded himself.

He walked back to the counter in the small space that was the kitchen to search for his keys. The apartment Parker lived in was a small studio. He lived on his own aside from his dog, a brown Labrador pit-Mix named Butch, so he didn't exactly require a lot of space.

The apartment was cheap, which is why he moved into it in the first place. He didn't make an enormous amount of money, but it was enough to support himself and his dog. Parker grabbed his keys from under a pizza box he had left on the counter overnight. He grabbed one of the four slices still left in the box and tossed it into the dog bowl. Butch who had been following Parker back and forth through the apartment whimpered as he sniffed the leftover slice that now occupied his doggy dish.

"Sorry buddy, I don't have time to make breakfast." Parker said as he knelt down to Butch and patted him on the head. "I promise you later on, chopped steak and some scrambled eggs. How does that sound?"

Butch replied by wagging his tail and licking Parkers' face.

"Oh, that's nasty." He said laughing. "Okay good boy, I've gotta go."

WARRIOR FROM AVALON

After leaving the apartment Parker jogged down the two flights of stairs to the parking lot where his truck was. The truck was the only other thing Parker devoted his paycheck to. It was an old pick up he had managed to acquire only a few months prior. It wasn't the most impressive truck, but it beat taking the bus to work every day like he'd done in the past couple of years.

The weather had been somewhat rainy, so Parker quickly climbed into the truck and after a few attempts he managed to switch on the ignition. The radio immediately came on and broadcasted the weather.

"…Rain was unexpected and baffled local meteorologists who were unable to predict the bizarre occurrence at such short notice. It is still unknown at this time how this weather pattern formed so quickly but we advise all drivers to be extremely cautious, as this strange storm is showing signs it could intensify throughout the day."

Parker switched off the radio as he backed out of his parking space and began his trip to work. After a short ride through the pouring rain he pulled into the parking lot of the local mall. He grabbed his duffel bag and jogged into the building headed for the nearest bathroom where he quickly changed into his security uniform. He stepped over the nearest sink and washed his face while taking a glance at his own reflection in the mirror. He simply brushed off his feelings of self-pity and made his way to the bathroom exit.

"Another day in paradise." He thought to himself.

Minutes later Parker entered the security booth to find his boss Jim Lloyd and a female guard waiting with an unpleasant look on both of their faces. He placed his duffel bag containing his casual clothing in a locker before he could muster up the courage to make eye contact with either of them.

"Our shift starts at 9:00 a.m. sharp." Lloyd spoke. "It's 9:15."

"I'm sorry sir." Parker responded. "The power must have gone out last night. It knocked out my alarm and…"

"I didn't ask for one of your sorry excuses." Lloyd said in irritation.

"It was a mistake; it won't happen again Sir."

"Honestly, I could care less if you're here or not, but since you decided to show up today why don't you just get to work. I'll have a write up ready before you leave this afternoon."

Lloyd exited the security room leaving Parker standing in front of the monitors displaying images of the shops inside the mall. The female guard moved over to stand beside him.

"It must be a gift." She said.

"What?"

"Being able to make someone so angry that easy."

"It's not hard to do actually." Parker replied. "He hasn't liked me since the day I was hired. Still not even sure how that happened."

"Just be on your guard around him. He's looking for a reason to get rid of you, so try a little harder at not giving him one."

"I appreciate your vast words of wisdom."

"You'd better honey." She said with a smile.

Kate was a middle aged African American woman with a big heart, and just about the only person Parker worked with he could honestly call a friend. She was the one who trained him when he first started. Anytime he had a problem he went to her. She had a somewhat gentle way about her, but she took her job seriously. During the first month on the job Parker had seen a large man trying to make off with a customers' wallet, but Kate spear tackled the guy before he could get down the escalator. She was an incredibly nice woman, the kind that baked cookies for fellow employees and volunteered at little league games as an umpire, but if someone negatively crossed her path, she could put the fear of God in them. Parker always joked she could be a bouncer at a nightclub if her security job ever went south.

"I'm off to do my rounds." Kate said. "I'll see you later kid. Try to stay out of the crosshairs while I'm gone."

"I'll do my best." Parker said as he sat down in the computer chair parked by the monitors. Kate walked out of the room leaving Parker to his job. He only had seven more hours until his shift ended. He silently prayed for the rest of the day to go smoother.

"This is only the beginning of better things to come." He assured himself.

It had been many years since Nimue had been to the meeting chamber of the Olympians. She walked along the enormous hallway leading to the chamber doors. Multiple paintings of Greek figures adorned the walls on both sides depicting a sort of historical record of events. One painting seemed to show an image of the Sun high in a bright blue sky with rays of light leading down to a beautiful mountain landscape. At the end of each ray of light was the image of a being that had light reflecting off of them. Nimue knew this was an artistic rendering of the Olympians coming to earth.

Another painting showed the construction of Mount Olympus and another seemed to show the creation of Atlantis followed by one final picture of the great city sinking beneath the ocean. At the end of the hallway was a large arched doorway that Nimue used to enter the chamber on the other side. The chamber itself had no walls aside from the one that held the doorway Nimue used to enter. The ceiling above her was held up by massive stone pillars. Straight ahead of her the floor stretched out nearly twenty feet and then dropped down. Nimue could see more clouds floating below her as she peeked over the edge of the floor. The sky that surrounded the hall was a mix of blue and pinkish colors. It was a beautiful sight to behold, one that she always treasured during her visits.

She turned her gaze forward as the clouds began to swirl and took the shape of five throne chairs. Gigantic figures, each one nearly a hundred feet tall began to appear and sat on the cloudy thrones.

Ares, the god of war.
Helios, the god of the Sun.
Demeter, the goddess of the seasons.
Poseidon, the god of the sea.
Zeus, the god of thunder and lightning, and the most powerful of all the Olympians.

"Welcome Nimue." Zeus spoke. "What news do you have to speak of?"

Nimue stepped forward and stood just a few feet from the edge of the floor.

"This has been coming for a long time." She said with a smile. "I have found him."
Zeus leaned forward with intrigue.

"Not this rubbish again." Ares protested.

"He is living on Earth at this very moment." Nimue continued. "I believe that the prophecy has begun and that now is the time to act."

"Do you have any evidence that he is the one?" Demeter requested.

"I have nothing to show certainty but ask for your trust in my selection."

"You show confidence in a mortal." Ares scoffed. "We cannot trust our future to them. They are as arrogant and self-righteous now as they were thousands of years ago."

"The Ancients prophecy is being fulfilled." Nimue continued. "Whether or not it is a mortal is of no importance."

"The Ancients have not been seen or heard from in millennia." Helios said. "Is their word even to be trusted? They weren't exactly our allies."

"We cannot risk it." Ares suggested. "Hades is in prison far from their reach. Forget the whole thing ever happened and let us get on with our own existence."

"No!" Nimue shouted. "Keeping Hades locked away does not solve the problem! All of the souls that have been trapped by him must be freed. This has gone on long enough. We can no longer leave the humans to be forgotten as if they never existed. They deserve to be set free."

"It's only a handful of mortals. Look how their descendants treat the world we left them. I could care less if they all died out."

"And Persephone?" Demeter asked Ares. "What about my daughter? She was trapped by that monster long before his exile. Doesn't she deserve freedom from that beast's control?"

"She chose her place at his side. She is accountable for her own actions."

"She was corrupted by that silver tongue!" Demeter said angrily. "He twisted her thoughts and turned her against us. Were it not for the deal I made for her I'd have gone after her long ago!"

"Enough." Zeus intervened. "You have all remained faithful to your promises. Even though our brother Hades corrupted his own soul we all have honored the law we set forth. It doesn't discount the fact that we all lost something when we sat back and allowed Hades to wreak havoc on the Earth. We stood aside and left the mortals to deal with something they couldn't have possibly prepared for. After Hades' exile we allowed the mortals to reign on earth like children. They are still young and still learning how to take care of themselves. I believe in the future they may even do better than we ever did. We hid the truth from them for a reason. However, Nimue is right. Continuing to ignore them doesn't remove the weight of guilt I have for what our brother has done. Those people were sacrificed for our sins, our lust for power, and we are just as much to blame for Hades' corruption as he is. It is our duty to mankind to do what is necessary to make things right again. At least this once. Nimue, what is it you are here to ask of us?"

"We need him. The mortal the Ancients' vision showed." She answered.

"What if you are wrong in your selection? We will not intervene again."

"I think I have found the right man."

"You think?" Ares asked. "Listen princess. The Ancients told of one, and I emphasize on the word ONE, person that has a slim chance of defeating Hades. Even the Ancients could've been lying. With all that is at stake do you want to take the risk?"

"The risk is well worth the reward should we succeed." Nimue said. "I've made my selection out of faith. My heart tells me my choice is right."

"Nimue," Zeus began. "Our involvement in this goes against everything we have become, everything we have sworn against. What I will be doing, I have vowed to never do again. We all agreed that the mortals must not be interfered with. If I break my vow, and your choice fails, you know as do I, Hades will be free again to reign over the entire Earth and he will seek vengeance on us for our part in this affair if it comes to that. Once this is done, it cannot be undone. You will be solely responsible for the outcome...."

"I'm aware of the consequences." Nimue interrupted. "I will gladly take the repercussions should this fail, but assure you, you won't regret this."

Zeus took a long deep breath and looked to Poseidon who had been sitting in silence.

"Time to weigh in Brother." Zeus said.

"If Hades is not defeated the gates of Elysian remain closed." Poseidon spoke. "All those who were killed by him will be tortured for eternity." He looked into Nimue's eyes. "However, I can see in your eyes you truly believe in this man."

"I do, Father." Nimue said.

"If you have faith in him, I have faith in you." He smiled and nodded his head. "I'm with my daughter on this one."

Zeus smiled and looked toward the others.

"Is everyone in agreement?" Zeus asked.

All but Ares nodded their heads in favor of Nimue's proposal.

"We will be breaking our own rules." Ares said. "This will mean war for us all. I always enjoy a good fight, but you had better be right about this or all the blood spilled will be on your hands." With that said, Ares nodded in favor of Nimue.

"Then it is settled." Zeus spoke. "Are you prepared Nimue?"

"Athena, Artemis, and Aphrodite are waiting for my word." She responded. "They will watch over him when he arrives. When the time comes, he will awaken, and his path will be presented before him."

"Then so be it."

"Let the hypocrisy begin." Ares said sarcastically.

"This is the path to peace." Nimue corrected him. "Something you'll have to learn to enjoy it seems."

She then bowed her head to the others as they each faded from the sky. Once they were gone, she turned and made her way to the exit with a smile on her face. She was ready to put her plans into motion. She felt she had waited long enough after all.

Parker finished his lunch and tossed the garbage in the nearest trash bin. He had another twenty minutes but decided to cut it short this time and return to work early. Suddenly his attention was brought to a lovely young blonde that he couldn't help but recognize.

"Jamie?" Parker asked. "Jamie Clark?"

"Yes?" She asked as he caught her attention.

"Remember me? Parker Wallace, we went to high school together."

"Oh right, Parker. Wow, how long has it been?"

"A little over ten years. You haven't changed at all, you look great." He said smiling.

"You haven't changed much either."

"Yeah?"

"Yeah, you're still a loser." She said with a laugh as she walked away leaving Parker with a blank stare on his face. He sighed and nodded his head.

"Yup. She hasn't changed one bit."

Parker never did have any luck with women. When he saw Jamie Clark, he could remember how she had made fun of him back in school, but he let himself believe for a few moments that maybe people change as they get older. Not this time it seemed. The radio attached to his belt screeched static and Kate's' voice came through. She had taken over Parkers' monitor duties while he went to lunch.

"Parker, come in." She said.

"I'm here." He responded.

"Sorry to interrupt your lunch but do you have a minute?"

"It's okay. I'm finished anyway. What do you need?"

"We've got what looks like a 'lovers quarrel' over by the sporting goods store."

"I'll check into it."

"Thanks kiddo."

WARRIOR FROM AVALON

Parker hooked the radio back onto his belt and made his way to the destination. Once there he found a young man, who was about his age, arguing with what Parker could only assume to be his girlfriend. The two began shouting as Parker approached.

"Whoa, you two need to calm down." Parker said. "I think you both should take this outside. You're disturbing the other customers."

"This is none of your business pal, just stay out of it." The angry man ordered.

"You're making it everyone's business." Parker replied pointing at the group of people as they gathered around them. "There's no reason to make a scene in front of all these people. Just take your friend and go settle this somewhere else."

"Get lost rent-a-cop!" The man said as he shoved his index finger into Parkers' chest.

Parker grabbed the angry man's wrist and twisted it until he was on the ground in submission.

"You're hurting my hand!" He cried out.

"I'm having a really lousy day so far and you're not making it any better." Parker said. "Now I'm going to ask again politely, take your business elsewhere or I'll make you..." It was then angry man's female friend decided to intervene.

"My boyfriend said to get lost!" She yelled as she balled up her fist and sucker-punched Parker in the face.

It was almost instantly that Parker went from being the hero for a lady in distress, to suddenly being rendered unconscious at the fist of said lady. There was a faint moment of confusion in his eyes before everything went black.

After regaining consciousness Parker noticed he had been dragged into the security room. Kate handed him a bag of ice with a somewhat sympathetic look on her face. He attempted to regain his composure while Lloyd and

Kate, along with two other store employees' in the monitor room, watched a recording of Parker getting decked by the young girl. The two employees continued to laugh as they replayed the video several times before Lloyd insisted they exit the room.

"This is unacceptable!" Lloyd shouted.

"What did I do wrong?" Parker defensively asked as he placed an icepack on his left cheek.

"You are supposed to display some semblance of authority, yet you couldn't even settle a simple domestic dispute? You not only embarrassed yourself but you're embarrassing me!"

"She caught me off guard. I wasn't expecting…"

"Save it! You are on a slippery slope here Wallace. Get your act together or I'll have you working in the food court passing out cookie samples!"

Lloyd walked out of the room and slammed the door behind him. Kate stood by Parker and gave him a soft pat on the shoulder.

"You all right kid?" She asked.

"I think she loosened one of my teeth." He answered running his index finger along the inside of his mouth.

"Actually, she knocked one out." Kate said handing him a napkin with a bloody tooth inside. "You spit this out onto the floor before you passed out."

"You've got to be kidding me! What's wrong with me?"

"There isn't anything wrong with you son. Some people just aren't cut out for this type of work."

"I thought I was doing good back there. I thought, you know damsel in distress, I could save the day. Once again, I tried to do the right thing, but I get my lights knocked out by a girl half my size."

"We weren't all meant to be heroes Parker."

"This is the kind of work I want to do. Policeman, fireman, security guard is fine, but why does stuff keep happening to me? It's like I'm cursed or something."

"Why? Because you can be too nice of a guy sometimes."

"Doesn't matter. I'll probably lose my job before the end of the day."

"Because of Lloyd? Kid, he likes to flex his authority and he's got to go after someone, you're just an easy target, but don't worry. I won't let you get fired for having a bad day."

"It isn't just Lloyd. I'm talking about my life in general. I'm in a get-no-where job making barely minimum wage. I have a crappy apartment. I'm almost thirty, and I've made it nowhere in life. I've tried, believe me. I've put the effort in everything I do, but it seems everyone is destined for something, but destiny doesn't even know I exist. It just ignored me completely."

"You're still young. You've got plenty of chances to make a name for yourself."

"I feel like I'm capable of so much more than this. I just don't have the opportunities to prove it."

"It's coming Parker. Never give up hope. Good things happen to those who wait."

"I've tried to be a good person all of my life. I always try to do the right thing and help people, but no one ever notices. Maybe I should be a jerk like Lloyd."

"You can't be a jerk like Lloyd."

"Why not?"

"Because it's in your nature to do the right thing. I've seen you go out of your way to help those in need. One day, someone is going to take notice of those good deeds. I have no doubt that you're destined for greatness, just be a little more patient."

Parker was silent. It felt good to hear someone believing in him. Kate always did have a way of making him feel better about himself, but this time Parker wasn't so easily comforted.

The rest of the day was smoother than the start. Parker had managed to stay out of trouble and avoided his boss as much as possible. Even going so far as to dodge him after work and avoid that writeup he was threatened with. He punched his employee code into the time clock and began his end of the day routine. After changing into his casual clothing, he made his way to the front exit of the store. People were running quickly to their cars, and some were even afraid to leave because of the storm. The thunder rolled across the sky as the wind blew shopping bags and empty soda cans across the parking lot. The weather had picked up considerably since that morning.

Parker zipped up his black rain jacket and pulled the hood over his head. He held tightly to his duffel bag as he darted across the parking lot through puddles of water toward his truck. He was thankful that he had a short drive home. He hadn't had time to let his dog out before he left, so there were probably a few surprises waiting for him inside. There was a dog door but with the weather like it was, Butch was most likely hiding under the bed. Parker flipped his wipers on the highest speed as he pulled out of the parking lot. The rain was coming down hard and the cars on the road were limited due to the storm.

Lightning flashed in the sky as Parker headed for the bridge leading home. The bridge was a multi-level with the traffic on the top headed in one direction while the bottom level headed in the other. Parker was driving on the lower level and was halfway to the other side when suddenly the bridge began to shake, and he was forced to slam on his brakes. The cars in front of him were stopped while some were even trying to turn around to go the wrong way. He wasn't sure if any of the cars ahead of him had crashed, but he could see people getting out of their vehicles to run away from something. He climbed out of his truck, not even bothering to shut off the ignition. People raced passed him as he waved someone down.

"What's going on?" He asked as he grabbed a guy by the jacket sleeve.

"The bridge is shaking apart." The guy said as he shoved Parkers' hand and raced away.

Parker watched as people continued to run past him. The bridge began to shake again, this time it was strong enough to knock everyone off balance and sent Parker clinging to the railing. He watched as cars and trucks slid around him and into the side of the bridge. A couple of empty cars on the upper level busted through the rails and dropped hard to the river below. Parker managed to regain his balance and was shocked when he looked toward the sky. An enormous funnel cloud hovered just above the bridge. It was the oddest thing he had ever seen. Lightning wasn't striking anywhere else but inside the cloud itself.

At the end of the bridge the top deck began to crack and collapse onto the one below. Parker held on tight as the bridge began to shake again as if it were attempting to knock him loose. After a moment it was calm again, only swaying slightly. He decided it was time to go and was about to join the other people and run for his life when he looked up and noticed a car just ahead of him. The front half had crashed through the rails and was hanging over the edge. After a second glance Parker could see the silhouette of someone in the drivers' seat. Without hesitation he darted as fast as he could toward the vehicle. After peeking through the rear window, he could see his old classmate Jamie Clark unconscious.

"Oh geez!"

He banged his hand on the glass shouting her name, but it was useless. He rushed to the back door on the driver side and pulled the handle only to find it locked.
He took off his jacket and wrapped it around his arm and with as much force as he could muster he jammed his

elbow at the window causing it to crack, but at the same time it sent a steady jolt of pain up his arm.

"Cheesy peaches..." He shouted in pain as he rubbed his elbow.

He quickly tossed his jacket on the ground and repeatedly kicked the glass breaking the window, but in the process managed to slip and fall onto his back. He received several tares through the leg of his jeans along with a few small cuts, but nothing severe. He stood up and reached into the car unlocking the back door. He struggled to reach Jamie, who was leaning forward against the steering wheel due to the forward slant of the car. Parker had no choice but to enter the car via the backseat. After retrieving his jacket and using it to slide the shattered glass into the floorboard he positioned himself behind her and cautiously leaned forward to stretch his hand out to her.

"Jamie!" He shouted. "Wake up!"

He was still unable to reach her. He leaned forward and reached between the driver side door and the seat to feel for the lever and lower the seat back into a lying down position. The car began to rock softly.

"Oh, this is bad." He said to himself terrified. "This is really bad."

He then started to reach for her once again, but the car protested at the extra weight and began to inch its way forward. He quickly reached down and pulled up the emergency brake hoping that by some miracle it would keep the car from rolling any further. He wasn't sure if it had worked but the car was motionless. Jamie started to show signs of movement as she began to wake up.

"Jamie!" Parker shouted.
She raised her hand to a bleeding cut on her forehead and then looked forward to see the beckoning river below. She began to scream causing Parker to cringe a little at the sound, like nails on a chalkboard to him.

"Seriously?" He asked. "Screaming isn't going to stop gravity! No wonder you flunked science."

"Parker?" She turned her head to see him pushing himself against the back seat hoping to balance out the vehicle. "What are you doing here?"

"Just thought I'd hitch a ride home; do you care to drop me off?" He asked sarcastically.

The car inched forward once more.

"Whoa, okay bad choice of words." He shouted. "I'm trying to help you, just don't move!"

Jamie leaned back in her seat as Parker stretched out his hand and placed it on her shoulder.

"Okay, okay. This is what we're going to do. Give me your hand, I'll slide out the door here, and then pull you out with me as quickly as possible."

"Will that work?"

"Let's hope so." He said easing his way toward the door, but the bridge began to shake once more. The car rolled forward again, but this time it wasn't stopping. The back end of the car began to rise upward, and Parker was thrown forward landing upside down into the front passenger seat. The car stopped moving as Parker slowly changed his position with his back resting against the dashboard. He looked out the rear window and could see a sharp piece of the broken railing had stabbed its way into the side of the car, preventing it from going over the edge.

The railing was now the only thing keeping them safe. The horn honked as Jamie used her hand to lift herself upward, keeping her from going through the windshield. If it hadn't been for her seatbelt halfway holding her up, she would've gone through much sooner.

"Okay, new plan." Parker said nervously. "Unbuckle your seatbelt and make your way toward the back. I'll give you a boost up and you can climb out."

He slowly changed his position once more where he could hold himself up with his legs and used his hands to help her do as he suggested. The time for playing it safe was over. He had to get her out of the car as fast as possible.

"Parker, I'm so sorry." She cried. "I didn't mean what I said."

Parker glanced up at Jamie and gave her a nervous smile and a wink.

"Okay, easy does it." He said holding onto her while she unbuckled her seat belt.

Parker boosted her up to the back door as she reached out. Suddenly the car shifted causing Parker to fall with his back against the dashboard yet again. Jamie held on tight and looked out to see the car edging its way over the side. The railing wasn't going to hold out much longer. She placed her foot on the back of the drivers' headrest and used it to push herself out the back door. Halfway in and halfway out she was then able to reach the bridge.

"Parker, I'm almost out." She shouted. "Somebody help us!"

"Jamie! Just keep going." Parker said as he watched her struggling to pull herself up. It was then he noticed the railing was about to break away. His eyes widened; she wasn't out yet. He forced himself upward and reached out for her foot. With one last burst of adrenaline he used every ounce of strength he could and shoved her from the falling car.

She quickly rolled onto the bridge and turned back to help Parker, but the car was gone. She screamed his name and peered over the edge to see the ripples in the water below. The car had broken loose and fell taking Parker along with it. She screamed and shouted for him as two rescue workers grabbed her by the arms and pulled her away. The rain and the wind had stopped almost instantly. Now that it had served its purpose the storm was over.

Hours passed by as people were escorted away from the area. Emergency rescue searched for survivors throughout the rest of the evening. Many people were rushed to hospitals with cuts and bruises but would make full recoveries. Day's passed as the search for Parker and any others the storm may have claimed continued.

Weeks went by as the local news reported on the strange incident. It was soon discovered that throughout all the damage the storm had caused there had only been one person missing from the devastation. Despite all the efforts made by police, friends, and co-workers, the body of Parker Wallace was never recovered.

CHAPTER THREE

Water erupted from Parkers' mouth as he woke to find himself lying on a wooden floor. He gasped for air as he flipped himself over onto his stomach and coughed up the rest of the liquid that once occupied his lungs. After a few moments he was able to catch his breath and survey his new surroundings. The room was dark aside from a small lantern hanging from the middle of the ceiling. Parker was overwhelmed with confusion. Just moments earlier he was inside a car hanging off the edge of a bridge.

The room he found himself in resembled that of a small cabin. The walls and floors were made of logs and there were two windows on opposite ends of the room he could see out of. However, it was too dark outside to see anything to identify his location. The room was empty aside from the lantern, a mattress lying on the floor against the wall, and a door leading outside. Parker started for the door but backed away when he heard footsteps on the other side. There were two knocks before it opened, and a man stepped inside. He was young looking, mid-thirties at least, and had short blonde hair. He wore old fashioned clothing, like something out of the 1800's. Parker thought maybe it was possible someone from a renaissance fair had dove into the river to pull him out. At this point nothing made sense anyway.

"Good, you're awake." He said with an English accent as he entered the room.

Parker remained silent and slowly backed away with caution.

"I'm glad to see you up and about." The man continued. "I brought you some food. I'm certain you're not hungry, but it tastes really good." The man held up a plate of grapes and a small turkey leg. He stepped forward and placed it on the floor when Parker made no attempt to take it from him.

"Well, that's for you." He said. "Whenever you feel like eating. My name is Lucas Vincent by the way."
He extended his hand, but Parker stood still.

"I understand that you might be a little hesitant right now." Lucas continued. "Most people are when they arrive here, but I assure you I mean you no harm. Once you have adjusted to the way things are here the rest flows along quite nicely." Lucas said smiling. "This would be a bit easier for us both if you spoke."

"Where am I?" Parker asked.

"Well for starters this is your new home. Or it will be."

"My home?"

"Absolutely. Everything here belongs to you." Lucas said surveying the empty room. "I see it is a bit lacking at the moment."

"How did I get here?"

"You were brought here after your unfortunate accident."

"Who brought me here?" Parker asked interrupting. "Did someone save me from that river?"

"No, I'm afraid not. Or at least not in the way you are thinking. The life you knew before is over."

"What do you mean over?"

"This is my first time welcoming someone here so bear with me if you will. The hardest part of greeting a new arrival can be difficult as they are usually very confused. I'll be as forthcoming with you as I possibly can." Lucas said as he cleared his throat. "The best way to put it is, you died."

"Died?"

"Yes. I'm sorry for your loss."

Parker didn't respond but stared at Lucas confused.

"What do you mean I died?" Parker asked.

"You my friend are no longer among the living. You're still you. You're not a zombie or anything." Lucas said with a slight chuckle.

Parker glared at Lucas as if he thought the man might have some sort of mental problem.

"If I were dead, wouldn't I know it?" Parker asked.

"Well, obviously not." Lucas replied.

"This doesn't make any sense. I'm not dead. I don't feel dead."

"I know this is a lot to take in and believe me, it can be quite confusing."

"Listen, I'm not sure what's going on here, but I think I should just go." Parker said as he headed for the door.

"I wouldn't walk out there if I were you." Lucas warned. "You're spirit and body are still adjusting here."

"No worries, I'm just going to find a phone and have someone come and get me. When I get to a hospital, I'll send someone for you too. You sound like you could use a mental evaluation. So, feel free to make yourself comfortable. What's supposedly mine is yours…" Parker looked around the room. "…or lack thereof. Stick around, I'll be back soon."

"You've got that part right."

Parker made his way passed Lucas and out the door. It was so dark outside he couldn't even see the ground in front of him. As Parker stepped off the front porch, he began to fall into absolutely nothing. It was then he could tell there was no ground to even fall on. There was no sudden stop and nothing to break his fall, but before he could scream his face slammed hard onto the wooden floor of the cabin. Parker groaned in pain and looked up to see Lucas turning away from the door he had just gone through with a mild grimace on his face.

"As I was saying." Lucas said. "Not the best idea for you right now."

"What just happened?" Parker asked as he pushed himself up off the floor. Parker stood up confused. He glanced over at Lucas and then darted out the door once more.

"That's not going to work!" Lucas shouted.

Parker ignored Lucas and rushed out into the nothingness once more only to fall and land yet again on the cabin floor. Without even looking at Lucas, Parker jumped to his feet and headed out the door. Lucas simply crossed his arms and looked up at the ceiling just in time to see Parker fall from thin air once again. Parker pushed himself up off the floor and looked at Lucas almost in a state of panic.

"You do that fast enough and you might even see yourself running out the door." Lucas joked with a sarcastic grin.

"What in the...?" Parker asked in a deep state of confusion.

"That is a circular loop." Lucas answered. "It's meant to keep you here until you're ready to join the community."

"A loop?" Parker asked.

"When you stepped out of the boundary area you just ended up right back to where you first woke up. It goes in a circle you see. That's why we call it the loop."

"How does that even work? Parker asked. "Does that mean I'm trapped here?"

"Right now, your mind is still tied to the living world. Your brain is simply trying to grasp onto your new reality. Normal physics that you've been used to do not apply here. Until you're ready to accept the fact you have moved on from the mortal world, you're not going to be able to leave this room."

"None of this makes any sense."

"I'm trying to tell you Parker. The quickest way to move forward, literally, is to let go of your old life."

"You know my name?"

"I know because it's my job to know."

"Your job?"

"I was assigned to you as your guide. My role is to explain how things work around here and to help you adjust."

"How much do you know about me?"

"Your name is Parker Wallace, a security guard with an unappreciative boss and your best and only true friend was a dog named Butch. You're an orphan, 5 foot 9 inches, blue eyes. You were never adopted and left the orphanage at an early age to establish your independence. You've never been married, no children and though you love to read, you rarely pick up a book that isn't a comic." Parker nodded his head in agreement.

"Take a seat." Lucas said pulling up a chair. Parker looked around him curiously. He hadn't noticed any chairs in the room before.

"Where did that come from?" Parker asked as he sat down in the chair Lucas had just pulled out for him.

"I understand what's going through your head right now." Lucas said sitting in a chair across from Parker, ignoring his question. "Believe me, I went through the exact same thing. I promise you, I'm here to help."

"All right, I'm listening."

"Do you believe in life after death?"

"Sure, I do."

"Good. That makes this a bit easier."

"You're serious? I'm dead?"

"As far as the world you knew is concerned, yes."

"This is heaven, right?"

"Not even close." Lucas said laughing. Parker felt a wave of nervousness wash over him.

"Oh, no wait." Lucas corrected himself. "That's not how I meant it. I apologize. Heaven is a fantastic place full of beauty and colors that can't even be imagined by mankind. It's completely different from anything you could possibly think it is. Though the stories are true, it is the perfect place, but this is not heaven."

"You've been there?"

"No, no. Not myself. Though I've heard about it. It's hard to get most people to talk about it because it's sort of hard to explain what it's actually like, but anyway. We do share some similarities here from what I understand."

"Such as?" Parker asked.

"You're new home for starters." Lucas said as he drew Parkers' attention to the interior of the small cabin around them. "Right now, your mind is building all of this around you."

"My mind is?"

"The things you need are being created at this very moment by your subconscious. Every person who lives here creates their own personal accommodations."

"I built a shack?" Parker asked disappointed.

"A step up from the previous residence if I'm not mistaken?"

"It is bigger." He answered nodding his head.

"See? Glass half full. The longer you're here the more things will begin to appear. Things you need, things you like, even things you didn't know you liked."

"Why can't I leave?"

"Your mind is still tethered to the other side. This reality is much different. The best thing you can do for yourself is to be patient and get some rest. I'll leave you here and come back when you've had a bit more time to get settled." Lucas said standing up.

"Wait a minute. You're leaving now?"

"No need to worry, I'll be back tomorrow."

"So, what am I supposed to do?" Parker asked motioning to the emptiness of the room.

"There is no need to panic or worry about anything. Relax, and get some sleep." Lucas said as he walked out the door. Parker watched as Lucas stepped off the porch and disappeared into the darkness. He slowly closed the door to the cabin, slightly nervous but more or less confused.

"Okay then." He said to himself. "Sink or swim I guess."

He looked up at the ceiling where the lantern had once been to find it had been replaced with a light bulb and a ceiling fan. Along the wall to the left of the front door, a refrigerator had suddenly caught Parkers' attention.

"He wasn't kidding." Parker said shocked as he walked over to the fridge and opened it up only to find a half empty jug of milk and an unopened can of tuna.

"Figures." He said disappointed. "Well, this looks like my fridge."

Parker closed the fridge door and scanned the room again to find counters had appeared behind him along with a sink as well. He smiled as he turned the faucet on, although when he did there was no running water.

"Be patient, he says." He muttered to himself. "Try to rest."

He picked up the plate of food Lucas had left on the floor and walked over to sit on the mattress in the corner. After eating a few grapes and taking a few bites off the turkey leg, he could feel himself getting sleepy. He placed the plate on the floor next to him and lay down on the mattress. He stared up at the ceiling thinking that any minute he'd wake up in a hospital having almost drowned. Soon he'd go back to his normal, yet uneventful life. It wasn't long after Parker couldn't keep his eyes open anymore, and he quickly fell asleep.

"The Answer is no." Arthur said slamming a cup onto the table.

Nimue stood in front of him with a disappointed expression on her face. Arthur had good reasons for not wanting to assist her. Even now after so much time had passed, his final battle against Mordred weighed heavy on his heart. He couldn't forget all the lives lost that night or like many nights before that. He led his soldiers into a battle he knew deep down was going to be one of the worst he had ever experienced, but he also knew where he would end up when it was all over. It didn't feel very fair. In his mind, the bloodstains on his hands would never come clean.

Arthurs' cabin was large and fully furnished with tables and chairs. There were books piled on shelves indicating a love for literature. The walls in the cabin adorned many types of medieval decorations, but where one might see the usual crossed swords or glass case of weaponry, Arthur chose not to have any sort of reminder of his previous life out for display. Nimue had gone to him for help but didn't expect him to be so uncooperative.

"I gave my life and soul to make sure that monster stayed locked away forever." Arthur said. "I won't allow him to be set loose again."

"His imprisonment was never going to last forever." Nimue replied. "Whether he escapes on his own, by way of his demons, or we take the offensive, one day he will be let loose again. It is only a matter of time. In this way at least we have a chance to stay a step ahead of him."

"You wasted your time bringing that boy here."

"He needs training Arthur. This is the purpose for which you were brought here, and he needs to begin soon. Without you Parker will not survive."

"If he's the chosen destructor of Hades then wouldn't he win regardless of his knowledge? I mean if it is his destiny after all?"

"You know it doesn't work that way. Prophecy is a foretelling of what could happen, but nothing is set in stone. You of all people know destiny can change in an instant. We rewrite the future with every action we take."

"Don't send him at all."

"We have to end this. This is our only way to atone for our past sins."

"Your past sins!" Arthur said pointing his finger to Nimue. "You and your family unleashed all of this upon us! Here we are centuries later still feeling the repercussions of your greed and lust for power."

"That's not fair." Nimue protested. "We did what we thought was right leaving humanity to live free."

"Then Hades runs loose, and you left us to our fate!"

"Zeus wanted to help, but by doing so he would've defied his own law! He'd be no better than Hades himself."

"Yet now he intervenes to send the boy here? Zeus just wasn't man enough to kill his own brother. He needs someone else to do his dirty work."

"It isn't about killing Hades; it's about saving those souls."

"We can't always save everyone. We're not at war anymore, but if you let him loose it will be the worst war this world has ever seen."

"I'm aware of what could happen." Nimue said. "I still believe in doing the right thing. Everyone wants to ignore this situation like it's a bad dream, but there are thousands of people Arthur, thousands that are trapped in that nightmare. The only problem is they can't wake up from it. They live in that endless darkness that we ignore. If we choose to leave them to their fate, then God have mercy on all of our souls. Especially when we have an opportunity to do something about it."

"We will add more souls before we could ever free one." Arthur said as he turned his attention to a fireplace near the wall to his left.

"I have nothing left to offer you." He continued. "If you wish to send more people to that abyss, do it without me."

"Then they will never see the Elysian Fields. They will never know the joys of heaven."

"It hurts me to say it Nimue, the words burn my tongue to speak them, but we cannot sacrifice more lives for theirs."

"I thought you of all people would understand. Do you even think of her anymore? Do you pray for her soul to find rest?"

"What makes you think I pray anymore?"

Nimue, saddened by Arthurs' words walked to the door and then proceeded through it like a ghost. Arthur knew she was right. In his heart, deep down to his soul, he wanted to help her.

"Coward!" He said to himself as he threw his cup into the fireplace. He stood up from the chair he had been sitting in and paced the floor. His eyes filled with tears at the thought of the loved ones he had lost. The wind began to blow outside and suddenly Arthurs' front door blew open and extinguished the flames in his fireplace. He stood in silence and darkness in sudden confusion.

"Arthur." A voice whispered.

He searched to see no one near him. The voice called out to him again. He felt the wind gently caressing his face as he walked out of his cabin and looked upward to see a small orb glowing a bright bluish color. The source of the voice was coming from the orb itself. Arthur had heard of the myth which surrounded the orb, but he never thought he'd see it. He was being invited to the Queens palace.

The Orb began to float away in the direction leading up a forested mountain path. Arthur followed behind as quickly as he could. He kept pace with the orb for a good six minutes before he emerged from the forest at the top of the mountain.

The path continued straight to the edge of a cliff overlooking the ocean. Arthur peered over the edge to see cascading waterfalls pouring off the mountain. He could also see the ocean waves crashing into the rocks below. Suddenly his attention was drawn to the appearance of a pearly white stairway leading up toward the night sky. At the top of the stairway resting on a cloud was a large white palace, home to the Queens themselves. Arthur was overwhelmed by its beauty.

    He watched as the orb ascended the stairway toward the palace and he followed it closely all the way to the top. The trip took nearly an hour as Arthur carefully climbed the stairway into the sky. There were no guard rails so he kept to the center as best he could.

    The closer to the top he got, the more he realized that the palace itself was bigger than he had thought. The doors stood over two-hundred feet tall and were nearly one-hundred feet wide. As Arthur approached them, they began to open on their own. Once inside he saw a long white hallway with marble walls and flooring that seemed to stretch on forever. There were hundreds of large doors along the hall, but it was the one straight ahead of him that caught his attention.

    He continued down the hallway and somehow, he managed to reach the door faster than he anticipated. It was as though he had walked the distance within a minute. As he entered the room, he couldn't help but be amazed. The room was so large that it could hold an entire village within its own walls. It was decorated just like the hallway outside with marble floors and columns that reached to the ceiling. Arthur gazed upward in wonder to see that instead of a roof there was a ceiling of stars and galaxies all shining brightly above his head. It was as if he were looking straight into the heavens.

    Nothing could have prepared Arthur for what he saw on the other side of the room. Three massive thrones sat along the wall and sitting there were three women. Each of them gigantic in size, dressed in matching gowns, though different in color, with golden belts, and they were all more beautiful than Arthur remembered. The Queens of Avalon were the ones who had brought him on their ship many years ago after his intense battle with Mordred.

Artemis, the goddess of the Moon, wore a yellow gown.
Aphrodite, the goddess of love wore red.
Athena, the goddess of wisdom, wore a gown as blue as the sky on a sunny day.

"My Queens." Arthur said kneeling before them.
"Arthur, we welcome you here with great anticipation." Athena spoke.
"It is my honor to be in your presence yet again."
"We have all been waiting patiently for this moment. It seems that the time has come for you to fulfill your oath to Zeus."
"I thought the bargain I made was for my soul in exchange for Hades capture?"
"Of course, it was, but what good is collecting a soul that you're not going to put to good use. You didn't honestly think you were going to live out eternity in that cabin of yours, did you?"
"I assume your request is the same as Nimue."
"We're aware of her mission which is why we have called you here." Artemis said. "Hades must be destroyed once and for all."
"I do not wish to be disrespectful, but this boy Nimue spoke of, he has no clue about any of this. He comes from a vastly different world than us. History has been rewritten to hide our dark past. He may not be able to accept the truth."
"We have no choice now Arthur, the process has already begun." Aphrodite said. "It's too late to stop what has already been set in motion."

"Why do you wish this weight be placed on my shoulders?"

"It is your purpose, Arthur." Athena answered. "This is just one of the many reasons we brought you here. You must teach him the ways of the sword. You were the most skilled swordsman of your time and we cannot afford anything less."

Arthur bowed his head in understanding.

"I will do what you ask without further protest. When do we begin?"

"In time you will know." Aphrodite answered.

"I understand."

"You may go now Sir Arthur, but remember, we have placed this burden not only on you but on the boy as well." Athena said. "Train him harder than any other, and once you have completely served your purpose, your eternal soul will be granted the peace it yearns for. Should we prove successful, you'll have the someone you yearn for as well."

"I understand my Queens. I will do my part as instructed."

Arthur then turned away and made his exit of the throne room to begin his long trip home. The Queens sat alone for a few moments before another man appeared before them. Sang, a middle-aged Asian man had been hidden behind a column out of sight.

"So, you've seen what is to come." Athena spoke. "How do you feel about this new path being presented before you?"

"My role in all of this has yet to be played out. Parker will need my assistance as well as Arthurs'. My experiences are tied to his and my knowledge is vital to his overall success."

"Is that why you were brought here?" Aphrodite asked. "What is it about this boy that makes Nimue so certain he's the one we need?"

"I assure you, there is no need to think otherwise. I have seen the man he is to become with my own eyes."

"This must all remain between us." Artemis spoke. "No one else must know of your origins. Not even Arthur and especially not Parker himself. We must ensure future events are not altered. Even the parts that you would wish to change."

"Of course."

"You may go now Sang and we thank you for all you've done."

Sang bowed his head and exited the room. The three Queens sat filled with more confidence than they had before. Nimue knew more than she had told them, but her reasons were sound. Parker would soon learn of his destiny. With the help of Arthur and the man known as Sang, Parker was more likely to be better prepared to face his future.

CHAPTER FOUR

Parker opened his eyes to a brightly lit room and stretched his arms. He hadn't slept that comfortable in an awfully long time. He sat up and looked at the changes in his surroundings. He was no longer on a mattress laying on the floor, but instead in an actual full-sized bed. Parker climbed off the bed to inspect the room around him. The inside of his cabin had gone from a barely empty room to a fully furnished home. Plants and paintings that Parker had been fond of were decoratively placed throughout the room. Tile floor separated the living area from the kitchen and a new dining table had appeared as well. There were shelves of books along the walls, some of Parkers' favorites from his childhood. There was even a couch in the living area on top of a new carpet.

All of the new furnishings seemed to make the room feel bigger than it was before, and some of it Parker didn't even realize he liked just as Lucas had explained, but all of it made him feel at home. He was amazed as he looked toward the kitchen to find a new door occupying the wall. He walked toward it and opened it up to find a new room had been built onto his cottage.

"Thank goodness." He said staring at a brand new fully functional bathroom.
Lucas entered the cottage after knocking a few times.

"Good morning sir." Lucas said looking around the room.

"You weren't kidding." Parker said with a grin.

"See what you can accomplish when you let your mind take control?" Lucas asked as he turned to see the fridge. "The first time I saw my own home putting itself together, it blew my mind." Lucas continued speaking as he opened the fridge door and reached inside. "Like this refrigerator, this is something I didn't have when I was still living on earth."

"It's half empty but feel free to help…" Parker stopped speaking when he saw Lucas pull out a bottle of water. "That wasn't in there before." Parker said confused.

"It's there now." Lucas said opening the fridge door wider for Parker to see inside.

"Last night there was nothing." Parker explained examining the fridge. The milk had been replaced with a full gallon jug and the tuna was gone. Instead Parker saw grapes, cheese, different varieties of meat, eggs, water bottles, and last but not least several cans of his favorite soda.

"This is incredible." Parker said.

"When you first looked inside, you're mind only produced what you needed at the moment. Now that you've been here for a while, you're starting to feel the true potential of this place."

"So, I'm creating all this stuff from pure thought?"

"Your subconscious mind will basically procure the things you need. Some things you didn't even know you needed. Before long, you'll be able to make things a bit more fluidly."

"Wow."

"Come on, let's try to go for a walk." Lucas said walking toward the front door. Parker followed him out onto the porch and stopped when he saw there was still no ground. This time the darkness was gone but Parker could see a bright blue sky in every direction of the cabin. He stepped to the edge of the porch and looked down at the endless sky.

"This is really cool and all, but I don't know if I'm ready." Parker said nervously.

"With that kind of thinking you'd be absolutely right." Lucas said walking off the porch and standing on the air in front of Parker. "You've got to let go some time. Now is as good of a time as any to take a leap of faith."

"You look like you're floating on air, so you do realize how crazy this seems to me right?"

"Of course I do. I was in your place once, but you can't just sit inside your cabin and let eternity pass you by. This place has so much more to offer."

"From this perspective, I'm not missing out on much."

"You're missing out on plenty, come on. Step off."

Parker stood at the edge. He felt overwhelmingly dizzy as he looked down. He had never been a fan of heights.

"Okay then." He said to himself.

Parker wasn't excited about landing face-first on the floor again. He thought to himself a moment and wondered if he had finally snapped and Lucas was just a figment of his imagination. However, in the off chance everything Lucas was telling him was real, maybe if he were willing to believe hard enough, then he'd see what Lucas saw. He stretched his right leg out in front of him and leaned forward.

"Here goes nothing."

Parker let himself believe as hard as he could that he was about to open his mind to a whole new reality. He felt himself leaning even further and opened his eyes to see that nothing had changed below him. He let out a loud yell as he fell face-first into the sky below and then felt a hard slap in the face as he hit solid ground.

"Ohhh, that's gonna leave a mark…" He said as he lifted himself up and dusted off his clothes. Parker then looked up to see he wasn't on the floor of his cabin, but instead on a stone walkway leading to a dirt path. He rose to his feet and checked his new surroundings. Lucas walked over to Parker and helped dust him off.

"You're the first person ever to not land on their feet." Lucas said. "I mean why would you lean forward like that as you step down? Honestly?"

"I didn't think it would actually work." Parker said.

"Some part of you did, otherwise it wouldn't have." Lucas said with a laugh. "So, what do you think?"

Behind him, he saw a path leading up to a large mountain reaching high into the sky with cascading waterfalls. Ahead of him Parker saw the path leading down from the mountain. At the very bottom was a village full of old-fashioned market stalls and people walking around. He could see a sign that read 'Café'. There was a dock close to the café itself and people sitting on the edge fishing. He then saw the vast ocean that surrounded the island and couldn't believe how beautiful the environment was. Birds flew overhead and sang their melodies. He could see the Sun rising beyond the ocean creating thousands of glistening sparkles on the water. He knew he wasn't looking at heaven, but he could imagine how close he was to it.

"What is this place?" He asked in awe.

Lucas stepped behind him and gave him a welcoming pat on the back.

"My friend, welcome to the Island of Avalon."

Lucas and Parker entered the village at the base of the mountain. It was a bit bigger than Parker had initially thought. There were so many areas where people could eat and relax. Parker felt as if he truly was in paradise.

"I think I'm gonna like it here." Parker said.

"The weather is always sunny and yet the temperature stays comfortable. The island is self-sustaining, and we can literally get anything we can think of as if by magic. Avalon is the true vacation destination."

"Yeah, it only cost you your life it seems."

"Not everyone came to this island the same way as you did. Some were born here."

"I guess some people are just born lucky."

"Seems that way I suppose." Lucas responded.

On the beach just below the outdoor café a dozen men were practicing some type of martial arts.

"Who are they?" Parker asked.

"They are the defenders of Avalon." Lucas said. "They train just about every day."

"Why would they need to do that? Are we not safe here?"

"The island is hidden, but there is always a need to be prepared."

"Prepared for what?"

"We'll talk about that some other time. No need to worry yourself about those matters."

Parker sat down at a nearby table while Lucas walked over to the café bar and ordered breakfast for the two of them. He returned to Parker and handed him a plate of eggs, bacon, and grits. He then handed him a cup of freshly squeezed orange juice.

"Enjoy." He said.

"Tell me Lucas, this place is great and all, but what's the purpose of all this?" Parker asked shoving a forkful of eggs into his mouth. "Did I win the lottery of death or something?"

"Nothing like that." He began. "Avalon is an island with its own community. Though since its creation it has served as a temporary resting place for those worthy of a second chance at life."

"A second chance to do what?"

"Many people live their lives with simple destinies and then there are others who have a greater role to play. Those people are brought here to educate themselves for use in the next life."

"Like reincarnation?"

"Not exactly reincarnation. When the time comes the chosen person will be taken back to earth as an infant, delivered by someone from Avalon. In life they'll grow up all over again. Only this time they will naturally develop all of the skills they learned here that will help them on their future journey. This is a resting place where people train their bodies and their minds until the day comes when they're chosen to return."

"So, when they return to earth do they remember any of this?"

"No one ever has. However, skills and knowledge acquired here will be passed along to them in the next life. They won't know how they have these skills, only that they are blessed with a 'natural talent' so to speak."

"Like instinct?"

"Exactly. Like you for example, your body was never recovered after your accident. As far as anyone you knew before, Parker Wallace died after falling into that river. After your time here you'll return to earth as an infant at later date, but you won't remember Avalon, or me, or anyone else you might encounter here, but your skills and knowledge will stay with you."

"That's pretty awesome, but what is it I'm supposed to learn?"

"Even that bit of information is unknown to me."

"Who would know?"

"The Queens would probably know."

"Queens? Would I be able to ask them?"

"No one has seen the Queens for centuries." Lucas said biting into his scrambled eggs. "When the time comes, you'll find out what you need to know. Until then, live it up. This place is paradise."

Parker took a sip of his orange juice and ate his eggs as he watched the men on the beach train with swords and daggers.

"What's your story?" Parker asked. "How'd you end up here?"

"In my life I was an archer." Lucas responded with a mouthful of toast. "I won a lot of tournaments, but when I was 33 I 'died' of dysentery."

"Dysentery?" Parker asked. "You died of the poops?"

Lucas looked up from his plate to see Parker holding back a laugh. He rolled his eyes and took a sip of coffee to wash down his food.

"It was a lot more serious back then." Lucas explained slightly annoyed. "In any case, I was about to fall dead in the middle of the woods and the next thing I knew, I was in my own cabin like you."

"I didn't mean anything by it." Parker said with a smile. "It could happen to anyone."

"I understand." Lucas said with a defeated grin. "I've been brought up to speed on the wonders of modern medicine. Could have used some Imodium back in my day, but then again I wouldn't be where I am now."

Parker smiled as he took a drink of his orange juice. The two of them continued to talk and joke as they finished up their meal. He turned his attention back to the fighters on the beach.

"You sure that's safe?" Parker asked.

Lucas had no response but looked on with interest. The two fighters struck at each other furiously. Parker watched as the intensity of the fight increased. Then with one swift move one man stabbed the other until the blade of his sword exited through the other man's back.

"He just stabbed that guy!" Parker shouted.

"It's all right. That happens." Lucas turned his head to the barkeep. "Can I get another coffee please?"

"Doesn't he need help?" Parker said standing up.

"Not at all, watch." Lucas replied.

Parker turned his attention back to the two men. Blood was pouring from the man's stomach as he lay on the ground, but suddenly the wound on his stomach began to heal and repair itself. The man then returned to his feet with the help of the man who had stabbed him. He wiped the blood off of himself and shook the other man's hand with respect.

"See, he's fine?" Lucas said. "Pain is easily overcome here. Eternal health and regeneration. Wounds heal almost instantly. It helps with the training process. Helps to build a tolerance to pain."

Parker stared blankly at the two men as they began to square off once again.

"Parker, are you all right?" Lucas asked. "You look a little pale."

Parker didn't respond, instead his eyes rolled upwards and within seconds he was out cold.

"Oh dear." Lucas said as he watched Parker drop to the ground unconscious.

The ship sailed in the dark and cruel waters of the abyss. Lightning lit up the sky in bright flashes as the thunder roared furiously. The hull of the ship vibrated with intensity due to the storm. The ship was a Balinger, a small sea vessel used during the medieval ages. The wood of the ship was of a darker color as if the wood was burnt, yet somehow seaworthy. The ship was crewed by the spawns of Hades, also known as the Ash demons. The crew worked feverishly to continue sailing through the storm. Should they stop for too long, the ship would surely be destroyed by the intense weather leaving the Ash to swim in the rough waters for eternity.

The demons that controlled the vessel had been sailing in the endless storm since the exile of their master Hades. They were monstrous creatures themselves. Their bodies were big and bulky with strong muscles, standing at nearly seven feet in height. Their faces were a cross between a wolf and a wild boar with tusks sticking up from the bottom of their mouths, sharp as knives, reaching up past their dog-like noses. Their eyes were filled with darkness and a hint of red around the pupils. They were soulless creatures cursed by the Olympians, destined to wander the timeless abyss for eternity, but that was about to change.

While the beasts worked as usual, the captain of this particular vessel walked around the ship checking over each of his crew to help maintain their assigned tasks. It was a routine that he had no choice but to follow. The ship would never reach land, nor would it find anything other than its own kind, cursed to sail forevermore, but if they wanted to survive, they had to stay afloat. However, something was different. There was a strange smell that alerted his senses and he found himself following it into his personal quarters.

He kicked open the door to the dark mess he called his room sniffing the air around him for the unfamiliar odor. He drew his sword when he saw a shadow moving across the wall. He shouted at the stowaway in the language of the Ash. It was a language that had been long forgotten by all except those who chose to study it. Their voices all seemed the same only slight differences in tone, but they all spoke with deep roaring growls.

"Show yourself!" The captain shouted.

A cloaked figure approached him slowly and responded in a feminine, but raspy voice. For some odd reason, not one voice was heard when she spoke, but three different voices in unison.

"As you wish." The figure spoke.

"How did you get on this ship?" He asked holding up the point of his sword to the cloaked figure.

"We have our ways."

"Then you have found your way to the wrong place. Now you'll be feeding my crew with your flesh and bones."

"You would threaten us before hearing our offer?"

He lowered his sword in curiosity. This being didn't show any sign of fear by his presence.

"Then speak quickly and make it good."

"We offer a gift, one that you may offer to your master."

"What gift?"

"It seems the Olympians have found a champion. They wish death upon you and the one you serve. We have come here to offer aid."

"I'm getting hungry and your flesh looks appetizing."

"Then how about blood? The blood of a Pendragon."

"Arthur?" The demon asked. "Who are you?"

"We are known by many names. Oracles, Moirae, Fates, or perhaps the forgotten name of the Ancients."

The demon knew the name from long ago. At the time, the Ancients were not in one body, but three separate women. Each one was beautiful in unique ways and each one was also very vain. Men would risk their very lives for a chance to look upon them, yet no man would ever be good enough for the Ancients. They were once known as powerful psychics making numerous predictions in the lives of the mortals. It was once believed that they held the power to control the very fate of every living person on earth. However, during the war between Hades and the mortals the Ancients predictions had stopped coming true. They sought out help from the Olympians to discover the cause of this but were denied any aid. Zeus had seen greed in their hearts and thought it best to leave them without their power.

It was after Hades offered his own assistance in exchange for their predictions, making them his own personal prophets. With their knowledge of the future he could change the course of history and shape it for his own ends. They had agreed to become his servants, but before they could be of any real benefit the fate of the Ancients had been left in the hands of Merlin and Nimue. Merlin used his power and cursed the three souls into one hideous body. For helping Hades in his attempt to take over they were banished to their home, trapped forever inside a mountain of crystal that was known to many as the Glass Tower. Using a special type of magic Merlin hid the Glass Tower from the rest of the world and only he himself would know its location.

"Why come here now?" The Demon asked.

"We want to finish what was started so many years ago." They answered.

"What do you know?"

"Our prophecy has come true. The visions are fragmented but clear, and the Olympians are counting on their new hero to stop lord Hades once and for all."

"A mortal destined to bring down the god of the Underworld?"

"Yes."

"Impossible!"

"It isn't! We have seen it! However, we have seen alternate futures as well. We can help Hades accomplish his goal."

"What is it you require of us?"

"He is still young, still lacking the knowledge and experience. Take him now. In his current state he will be no match for Hades, but if you wait until it is too late, then his chances will increase."

"Where can I find him?"

"He resides on an island hidden from the Earth and hidden from time itself. Be cautious, the island is of old power. It will not be as easy as you think. They are cunning."

"We are unable to leave this realm; how do you expect us to find this island?"

"We have friends in high places, but you get nothing until you have made a promise to us."

"What promise?"

"Even at this moment we are trapped inside our tower. Prisoners like you and we are also trapped in this abomination of a body. Our minds cannot break free of this. The constant thoughts of three minds all at once is driving us insane! We will help you, but in return we want Merlin. Bring him to us, alive so that he might free us of this curse!"

"Where can I find Merlin?"

"Unknown at this time, but when he has been located you will bring him to us."

"Deliver us from this realm and you shall have what you seek."

"Deal." The Ancients said with a smile. "You only have one chance, do not waste it."

Even in the dark the demon could see their slimy and snake-like face under their dark hood. The Ancients finally disappeared into a black fog and the demon marched his way to the top deck shouting at the others, ordering them to change course.

"The winds are about to change!" The captain shouted. "It's time to bring back our master and punish the one responsible for our cursed fate! Let the war begin!"

The demons shouted and cheered as the rain sprayed their ugly faces. Soon they would see the way out of the endless ocean and get their revenge on Arthur himself.

CHAPTER FIVE

Parker slowly began to regain consciousness. He could feel a gentle breeze blowing against his face as he lay on the ground at the center of the café. The darkness was starting to fade, and things were beginning to get brighter, and...something smelled terrible. He opened his eyes and grimaced at the foul thing being held before him.

"What is that?" He asked grabbing his nose.

Lucas held a bright red and green flower inches from Parkers' face and pulled it away at Parkers' request.

"This is a flower that gives off a putrid smell." Lucas said. "We use it to revive the unconscious with its odor."

"It smells like a...what does that smell like?" Parker asked.

"We tried to think of a name but couldn't come up with a word ill enough to describe it. Are you well now?"

"I think so, but I'll smell that for days."

Lucas helped Parker to his feet. A small crowd had gathered around him. Among them was Arthur.

"All right everyone, give him some room to breathe." Arthur spoke waving everyone away. He walked forward and shook Parkers' hand. "Quite a fall you took."

"Yeah, I guess I'm a little squeamish."

"You'll need to get over that. I suppose Lucas didn't go over everything just yet."

"One step at a time, I didn't want to overwhelm him on the first day." Lucas said defensively. "Parker, allow me to introduce you to Arthur, one of our oldest residents."

"Nice to meet you." Parker said shaking Arthurs' hand. "What was the deal with that guy back there?"

"No one dies on Avalon." Arthur explained. "This island has a healing capability that allows us to regenerate from wounds faster than normal. It makes us stronger and more tolerant to pain. It also allows us to train much harder."

"I can see how that would be useful." Parker said.

"Lucas, I'd like to speak to you a moment in private if that's all right." Arthur said.

"Sure. Parker, why don't you take a walk around and explore the island?"

"Yeah okay. I'll catch up with you later." Parker replied.

Parker walked away from the two men and headed up the mountain path.

"Is everything all right, Arthur?" Lucas asked taking a seat at his table.

"We need to talk about our new friend." Arthur replied.

Parker continued along the path taking in the amazing sights. He started for his own cabin at first but detoured when he noticed a large garden just off the path to his right. Waist-high hedges circled the garden with a floral arched doorway displaying several types of roses, red, white, yellow, and mostly blue. To get into the garden, he had to cross a small narrow bridge. A few feet below the bridge there was a stream that couldn't have been more than a couple of feet deep.

In the center of the garden stood a large tree full of green apples. It was the apple tree that caught Parkers' attention in the first place, but he couldn't help but gaze upon the different flowers that adorned the beautifully kept garden. There were roses, poppies, lilies, daisies, and even several flowers that Parker had never seen before. Not just one of any kind either, but dozens of colors. After looking over the garden, Parker stepped toward the tree and reached up for an apple. He grabbed the one hanging from the lowest branch, but no sooner had he pulled one from the tree another grew in its place just as quickly. Parker smiled and took a large bite from the apple.

"What are you doing?" A female voice asked with an English accent.

Parker turned sharply, startled by the sudden voice. A slender woman stood in front of him. She had to be in her early twenties with auburn colored hair that hung just barely past her shoulders and she had the brightest blue eyes Parker had ever seen. He was quite taken with how beautiful she was. Never had he seen someone so lovely.

"Oh sorry, I saw the tree…" He said trying to quickly swallow some apple. "I didn't know it was private property."

"I don't mind people taking anything from here, but I do appreciate them asking me first." She said.

Parker swallowed the rest, hoping he wouldn't choke on his stolen fruit.

"I really am sorry." He said sincerely. "I didn't mean to overstep…"

"No, it's all right." She replied. "I don't mean to sound rude. I just try my best to care for this garden, and some people are less careful when taking things from here."

"I love flowers and apples. I think you've got a fantastic landscape here. Must be really good soil."

"Thank you. The garden belongs to the Queens, but I tend to it for them."

There was an awkward moment of silence while the young woman placed an empty basket on the ground beside her.

"My name is Parker, Parker Wallace." He said extending his hand.

"I'm Eva." She said as the two shook hands and smiled.

"So, you live around here?" He asked, immediately regretting it, thinking to himself where else would she live dummy?

"I do, I have a small cabin just up the mountain." She answered. "You seem somewhat familiar to me, have you lived here long?"

"Technically it's my first day."

"Oh, well then, welcome to Avalon."

"Thanks. Apparently, I had a death in my.... well me. I died recently." He said not so smoothly. "How long have you been here?"

"I grew up here." Eva responded with a grin.

"Really? Then you were born here?"

"Not exactly. I was found when I was just a few months old. I somehow ended up here and the Queens allowed me to stay. I try to repay their kindness by tending to the garden and watching over the horses."

"Sounds like a great deal, I like horses, apples, flowers...." Stop talking, Parker thought to himself. Eva couldn't help but smile as Parker fumbled through the conversation. Obviously, he was a bit nervous, but she was flattered none the less.

"Would you like to help me feed them?" She asked. "I was just about to head that way."

"Sure." He answered, relieved that she hadn't been put off by his awkward approach.

Eva grabbed a basket sitting on the ground and began picking several apples to place inside of it. Parker watched as they instantly grew back, still amazed by the sight. Afterward, she walked through an exit at the opposite end of the arched entrance and Parker followed. They entered a large grassy field where two horses were prancing around. After seeing Eva enter the area the two horses moved toward her. Parker watched as they walked up to her and brushed her arms with their noses showing their compassion for her.

"These are my babies." She said patting them both on the neck. "This is Midnight and Serenity."

Midnight was a Clydesdale with dark-colored hair while Serenity was a pony, white as snow. Midnight walked toward Parker and nudged him with his nose nearly knocking him off balance.

"He wants you to pet him." Eva said laughing.

Parker patted Midnight on the neck gently while Serenity slowly moved toward him as well. He held his half-eaten apple up to Midnight who grabbed it from his hand and finished it off rather quickly.

"He let you feed him." Eva said with a surprised smile. "Normally he doesn't let anyone that close. I guess they like you."

"That's a good thing, right?" Parker asked.

"Animals can tell you a lot about a person. If my horses didn't trust you then I wouldn't either. They look out for me and I look out for them. It's safe to say that I value their opinion."

"Glad we all got off to a great start. I definitely believe trust has to be earned and not given."
Eva smiled at Parker.

"Not that you can't trust me." He corrected himself nervously. "I'm a trustworthy guy, but other people have to earn trust. Build bonds and...." Stop talking he again told himself.

"I'll try to remember that. That's good advice." She said with a subtle laugh.

Parker smiled at Eva, but shook his head, annoyed at himself. In his head he could remember how awkward he was when talking to a beautiful woman. He didn't want to repeat the same mistakes. He reminded himself to choose his words more carefully. Midnight broke away from the group and began to run around in circles. He swayed his head back and forth as if he were dancing around begging for attention. Eva and Parker couldn't help but laugh.

"Nice moves show off." Parker said. "He's a better dancer than me, that's for sure."

After treating the horses to the apples, Parker and Eva left the field and made their way out of the garden.

"I appreciate you letting me help you out." Parker said politely. "That was fun."

"Well I appreciate the help." Eva responded. "In fact, I like to occasionally take them for walks. Have you ever ridden a horse before?"

"I can't say I have."

"I could teach you to ride if you'd like. You think you might be up for that sometime?"

"Absolutely, just say when and I'm all yours…theirs…. I'd love to take them out for a ride." Parker said, again reminding himself to think before speaking.

Eva seemed to be interested in him, but he wasn't exactly sure. Maybe she was just being friendly to the new guy. She was definitely a nice woman with a gentle soul. He wasn't going to turn away a new friend, especially one so lovely and caring.

Suddenly the light in the sky started to dim. Clouds were moving in overhead and the wind began to pick up.

"It looks like it's about to rain or something." Parker said.

"That's odd." Eva spoke.

"What's odd?"

"It doesn't rain here."

A bell began to ring in the distance. It seemed to be coming from the center of the village. Eva was slightly puzzled after hearing the sound.

"That's a warning bell." She said.

"Warning for what?"

"I'm not sure."

She walked down the path a little and noticed several people running toward them. It was only the shop owners and fishermen from the village. Eva managed to catch the attention of one woman rushing past her.

"What's going on?" Eva asked.

"It's them." The woman said in a panic as she continued running away. "They've found the island!"

"Oh no." Eva said softly.

"What is it?" Parker asked.

Eva looked out through the trees toward the ocean. In the distance, she could see a dark ship headed toward the docks. There was a sudden smell of burning wood that swirled in the air around them.

"Ash demons." She said.

"What's an Ash demon?" Parker asked.

"Come on!" Eva said ignoring his question and instead grabbed him by the hand and almost literally dragged him behind her.

Lucas and Arthur joined the dozens of men near the docks ready to fight. Arthur walked toward the front of the group with Lucas right behind him.

"That was fast." Lucas said looking at Arthur.

Arthur had told Lucas about his conversation with Nimue, and how the Queens had called him to serve after all his years on the island. Arthur would need Lucas' help as well. However now he had to figure out how to resolve their current situation and fast. Arthur turned to the warriors that stood ready. He looked to the man who was their master.

"You know what to do." Arthur said to the master fighter, who nodded in understanding.

No sooner had the ship arrived the ash demons poured onto the dock. Arthur and Lucas drew their swords as did the men behind them.

"Attack!" The Master ordered.

The demons and the fighters' swords clashed so hard sparks flew into the air. The large creatures threw several men into the water and onto the beach. Slowly but surely the demons forced their way onto the island. Fighters all over defended against them as best as they could, but the demons were savage and brutal. They knew they wouldn't be able to kill any of the villagers due to the healing nature of the island, so they attacked strong while a smaller group of Ash demons ran for the mountain path to search quickly for their prize. The captain of the ship eyed Arthur and charged at him with rage.

Eva and Parker entered her cabin. Without the sunlight pouring in through the windows and a lack of lighting inside, it was too dark for Parker to really see anything.

"What is going on?" He asked as Eva dropped down and began to move her hand along the wooden floorboards. "Are you all right?"

Finally, she found what she was looking for, a small trap door located in the floor.

"Hurry, get in." She said as she pulled Parker downward and shoved him under the floor, climbing in beside him and closing the hatch above them.

The space they were in was tight and the two had no choice but to lay on their backs looking up through the tiny cracks in the floor. There was hardly any room to move at all. Their shoulders were touching the inner walls of the secret room as well as each other's. Only a space of a few inches separated them from the roof of their hiding spot. Parker wished he hadn't had such a big breakfast.

"Not that I don't enjoy being this close to you, but this is very uncomfortable." Parker whispered.

"Shhh, don't talk." Eva responded. "I can hear them."

A growling and snarling noise could be heard just outside the cabin.

"What is that?" Parker asked.

With one kick, the door was forced open and two demons entered. Eva pressed her hand against Parkers' mouth to keep him quiet as his eyes widened at the sight of the monsters above him. His heart began to pound in his ears as the demons searched the room kicking over furniture, breaking glasses, and other objects occupying the space. After a few minutes of searching they gave up and moved on to the next cabin.

"Those are Ash demons?" Parker asked Eva in a whisper.

Eva pushed open the trap door and sat up from the ground. Parker sat up beside her licking his lips and wiping off his mouth.

"What kind of lotion do you use?" He asked.

"Sweet Coconut." She answered.

"Smells great."

"Thanks."

"Tastes terrible." Parker said as he climbed up onto the floor and helped Eva out of the trap door.

"I think they're gone." She said. "If they're here, something bad must have happened."

"What do you mean? I thought this was a safe place."

"We should get to the shelter. There's a secret path that leads to the other side of the island. Most of the other villagers would have gone there."

"All right come on."

They cautiously walked out of the cabin only to find the two demons standing on opposite ends of the door waiting for them.

"Run!" Parker said shoving Eva forward as the demons swung toward him, but he managed to duck in time for the monsters to hit each other. He rushed to Eva and grabbed her by the hand. The demons quickly recovered and chased them down the mountain path. Parker had no idea what they wanted or why they were after them, but he knew he had to get Eva away from them as quickly as possible.

Arthur was growing tired as the captain swung hard and furiously as if he were attempting to knock the sword from Arthurs' hand. Lucas could see Arthur struggling, but there was no possible way he could offer aid. Arthur slammed the hilt of his sword into the demons' stomach and attempted to run away but another demon managed to trip him, forcing him to the ground. The fight wasn't going well as most of the men had either been disarmed or knocked unconscious. Arthur knew the battle was almost over, they had been caught off guard, which was no excuse for an island of men who devoted so much time to training for such events, but it was obvious they had lost. The captain swung hard and finally forced Arthurs' sword from his hand.

"What do you want?" Arthur shouted at them.

The captain shouted orders to his demons to stop their attack. The Ash disengaged from the battle and rounded up the village defenders. The fight was over. The captain stared annoyed and angry into Arthurs' eyes.

"Where is he?"

"I'll keep them busy while you get to safety." Parker told Eva as they stopped near the garden.

"What are you going to do?" She asked in concern.

"I haven't figured that out yet." He responded as he motioned for her to run.

He watched her closely until she was out of sight and then turned back to see the two demons approaching quickly.

"Whoa!" He yelled as he darted for the garden entrance. The demons followed him inside quickly, but Parker was already hidden out of sight. One demon ordered the other to search the area. He unsheathed his sword and began to chop at the flowers surrounding him, hoping to force Parker from his hiding place.

Just as the demon stepped toward the apple tree, the bucket Eva used to carry apples slammed into his face knocking him to the ground. Parker stepped out from behind the tree with the bucket in his hand.

"How do you like them apples?" He retorted.

The second demon appeared behind Parker and grabbed him by the arms, lifting him off the ground.

"Whoops!" Parker yelled as he kicked his feet trying to break free, but it was no use. The demon was still stronger. The other demon rose to his feet.

"Take him to the captain." He said in their unknown language.

Moments later, the two demons approach the docks with Parker as their captive. Parker could see the village warriors had also been subdued. Arthur, Lucas, and worst of all Eva were restrained with the others.

"Now hold up a minute!" Parker shouted as the demon tossed him onto the ground in front of the captain.

"What do we have here?" The captain asked. "You smell important."

Parker looked at the captain curiously as he crawled away toward the others.

"I don't understand what he's saying." Parker said shaking his head.

"It's me you're after." Arthur said standing to his feet. "Leave everyone else out of this."

The captain turned his attention to Arthur. Arthur knew the language after years of study. However, everyone else around them were oblivious to the conversation.

"We didn't come here just for you Arthur." The demon captain said. "We want the one the Ancients spoke of. The one from the vision Nimue tried to hide away."

"What is he saying?" Parker asked Lucas.

"I don't know." Lucas whispered. "Just stay silent."

"How did you get here?" Arthur asked.

73

"As it turns out, you have more enemies than you thought."

"No one here needs to suffer. I'll go with you without incident. Just take me and we'll go."

"We want the boy as well and then we will leave."

"I'm not agreeing to that."

"I know it's him." The captain said pointing at Parker. "Confirm it and we're done here."

"I'm not sure of any Ancients, or boy that you're looking for."

"This island prevents us from killing anyone, but how much pain can they endure?" The captain asked as he inspected the men around him. "We've got nothing but time."

He stopped at one of the villagers and thrust his sword deep into his back. The blade stuck out of his chest, covered in blood.

"Stop this!" Arthur shouted.

"Bring another blade!" The captain shouted.

"This is insane." Parker said to himself.

The captain shoved another sword into the villagers' body as he screamed in pain.

"That's enough!" Arthur ordered.

"Another blade!"

Parker shut his eyes as a demon handed the captain another sword and he continued the man's cruel punishment.

"Perhaps we shall remove his head! That should take some time to heal."

"All right!" Arthur yelled as he stepped toward the captain and pointed to Parker. "You're right. He is the one you're after."

The captain turned and snarled as Arthur slowly made his way to Parker.

"I'm sorry kid." Arthur said softly. "I don't have a choice."

"No." Eva muttered under her breath.

The captain ordered one of his demons to grab Parker and Arthur. The demon grabbed Parker by the shirt and began pulling him toward the ship.

"What's going on?" Parker asked frightened, trying to resist being dragged aboard.

Lucas and Eva both looked on with concern. The demons removed the swords from the villager and threw him toward Lucas.

"What of the rest of them?" A demon asked. "We could bring them along."

"We have what we came for." The captain said. "Let's not linger any longer."

Arthur and Parker were both taken aboard the ship. The demons were cautious about turning their backs toward the village warriors. It would be best to get out of there quickly before the warriors had a chance to turn the tables. Before being hauled below deck Parker caught a glimpse of Eva attempting to run after the ship, but Lucas and another villager were holding her back. She watched in horror as the ship departed the dock. Lucas put his hand on her shoulder.

"Why would they take them?" She asked jerking away from Lucas. "Why would you let them? We could have fought them off. I don't understand how you could lose so easily. This is supposed to be the safest island in existence."

"Have faith my dear." Lucas said as he pointed to the ship. "We haven't lost anything yet."

Eva turned her attention back to the ship as it gained distance. Then her eyes were drawn to the silhouette of a figure climbing on the outside. It was too small to be a demon, but before she could make out who the figure was, they disappeared inside a porthole out of sight. She turned back to face Lucas with a curious look on her face.

"Have faith." He repeated with confidence. "We're always prepared."

CHAPTER SIX

Arthur and Parker found themselves locked in the brig of the ship; their wrists chained to the wall. Parker pulled and twisted in an attempt to free himself, but it was no use. The two men were trapped.

"You're not going to break free from that." Arthur said.

"Unlike you I don't plan to give up so easy." Parker said angrily.

"Very well. I suppose you think I should have let them decapitate that man just for the fun of it."

"I thought you all were fighters." Parker said as he continued to pull at his chains. "Those things shouldn't have even got that far. What a joke."

Parker was caught off guard a moment as he suddenly felt a sharp pain in his stomach.

"Ow, my stomach hurts." Parker said. "Where did that come from?"

"They've gained some distance from the island now." Arthur responded.

"What does that have to do with it?"

"The further away you are from Avalon the healing ability becomes useless. It makes us more vulnerable. I assume they'll take us as far away as possible before they try to execute us. Or they'll take us to the Underworld to be tortured. Or maybe even snack on us for a while."

"That's quite a picture you're painting Picasso."

Parker felt that his stomach pain was the least of his worries at this point. Arthur seemed way calmer and more collected than he should have been.

"Why did you give up so easily?" Parker asked.

"I didn't." Arthur answered.

"You did. then you gave me up with you, which by the way made no sense! Why would they even want me anyway?"

"They have a score to settle with me, but you they need to stop before you can do any damage."

"What damage? I didn't have a grudge with them. I don't even know anything about them."

"That doesn't matter. They know something about you that you haven't discovered yet."

"I'm a nobody. I shouldn't even be here."

"You taste the same to them regardless. Whether you're someone important or just another man in their way, you're a piece of meat now."

"That's just great." Parker said sarcastically. "Sounds like my kind of luck. Find an island paradise just in time to be a demons' main course."

Parker finally quit tugging at his chains and sat on the floor across from Arthur. The chains would not allow his hands to drop, forcing Parker to hold his arms above his head.

"Who are these guys?" Parker asked. "Eva called them Ash demons?"

"Spawns of Hades." Arthur answered. "Soulless creatures devoted to destroying the world in the name of their master."

"Hades? Like from Greek myth?"

"It's no myth."

"It's fantasy. They make movies and about them and teach us that stuff in high school."

"I'll let the myths know that they are just fantasy when they come back to eat us."

"Or maybe you and I could figure a way out of here."

Arthur looked around the room. There was nothing but the cell door and the chains holding them captive.

"I don't see a way out." Arthur said.

"Well don't strain yourself old man." Parker said slightly annoyed at Arthurs' lack of concern for their situation.

"That hurts. Did you make that observation all by yourself?"

"How are you so calm?"

"Who says I am?"

"You just look like you're waiting for a bus or something. I suppose you're used to this kind of thing. You even said they have a score to settle with you. What did you do to them?"

Arthur looked away in hesitation. Nimue had told him a little about Parker, but he couldn't see what made him of such importance. He looked like just an average guy who ended up in the wrong place at possibly the right time. Parker could sense that Arthur didn't trust him. They had just met and ended up together on the ship, but he had to have answers. He was in this situation because of Arthur after all.

"Look, instead of me sitting here asking a thousand questions, why don't you just explain to me what's going on." Parker said. "You obviously have history here."

"During the time you know as the Dark Ages, Hades started a war with the mortal world." Arthur replied. "The other Olympians had stepped aside long ago in order to give mankind its freedom, but Hades refused to let go of his power and sought to destroy everything that man possessed, but his campaign was ended. He and his demons were captured and locked away where they could cause no more damage."

"That's good right?"

"It was, but while they were still on earth, Hades captured the souls of thousands of men, women, and children."

"How could he do that?"

"Hades was the ruler of the Underworld. After someone's death he had the ability to take anyone's soul as long as they were within a certain range."

"Within range?"

"His power has limits, or else he could simply wipe out everyone and then he'd succeed."

"Makes sense I suppose."

"The souls he captured have been locked in the Underworld, unable to move on or be at peace ever since. The only way to set them free is to destroy Hades once and for all."

"What does that have to do with you?"

"I had a part in locking him away. I traded my own soul to his brother Zeus for Hades capture."

"Traded to who?" Parker asked in surprise. "You said Zeus?"

"Zeus yes."

"Zeus? As in the god of Olympus? That means they're all real?"

"All myth is based on some truth. They aren't Gods, but it isn't hard to see why people thought they were."

"Okay, so where do I fit in? That's the part that makes the least amount of sense."

"Before his imprisonment, a trio of women known as the Ancients predicted his downfall by a single man who would have the ability to destroy Hades and set our people free."

"That man, being you?"

"No, I only helped imprison him. I can't destroy him."

"So what? They think I know where this guy might be?"

"No, you're here because you are that guy."

"Me? Talk about scraping the bottom of the barrel. Seriously I'm not the guy they're looking for, I've never done anything to suggest otherwise."

"That's not true then is it? Lucas told me you saved a woman by giving your life for hers."

"What woman?"

"The woman you helped on the bridge before

dropping into that river. Lucas told me all about it."

"That just happened. It wasn't.... You're more of a hero than I am. You fought these things before."

"I only played a small part in their capture. I tried to fight them before and nearly died in the process, but I failed because it is not my destiny to defeat them. It's yours."

"If you couldn't win then, how could I? I can't fight a demon; I wouldn't even know how."

"You can be trained."

"No, I can't do this. They made a mistake. You all did. I'm not who they think I am. I'm just a normal guy. I'm a security guard, and not even a good one. I don't even belong here." Parker was even saddened by his own words. The thought of what he just said impacted him more than it did Arthur. "I haven't really belonged anywhere."

Arthur was silent a moment. He didn't know the man sitting beside him any more than Parker knew him. Yet he felt Parkers' sadness deep down. His eyes were filled with what seemed like a longing to be someone, or even have a place somewhere. One thing Arthur knew for sure was that this young man knew heartbreak.

"Maybe you're right." Arthur said. "Maybe you aren't the right man. There is no guarantee that you could help us win this fight, but the people who pulled you from that river believe otherwise. You are here for a reason. Someone saw something in you, and I have to believe that anything is possible. There are so many souls trapped in the Underworld and going up against Hades will sacrifice more lives, and if that happens, the only way to save them all is to destroy him for good. Those souls deserve freedom Parker and their fate rests on both of our shoulders whether we like it or not."

Parker struggled to understand what he had just been told. He still didn't believe what Arthur was telling him. They had made the wrong choice that much was certain, but he couldn't help but ponder on the thought of what was the right choice? He felt he could just make things worse.

"What am I supposed to do?" He asked.

"That is for you and your conscious to decide." Arthur answered. "I will do my part to help you, but while you're thinking it over it's time for us to go. Get us out of here Sang."

"What?" Parker asked.

Suddenly, Sang dropped down from the ceiling just outside the cell.

"The portal is open." Sang said as he kicked open the cell door. "We have less than five minutes." He unsheathed a sword from over his left shoulder and swung at the chains holding Parker and Arthur freeing them from their restraints.

"He was out there the whole time?" Parker asked.

"You asked why I was so calm?" Arthur answered.

"Ten minutes sooner couldn't have hurt any."

"What about the crew?" Arthur asked Sang as he got up from the floor.

"I've taken down a few, but it's best to just go quietly and as soon as possible." Sang responded.

"Anyone care to explain to me what's happening?" Parker asked.

"This is Sang." Arthur answered. "He jumped on the ship while the demons were distracted with us."

"You planned this the whole time?" Parker asked with a blank look on his face.

"Your arrival was the beginning." Sang said. "I knew the Ash would come for you; it was only a matter of time."

"Then all of those fighters back on Avalon?"

"They were told to hold back." Arthur replied. "We had to make it look like the demons won."

"Why?"

"Demons cannot travel between worlds on their

own." Sang said. "They had to have had help. It takes some great power to do so. We needed to track them and create our own portal back to the island."

"Okay, nice plan."

"You think we wouldn't be prepared for something like this?" Arthur asked.

"Wouldn't the demons know that?"

"They aren't the brain, they're the brawn."

"A little bit of a heads up in the future might be nice."

"I wanted to see how you did under pressure."

"And?" Parker asked.

"I guess we'll have to work on that." Arthur answered

"We must hurry." Sang suggested. "I've rigged the ship with explosives."

Sang opened a door leading into the interior of the ship. Arthur and Parker followed behind him cautiously.

"Move when I say and don't make any noise." Sang spoke, mostly to Parker, who shook his head in understanding.

As the three men made their way onto the top deck they headed for the quarterdeck of the ship. It was the area of the ship above the captains' quarters with stairs on either side to access it. Sang ducked as he silently instructed the others to do the same. Four demons stood directly on the deck above them. One demon held the wheel while talking to the others. Parker sat with his back against the door leading into the captains' quarters. He slowly raised his head to peek into the window only to see the captain sleeping.

"Wait here." Sang whispered as he slowly climbed the stairs.

He had no choice; it was their only way out. He quickly jumped toward them and kicked one demon in the stomach. The other three drew their swords and swung at him simultaneously. Sang performed a backward flip maneuver causing the other three to stab the other demon rather than Sang. He then shoved the demon down the stairs with the three swords sticking out of his chest. Parker watched as the demon then crumbled away leaving only a pile of ashes in its place.

"Right, I get it now." Parker whispered to Arthur. "Ash demons. That's clever."

Arthur rolled his eyes. The remaining demons attempted to attack Sang who swiftly moved through them all with rapid punch and kick combos. His fighting style mimicked that of Brazilian martial arts known as Capoeira, though his style seemed more intense. Each punch thrown in his direction was used to throw the demons off balance. He then kicked one demon in the head, sending him spinning into the air and onto his back. The next demon attempted to kick Sang's feet out from under him but Sang threw his legs into the air and all his body weight shifted onto his right hand which he used to hold himself up.

He moved his legs around the demons' head, twisting it and snapping its neck causing it to crumble into a pile of ash. Finally, the last demon approached him and with one swift motion Sang punched him hard in the chest sending the monster onto its back. Parker watched the entire display in astonishment. He had never seen anything like that outside of an action film. All the noise above however caused the captain to wake up. Parker took a glance through the window only to lock eyes with the captain himself.

"Time to go!" Parker shouted.

Arthur and Parker moved up the stairs toward Sang and looked over the rear edge of the ship.

"Wait a minute!" Parker said.

"We have to jump!" Sang shouted.

"Just a second!"

Suddenly at the back of the ship straight below the

three men, a whirlpool began to appear.

"There's our ride!" Arthur yelled. "It'll take us back to Avalon!"

The whirlpool grew bigger until it was a tunnel wide enough to carry the trio home. Then there was an explosion at the bow of the ship, followed by another just below deck.

"Now!" Sang shouted just as he jumped into the whirlpool.

Arthur grabbed Parker by the shirt and jumped, dragging him over the railing behind him.

"Cheesy peaches!" Parker shouted as he fell into the whirlpool.

The ship exploded into nothing but debris of wood and fire. The demons aboard the ship were caught in the explosion and quickly turned to a cloud of ashes drifting down onto the surface of the ocean waves.

Parker opened his eyes to see Sang and Arthur sliding ahead of him inside the tube of water. He was immediately reminded of a water slide at some theme park. The tube carried him and the others deep under the ocean. As he looked back, he could see the destroyed ship through the surface of the water behind him, which was now several yards away.

Schools of fish, sharks, and stingrays could be seen all around him. Parker felt a rush of adrenaline, like being on a rollercoaster underwater. After going on for a couple of minutes another whirlpool began to open just ahead of them. The tube was reaching its end as water engulfed the three men and began to propel them forward. All three of them shot into the air and hit the wet shore below. Parker crawled forward out of the water and rested his head on the sand.

He pushed himself up and sat on his knees looking ahead of him. Lucas, Eva, and the rest of the villagers stood in front of him. The underwater tube had carried them all the way back to the island with great speed. Arthur and Sang walked away from the beach, leaving Parker to gather his thoughts.

"I may have overdone it a little on the explosives." Sang said with a slight grin.

"Seemed fine to me." Arthur responded with a smile.

Lucas and Eva ran forward to help Parker to his feet. Wet sand covered the entire front of his body.

"Welcome home." Lucas said patting Parker on the back. "That must have been quite an adventure for you."

"How do you feel?" Eva asked. "Are you okay?"

Parker didn't answer at first, but instead had a somewhat blank look on his face. He was dizzy from the ride and somewhat disoriented. He looked at Lucas and then at Eva and then passed out onto the sand.

"Oh dear." Lucas said. "I'll go get the flower."

CHAPTER SEVEN

Once they had arrived back on Avalon, Sang retreated to his cabin near the top of the mountain. Parker was somewhat uneasy after being so far from the island and needed some time to rest. Most of the day had passed and Arthur decided to leave the others to talk at the café. He decided to walk to the middle of the island, deep into a forested area and found himself at the edge of a small lake. The deepest part of the water was at least sixteen feet. He picked up three stones lying on the ground next to him.

With a swift fling the first stone skipped across the lake five times before dropping beneath the surface. The second stone skipped four times. Arthur flicked his wrist and the last stone skipped three times before a hand popped out of the water and caught it as if it were a softball. Arthur watched as Nimue slowly rose out of the water and began to walk barefoot across the surface leaving ripples as her footprints passed over. This time she wasn't just a spirit presence. She stood in front of Arthur in full physical form.

"You do know that skipping stones across my roof is like the screeching of a harpy to me." She said with a slightly irritated look on her face but maintained a smile. "It's slightly annoying."

"Given that you live under a lake, this is the only way I know how to knock." He said slyly.

"Glad you made it back safely." She said.

"We have you to thank for that. I don't suppose sending a boat would have been enough?"

"I thought the tunnel would be more efficient."

"It was, but my stomach is still churning a little from the trip. Poor Parker, what a delicate lad."

Nimue reached the shore and placed the stone on the ground next to Arthur.

"You're really here." Arthur said somewhat surprised. "I would've guessed you'd be back with the other higher beings."

"I thought it best we talk in person this time." She replied.

"I suppose you were able to find out how our friends found us so quickly?"

"It took some time to confirm, but yes. The Ancients are involved once again, yet they aren't powerful enough to open a door between worlds like that. They had help, but I don't know who from. They knew we'd try to track them and shut us down fast."

"I thought you and Merlin took care of the Ancients long ago."

"We did what we needed to do. They've had a long time to let their hate build, and with all that's happening now I suppose their involvement shouldn't be a surprise."

Arthur stood up and walked away from Nimue in frustration.

"You should have known they'd try something like this one day." He said turning back to Nimue with an accusing gesture. "They're the ones who showed you the prophecy and we knew which side they were on. Merlin should have destroyed them when he had the chance."

"Merlin is not a murderer." Nimue said reminding him of his old councilors' nature. "He's a fighter to be sure, but he wouldn't kill anyone he didn't have to. You know him better than that."

"Yes, and look where he ended up, stuck in a bloody tree."

"Arthur. We all did what we had to do to get us to where we are. Merlin had to take a different approach, but he will be ready when we need him again."

Arthur stood still and looked into Nimue's eyes.

"Of course, I forget you have this all figured out and you can't share your knowledge with me."

"You don't seem to understand how lucky we were. We had a brief look into the future and saw one of many possible outcomes. If we aren't careful, we could make it worse in so many ways. I didn't know that the Ash demons would be sent here so quickly upon Parkers' arrival."

"But Sang knew."

Nimue stared at Arthur, not sure how to respond.

"What is it you're not telling me about him?" Arthur asked.

"Sang is a vital part of all this." She answered. "You know what you need to know, and if you don't trust me, you can at least trust him."

"I barely know him. He showed up not long ago himself. Refused any kind of introduction to the island. He isolated himself from the rest of us and now all of sudden he's taking an interest in this boy same as you."

Arthur sat on a nearby stump and Nimue took a seat on the ground beside him, her toes lightly touching the water.

"Knowing too much is dangerous, even for you." Nimue said softly.

"Will anyone else come for him?" Arthur asked.

"Whoever sent the Ash demons can't do so again without exposing themselves. They know we're watching now. You should all be safe for the time being."

"I don't want any more surprises from our side. If there is something that could cause harm to anyone else on this island, I need to be kept in the loop."

"I understand, and you're right. I'll try to be more generous with what information I can."

Arthur nodded his head in agreement, but he was still a bit upset about how the situation played out. He had only known Sang for a brief period. They weren't exactly friends, but Arthur knew he was good man from what few conversations they had.

"That said, there is something else you should know." Nimue said.

"What is it?" Arthur asked.

"A gateway was opened on earth some time ago. A large army of Ash demons poured through."

"You think whoever helped the Ancients saw to that as well?"

"No, this was something else. Someone was able to come into possession of an orb."

"The Dark Light? I thought it was hidden away a long time ago."

"It was and that is what bothers me."

"What do you mean?"

"The timeline is in a constant flux. I've been so focused on the future that I somehow missed something in the present, or perhaps the past."

"Has something changed?"

"It's hard to say. The vision is consistent, and I can tell you for certainty that Parker has an important role to play."

"I'm not sure I believe that's true."

"Regardless of your beliefs, you have a job to do."

"Does Parker know how much time has really passed since he's been on the island? Does he know how long he's been kept in the dark?"

"No, and it would be unbelievably bad to reveal that information to him now. Everything is happening so fast for him that I fear he might be overwhelmed already. Perhaps I should have gotten to him sooner."

"I thought you just discovered his existence." Arthur said in confusion.

"I did." Nimue corrected herself. "I... only meant that I wished that I could have found him sooner."

Arthur decided to brush off Nimue's slight nervousness in her voice. With all that has happened, perhaps she was just as rattled by the events as the rest of them were. Not that she'd be willing to tell him either way.

"He's not like us Nimue. He wasn't born during our time. The things that existed then don't exist anymore."

"He has more of an open mind than most others. He's more like you than you might think. All he needs is time to adjust."

Arthur sighed with frustration as Nimue put her hand on his shoulder in an attempt to comfort him.

"It's going to get worse Arthur. It is going to get so much worse, but it can be fixed as long as we keep fighting. We have to do this."

"I wish there was another way." Arthur responded.

"I do as well, but we were blessed with this vision of the future. We were given the gift of time to prepare and plan. We have to push harder than ever to ensure Earths survival."

"You know I have no fear of death, but when my time comes to return, if Hades gets to me before Parker can…"

"Do not worry." Nimue interrupted. "You're strong enough to take care of yourself."

There was a moment of silence between them.

"Did you speak to him about his destiny?" She asked.

"I did." Arthur replied.

"How did he respond?"

"Exactly how I thought he would. It's going to take him some time to think about what lies ahead. How do you tell someone they're the only hope for the future of mankind?"

"He needs to begin his training soon."

"What if he decides not to do it? What if he chooses to do nothing? You're plan comes crashing down if he simply says no. I'll sure not force it on him."

"He will fight for us."

"How do you know that?"

"He is Parker Wallace." Nimue said as she stood up and walked to the center of the lake.

"That doesn't even make any sense!" Arthur

shouted. "What of Eva?"

"As far as she is concerned, destiny will do the job for us." Nimue said as she smiled and lowered herself into the water, vanishing beneath the surface. Arthur stood up and walked away from the lake and continued to ponder on Nimue's words.

After a decent meal with Lucas, Parker and Eva took a stroll on the beach. Lucas sat at the café, having fallen asleep with his legs on the table, his head leaning back, and his mouth wide open. The sun had set, and the galaxy of stars lit up the sky. There were even more stars than Parker had ever seen in his entire life.

"Quite a day." Eva said trying to break the silence.

"You could say that again." Parker responded.

"Are you all right? You've been quieter since you came back."

"I have a lot on my mind." Parker answered.

"Are you thinking about your life? The one you lived before coming here?"

"It's hard not to, but it's strange to me that I don't even miss it."

"Didn't you have a family or anyone you cared for?"

"My dog." Parker chuckled. "He was my only family. I hope someone's looking after him now. We didn't have anyone else."

"No wife or girlfriend?"

"Not even close." Parker said with a shy laugh. "I was pretty much on my own. Never had too much luck talking to women."

Eva put her arm through Parkers' as they walked along the edge of the beach.

"I think in your own special way, you're very charming." She said with a sweet smile as she looked into his eyes.

"Thanks." He said as he smiled back at her. "I don't know how you'd come to think that, but I'll take it."

"We've definitely got to work on your confidence." She said as she playfully poked him in the side with her finger.

Parker and Eva enjoyed walking arm in arm while gazing up at the starlit sky. Although they had only just met, they were already beginning to feel comfortable in each other's presence.

"This is the first chance I've had to look at the stars since I got here." Parker said, amazed at how many he could see.

"Avalon is closer to the heavens than most places." Eva said. "Nowhere else in the world could you see this many stars all at once. I absolutely love stargazing."

"Where I lived before, I couldn't see any of them. There was too much light pollution, but I was really into astronomy when I was younger. Stargazing was a fun hobby, but later I just didn't have any time for it."

"I always find myself looking up at the stars any chance I get, imagining what wonders could be out there, what worlds I could see."

"Exactly."

"What astronomy knowledge do you have?" Eva asked. "Retain anything interesting from your childhood?"

"Maybe a little." He said pointing toward the sky. "That one there is called Orion, the Hunter."

"Very nice, what about that one?" Eva asked pointing.

"Leo, the lion. In Greek mythology it's said that Hercules himself killed it and placed it in the sky."

Parker thought for a moment about his conversation with Arthur. He was beginning to wonder how much of the legends were actually true. Obviously not that one, because that wasn't how stars worked, but the thought of Hercules as a real person was starting to look more interesting.

"How about another one?" Eva asked.

"Okay, you see that bright one?" He asked pointing up. "It's called Polaris, the North Star. It's the brightest star in the constellation Ursa-Minor. It's also a guiding star because travelers would use it to find their way north when they got lost."

"You know a little." Eva said smiling.

"I read a few books, seen a few movies."

"What are movies?"

"You don't have movies here?" Parker asked as Eva shook her head. "They're moving pictures that tell stories. Instead of reading books you watched the story unfold on a screen with people acting out the parts like a performance."

"What about using your imagination?"

"People still do. You could see things from a director's perspective on a particular story, and most were good. Some could have been better."

"Sounds interesting I suppose."

Parker immediately knew he'd have to speak to Lucas about the possibility of acquiring movies to show Eva if it was even possible. The two continued their walk together until Parkers' thoughts began to wonder again. He couldn't get his mind off what Arthur had said to him.

"I want you to know that I'm here if you need me." Eva said sensing some distress in Parkers' eyes. "I'm a very good listener and you can always count on my help for anything."

"There is something I could use a little more information on." He said.

"Of course."

"Do you know anything about Hades and the Underworld?"

"Only the stories I've been told."

"Such as?"

"Scary stories honestly. The kind that keep you awake at night because unfortunately they're all true."

"You mean the stories about the people trapped?"

"Why do you want to know about them? I should warn you it's not a happy topic."

"It's something Arthur mentioned when we were on that ship."

"I'm surprised he brought it up. Arthur doesn't like to talk about that with anyone."

"Why?"

Eva paused a moment as if she were contemplating on telling Parker the story at all. It was a tale of sadness and loss. Arthur wasn't keen on talking to anyone about his past. Eva and Arthur had known each other for a while, but not well enough to share stories that personal. Eva heard most of her knowledge of Arthur and his knights through hearsay and from Lucas as well as gossip from the other villagers.

"Arthur was one of those who wanted to find a way to help them, but no matter how hard he tried, he failed. He was devastated that he couldn't save her."

"Her?"

"His wife, Guinevere."

Parker stared at Eva curiously.

"Guinevere?" He asked. "You don't mean Guinevere like, Arthur and Guinevere? As in King Arthur?"

"Yes." Eva answered.

"Oh wow!" Parker exclaimed. He couldn't believe it. King Arthur was the real deal, and he met him personally. "That's incredible. I never would have thought Arthur was THE King Arthur."

"Oh, you've heard of him?"

"He's a legend where I come from. Most of the stories are pure myth, but to find out he's real, it's incredible."

"During the war," Eva continued. "Arthurs' wife was murdered by Hades and his demons. Hades captured her soul and trapped it just like many others. He searched every way possible to try to get her back, but more lives were claimed in the process."

"Arthur blamed himself?"

"It saddens me to think of how he must feel. I don't believe anyone has ever loved someone as much as he loved her. I know he'd do anything to save her from that fate, and the others, but it may not be possible."

"It's not his destiny." Parker said, thinking again about what Arthur had told him before. Thoughts raced through his mind about everything he had experienced thus far. He thought about his supposed death, his arrival on Avalon, and what it all meant. Was he meant for a greater purpose? Is this what he was destined to do? If he said yes and decided to fight against Hades, what if he lost? How could he risk everything if there was no guarantee he could win? If he said no then all those people would have no hope of getting out, or would they?

Would anyone else be up to the challenge he had been presented with. Could they succeed where he might fail? If King Arthur himself couldn't do it, what chance did he have? How could he live with himself if he did nothing to help them when it was supposedly in his power to save them?

He looked into Eva's eyes. Once again, her beauty struck him almost leaving him breathless. He could feel the butterflies in his stomach. He felt he could be happy on Avalon with Eva at his side. He wanted to get to know her better, but his conscience quickly pushed his desires away.

"I have to do something Eva." He said. "I'm not sure how it's all going to work out, but I think it's the right thing."

"Are you all right?" She asked.

"Yeah. Is it okay if I see you again soon?"

"I'd like that." She said with a smile.

Parker pulled her hand to his lips and kissed it

before he walked away from the beach. Eva looked down at her hand and smiled. She didn't have many friends on Avalon despite her growing up there, aside from Lucas and a few others. She didn't know what it was, but Parker made her feel safe and secure. There was something familiar about him. She felt she could trust him and that somehow, she knew that it was the start of something bigger.

Arthur sat in his chair near his fireplace. He slowly began to sip a hot cup of coffee when he heard a knock at his door. He opened it to find Parker standing on the other side.

"Tell me something." Parker said. "Do you believe I'm the one to set them free? Do you really think I have what it takes?"

"It doesn't matter what I believe." Arthur replied. "The Olympians vouched for you themselves."

"I'm asking you. Do you think it's possible I have a shot of being the man they hope I am?"

Arthur stood silent for a moment.

"Not yet I don't, but it wouldn't be the first time I've been wrong." Arthur answered finally. "Prove to me that you are. Prove it to us both."

Parker nodded his head in understanding. He stepped into the cabin and sat in a chair near the fireplace.

"I lived my whole life thinking I was nobody." Parker began. "I felt like I had no purpose, like God himself had completely forgotten about me. I grew up in foster homes, never got adopted. I just assumed nobody wanted me. Then I come here and find out that powerful people believe there is something great hidden inside me. People of legend believe in me. They believe that I'm meant to do something completely beyond my capabilities. I'm not the guy they need, but I'd like to be. That feeling it gives me, makes me scared, but it also feels good to be important to someone."

WARRIOR FROM AVALON

Arthur looked at Parker with a glimmer of respect, not expecting him to agree to what was being asked of him.

"I want be better than I was before." Parker continued. "I want to be the guy they think I am. I want to be a hero like you are in the stories they tell about you."

Arthur was humbled for a moment by Parkers' words. He knew Parker must have learned of his history either by Eva or by Lucas.

"Are you certain?" Arthur asked. "If you choose to do this, you understand that you will be taking the weight of this burden on your shoulders. Once I've taught you everything you need to know, you'll be completely on your own. Those lost will be dependent on you. Should you fail then you will join them in their fate. You will go to Hades to fight him to the death. There will be no coming back from that. Do you think that is something you can handle?"

"I understand the risk, but what kind of person would I be if I refused to try?"

"It's my responsibility to prepare you as much as possible. I warn you; it's not going to be easy. You will be trained harder than anyone else I've ever worked with."

"When do we start?"

Sang suddenly stepped out of the shadows from behind Parker and nodded his head at Arthur. Parker turned to see Sang behind him sipping on his own cup of coffee and turned back to Arthur.

"Immediately."

Moments later, Arthur and Parker had followed Sang back to his cabin. The back yard was lit up with spotlights enabling them to see even in the dark. There were numerous amounts of training equipment ranging anywhere from dojo mats, breaking boards, punching bags, and wooden dummies. Weapons adorned a long shelf to the side. Many of these included daggers, spears, makhaira (a type of short sword), butterfly swords (not to be confused

WARRIOR FROM AVALON

with the knife), broadswords, long swords, and even a Sidesword, often called a cutting rapier by most collectors. There were even handguns and other firearms off to the side.

"You're either well prepared, or you're really paranoid." Parker said.

"Everything you see here; you will become an expert with by the time we are done." Sang replied.

"Do you have padding, or protective gear?" Parker asked hopeful. "I bruise easily."

Sang didn't respond verbally, but instead looked Parker in the eyes, showing no sign of interest in his attempted humor.

"You don't know unless you ask." Parker said.

Arthur stepped in front of Parker and crossed his arms while Sang prepared on the side.

"As of right now, you are in training." Arthur said. "Sang and I are your instructors. You do what we say, when we say it. Is that clear?"

"Absolutely."

Arthur punched Parker as hard as he could in the stomach. He went to the ground gasping for air and coughed hard.

"You will be trained more thoroughly than anyone else on this island. We will not hold back because YOU cannot afford to fail."

Arthur then kicked Parker in the face sending him rolling onto his back. Sang stood beside Arthur and placed his hand on his shoulder as if to say enough. Arthur walked away allowing Sang to proceed. Sang pulled Parker to his feet but didn't let go of his arm. He then shoved his right knee into Parkers' chest and flipped him forward sending him to the ground yet again. Parker coughed even more as he spit blood from his mouth. He had never been in a real fight before. His body was taking a beating it wasn't used to.

WARRIOR FROM AVALON

"Before we can begin, we must break you in every way possible." Sang said. "You must learn to carry on through the pain. You must learn to treat every broken bone. Every injury is just another challenge. When we are finished, you will be a force not to be taken lightly. We will cover as much as possible in truly little time, so be ready, because this is just the beginning."

Arthur stepped forward once more, shouting as he attacked Parker with rapid punches and kicks. Each time Parker hit the ground Arthur would pick him back up, and then hit him even more forcing him right back down. He then reached down and grabbed Parkers' arm, snapping it at the elbow forcing him to scream in pain.

"There are monsters in this world, and when we are finished, they will be afraid of you." Sang spoke as he watched Arthur slam his foot down on Parkers' kneecap. Parker was bloody as he hit the ground. His face was cut, his bones were broken, and his eyes were already swollen shut.

"You will become the warrior you are meant to be."

CHAPTER EIGHT

Hours later the sun began to rise. Arthur and Parker circled each other on the dojo mats as Sang watched patiently from the side. Parkers' bones had already healed, and they were broken again. Now he was bruised and bleeding, wishing that the healing ability would do its job much faster. He threw a right punch as Arthur leaned over to dodge the attack. He returned with a swift uppercut to Parkers' jaw knocking him off balance.

"Pay particular attention to your opponents' movements." Sang said. "You must know where his arms are before he does."

Arthur threw a quick jab at Parkers' face, but Parker leaned left avoiding the punch.

"Very good." Sang said. "Now do it again."

Arthur threw another jab which Parker avoided, but immediately Arthur followed with a left cross knocking Parker to the ground.

"This fight was over quicker than the last one." Arthur said.

Parker tried to shake off the previous strike as his eyes were seeing double. He rubbed his temple with his fingers to try to regain his composure. Still dizzy, he stood up and turned to Arthur.

"I'm not done yet old man!" Parker shouted. "What are you fifty…or like six hundred years old now?"

"Do not become overconfident in yourself." Arthur replied with a grin. "You're still no match for me…kid!"

Parker moved forward with two quick jabs, which Arthur was able to avoid easily. He then quickly followed with a right hook, but Arthur ducked. It was then Parker used the opportunity to bring his knee sharply to Arthurs' chin, which landed perfectly knocking him off balance.

"That was unexpected." Sang said to himself with a smirk.

WARRIOR FROM AVALON

Arthur shook it off and ran forward to attack with a series of jabs, which Parker avoided or blocked. He followed with an uppercut, but Parker leaned back to avoid that as well and then forced three quick jabs to Arthurs' face. The jabs were painful, but Arthur had been hurt much worse than that. He stepped forward as Parker took a step back as if he were not interested in continuing the fight.

"Do not hold back!" Arthur yelled as he stood up.

"I'm not!" Parker responded.

"Those hits should have knocked me out. You have to put more power into your punches."

"I'm trying. Maybe I'm just not as strong as you thought."

"No, you're just too afraid of hurting me, but that is what this island is for. We can kill each other and shake it off and do it all over again. Now hit me harder!"

Arthur jabbed twice and tossed in a right hook for good measure. Parker spit blood and charged at Arthur with a jab and an uppercut.

"Harder!" Arthur shouted as he wiped sweat from his forehead.

Parker was starting to get a little angry. He moved forward throwing as many punches as he could. Arthur was able to avoid a couple, but Parkers' speed ensured he landed a few blows to Arthurs' face.

"It's not about just being fast kid!" Arthur explained. "You're punches have to hurt! You have to put everything you have into each strike!"

Parker tightened his knuckles. He had never felt such pain before. He moved quickly toward Arthur yet again and punched as fast and as hard as he could. Several of his punches were easily dodged, but the very last hit found its mark. Arthur had finally felt the pain he had been waiting for. He moved toward Parker and swung a left hook, but Parker ducked and returned with a right cross. His fist slammed into Arthurs' face, knocking him to the ground with force. Arthur looked up, his eyes trying to focus. Blood finally peeked out from a cut on his lip.

Arthur wiped it away as he sat on the ground and locked eyes with Parker.

"That's more like it." He said with a smirk. "But it's still not enough."

"You've gotta be kidding me." Parker said in between breaths.

He took in as much air as he could as Arthur rose to his feet yet again. The two men battled with bare fists for several more hours. Parker was exhausted from the lack of rest, and to his surprise, Arthur had the energy of a toddler hyped up on candy.

"Enough." Sang finally said to Parkers' relief. "We will continue in a few more hours."

Parker didn't care that his training would continue so soon. He was simply happy to hear he was about to get a break, and it wasn't one of his bones. After they were finished, Parker washed his face in the kitchen sink as Arthur entered one of the guest rooms of Sang's house. Sang walked up behind Parker and patted him on the back.

"You're a quick learner." He said. "You should rest here. Sleep in the other guest room. We will begin again very soon."

Parker nodded his head and started to walk away. His eyes were bruised, and his left eye was partially swollen shut. He held his ribs as he walked away slowly.

"One question?" Parker asked with a sore mouth as he turned back toward Sang. "I've never had any kind of training before. If Arthur wasn't holding back, how did I manage to do so well so fast? I'm not that quick of a learner."

"You may just surprise even yourself." Sang began. "Avalon does help you in many ways. You heal faster, but it also makes your mind more receptive. Where it takes normal people weeks or months to learn to fight, you will be able to learn in a matter of days or even hours depending on how dedicated you are to the training. We've much to cover while we have the chance."

"How is that possible? What is it about this place?"

"Avalon is a place of old magic. It was created by the Queens during the rule of the Olympians. They wanted warriors to fight important battles. After Zeus had decided to end their rule, this place became less important. However, events transpired as time moved on and the Queens still offered brave individuals like you a place to live as a warrior should. Free from the burden of battle, but always prepared to fight one."

"There has to be a purpose to all of this." Parker said. "You don't just keep a place like this and train on a daily basis for nothing. What are they preparing for?"

"Some say there is a war coming. Mankind may yet face its greatest battle. When that time comes, we will need fighters. I think some are hoping you may prevent that war from happening at all. Which is why you don't have time to waste. We must work extremely hard with what time we have. Soon enough, you will be taken to another destination. They will send a ship and then you will put everything we teach you to use."

"Right, lucky me." Parker said sarcastically.

"Get some rest. We're just getting started."

Parker turned and entered his room, which consisted of just a blanket and a pillow. There was no furniture anywhere. He already missed his own bed and wondered if he'd made the right choice. The days ahead were going to be very interesting.

It was only five hours later as Parker slept soundly on the floor. He was so tired from earlier that he was asleep in a matter of seconds. Suddenly he felt a rush of icy cold water poured over his entire body. He snapped out of his dreams and looked up to find Sang and Arthur standing over him, both with empty buckets in their hands.

"Rise and shine." Arthur said.

"Was that really necessary?" Parker asked.

"It was amusing." Sang answered.

"Glad you guys have a sense of humor. I was starting to worry. Can I have a towel please?"

"No need for that."

Not long after, Parker was floating in a glass tank of water. It wasn't large, but it was enough for him to submerge his entire body inside. Sang stood on a ladder just outside the tank.

"I don't remember seeing this here before." Parker said, teeth chattering at the coldness of the water.

"It wasn't." Sang said as he closed the lid. "I got it just a bit ago. Remember, we can get anything we need here."

Parkers' head was forced underwater and he slowly pushed himself to the bottom. Arthur stood on the outside of the tank, looking at him through the glass. Parker gave a thumbs up to indicate he was still all right, but after a few moments he started knocking in a panic. Arthur continued to stare at him without trying to help. Parker moved upwards in the tank and started to push on the hatch but Sang had locked it from the outside. He banged on the glass as hard as he could, but it was no use.

"It's been less than a minute." Sang shouted. "You'll have to do better."

Parker pounded on the glass. Another few seconds passed, and he was unconscious. Arthur nodded his head toward Sang who unlocked the hatch and reached in to pull Parker to the surface. It didn't take long for Parker to spit water out of his mouth as he gasped for air. He recovered quickly and slapped Sang's hand away.

"Are you guys' crazy?" He asked.

"We warned you when this all began." Sang said. "You have to push yourself as hard as possible."

"This isn't going to work."

"This is the only way to prepare you for what lies ahead."

"By drowning me? Been there done that! That's how I got here."

"You're still alive." Arthur spoke. "You can keep trying until you get better, or Hades is going to kill you, and there is no coming back from that. You must force yourself to go the extra mile and succeed where others have failed. It's not going to be easy, but it's your only chance of survival. You made the choice to go through with this. So yes, we're going to drown you, stab you, and kill you in every way we can think of, again and again until we're satisfied. You wanted a purpose; you want to be better? Stop complaining and prove me wrong about you. Forget about being a hero like I was. I want you to be better than that."

Parker took another look at Sang and then glanced back at Arthur. They were right. He had to try harder. He had no choice but to shake it off and keep going.

"Close the lid." He said before taking a deep breath and sinking to the bottom again as Sang shut the hatch. A knock was heard at the front door and Arthur walked through the house to get it. He opened it up to find Eva standing on the other side.

"Hi." She said. "Lucas told me that Parker was here."

"He is." Arthur confirmed. "He's a bit preoccupied at the moment. Perhaps you should come back later."

"I'm aware of his training. Word travels fast."

"On an island this small it's hard to keep anything a secret."

"Is he allowed to leave at all?"

"He's not a prisoner, just now isn't a good time."

"How are you training him today?"

"We're drowning him." Arthur said casually.

"Oh." Eva said slightly unexpected, but she understood. "When he is available, would you ask him to find me later?"

"Of course."

Eva started to walk away but turned around to see Arthur once more.

"I'm not saying to go easy on him." Eva said. "Just look after him."

"I will." He replied sincerely.

She nodded her head and continued away from the cottage. Arthur watched her leave and then closed the door. As he walked back out to the tank, he could see Parker still holding his breath under the water. They continued to train him to hold his breath a while longer. By the time Arthur had prepared them some breakfast, Parker was able to hold his breath a total of two minutes. Not bad for a beginner.

After a good break for breakfast, the training continued. Now the three men were in a heavily wooded area just behind Sang's house. Arthur was hidden in the trees somewhere in the woods while Parker stood blindfolded in the center of a small clearing.

"Listen very carefully to your surroundings." Sang said quietly. "Remember, a fight can break out at any moment. Always be vigilant and focused."

Suddenly a sandbag swung out from one of the trees and slammed right into Parkers' face.

"Crap!" He said rubbing his mouth.

"You're meant to dodge the sandbag." Arthur shouted from somewhere in the trees.

"Why can't I do this without the blindfold?" Parker asked.

"If you can do it with a blindfold, then without one should be easy as pie." Sang answered.

"I've never made a pie in my life."

"Don't start."

The sandbag retracted into the tree, and another one dropped from a different direction. Parker leaned forward but the bag still brushed against the back of his head.

"Your reflexes are getting better, but you still need work." Sang said.

"What should I do?" He asked.

"Listen."

"I can't hear anything."

"You're not listening."

"You want me to listen, but there isn't anything to listen to. Until it smacks me in the face, that's when it makes a noise."

"Just try again but think about your location. Think about the type of noises you should be hearing, listen for what doesn't belong."

After a few quiet moments passed by another sandbag dropped, Parker heard the rope holding the bag creak. He quickly moved to the left and managed to dodge the bag altogether.

"I did it!" Parker shouted.

"Very good." Sang shouted. "But sometimes, you might have multiple targets!"

Suddenly, Parker could hear more than just one sandbag swinging in his direction. The first one he missed with ease, but six others hit him from all sides.

"This is going to take a while." Arthur said pulling a lever to retract the bags.

Eva sat in the garden holding a blue rose when she saw Parker enter. She smiled and stood up to hug him as he approached.

"I was starting to think they would never be done with you." She said.

"You and me both." He replied. "I'd have been here sooner if it were up to me."

"How is training?"

"Brutal. Thanks for asking."

"Well, it is only the first day."

"A couple of days on Avalon and I haven't even had a chance to enjoy it."

"Well let's fix that." Eva said as she grabbed Parkers' hand and the two of them walked together down to the village. Their first stop was the café where they enjoyed a nice dinner together. They sat at the table closest to the edge of the dining area overlooking the beach. They slowly ate their meal while enjoying a conversation about their life experiences. It seemed Eva was more intrigued with Parkers' life story than he would have thought. Her experiences were limited to the same island she had lived on for twenty-four years. Parker had a few more stories to offer, though some not as entertaining to him as they were to her. He ended his long-winded rant and gave her some of the details of his training. As difficult as it was, he'd learned quite a bit so far.

"I'm proud to hear you're training so hard." Eva said. "You seem to be doing very well."

"I'm not sure how well I'm doing just yet." Parker said. "Arthur and Sang don't seem too impressed."

"You literally just got started. I'm sure they would tell you if you were doing something wrong."

"Believe me, I know they would. They have, a lot actually."

"Don't you think it's going well so far?"

"I don't know just yet. This is all happening so fast I don't know what to think anymore. First, they tell me I'm dead or something, living on an island paradise, and then I'm chosen to kill a mythological figure from the dark ages. It's a little farfetched even from my perspective. I don't even know what to make of it all. I've had so much information crammed into my head lately and if it weren't for the pain I've been put through, I'd say I was dreaming."

"You have to start believing in yourself. If you can't

do that then your doubts will be your downfall."

"You're right. I mean of course I know that. It's just been a strange couple of days. It's a lot to take in, you know?"

Parker reached across the table and placed his hand on top of Eva's.

"Thank you for looking out for me." He said with a smile.

"Of course. You're starting to grow on me." Eva said as she placed her other hand on top of his and smiled as she looked him in the eyes.

"Wow, now that's beautiful." Parker said sincerely.

"What is?" She asked.

"Your smile." He answered. "That makes it all worth it."

Eva blushed as she looked away toward the setting Sun with a big grin on her face.

"That was pretty cheesy wasn't it?" Parker asked with a laugh, and a little bit of regret.

"So cheesy!" Eva said laughing. "I still liked it though."

The two of them laughed and continued their meal together. By the time they had finished eating the Sun had completely set in the distance. They cleaned up their table and made their way down to the beach for a stroll in the sand. It was only moments later they sat on a couple of chairs not far from the tide and gazed at the stars above. The two talked for hours while they counted the shooting stars overhead. Both had plenty of stories to tell and even spent a bit of time telling jokes. At some point, Eva reached for Parkers' hand and held it tight. It wasn't long until they were fast asleep in their beach chairs.

Parker woke once throughout the night, only to find Eva still sleeping soundly beside him. He looked up at the sky to see the North Star shining brighter than he had ever seen it before. This was a memory he would treasure forever.

"This is only the beginning of greater things to come."

CHAPTER NINE

Parker had been training for nearly three months in the styles of Capoeira, Taekwondo, Shaolin Kung Fu, Jujutsu, drunken boxing, Wing Chun, weapons of many different sorts, and much more. In the short time he had been given, his skills were impressive to say the least. By the time Sang had finished his lessons Parker was able to hold his own against his teacher. It was then he spent his time with Arthur, learning to use a sword and dagger among other bladed weapons. Even Lucas had stepped in to teach Parker one of his greatest strengths, which was archery.

Parkers' training for the day hadn't started yet. He was more confident in his abilities, but he was beginning to get more nervous about what was going to happen next. He stood at the highest point of the mountain, a large cliff that overlooked the entire island. It was the same cliff where Arthur had ascended the stairs to meet with the Queens. Parker stared out toward the ocean which seemed to go on forever as he listened to the sound of the waterfall below him. Moments later Sang slowly approached behind him.

"Arthur would like to go over a few more things today." He said standing beside Parker.

"I'll be there soon." Parker responded.

"You've done well, but we've still more to do and not much time to do it."

"No problem Sang, just give me a minute please."

"Collecting your thoughts?" Sang asked.

"I'm just taking a moment for myself."

"Anything you wish to share?"

"Not really. I'm just trying to let my brain catch up with the rest of me."

"I know you will be all right."

"There is a subtle difference in knowing something and making a guess. You can't possibly predict the outcome Sang."

"I'm not guessing." Sang said with confidence.

"I feel more scared now than I have in my entire life. I used to think going to the dentist was scary. Maybe I'm just a coward."

"The Parker Wallace I know is not a coward."

"That's just it, you don't know me. You don't know anything about me. I worry that I'll lose my nerve. I don't trust myself."

"I know you better than you might think my friend." Sang spoke as he stared over the edge of the cliff. "You have a long life ahead of you. The battle that lies ahead may seem like a challenge now, but it is nothing compared to what awaits you. It will be rough, but you will show true courage, and strength. You are a man that fights for the people. No matter how bad things seem to get, you always push through. You fight for humanity. Even when it seems you're on your own, where most men would lay down and die, you will stand tall. Keep the faith, trust in yourself because you may even be surprised at what you can achieve."

"You talk like I've already done this stuff. How can you be so sure that I'm that guy?"

"I have faith."

"Faith?"

"Never underestimate it. I've seen with my own eyes what the power of faith can do. God is with you, always remember that."

Sang gave Parker a friendly pat on the back and left him standing alone at the cliffs edge.

Parker was unsure of what his friend was telling him, but somehow the nervous feeling in his stomach began to ease off. It didn't ease off much, but enough to make him feel a little better about himself. It was a good feeling to have someone who believed in him like that, besides Eva of course, who without a doubt was Parkers' biggest

WARRIOR FROM AVALON

supporter. He had never doubted that God existed either but given how his life had turned out so far, he felt a distance from him. He simply shrugged off his emotions for now. After all, he had bigger concerns to deal with.

Parker stood ten feet in front of Arthur on the beach. Both had their swords drawn and ready. Sang, Eva, and Lucas stood on the sidelines watching in anticipation and nervousness. Arthur was ready and nodded to Parker. They both moved toward each other slowly until finally, Arthur made the first move. Parker was quick in blocking Arthurs' attacks. He could feel the power behind the swing as the blades connected. Arthur attacked again and again. Parker ducked as the razor edge of the sword rushed over his head.

The two men spared with each other furiously as their swords clashed. Sparks flew everywhere as the blades connected with extreme force. In one swift motion, Arthur knocked Parkers' sword from his hand and kicked him to the ground. Parker rolled away as Arthur plunged his sword into the sand missing him by a few inches. It was then Parker seized the opportunity to kick Arthurs' sword from his hand. Arthur took a few steps back as his sword went flying several feet away. Parker then pulled a small dagger from a sheath tied around his pant leg. Arthur did the same and immediately slashed Parker across the face.

He stepped away as blood slowly trickled down his cheek. He wiped it off and the wound healed rapidly. Parker then rolled forward and swung at Arthurs' legs, but he jumped to avoid it. After several steady attacks Arthur knocked the dagger from Parkers' hand and darted around him in an effort to get behind him. He brought the dagger to Parkers' throat.

"Consider this a loss." Arthur said.

Parker could feel the coldness of the blade against his neck, but he wasn't ready to surrender just yet. There had to be a way for him to win. He looked down at his feet to see his sword partially buried in the sand. Parker positioned his foot under the sand and planned his next move very carefully. He quickly scooped his sword up with his foot and caught it out of the air and then maneuvered the sharp point at his own stomach. He pulled the blade into his own body with all his strength. The tip of the blade slid straight through Parkers' stomach and stabbed into Arthur as well. Parker reached up to grab the dagger from Arthurs' hand and quickly jabbed it into his leg. Once Parker removed the sword from both of their bodies, the two men quickly dropped to the ground. Parker regained his composure fast and stood over Arthur with the point of his sword inches away from Arthurs' neck.

"Care to repeat that?" He asked with a smile.

Arthur nodded his head and smiled as he held his stomach tight with both hands. Parker nodded as well and dropped his sword to the ground, and then he dropped to his knees struggling to catch his breath. Eva ran to Parker while Lucas and Sang ran to Arthur. After a few moments, both men slowly began to recover. Parker stood up in the sand with Eva's help and looked Arthur in the eyes. He could almost sense a bit of pride from his teachers' expression.

"That was a very dangerous move." Sang said. "But also, brilliant."

"Just remember Parker." Lucas spoke. "When you leave this island, you will not survive tricks like that."

"It doesn't matter what happens to me." Parker said.

"Of course, it matters." Eva answered.

"When the odds are against me, I'll do what I have to do to win. I can't afford to fail."

Arthur looked at Parker and smiled. He was impressed with the fact that Parker was willing to do what was necessary to win. Maybe there was hope for him after all.

WARRIOR FROM AVALON

"Well done." Arthur said. "Now, let's go again."

While Arthur and the others were impressed with Parkers' dedication to the cause, Eva on the other hand wasn't so pleased. She distanced herself from the group leaving Parker standing alone. The others were ready for the next round, but Parker was concerned for Eva.

"You okay Arthur?" Sang asked helping Arthur to his feet.

"No, the little bugger stabbed me." Arthur replied.

"Just a minute." Parker said as he left the beach to catch up to Eva. She had stopped just up the path from the village, barely hidden behind a tree as tears flowed down her cheeks. Parker slowly approached her and put his hand on her shoulder. She brushed his hand away and turned from him.

"You've got bigger concerns than my feelings." Eva said slightly agitated.

"I'm sorry Eva." Parker said sincerely. "I didn't mean to upset you."

"Why should you be sorry? You're doing exactly what you're supposed to do. You've got a fight to win by any means necessary. I'm the one who should be sorry."

"No, you shouldn't."

"But I am!" Eva said crying. "I'm sorry that you have to go away to fight. I'm sorry for worrying that you may not return, and I'm so sorry that I'm falling in love with you."

The words wounded Parker more than they flattered him. He understood all too well. During the time of his training, he hadn't considered how close he and Eva were after spending so much time together. He put his arms around her as she buried her face into his chest.

"Promise me you will come back." Eva said sobbing.

"I don't know if I can make that promise." He responded with tears of his own. "The one thing I can promise is that I will always love you as well."

Parker placed his fingers on Eva's chin and turned her face so that she could look him in the eyes.

"I promise I'll fight with everything I have, not just for myself, but for you." He said. "I'll fight harder than I ever have before."

Eva wrapped her arms around Parker as tight as she could. He returned the favor with a kiss on her forehead.

"No matter how far I go, my heart stays with you." He said.

Eva hugged him even tighter as the two of them stood silently in the moment and even though they didn't know it, they were both thinking the exact same thing.

"Don't let go."

After taking some time to heal, Parker and Arthur continued their training. After several hours of battle after battle, with Parker winning some fights, and Arthur winning a bit more, the two men decided to call it day. Arthur was the best swordsman, but Parker was more than capable of holding his own against him. With more experience, he may even surpass Arthur himself.

Later on, after the training had ended, Parker and Eva decided to take some much needed alone time together. The two of them made their way down to the dock and sat just at the edge. Eva let her feet dangle into the water as they held hands tightly. A ship was coming soon, and Parker wanted to get as much time with her as possible. She had decided to stay by his side for the remaining time he had left. Silence surrounded them aside from the sound of the ocean waves moving up and down the shore. He placed his arm around her and held her close.

"What happens next?" She asked.

"I'm not sure." He answered, hesitant at first.

Arthur and Sang had spoken to him about what he must do. He wasn't ready to go. His decision to be trained seemed a little too rushed now that he could reflect on the last several weeks. He finally found someone who gave him a sense of peace. Here was a woman, a beautiful woman at that, who thought so highly of him, and he had to spend most of his time training for a fight against the god of the Underworld. Parker shuddered at the thought. He and Eva just leaned against each other until they both fell asleep where they sat.

    The morning had arrived sooner than he wanted. As Parker looked out toward the ocean, he imagined it was only a matter of time before the ship would arrive to take him away. He could feel it getting closer somehow. He could feel his fear building up inside him, forcing a quick shiver over his whole body. Eva woke up and looked at him with concern.

    "It's just a little cold out here." He told her, passing it off as a cold chill.

    "You're worried." She said. "I know. I am too."

    "I'm trying not to be."

    "We both need to remember to stay confident. You've been trained by the best teachers you could have asked for. There are none better."

    "I'm trying to push down those feelings. Like I just want to run away. I'd give anything to stay here with you."

    "I believe in you. I've seen you fight. I've seen your focus and determination. You're not going to fail. You are going to get passed this, and you're going to come back to me."

    "Eva, whatever happens…"

    "Don't start talking like that." She interrupted. "You are going to win."

    Parker stood up and helped Eva to her feet. He reached into his pocket and pulled out a beautiful necklace. It had a golden chain with a pendant, and in the center was a small diamond that sparkled brightly in his hand.

    "Lucas helped me put this together." Parker said

holding up the necklace for Eva to see. "You really can get anything here. I wasn't sure when I should give you this, but I wanted you to have something to remember me by. Just in case."

"It's beautiful." She said as Parker placed it around her neck. She held it in her fingers and noticed a small inscription on the back of the pendant. With tears in her eyes she read the word "Polaris."

"You have truly been there for me more than anyone else I've ever known. You make me feel at peace when I'm with you, so much that it feels like home. You are my guiding star." Parker said. "Wear it for me so that I can find my way back to you."

Eva embraced Parker with tear-filled eyes and held him tight. Moments passed by as Eva caught a glimpse of an object floating in the distant ocean.

"Oh no." She said as the ship they had been dreading slowly appeared on the horizon.

Having seen it for themselves already, Arthur, Sang, and Lucas walked up behind them but did not interrupt. Lucas had a large duffel bag hanging off his left shoulder. Parker finally let Eva go and stepped back to see the others approaching.

"It's here." Lucas said directing Parkers' attention to the ocean.

The ship was a medium-sized Trireme. In ancient times the Trireme was a popular vessel that used manpower and oars to propel the ship, but this one had no oars or manpower to drive the ship.

"I can take some supplies?" Parker asked.

"I've already got you covered." Lucas said dropping the bag from his shoulder.

Moments passed and the ship came to a stop beside them. A ramp removed itself from the ship and placed itself on the dock as if by magic. Any other time Parker might find that impressive but instead turned his attention to his friends standing behind him.

"I appreciate all that you've done for me." He said to Lucas as he reached for the bag. "Thank you, all of you, for everything."

"You're welcome." Lucas said as he snatched the bag up before Parker could grab it and began walking up the ramp onto the ship.

"Wait, where are you going?" Parker asked.

"We're tagging along." Arthur said as he followed behind Lucas.

"We cannot enter with you when we get there, but we can share in the journey." Sang said.

"Why not enter with me?"

"We will not be allowed." Sang continued as he walked behind the other two. "You won't need us anyway, but we'll be close by for moral support."

Parker grinned and felt a wave of relief that he didn't have to make the trip solo. He turned to Eva and smiled for a moment before boarding the ship with the others. Sang walked up behind Lucas and placed his hand on his shoulder.

"Arthur and I could handle this." Sang spoke. "Are you sure I cannot convince you to stay with Eva?"

"I'm sure." Lucas responded slightly confused. "I'd like to show my support to Parker."

"Very well." Sang said.

As soon as the group was standing on the top deck, the ramp removed itself from the dock and the ship began to depart. Parker stepped to the railing on the deck and looked over to see Eva with teary eyes waving goodbye.

"Who's controlling the ship?" He asked.

"This ship has no crew." Arthur answered. "It controls itself."

Parker stood at the stern of the ship watching the island fade away until it was out of sight. Lucas gave him a pat on the back.

"You should try to rest a little." Lucas said. "It'll be a while before we reach our destination."

"Easier said than done." Parker said.

"I've brought plenty of food as well. So as the effects of the island wear off, at least we'll be prepared."

Parker nodded and glanced over to see Arthur looking out toward the sea and walked over to join him.

"Do you mind if I ask you a question?" Arthur asked.

"Sure." Parker replied.

"What's motivating you to do this now? You don't know any of those people you're hoping to save. You have no stake in this, but you trained hard and seem to be willing to die for this. You could easily forget it all and stay with her if you truly wanted. Why would you go through with it?"

Parker was silent a moment. He had been asking himself that same question since the night before his training started. Then the answer reminded him every time of what he was fighting for.

"I guess it's love." Parker answered.

"Love?"

"I'll be honest with you. I'm terrified of what's about to happen, but when you told me what my role was in this, I couldn't just walk away. It's not who I am, or it's not who I want to be."

Arthur looked at Parker curiously.

"I know about your wife." Parker continued. "All those people trapped in the Underworld, and she's one of them. I try to put myself in your situation. If it were someone that I cared about, if it was Eva down there, then I'd do whatever it took to set her free. I'm fighting for her and Guinevere. I'm fighting for you."

"It should never have been your burden to carry."

"But it is my burden now, and I'll carry it. I may not make it back from this, but I promise you, I will do everything I can to save her, no matter what it takes. You've given me a fighting chance, and I'll always be grateful for that. All I ask is that you look out for Eva."

"If it were possible for me to take your place, I'd gladly do so. For what it's worth, I'm immensely proud of you. You're not the same man I knew on that Ash demon ship. You're someone I can gladly put my faith in."

"That's nice to hear coming from the legendary King Arthur."

"Any time, Sir Parker Wallace."

"Did you just knight me?" Parker asked with a big smile on his face.

"We'll have a formal ceremony when we get back." Arthur said with a smile as he patted Parker on the shoulder. Arthur turned and walked away, leaving Parker to stand alone. He was more confident than before, but there was still doubt deep within him. He glanced up to the sunlit sky and felt the warmth of it on his face, almost as if it were the first time, he'd ever truly appreciated it.

"I know I haven't done this much." He began to pray. "I don't even know if you're paying attention to me at all. All I ask is that you give me the strength and courage to see this through. I don't care if I live or die afterwards, just help me get it done. Help me do what I'm meant to do. Help me be the man they hope I am. If anything happens to me, grant Arthur peace, and help Eva find a good man. Amen."

It was early the next morning when Parker woke and made his way out of his bunk to the top deck of the ship. He leaned on the side of the railing and looked up at the sky. Dark clouds blocked the Sun from shining through to the ship. Arthur was already awake and moved over to join Parker.

"We're getting closer to the island prison." Arthur said.

"No, we're already here." Sang said from the bow of the ship.

Arthur ran to join Sang as Lucas walked up from below deck yawning and quickly composed himself as he followed behind Arthur.

"Parker, come here." Arthur shouted.

He did as he was told and stood beside Lucas looking out to see the Island in the distance. Ashes began to rain down from the sky the closer they got. The Island looked like a large volcano that was just on the cusp of eruption, with lava flowing down the mountainside into the ocean below, causing a constant amount of steam to rise from the shore.

"Heads up!" Lucas shouted.

Small balls of fire began to drop on the deck of the ship forcing the men to run and hide under shelter as bits and pieces of the ship caught fire. Parker and the others did their best to put out the flames. Every few seconds a spark would hit their bare skin causing them to smack at their arms like they were swatting at mosquitoes. The sparks continued to rain down as the ship passed into a cave where a dock awaited at the far end. As the ship stopped near the dock the ramp connected on its own. Parker gazed at an entrance inside the cave. It had an arched doorway that lead to a circular staircase moving upward, beyond that was yet to be seen.

"I guess this is it." Lucas stated.

"I need a weapon." Parker said.

"We can't provide you with anything from this point on." Arthur informed him.

"Well, I can't fight without something."

"It's all right." Sang said. "Everything you need awaits you on the other side. Though this may be a prison for Hades, there are rules that must be followed. You will not fight without a sword."

"How do you guys know this stuff?"

"This place has been here for a while." Arthur said.

"We know how this goes."

Parker felt a rush of fear wash over him.

"If you say so." He said softly.

"Remember everything we taught you." Arthur said. "Keep your wits about you. Fight hard and fight smart."

Lucas motioned for the men to join with him. They formed a small circle around Parker and put their hands on his shoulders. Parker wasn't sure what they were doing at first, but once he realized, it gave him a sense of calm that he sorely needed. Parker joined in and bowed his head as Lucas began to lead them in a prayer.

"Dear God, we come to you in a time of need." Lucas prayed. "We ask for protection for our friend Parker. Give him the strength he needs for the trial ahead. Let his mind be alert and his skills be great. We ask that you stay at his side and grant him safe passage so that he may return home safely to those who love him. Guide his mind and his hands to rise where others have fallen. Fill him with calm and peace as he faces the task at hand. We ask this in Jesus' name, Amen."

"I appreciate that." Parker said.

"You are on the side of righteousness." Lucas said. "Remember that God walks with you where we can't."

"Be safe." Sang said.

Parker nodded his head toward his friends and walked down the ramp onto the dock. He slowly moved toward the entrance and took one final look back and then began to proceed onto the stairway. As soon as he entered the door, the cave began to shake as a door over the entrance to the stairs dropped down blocking Parkers' way out. Sang, Arthur, and Lucas could do nothing else now but wait.

CHAPTER TEN

Parker made his way up to the top step and looked behind him. He knew he couldn't go back even if there was a way. The passage he was in was so dark he couldn't even see his hand in front of his face. The darkness made him uncomfortable like he was trapped in a nightmare, only he wasn't going to wake up from this one. His eyes slowly adjusted to the darkness as he managed to see something sticking up out of the floor in front of him. The closer he walked to the object, the brighter the room seemed to get with a bluish glow.

There was a handle sticking out of an iron slab. The handle was the source of the glow and the light allowed Parker to see symbols molded onto it. He touched his hand to it and slowly began to pull it from the iron slab until he realized it was a sword. As he removed the sword from the iron slab it began to glow an even brighter blue color. Parker was amazed at the sword not only because of its beauty but because the blade itself wasn't made of steel or any kind of material he had ever seen in a sword.

Instead, the blade was made entirely of water, but the hilt was black, and the cross-guard was shaped like angel wings. He could also see through the blade clear as glass. He rubbed his finger along the edge feeling that it was solid and very sharp, but Parker could also feel the wetness on his fingertips as he touched it. He looked to the floor where the sword had been and saw the iron slab sinking into the stone ground. He held the sword tight as he stepped forward holding it out in front of him as a source of light.

Just as he stepped a few feet forward fire erupted from all around him, climbing the walls on both sides. He looked to the ceiling to see the flames moving along above his head, escaping through narrow holes that lead the smoke and excess fire outside. Parker was standing in a long narrow hallway that stretched about one hundred yards straight ahead. It was at most ten feet wide from either side, with a fifteen-foot high ceiling, and an arched doorway at the opposite end. The wall holding the door itself was also engulfed in fire. The ground was made of cobblestone with ashes scattered all across, as well as steel grates allowing strong pockets of steam and bursts of hot air into the room, helping to sustain the brutality of the environment.

Three chains were spaced out, stretching across the ceiling, slightly drooping down, and turning a burning red color from the heat around it. Parker knew he couldn't touch the chains, but they served a purpose that much was obvious.

Lucky enough for him, the floor itself wasn't on fire, but the longer he stood in one spot, the hotter it became on the bottom of his boots. Sweat was already pouring off him and the floor was starting to heat up even more by the minute. There was no way he could hang around here for too long.

"Starting to get a little toasty in here." He said to himself as he began to walk forward.

Swish

A flaming arrow flew straight past Parkers' right arm just grazing him above the elbow.

"What the...!" He said as he grabbed at his arm and ducked down to the ground.

He felt a little foolish for a moment. He should have known it wouldn't be a casual stroll ahead of him. He took the Aqua-blade and tucked it between his belt and jeans so he wouldn't have to hold on to it. With his hands free, he might be more maneuverable. He stepped forward again only this time with more caution. Another arrow shot out of the fiery wall ahead of him and was headed straight for his chest. He stepped left allowing the arrow plenty of room to fly by but in the process, he moved too close to the wall, where his shirt sleeve caught fire. After slapping at his arm to put out the fire, he moved back to the center of the hall and walked forward another few steps.

Three more arrows shot out, one aimed at his head while two others were aimed at his knees. He ducked down allowing the first one to fly over his head and performed a forward flip above the other two landing on his back. As he lay on the ground a giant fiery pendulum dropped from the ceiling swinging side to side and through the wall, as if neither the wall nor the pendulum was solid in form, but the heat from either would surely be enough to cause Parker almost certain death.

As it entered the wall to Parkers' left, he quickly rose to his feet and moved forward just in time for it to swing and miss his back by mere inches. He moved forward a couple of steps to get away from the fiery pendulum. He looked up to see the chains on the ceiling above him. He wasn't exactly sure what he was supposed to do or what purpose the chains served, but his instincts told him his next move. He took the Aqua blade from his belt and cut the chain above him.

Suddenly a stone door dropped from the fiery ceiling blocking off the passage behind him. At the end of the hall, the arched doorway slowly rose to reveal a small opening underneath. Parker was relieved he made the right call. The chains were the key to unlocking the door ahead. By cutting each one the path behind him would be blocked, but the exit ahead would open more for him to get through and escape.

Parker could feel the bottom of his boots getting hotter by the minute and soon he wouldn't be able to stand the heat any longer. He moved forward again, and fifteen arrows shot out of the wall. This time it only left him just enough space to lay flat on his stomach. Parker had to press his face against the floor causing a slight burn on his cheek. His shirt began to heat up while he waited in agony for the arrows to pass just inches above him. No sooner had they gone over, he jumped to his feet, dropping his sword as he rubbed his arms and face. He quickly patted down his shirt to stop any flames that might have built up while he lay on the ground. Parker picked up his sword and placed the blade flat to his cheek. Not the best idea, but the coldness of the Aqua-blade gave his burn a bit of temporary relief. He was in a miserable situation and he had no choice but to keep going. He had to get through this fast, or at least faster than his current speed.

He then quickly ran forward as more arrows shot toward him, but he managed to dodge them all with ease. He was only a hundred feet away now and his eyes were starting to blur from all the heat and sweat. He stepped forward as another fiery pendulum dropped from the ceiling. As it swung back and forth from one side to the other Parker jumped passed it quickly and turned to see it continuing to swing, but as he turned to move forward, two more pendulums dropped down in front of him, both of them placed close together, and instead of swinging side to side they were swinging toward him and then away. One got so close that He was forced to lean back and was almost grazed by the pendulum behind him.

"This is getting ridiculous!" He said to himself.

As Parker watched closely, he noticed that the pendulums weren't moving in unison, but were in fact swinging with slightly different variations in timing. He wiped at his eyes to remove the sweat while trying to watch the movements of the pendulums and work out the right combination of steps in his head. As the first pendulum swung forward, the second swung backward, giving Parker a few seconds to react. He waited for them both to move a few more times and leaped passed them, cutting the second chain above his head in the process. He stepped forward as another stone door closed behind him.

The arched doorway ahead opened a bit more. As he moved forward again, five pendulums dropped from the ceiling, all of them swinging in different directions. The first swung back and forth, the second side to side, and the third swung back and forth while the fourth and fifth swung side to side. He studied the motions carefully until finally, he could see a pattern. They weren't in sync at all times, for one brief moment, each pendulum would allow him enough time to slip by if he were quick. He ignored the burning pain at his feet a few more seconds so he could plan out his timing as best as he could.

"Here we go, here we go." He said as he stepped forward and dodged the first and second pendulums.

He stood at the second pendulum a couple seconds longer giving the third one time to pass by him. Just as soon as the fourth and fifth both went in opposite directions Parker leaped forward passed them and finally reached the end of the hall. He looked back at the traps behind him and immediately remembered the training Sang had put him through with the sandbags and how it helped in his current situation. He finally cut the last chain but was surprised when there was no door dropping down behind him and the arch doorway wasn't opening enough for him to get through. He thought about trying to squeeze underneath, but the gap between the door and the floor was too narrow. The door was also too hot to touch, and way too heavy for him to lift.

He looked around him in a slight panic, only to see there were no symbols or handles anywhere. It was either a puzzle of some kind or the whole thing was rigged as a terrible joke. After all he had just been through to get this far, there had to be a way out. It was then he noticed on the right side of the door there was a small hole that he could barely notice due to the flames around it.

BOOM

A blast erupted from behind him and the entrance became a large stream of lava that began to flood toward him. The stone doors that once protected him were being knocked over as he quickly studied the door to find an answer to open it. It was then he realized that the hole was just the right size for the Aqua-blade. He quickly took the sword and slid it into the hole, checking behind him to see the flow of lava rushing toward him. He twisted the sword like a key and suddenly there was a loud hissing sound and the room went dark once again.

Parkers' breathing was rapid, and he had no explanation for what had just happened, but he did it. The sword was a key as well as a weapon. The room became cooler and suddenly he could feel air blowing against him. He grabbed the handle of the sword as his heart pounded in his ears and pulled it from the lock. He finally allowed himself to relax a little as the fiery hallway had gone black but was now beginning to glow as dark blue as the sword he was holding. The walls and ceiling suddenly became water, as well as the door he had just unlocked. He looked to either side of the hall to see fish swimming around as if he were standing in the hall of an aquarium.

A stingray swam close to the edge of the watery wall and Parker stuck his hand through to touch the creature as it passed by.

"How is this even possible?" He thought to himself.

There was nothing to hold the water back from collapsing on top of him and yet it was holding itself up all around him. He turned back to the watery exit and saw a room on the other side. He took a deep breath and stepped through the watery door and took a quick look around. The room he was in was much larger and was more like the fiery hallway he had just passed through, but thankfully the walls were made of hot stones instead of flames. Large pillars held the ceiling in place and in the center of the room was a large fountain, but instead of water, it was oil that was flowing through it. Parker would have much rather gone back through the water door and exited the way he came in, but just as the thought entered his mind, the watery door splashed down to reveal a stone wall where the door had once been.

"Perfect." He said to himself.

He looked around the room to see there was no other way out. As he searched around him, his attention was drawn to a small stairway leading up to a wall where three large chains dangled against it. He gripped the Aqua-blade tight as he noticed some type of mural or symbolic painting behind the chains. As he stepped closer to look at the mural, he felt a cold shiver cover his entire body, despite the heat from the room he was in. There were many pictures of a single figure without a face. It showed the figure sitting in what looked like a car falling from a bridge-like structure into a river, and then the same figure standing in a garden of flowers next to another figure that Parker could only assume was a woman.

"You've got to be kidding me." He said to himself.

The pictures continued depicting key moments in Parkers' memory, his escape from the ash demons ship, his passage back to Avalon, and another of him training on the beach with Arthur. He was amazed as he realized he was looking at a mural of his own experiences.

"This is me." He said to himself.

From his accident on the bridge to his training with the others, Parkers' life was depicted on the wall in front of him, but there was nothing else of his life before. It was then he noticed another picture at the bottom of the mural that he wasn't familiar with. It was the figure of him, gazing at the mural itself, with a large creature standing behind him.

"If this is supposed to be me, then this picture is me looking at this right now. Then that is…"

ROAR

"Oh, cheesy peaches."

Meanwhile on the outside of the cave, Lucas stood by the railing overlooking the dock.

"How do you think it's going?" He asked.

It had begun to storm just outside the cave. Sang sat in the center of the ship, meditating. It was all he had done since they had arrived, and he showed no signs of concern as to what was happening around them.

"I think he's still alive." Arthur answered. "He's a

smart kid, he'll make it."

It was then that Sang opened his eyes and picked up a sword that had been lying next to him.

"Something is wrong." Sang said as the ship suddenly began to move away from the dock.

"What's happening?" Lucas asked as he looked over the edge. The sudden movement puzzled him as well as Arthur.

"Why are we leaving?" Arthur asked.

"I don't understand." Lucas said diverting his attention to Sang. "Parker hasn't returned yet. Does that mean he's failed?"

"It seems our job here is finished." Sang answered. "Parker is alive, but we are of no use to him now."

"How could you know that?" Arthur asked.

"Because I do."

"What's happening Sang?" Lucas asked.

"There is nothing more we can do here." Sang replied. "The ship is taking us back to Avalon."

"We have no idea what is happening in there!" Arthur shouted. "We can't leave yet!"

Just outside the cave entrance, Sang could see a ship passing by very quickly. Parker was officially on his own. Now it was them who were in trouble.

"In just a few moments we are going to be attacked by ash demons."

"Ash demons?" Lucas asked. "How are they here?"

"I imagine they are a part of the fleet that tried to take Arthur and Parker months ago." Sang answered. "They are here to ensure Parker fails. They must be stopped."

Lucas and Arthur sprang into action as the ship moved toward the exit of the cave.

"Parker will be trapped here with no way back." Lucas said as he ran toward a small lifeboat hanging on the left side of the ship.

"We need rope!" Arthur shouted. "Quickly!"

The men searched for anything they could use. Arthur spotted the anchor with a rope tied to the end of it. He cut the rope from the anchor using a dagger he kept on his belt.

"Take this." He shouted tossing the end of the rope to Lucas. "Tie a lasso!"

Lucas did as he was told and tied the end of the rope as he ran toward the railing of the ship. He tossed the lasso to attach it to the dock. The first toss missed the post, but the second was spot on. Arthur pulled the lifeboat down and ran toward Lucas.

"We're running out of time here!" Lucas shouted.

Arthur took the end of the rope from Lucas and tied it to the lifeboat. No sooner had they finished, the boat ripped from the ship and plunged down into the water below. No matter what happened next, Parker would have a way to escape the Island at least.

"Do you see them Sang?" Arthur asked.

"Grab your sword and get ready." Sang replied.

Arthur and Lucas grabbed their weapons from the duffle bag Lucas had brought with them. Once the ship exited the cave, they could see a large black ship floating around the corner only a few meters away. Ash demons stood on the deck with weapons in their hands.

"They're here." Sang said as the demon ship crashed into theirs.

"Kill them!" A large demon ordered as it and others stormed the ship.

Arthur sliced at one demon in front of him and then another behind him as a third demon approached him and took a swing at his head. He managed to duck just in time while shoving his sword into the demons' gut then pulling it out to cut off the demons' head. The headless monsters body quickly crumbled to ash and blew away as the wind picked up what was left.

Sang dodged three demons that chased after him,

each of them swinging their swords at him one after the other. As one of the three attempted to shove their blade into his chest, he grabbed its arm and moved it into the path of another demon, killing it instead. Lucas had grabbed his bow and arrow and made headshots at any Ash demons coming toward him. Once he had run out of arrows, he pulled a dagger from his belt to fight off some more. During the fight, Lucas made his way around the ship collecting his previously fired arrows so that he could continue to use his bow.

"This is the only sad thing about being an archer." Lucas said.

Arthur continued to cut off the heads of each demon that attacked him. Sang used one demon to plow into another that stood in front of him, knocking it over the side of the ship leaving only one demon left. Lucas turned to see Sang looking for more to fight, and while his attention was elsewhere, the largest of the Ash demons approached behind him and jammed its sword into Lucas' back. Lucas shouted in pain as Sang and Arthur turned their attention to his cries. He took a couple of steps forward and turned back to see the final demon standing with a smile on its grotesque face.

"You lose!" The demon smirked as he pulled a tiny device from his side and pressed it. The demon ship exploded behind them sending a cloud of smoke into the rainy sky. With as much strength as Lucas could muster, He drew back his bowstring and shot a final arrow into the demons' head, causing an explosion of ash to fill the wet air.

"Lucas!" Arthur shouted running to his aid.

Sang watched as the Ash demons ship slowly sank beneath the ocean waves. Sang had known they weren't there to kill them, but to attack Parker. Hades intended to cheat. More importantly, the demons wanted to ensure Arthur and the others would not be going to Parkers' aid. After ensuring they weren't being pursued, Sang rushed to Arthurs' side to help Lucas.

"It's just a scratch." Lucas said in a painful groan. "I don't suppose you have a band-aid?"

"Arthur, help me get Lucas to his bunk." Sang said. "We must return to Avalon."

"What about Parker?" Arthur asked angrily.

"We can't do anything for him now."

"We have to go back for him." Lucas said.

"Everything we hoped for has been placed on Parkers' shoulders!" Arthur said.

"We've done everything we can." Sang replied. "Parker is no longer our concern. We were able to fight off the demons, but we can't wait for Parker any longer."

"We can't just leave him behind!"

"We have to go. Parker will be okay, Lucas will not…."

"How are you so sure!" Arthur shouted as he pulled out his dagger and placed it near Sang's throat. "You've been keeping things from me since the beginning. You know things that you can't or won't explain. It's time to come clean with me. Or I'll slit your throat and toss you over the side myself."

Sang stared into Arthurs' eyes knowing that if he didn't answer that Arthur would, and could, cause him harm. He had served his purpose in helping Parker prepare, but he had kept very many things from Arthur in the process. Anything he could have told him may have jeopardized Parkers' chance of success. However, Arthur had become a friend, and he deserved some shred of truth.

"Very well." Sang began. "I'll tell you what I know, but right now we have to get Lucas back to Avalon or else he's going to die."

"Parker still needs us." Arthur said.

"Then make your choice Arthur!" Sang shouted in frustration. "Lucas is dying right now, and he needs us more. If we turn back, he will die. We do not have time to save them both."

"Parker is more important." Lucas said softly.

"Arthur, you have to trust me." Sang said as he slowly moved Arthurs' dagger from his neck. "You have to believe in him."

There wasn't time, and there wasn't a choice, Arthur helped Sang move Lucas below. Lucas would be fine as long as they could get him to Avalon in time, but Arthur wondered if it was really the right thing to do. Was Lucas' life worth more than Parkers'? Even Arthur had no right to weigh the lives of either man. There was more going on than he could know, and as soon as they arrived on Avalon, Sang would have to answer a lot of questions.

CHAPTER ELEVEN

Hades' was even more frightening than Parker had imagined. He had evaded the large beast long enough to hide in a large hole in the wall. He needed a moment to get his bearings. Parker watched as the large monster hunted for him around the room. Hades height reached eight feet tall, with broad shoulders, and was bulging with muscle. His face was a cross between a man and a bull with two of his bottom teeth sticking up sharply from his mouth, similar to the Ash demons but way more ferocious. He had long horns about fifteen inches in length on the top of his head. His eyes were bright red with flames rising out of them as if they were made of pure fire.

"A Minotaur." Parker said softly.

Around his arms were strange irritations against his skin. Parker could see the imprints on his arms and then looked toward the wall where the chains had been hung. It was then he realized the irony in what he had done. In his attempt to escape the flaming hallway by cutting the chains and opening the door, he had also loosened the chains which held Hades captive.

"Well, that is just unfair." Parker said to himself.

He couldn't hide in the hole in the wall forever. He may have released the monster from his chains, now it was his responsibility to put the beast down for good. He waited for Hades to gain some distance across the room before he worked up the courage and stepped out to face the Demon King.

"Hey ugly!" Parker shouted to Hades. "Your mother was a Texas Longhorn!"

Hades turned to face the source of the insult and growled in anger. He slowly moved forward until they stood just several feet away from each other as he reached to his side and pulled a sword from a scabbard attached to his hip. Hades sword had a dark black hilt with skull-like symbols etched around the grip. The blade was the exact opposite of Parkers' Aqua-blade. Instead of water, it was made of nothing but fire. Parker held his sword tight and was ready for an attack. Hades was large, but Parker swallowed every ounce of fear he had inside him and stood his ground. He already made it this far and wasn't going to die without a fight.

Hades forced a loud roar once again, and Parker decided that for the moment, running wasn't that bad of an idea either. He jumped out of the way as Hades charged forward swinging his sword. Parker ran to the other side of the room to hide behind one of the four large pillars, buying himself more time to think. His strength wasn't going to be enough to get him through this. That monster would rip him apart without any real effort. Hades poked his head around the pillar to see Parker and snarled.

"The mother line was uncalled for, right?" Parker asked, knowing full well that Hades had no interest in what he had to say.

Parker jumped up to swing his sword at Hades head who blocked it with ease. He backed away as Hades moved toward him pointing the tip of his blade at Parkers' chest. Parker aimed the tip of his sword toward Hades in retaliation. The two blades slammed together causing steam to erupt toward the ceiling. Parker could barely hold the beast back and knew that Hades was merely playing with him. His size alone was all the advantage he needed to get the best of Parker. Once again, he knew strength alone wasn't going to help. Parker was going to have to be faster and use his brain.

Parker sidestepped, allowing Hades' own momentum to knock him off balance and send him crashing into the wall behind him. Hades swung his blade blindly behind him hoping that he'd strike his adversary, but Parker was already out of reach and standing in the center of the room planning his next move. He followed as Parker stood firm ready to defend himself. Their swords clashed repeatedly. Hades barely missed Parkers' head as he ducked and jammed the tip of the Aqua-blade into Hades' leg. The monster let out an earsplitting roar and swung his blade at a downward angle, but Parker managed to roll out of the way causing Hades to hit nothing but solid ground.

He kicked to his side connecting his foot to Parkers' back launching him several feet away. Parker returned to his feet as Hades continued to lunge at him, but Parker dodged him and ran behind him swinging his sword making a large cut on the beasts back. Hades swung his large fist backward knocking Parker to the floor and forcing the Aqua-blade out of his hands. He looked up to see Hades charging at him once more. The Aqua-blade was several feet away, but Hades wasn't about to let Parker near it. He jumped up quickly and ran to the fountain in the middle of the room, keeping it between him and Hades. The monster jumped high over the fountain, landing behind Parker, and quickly grabbed him by the back of the neck. He then shoved Parkers' head into the fountain of oil. Parker flailed his arms wildly as he tried to break free from Hades strong grip.

He slammed his fist into the beasts' strong knuckles, but Hades just let out a monstrous laugh as Parker began to weaken. After just moments with his head under the oil Parker stopped squirming. Hades lifted him out of the fountain and glared at the weak being in his clutches. Parker was still, blood and oil dripped from his face. Hades smiled in victory, but suddenly Parker opened his eyes and spit a mouthful of oil into Hades' face causing the flames of his eyes to burst out of control. He dropped Parker to the ground and then released his sword to reach for his eyes with both hands.

"Blech!" Parker said spitting the remainder of the oil from his mouth in disgust.

He used the time to his advantage and raced to pick up the Aqua-blade. Parker needed a plan, that little move was only going to slow the beast down. He surveyed the room and smirked at an idea. Moments later, Hades picked up his sword and searched for his prey. His eyes were burning, and he couldn't see Parker anywhere. He had lost precious moments and this mortal was starting to get the best of him. He had underestimated Parker before and now he was more cautious. He slowly turned around trying to look in every direction, but he found no one until finally, Parker erupted from under the oil in the fountain, having submerged his entire body underneath, holding his breath as long as he could.

Using the surprise attack, Parker splashed oil into Hades' sword causing the flames to explode every which way. He then jammed the tip of his blade into Hades' stomach and pushed it in as far as he could. Hades roared in pain and dropped his sword grabbing Parker with both hands and lifting him into the air. Hades began to squeeze Parker in an attempt to crush him with both hands. Parker grunted as he slammed his fists as hard as he could into Hades face and arms. He looked into the monster's eyes, which were glaring back at him with hate. He looked at his own hands, which were still soaked and dripping with oil. He then jammed his palms into Hades eyes and pressed down as hard as he could. Hades held Parker tight in his massive arms as both of them fought to overcome each other. The fire from Hades' eyes was beginning to burn the palms of his hands.

Finally, Hades could stand it no longer and had no choice but to let go, dropping Parker to the ground. In one quick motion, Parker reached out and removed the Aqua blade from Hades' stomach, spinning it around in his hand. He then forcefully plunged the tip of the blade into Hades' left leg, and then into the right leg, forcing Hades to drop to the floor. Parker stood before Hades holding his sword tight in his hand. With Hades kneeling on the ground in front of him, Parker stood tall, glaring straight ahead at the beast.

"You think you've won?" Hades asked in a low

roaring voice.

"Now you wanna talk?" Parker responded, cautiously watching for any surprises.

"I've waited for this moment since before you were even a thought."

"I guess it didn't turn out the way you imagined. It's time to release your prisoners. Do it now and maybe you can walk away from this."

"You really haven't got a clue do you boy? You think this war is over? This is just the beginning." Hades let out a roaring laugh.

"What are you talking about?"

"I'd hate to ruin the surprise. I'll be seeing you!"

Parker raised his blade high, ready to jam the point into Hades' skull, but before he knew it, Hades had reached up tearing off a sharp piece of his own horn and jammed it into Parkers' stomach. Parker took a step back to look down at the wound in surprise.

"Sooner than you think." Hades said laughing.

Parker looked back up at Hades, ignoring the pain as much as possible, and brought the Aqua-blade down as hard as he could, crushing it into Hades' skull. He took several steps back as the flames in Hades eyes began to burn out leaving nothing but a horrible blackness in his eye sockets.

Parker watched Hades flesh began to darken as ashes covered his entire body and then began to fall apart. Hades' monstrous arms dropped down to the stone floor and broke into millions of ashy pieces. Then the rest of Hades' large body collapsed to the floor blowing away into the air, allowing the Aqua-blade to drop to the ground pointed tip first and stuck into the stone floor. A small red orb of light was all that remained. Parker watched as the orb hovered above the ground where Hades had died. Slowly the orb burst into a cloud of dark smoke and flew into the air where it exploded into a huge flash of light. It was so bright that Parker had no choice but to shield his own eyes.

Once the brightness was gone, he looked at the blazing sword on the ground. He quickly grabbed it and pressed it to his stomach to cauterize the wound. After a few seconds, the sword itself shattered in Parkers' hand as it turned to ash itself. Looking over at the Aqua-blade, he watched as it also splashed down into a wet spot on the stone floor, disappearing into nothingness.

He inhaled a deep breath of air and held his stomach tight with both hands. He looked toward the wall where the chains had been earlier. It began to shake until finally it broke apart revealing an arched doorway. Parker could see on the other side was a stone stairway that went down. He slowly moved toward it, holding his stomach with bloody hands. He made his way down the steps, which seemed to circle back toward the entrance he had started from.

It was sure enough at the bottom of the dark stairway an exit appeared from nowhere and Parker was able to make his way to the dock in the cave. The ship however was gone, and He couldn't help but wonder what had happened. He walked to the edge to see a small boat floating in the water with a rope holding it to the dock. Something went wrong, but his friends had left him a lifeboat. He grabbed the rope lassoed around the post and used what was left of his strength to pull the boat toward him.

Once it was close enough, he tossed the rope and slowly climbed into the boat. He picked up one of the two oars that had been lying inside and rowed his way toward the exit of the cave. He had no idea how to get back to the island, but he kept a little bit of hope in the back of his mind that somehow, he would find a way. He could feel the pain in his stomach with every row of the oar, but he couldn't let it get to him. On the outside of the cave the dark clouds of ash had dispersed, and he could see blue sky above him. Once he had gained some distance, he could hear a rumbling noise behind him. He turned his head to see the volcanic island sinking into the ocean. He then looked high above him to see that somehow, even in the sunlit sky, the stars were shining brightly. Even more so, the North Star outshined them all. He couldn't help but smile as he thought of Eva. He had even more hope and almost felt certain that he would find his way back to Avalon. Unfortunately, the wound he had sustained would soon cause him bigger problems.

Hours passed as Parker found himself adrift in the middle of the ocean. The sunlight poured heat down on top of him. He couldn't force himself to row anymore. He had to take a break, leaving the current to carry him along. He could feel his heart beating faster as he coughed violently and spit up blood. He pushed his hand against his wound as hard as he could, but the pain would not stop. He was more tired than ever, and he couldn't keep his eyes open much longer. Just ahead of him, he could see a large waterfall. His adrenaline kicked in for a moment. Surely his eyes were playing tricks on him. He was in a boat in the middle of the ocean after all. It was impossible for there to be a waterfall.

He grabbed an oar and began to row as hard as he could. The small dinghy inched closer and closer to the falls. It wasn't long until the boat went over the rushing waters, flipping over entirely, forcing its occupant into the air. Parker watched as the boat dropped quickly beneath him. As he fell in with the falling water, he could see the Earth below him. He was high above the world, but not quite in space itself. He fought as hard as he could to keep his eyes open and alert, but it was no use. Everything began to fade in front of him as he fell towards the Earths Ocean below. His body turned upwards toward the sky and Parker could see the waterfall slowly fading away, changing into an enormous cloud floating above him. Darkness overtook his sight, his heartbeat slowed until finally, it just stopped beating.

Parker woke to find the pain in his stomach had dulled. He could still feel the burn from the blade, but the overwhelming pain was gone. He opened his eyes, only to find himself in darkness. He looked up at a ceiling of a large cave to find it covered with stalactites. He took a deep breath of air but coughed at the foul stenches he had inhaled. He rolled over onto his side and gasped when he nearly rolled off the edge of a cliff. He reached back and grabbed onto the ground behind him, trying to pull himself back, sliding away from the edge. Looking over he could see he had to be around three hundred feet high.

As he slowly slid himself away from the edge, he was able to see that he was in something much worse than a dark cave. The grim environment spread out for miles, and from his perspective, it went on forever. Small Volcanic peaks were scattered along the rocky and harsh landscape. He could see a river of black water flowing in the distance, as well as a waterfall of lava. The river reached around the area Parker could see and went on much further into the distance. It was a world below the surface. Parker had a feeling of terror deep inside himself as he put his hand over his wound. It was then he knew exactly where he was.

"The Underworld." He said to himself.

Parker surveyed the area to see a rocky stairway that led from his current location to the ground below. There was no other way down, and no other choice. He began the trip down the stairs, which took a while to reach the bottom. Once he was at ground level there was a path that led through a narrow passageway. He decided that his best option at this point was to follow it. The passage wasn't long at all, and once on the other side, Parker was shocked as he saw on either side of him were thousands of people, crammed and chained together standing shoulder to shoulder. He walked over to a woman and looked into her eyes to see them clouded over. Parker waved his hand in front of her face only to get no reaction. All the people around her appeared the same way.

It was as if their minds were lost and unaware to the world around them. They were all shackled together with chains around their ankles, wrists, and necks. There were rows upon rows of them, stretching on like a field of people, so far that Parker couldn't see the end of them.

"The lost souls." He said. "Why are they not free?"

As he continued along the path, the horrors began to get worse. People were being tortured all around him. He stopped to see one man, strapped tightly to a tree, with spikes sticking into his back, and some so long they stuck straight through him. Parker ran over to help the man by grabbing his hand.

"Let me help you." Parker said.

"No, don't touch me!" The man shouted.

As soon as Parker had barely touched the man's hand, the spikes dug further into his back, and deeper into his body.

"No, leave me alone!" He screamed at Parker.

"I'm sorry." Parker said backing away from him. "I didn't know."

The man screamed and spit at Parker as he backed away. He could see no way to help the man. His screaming caused Parker to panic as he didn't know what else to do. His heart was heavy, but he had no choice but to continue onwards moving along the path once more. A little further down he saw an old man, wearing old ragged and dirty clothing, standing next to a well pulling a rope to bring water to the surface. His hands were calloused and sore. The bucket hung just out of reach, and was full of cool clear water, but no matter how fast the old man pulled the rope the bucket would not move an inch.

"I've almost got it." The man repeated to himself. "I've almost got it. I've almost got it."

Parker walked over to the well and reached out for the bucket, but just as he was about to touch it, the bucket dropped back down into the well. Parker looked inside to see nothing but a dirt floor at the bottom. The old man screamed in protest.

"I almost had it!" He shouted as he shoved Parker away. The old man picked up the rope and began to pull it up to the top once again.

"I almost had it!" The old man repeated to himself.

Parker knew he shouldn't have even gotten that close. He was angry at himself for even trying yet again. After shrugging off yet another failed attempt at humanity, Parker continued up the path further and saw a woman sitting in front of an apple tree. The apples looked healthy and delicious, but each time she touched one, it would shrivel up and turn to dust. Parker felt a wave of sadness and anger. He wanted to help them all so badly but knew that if he interfered anymore, he'd just make things worse.

CHAPTER TWELVE

Nearly a mile away, Parker could see the end of the path with a small set of stairs leading up to a large stone platform. At the top of the platform sat an enormous black throne. The throne was the biggest chair Parker had ever seen, and he was certain that he didn't want to meet the person big enough to sit on it. Just as he had reached the bottom of the stairs, a young woman stepped directly in front of him. She looked to be in her late twenties, possibly early thirties. She was covered in dirt and soot as if she had been exposed to a fire, but it did nothing to hide her beauty. She wore a long purple dress that was ragged and torn with burn marks at the bottom. Her eyes looked up toward Parker as she held out her hand to him. He approached her cautiously and stopped just a couple of feet away from her.

"It isn't time yet." She said.

"Time for what?" Parker asked.

The woman grabbed his hand and pulled him to a small hidden area behind the stairs where they could remain out of sight to anyone or anything that might be passing by.

"You're not supposed to be here now." She continued.

"This is the Underworld isn't it?" Parker asked.

"Yes, but it's much too soon for you to be here."

"What are you talking about? What's happening?"

"You have to go. They will be looking for you."

"Who?"

"Death is coming for you."

That made Parker feel a little more than unsettled.

"It's all right." She assured him. "It is not your time, but you have to get away from here or else they will find a way to keep you here."

"Who are you?" He asked.

"I am Guinevere."

"Guinevere? You're Arthurs' wife!"

"Arthur?"

"He helped me. He trained me so we could get you all out of here."

"Where is he?"

"He's on Avalon. If we can get out of here, I can take you to him."

"No. It isn't time."

"Why do you keep saying that?"

"I have to stay here. I have to serve my purpose."

"You've been here long enough. Why would you want to stay here? You're supposed to be free now."

"I have to keep this safe for you."

Guinevere reached into her dress pocket and pulled out a small leaf, but it wasn't like any leaf Parker had ever seen before. It was dark blue, with a bright red stem. She held it out to him.

"I won't let anything happen to it." Guinevere said holding it out to him.

"What is it for?"

"Nimue gave it to me. She told me to keep it safe until you needed it."

"I don't understand. Who is Nimue?"

"Please hurry. We will meet again." She said as she returned the leaf to her pocket.

"What are you saying? How are you not like the others?"

"You must go now. They will try to stop him from taking you, but everything will be okay."

"Taking me where?"

"Back to the fight."

"Guinevere, I made a promise for you."

"A promise that you will no doubt keep." She said as she placed her hand on his cheek. "I knew you would come, and you have, and that means more to me than you will ever know. Please, go and live. Continue your journey and know that I believe in you."

She gently shoved Parker and he began to walk away but turned back to see her one last time.

"Arthur loves you, and he misses you." Parker said.

Guinevere had tears in her eyes as she turned and ran away, leaving Parker behind. He couldn't imagine what she'd been through, or why she wasn't like the others. She had a purpose, one that he would eventually discover for himself.

Parker reached the top step and made his way toward the throne when suddenly twenty Ash Demons came out of different hideaways and doorways in the platform walls. They quickly surrounded Parker with their weapons drawn. He started to reach for his own sword and then realized that he didn't have one. He began to calculate in his head as he counted the enemies around him. Arthur and the others could hold their own against these things. Having been trained well by them, Parker should have no problem either. He waited patiently when the first demon attacked, he'd take its sword and use it for himself given the chance. The leader of the demons approached him and stopped just a few feet away.

"You don't stand a chance here welp." The Ash leader said in English. "This is our realm."

"What do you want with me?" Parker asked.

"We plan to deliver you to Hades. He's been carefully deciding how you will spend your eternity here."

"Hades is dead."

"You know so little about the way of things boy. You destroyed the vessel, but you have yet to meet the real god of the Underworld."

"Fart nuggets." Parker muttered under his breath.

"Show him what it feels like to be ripped apart, over and over again."

The leader watched as its twenty demons all charged after Parker at the same time. Parker punched the first one in the face as he kicked another, but it was no use. All the demons overpowered him at once and he was taken to the ground without mercy. It was then, just as one of the demons attempted to stab Parker in the chest, a loud pound against the ground could be heard, followed by a bright green flash of light. Instantly, every demon that had been attacking Parker flew into the air with great force.

The leader of the demons stepped forward and Parker quickly backed away from him until he bumped into the source of the noise. Parker turned to see a long staff stuck into the ground. Decorating the staff was a carving of a snake slithering up until it reached the top, where a long blade adorned it. Then he noticed it wasn't a staff at all, but a scythe and the snake that swirled around it looked as though it were alive. Parker looked to see the person holding it. He was seven feet tall, wearing a black cloak with the hood pulled over his head. Parker couldn't see much of his face, but what he could see was mostly bone and teeth. His hands and feet were pale and looked as if some of the skin had been peeled off.

"Thanatos!" The leader shouted. "You have no business here."

"Oh, but I do." Thanatos answered with a growling and raspy voice.

"Hades won this fair and square." The leader continued. "The boys' soul belongs to him!"

"Fair and square? That is debatable, besides Hades has no right to a living soul."

"That is impossible. How could he be…?"

"That is irrelevant and of no concern to you." Thanatos interrupted. "What matters is that I've come to take him back where he belongs."

"You're not taking him anywhere reaper!"

The leader pulled out his sword and charged at Thanatos with a loud battle cry. Thanatos raised his scythe as it lit up a bright green light, and then pointed it toward the demon leader, a blast shot out and hit the demon launching him onto his back, cracking the ground beneath him with the impact of his body.

"Do you wish to challenge me?" Thanatos asked. "The Underworld revolves around your masters' rules, but he has no control over me. If I say this one lives, this one lives."

"You mettle in affairs that are beneath you." The leader grunted as he stood to his feet. "Are you an errand boy for the Olympians now?"

"I care little for this feud of the gods. I'm here to do my job as this is how it has been since the beginning of time, and neither man nor demon will stop me. If you want this boy, you must challenge me for him, but you have to wager your soul in exchange."

The leader was silent at the words.

"Oh, that's right." Thanatos continued. "Ash demons have no souls. I guess a fight is the only other option. Care to indulge an old man in a quick duel?"

Thanatos held out the bottom of his scythe to Parker and helped him to his feet all the while staring into the eyes of the demon leader.

"That's too bad." Thanatos said, belittling the leader. "I was hoping for a bit of fun."

"I appreciate your help." Parker said.

"Do not be thanking me." Thanatos replied. "You owe me a debt. I would see you live to make the bargain."

Parker looked up at Thanatos in confusion. He wasn't aware of any debt and he certainly didn't ask for his help. Before Parker could ask any questions, Thanatos took his finger and slowly moved it across the wound on Parkers' stomach. Parker could feel the heat rising from within his own body until he felt the urge to scream in pain. A small shard of Hades horn that had been broken off deep in Parkers' stomach popped out. Thanatos held the shard in his hand until it disintegrated into nothing.

"This was only a pit stop for you, but rest assured we will meet again at another time."

WARRIOR FROM AVALON

Thanatos then touched Parker on the chest and suddenly green light covered his entire body. Parker was in agonizing pain and couldn't stop himself from screaming. Seconds went by like minutes, and then just as quick as it started, it was over. Parker opened his eyes to see a large, forested area all around him. Suddenly he was standing under a beautiful oak tree. He felt his stomach to find that the wound had been healed. There wasn't even a scar. He wondered if he'd been sent back to Avalon.

He started walking through the woods until he heard the sound of gentle music playing in the distance, like a ballet or opera. The lovely sound grew louder as he found himself standing in front of a small lake in the middle of the forest. A waterfall rained down at the back of the lake as the Sun shined down through an opening in the trees creating a rainbow within the falls, and that is when he saw her for the first time. A young woman stood on top of the water dancing to the music. He watched in amazement as she moved from ripple to ripple until the music ended and she bowed to end her performance.

"You're right on time, Sir Wallace." Nimue said without even looking up at him.

"You know me?" He asked.

"I have known you for quite some time actually, though we haven't met officially."

She waved her hand toward him, motioning him to come closer.

"I'm good here thanks." He said waving back to her.

"Come now. I don't permit just anyone to walk beside me, least of all like this."

"Okay." He said with a slight uncertainty.

Parker stretched out his foot and walked softly expecting to fall into the lake, but instead he stood above the water as if it were solid ground. He carefully walked out to the middle to stand next to her.

"Allow me to formally introduce myself." She said.

"I am Nimue, or known to some, The Lady of the Lake."

"Nimue? That's the name Guinevere mentioned." He said.

"I'm sure she did."

"What's going here? Are we on Avalon?"

"Not Avalon, currently you're standing on the border of the Elysian Fields."

Parker smiled at the beauty around him.

"Am I dead?" He asked. "Again?"

"Not at all." She answered with a smile. "You are very much alive."

"Why am I here? I thought this was locked off to everyone."

Nimue held Parkers' hand as they walked along the water.

"Only to those held captive by Hades, but you on the other hand are different. I brought you here myself, with a little help from Thanatos."

"Why?"

"You have a destiny to fulfill, one that was chosen before you were even born."

"I already fought Hades, and I failed. He's still alive somewhere in the Underworld and it's my fault. I did something wrong."

"You didn't fail Parker. You did as you were meant to do."

"He was set free because of me."

"Hades was imprisoned, not just on the Island of Fire, but in the body of a Tulpa. A vessel created by Zeus to house the soul of Hades."

"What is a Tulpa?"

"A Tulpa is a vessel that can be created by the pure will of a powerful being. It can be used to house a soul, but it is never meant to be permanent. By destroying the Tulpa, you released his soul to return to the Underworld, but Hades' true body had been destroyed long ago, so he had no vessel to return to. You may have set him free, but he is nothing more than a spirit with no body."

"So then, where is he?"

"Hades has desires upon the earth. I imagine he's out there somewhere, plotting his next move. He's had quite some time to think about it."

"This isn't the way it was supposed to happen." Parker said with regret.

"Actually, it was." Nimue responded. "He had to be released."

"I was supposed to destroy him entirely. Not set him free. If that's the case, we should have just left him where he was! We should have found another way."

"Hades has a hold on all of those souls you saw in the Underworld. Destroying his vessel does not relinquish his power over them. Only by destroying him entirely will we unlock the gate for the others."

"Then we're not any closer to when we started."

"This was merely the beginning Parker. Your mission was never going to be this simple."

"I don't remember it being that simple. He nearly killed me!"

Nimue placed her hand on his shoulder.

"I understand the weight of what you carry, and I know you were so ready for this all to be over, but the journey ahead is quite long I'm afraid. Unfortunately, I must now ask more of you."

"What more use could I possibly be?"

"Come with me. I'll show you what waits." She said as they walked together under the waterfall.

Nimue could feel Parker tighten his grip as they passed through to the other side. As they went under the falls the water split apart for them like a curtain. Once they were through, they found themselves in a large field of grass. Parker looked around and was suddenly alone as Nimue had disappeared entirely. Even the waterfall was gone, leaving nothing but an open sky and hills of grass around him like

WARRIOR FROM AVALON

he had been teleported somewhere else. A few moments passed and suddenly he dropped to his knees in heartbreak at what he saw scattered along the landscape. Hundreds of bodies lay dead on the ground all around him.

"What happened?" He asked with sorrow in his voice. "Why would you bring me here?"

"This is the world today." Nimue said stepping into his view. "What you knew when you awoke on Avalon is that you were in an accident in the year 2022. The world has changed since then."

"What are you talking about?" He asked as he stood to his feet. "I've only been gone a couple of months."

"You have been gone centuries Parker." Nimue corrected. "After your supposed death on the bridge, you were taken to Avalon and placed in a state of deep sleep. You've been unconscious for a little over three hundred years."

Parker could feel his stomach tying itself in knots.

"I don't understand. Why?"

"The year is 2332. A new Dark Age has claimed the world."

"How is this possible?"

"Years have passed since darkness was released on the Earth. Ash demons roam free, plaguing mankind once again and a war is coming that we all must fight."

"What war?"

"The greatest war the world has ever seen, and you are one of many that have been chosen to fight it."

"You have it all wrong. I'm not a soldier. I tried to tell Arthur and the others. I'm just a nobody."

"A nobody who defeated the god of the Underworld in combat."

"I prepared for that. What you're asking of me is too much."

"I know you Parker. I know you in so many ways that you don't even know yourself. I know what rests in your heart. You have so much courage buried inside of you. I've seen your true potential for myself."

"How do you know what I'm capable of? You just met me."

"I've seen you achieve many great deeds. I've seen your future in fact. The feats you accomplish out of your own determination and courage. You are going to save so many people. It's been your destiny, as well as Eva's."

"What does Eva have to do with any of this?"

"She was found many years ago. Like you, she was placed in a deep sleep until we saw it fit to wake her. Her role in this future is just as important as yours, even more so. Your destinies have been intertwined and you have become her protector. It is your job to keep her safe along your journey together because, in the end, the world will need the both of you."

Parker remained silent.

"I know this is a lot to take in." Nimue continued. "You want the answers, but I cannot reveal to you what lies ahead, I can only guide you in the right direction."

"What is it that I'm supposed to do?"

"Live again, fight for humanity. Stop this world from descending further into chaos and follow your destiny. You can stop Hades once and for all, free those souls from the Underworld and prevent more of this from happening." She said pointing toward the fallen soldiers.

"I'm just one man."

"You'd be surprised at what one man can accomplish." She said putting her hand on his cheek.

Parker closed his eyes tight and thought of Eva. Nimue could read him as if were a living book. He looked around him at all the death and destruction. It was the same story all over again. If the world could be saved, and it was his job to help, what could he say?

"I've never been important to anyone before. I don't see myself the way you all have, but if you believe it's possible, then what else can I do? I'll do everything I can."

"Understand me. This will be a long and dangerous path, but the end goal is what will make all of our sacrifices worth it."

"Peace?"

"Hope. Hope for a future that can find peace. Everything you have fought for and will fight for can be won. I have faith in you, but you must also have faith in yourself."

"You're not the first to tell me that." Parker said as he nodded.

"It's time for your return to Earth. Your greatest journey begins now."

"Wait." Parker said. "What about Guinevere and the others? Where do I even start?"

"It will take time, but your path will be presented before you." Nimue said as she reached for his hand and slowly the two of them disappeared into the air.

The crying could be heard in the night sky as an infant child lay on the ground by a lake. Nimue stepped toward him and looked down with her finger over her mouth to shush the baby. She was transparent, only there in spirit form.

"Don't worry." She said. "Your new family is almost here."

Nimue then raised her hand into the air. A bright light began to emit from her fingers and shined deep into the forested area around her. The light from her hand began to blink on and off. It was then Nimue could hear a man somewhere in the woods speaking inaudible words.

"He's a good man." She said to the baby. "He and his wife will take great care of you until you're older."

Nimue began to walk away from the baby, moving into another part of the forest just out of sight. The man from the woods came into her view and saw the baby lying on the ground in front of him. Behind him from the woods emerged a woman of about thirty-years old and a child of six.

"What is it Frank?" The lady asked.

Frank, a scruffy Scottish hunter in his early forties, picked the baby up from the ground.

"It's a child Lora." Frank said holding the baby in his arms. "Just a child lying here in the middle of nowhere."

"What was that light Daddy?" The little boy asked.

"I'm not sure Isaac, but I think it was someone trying to get our attention."

Frank walked over to Lora and placed the baby in her arms.

"Who would leave a baby out here all alone?" Lora asked.

"Someone who doesn't want him I'm afraid." Frank answered.

"That's awful. Why would they just abandon him like this?"

"The worlds a dangerous place Lora, some people just can't handle another mouth to feed."

"We should take him with us then. We can provide for him can't we Frank?"

"We can and we will."

"I'll look out for him Mom." Isaac said.

"We all will sweetie." She said with a smile.

Nimue watched from the shadows with a smile on her face.

"What's his name?" Isaac asked.

Frank looked at the blanket the baby had been wrapped in and could see a small note sticking out from underneath. He reached for the note and read it aloud.

"This is Parker Wallace. Look after him, as he will one day look after you. Protect him with all your being, so that one day he will do the same for the world."

Lora rubbed her thumb against baby Parkers' cheek.

"Parker Wallace." She said with a smile. "Welcome to the family."

Nimue watched as the family carried baby Parker back the way they had come through the woods.

"I'll be watching over you Parker, as I always have." Nimue said softly. "We'll see each other again."

She then stepped out toward the middle of the lake, and slowly sank beneath the water.

Eva sat on the beach looking out toward the ocean while Arthur and Lucas sat at the café. It had been a couple of days since they had returned to the island and couldn't help but feel that more should have been done. Sang and Arthur had talked once they had returned to the island, and Arthur was still unsure of Sang's actions. It was a problem for Arthur, but in the end, Sang assured him that it was the best course of action. Lucas had been taken home to heal and rest as soon as he'd arrived. His wound healed rapidly, and in no time at all he was back to his normal self. It still didn't make him feel any better that they had left Parker to his fate.

"I try to think of what else we could have done." Lucas said.

"There wasn't much we could do." Arthur spoke. "The ship detected the demons' presence. It chose to bring us back."

"You could have found a way to turn around. You could have saved him."

"No, I couldn't have done that to you my friend." Arthur said patting Lucas on the shoulder.

"What if Hades won?" Lucas asked.

"I refuse to believe he did." Arthur answered. "Time will answer."

"How did the demons get out again? The portal was sealed after they took you the last time. It couldn't have opened again."

"No. The Ash Demons aren't prisoners anymore. Someone let them all out and they went for us."

"Who would do such a thing? Who would release

them again?"

"I'm not sure, but it does mean that this island must be on alert from now on. Watchtowers must be set up. Patrols. Just to be safe."

"You think they'd try to come back again?"

"I don't think so, but it doesn't hurt to be more prepared."

Lucas took a sip of coffee he had sitting in front of him.

"Do you think we should join her?" Lucas asked looking toward Eva.

"It's not our company she seeks." Arthur answered.

Eva let her feet stretch out as the tide rushed to her ankles. Tears continued to roll down her cheeks. Her heart was broken at the thought of losing Parker. She wanted to believe that he was still out there somewhere, but after the others had returned without him, she wasn't so sure. After two days had passed, she could do nothing more but look to the sea and mourn. The wind began to blow her hair and the waves began to slow to a halt.

"Eva." A voice whispered.

She stood in the sand and looked out toward the ocean.

"Eva." The voice whispered again.

Sang had been standing on the cliff near the highest point of the island. He looked down to see Eva on the beach moving closer to the waves. He had been visiting that very spot at the same time every day since their return and he would simply wait. It was only then he smiled with a sense of pride. The waves began to rush toward the beach faster and faster as Eva stood looking out toward the horizon.

Arthur and Lucas walked to the beach and stood behind Eva as Nimue slowly walked out of the ocean and onto the shore.

"Nimue?" Eva asked.

"It's good to see you again Eva." Nimue responded. "It's been a long time."

"Please tell me you have news." Eva said hopeful.

"Parker is alive." Nimue said with a smile.

Arthur held Eva's hand as tears of joy streamed down her face.

"I come not only to inform you of your friend, but others are needed as well." Nimue continued. "Eva, you were brought to this island many years ago, but you were always meant to serve a greater purpose."

"What purpose?" Eva asked.

"Parker has returned to Earth, and I ask that you go there as well, just as he did. He will be there waiting for you, to protect you and he will need your protection as well."

"If this is my calling. If this is the reason I was brought here so long ago, then so be it. I will do whatever I have to do for him."

"Then it is time."

Eva turned to the others and said her goodbyes until Nimue took her by the hand and they both began walking toward the waves. Nimue looked back to Arthur and smiled.

"I will see you again very soon, Sir Arthur."

Then, as Nimue and Eva both stepped into the ocean, they vanished beneath the waves. Arthur and Lucas smiled after hearing the news of their friend. No longer did sadness dwell within them, but happiness that Parker was alive. He had done what he was meant to do. He had survived his encounter with Hades. Arthur felt a deep feeling of pride in his heart. Even though he had no idea of what was to happen next, he finally allowed himself to hope again. He could feel it deep in his very soul. Someday his wife would be free once more. In time, she would be at peace, and it would all be worth it.

CHAPTER THIRTEEN

The year was 2362, and the world had changed drastically since civilization fell apart. Technology had thrived until suddenly, human progression just stopped. Cities and countries unraveled after the world was plunged into chaos. It wasn't something anyone had expected. An orb known as the Dark Light, an object of overwhelming power, was used to release the ash demons from exile and had since gone missing. Immediately after the ash arrival on Earth, they took possession of the oceans by extreme force, only setting foot on land when necessary.

People all over the world had moved as far inland as possible, leaving much of the coastal cities and towns deserted. However, some people sought to take advantage of this situation and created their own kingdoms to maintain a sense of power. All those who dared to oppose were exiled or killed. Many communities managed to find places in between, hoping to fight off whatever threat might come their way. This included a more modernized pirate society in the world. With the Ash laying claim to the oceans and coastal cities, the pirates weren't stupid enough to challenge them for control, so they moved inland as well, claiming the smaller cities for themselves. The pirates would set up outposts and send out salvage teams. They would either find what they needed or steal it from someone else. Often, they would take everything, and trade the leftovers to other pirates from other towns. There was no order, there was only lawlessness and greed. It seemed there was very little hope in the world as it had become a new age of darkness.

The apartment building was dark and dreary as Parker entered the narrow hallway, stepping on old newspapers and other scattered debris that had been there for decades. He reached over his shoulder and pulled a shotgun from his backpack and switched on a small flashlight he had taped around the barrel. The shotgun was an old pulse weapon he had found several months earlier on a salvage trip in a small city near Kilkenny Ireland. Pulse guns, or numb guns, were extremely difficult to find. A Pulse gun, once charged, could fire a numbing shot into a person's body. The affected area, when hit would cause temporary paralysis for at least a couple of hours. Taking a hit directly to the head would render the person unconscious completely for almost the same amount of time. The guns never ran out of power but depending on what type of weapon was being used, a person could shoot several rounds before the weapon became useless and had to be recharged by shutting it off for a few hours.

    The pulse material itself was generated inside the gun through a combination of synthesized regenerative chemicals that included Atracurium, a type of pharmaceutical anesthetic that originated from the idea of curare darts. Once a pulse was fired, the gun would automatically regenerate the material inside itself. Pulse tech had been invented long before as a medical anesthetic, until the technology was adopted by the government as a replacement to all lethal weaponry. It was considered a medical breakthrough, but turned into a weapon and was an innovative idea that helped reduce the number of murders by eighty percent the year they had hit the public market, but muggings, robberies, and other atrocities were at an all-time high. Though the Pulse gun was effective, it didn't work on Ash demons. The only lethal way to kill them was to carry some type of blade.

    Parker carried three sharp edge weapons. One was a long sword, which he kept in a sheath on his back, which would crisscross with his shotgun when both were holstered. Another was a dagger he kept sheathed to his belt next to a pulse style handgun modeled after a 9mm Glock yet more stylish, and lastly he carried a small blade hidden in the bottom of his right boot that popped out at the touch of a

WARRIOR FROM AVALON

button.

The light shined down the hall as Parker slowly made his way to the stairway directly ahead of him. From the look of things, the city pirates hadn't cared enough to check the building out, or Parker had managed to get to it before them somehow. Most cities were too large even for them to cover every building. Either way, he was going to check the top floor first and work his way down. He reached the seventh floor and proceeded to the end of the hall.

He slowly twisted the knob and entered the room while shining the light around carefully. He began checking behind doors and in closets to make sure there wasn't an ambush waiting for him before he conducted his search for supplies. The apartment wouldn't take long to scavenge considering the size. Once Parker was satisfied that he was alone he began searching for any items that might be of use. His first stop was the kitchen.

Many of the cabinets were half-empty aside from old, spoiled bread, some canned goods that Parker tucked into his backpack, and an old box of cereal with a holographic video displayed on the front cover. Parker watched as a cartoon began to play when he picked up the box. The digital cover showed a monkey being chased around a forest by the stereotypical hunter with a large gun. Although it was heavily distorted, the audio from the box repeated a slow monotone recording.

"Monkey Chunks, the new chocolate cereal with banana-flavored marshmallows. Fun in a bowl that will make you go bananas!"

"That sounds disgusting." Parker muttered to himself with a slight Scottish accent as he tossed the cereal box away.

After moving out of the kitchen he made his way to the bedroom. All he had managed to find was an old, dusty leather jacket. It wasn't much, but it was clothing. It seemed too small for him, but someone could use it. He took the jacket, rolled it up to save space, and shoved it into his backpack. He decided that whoever had lived there long ago must have packed up and left in a hurry. Parker didn't waste any more time in the first apartment. Once he had salvaged anything useful, he moved on to the next place.

It took him nearly an hour to check the top three floors, but it wasn't a total loss. He had managed to find several items of clothing that would help a lot of kids he knew, plus a couple pairs of jeans that he wasn't too proud to keep for himself. He had spent enough time scavenging and figured it would be best to call it a night. He would come back later to collect whatever else he missed. He headed for the stairway once again but was stopped when someone grabbed his backpack and yanked him into one of the other apartments. Parker hit the ground hard dropping the pulse gun on impact. Before he could make a grab for it, a dark figure approached and kicked it out of his reach.

A second figure appeared moving toward him, so he swept his leg underneath the figure knocking him to the ground and he quickly jumped to his feet. Suddenly he could see the light from his own weapon being pointed at him and he was forced to stop his attack. Parker slowly raised his hands into the air in submission.

"Well now, what do we have here?" A male voice asked with a hint of an oriental accent. "The infamous Parker Wallace."

"I'm sorry." Parker said calmly. "You must have me confused with someone else. My name's Archibald."

"I don't think so." The man said holding up a small handheld ID scanner with Parkers' photo and other information on its screen. It was a handy device, and one of the only few pieces of technology that had managed to survive over the years. Parker had been caught by a small group of men a few months back, and before he had been able to slip away, one of them had input his photo and description into the scanner. Once the information was entered, the one and only self-sustaining satellite, which surprisingly orbited the earth and still worked, managed to pass the info to every scanner on the planet.

"Parker Wallace..." The man began, "...Caucasian, dark hair, blue eyes, five foot nine, wanted for terroristic attacks, theft, and other acts of violence against King Roland and the city of Dublin."

"King Roland?" Parker scoffed. "That's that dictator guy, right?"

"Disarm him." The man shouted to one of his thugs.

Parker surveyed the room. The light from his gun being shined in his eyes made it difficult to see, but it was also enough brightness that he could look for an escape as well as count how many men he would have to take out should a fight erupt. He counted six men altogether. Two of them approached him to take his long sword, handgun, and dagger but neglected to check his boot for the hidden blade.

"Try not to hurt yourselves, those things are sharp." Parker said.

"I wouldn't be wisecracking if I were you." The man said stepping into the light to reveal his face.

"Jiao-Long Feng. What is a dirty little cement crawler like you doing on this side of the city?" Parker asked. "I thought you guys avoided the coastal areas?"

"One of my lookouts spotted you entering the city. I'm here to claim the reward that has been placed on your head."

"Oh yeah? What's the claim up to now?"

"It's alot."

"Yeah, what do you need a reward for? You just steal what you need from someone else anyway."

"Very true, but I also just don't like you."

"Come on Feng!" Parker said with sarcastic exaggeration. "You'd get bored with me gone. Besides, I heard you got promoted to running your own little town, congratulations! Which family member was it you had to kill to get that spot?"

One of Feng's men slapped Parker in the back of the head for his disrespect.

"That one, I'll let slide." Parker said angrily to the man who hit him. "Hit me again and I'll break your wrist."

The man approached and popped Parker in the back of the head again, then stared him in the face to show him he was not afraid.

"Okay." Parker nodded. "Hang tight, we'll get there."

"Say what you like." Feng spoke unhampered by Parkers' remark. "Pretty soon, you won't have a tongue to speak with. I've sent one of my best messengers to find captain Steel and inform him of your capture. The way I hear it, he's extremely upset with you and your friends."

"Steel? Oh, that's right. He's one of Roland's guys, the bald one. I mean have you seen the shine off that guy's head. Whew, could brighten up a city block with the right lighting."

"Keeping laughing. We're taking you back to our base, and once Steel arrives, he's taking you with him and we'll get our reward for your capture."

"You think you're in Roland's good graces out here? Your little band of thieves isn't going to last forever."

"No, Roland needs people like me. You see, he can rule inside those walls of his, but out here in the city ruins, I am King. Guys like me get things done. It's why we're allowed to operate freely."

"What happens when you've served your purpose? What happens when he decides that you're no longer useful out here?"

"Then I will show Roland how things work, in the real world."

"You keep telling yourself that Feng. I'll be there when you realize just how small a fish you are in this big pond."

167

"You are not better than me Parker." Feng said with anger. "I have an army to do my bidding. What do you have?"

"A charming personality?"

Feng scoffed and motioned for one of his men to escort Parker out of the room.

"Take him to the holding cell." He ordered. "And keep a close watch on him, he's crafty."

Two of Feng's men grabbed Parker by the arms and began pulling him to the door. Parker watched as the light from his gun followed him closely.

"It was really good thinking you could catch me with my own gun, too bad the battery is dead." Parker said before head butting the man to his right. Once his arm was free, he slammed his right fist hard into the other man's face, then grabbed his wrist and broke it.

"Told you that would happen." He said with a smile.

Parker turned to the man holding the shotgun. He watched as he tried to pull the trigger, but Parker grabbed the barrel of the gun and pointed it at the man's leg. A pulse shot out and the thug fell to the ground. Parker then pulled the gun from his hands and slammed the butt of it into the man's head knocking him out.

"Oops, I might have been bluffing." Parker said with a smirk.

Feng began shouting orders in Japanese to the last two men in the room. Parker saw them both racing toward him. He aimed with the pulse gun but as he pulled the trigger it let out a low mechanical hum that indicated the battery was indeed depleted.

"Cheesy peaches, guess it wasn't much of a bluff." Parker said as the first man entered his reach.

Parker kicked him in the stomach forcing him to double over. As the second man approached, He threw the shotgun at his face distracting him so Parker could perform a series of punch and kick combos until he finished by clotheslining the man to the floor. Feng darted out of the apartment door as Parker turned around to finish off the man he had kicked in the stomach. Unfortunately, he had managed to regain his strength quickly while Parker was distracted and was now ready for a brawl.

Parker punched hard as the man ducked and buried his elbow into Parkers' ribs. The two men continued smashing each other's faces with their fists until Parker was backed against the wall. The man jabbed hard, but Parker ducked allowing his fist to slam into the wall behind him. Parker placed his hand on the back of his opponents' head and slammed it into the wall forming a hole. He continued slamming the man's head until he crashed through the hole all the way into the next room and got stuck. It still wasn't enough to stop him. He kicked backward at Parker who managed to sidestep just in time to avoid being hit. Parker stood back and couldn't help but laugh as the man struggled to free his head from the wall.

"Stuck huh?" Parker asked as he entered the next room. He could see the thugs head sticking through the other side as he struggled hard to pull free.

"Yep, that's in there pretty good." Parker said as he patted the man on the back. He looked around the room and found a long piece of 2X4. He stood next to the thugs' head and took aim.

"No worries friend, I'm gonna get you out of there!" Parker said as he swung the makeshift bat knocking the man free from the wall and breaking the piece of wood into splinters. Parker entered the next room to see his fallen adversary unconscious on his back. He held up the now smaller piece of wood and then tossed it on top of the thug's chest.

"Take a nap, you earned it." Parker said. "I win."

Parker gathered up his equipment as quickly as he could and ran for the door. No sooner had he entered the hall he felt a solid object crash into the back of his own head. He fell to the floor, dropping all of his gear and hit face-first on the flat surface. He rolled over onto his back and looked up to see the blurry face of his attacker standing over him, holding the weapon as if they were ready to hit him again. He squinted his eyes, hoping to focus on what slowly became a familiar face.

"Eva?"

Her face was clear for just a few seconds before turning back to a blurring figure. Parker struggled to raise himself up from the floor, but it was no use as the impact to the back of his head finally rendered him unconscious.

CHAPTER FOURTEEN

It was almost an hour later when Parker woke in a holding cell. He was lying flat on his back staring up at the ceiling after he finally managed to open his eyes again. He slowly raised himself from the floor and held the back of his head. One of Feng's guards, Trigger, sat in a chair by a desk in the small room. Parker was locked in an 8X8 cell with not even a bed to sit on. Trigger had been a guard for Feng for a few years. He didn't even remember his real name since it had been so long since anyone had used it. They called him Trigger because of an accident he had when he was younger, which cost him his right trigger finger. He stood up from his chair after seeing Parker had woken up.

"I wouldn't be getting up too quick, you took an awful knock to your noggin." Trigger said in a thick Scottish accent. "You're a tough one to wake up so quick after that little pop to the thinker like that, aren't you?"

"Have you got any water?" Parker asked.

"Sure." Trigger said as he placed a cup of water on the floor outside the bars.

Parker grabbed the cup and sipped on it for a few moments before standing up.

"Been a while Trigger."

"Too long. You're still as ugly as ever."
Parker couldn't help but laugh.

"You shouldn't talk down to prisoners." Parker said with a sly smile. "They may riot on you."

"You plan on breaking out, do you?"

"Eventually."

"Consider yourself lucky, most of the prisoners they bring here are killed. That makes you something special."

"Prisoners are just another mouth to feed. I imagine that's a bit too time-consuming for Feng. If he's killing more people, then I suppose he's lost all traces of his humanity."

"Lately, they just take them somewhere else."

"Take them where?"

"They don't tell me that, nor do they tell me why."

"You are just a wealth of information Trigger. What do they keep you around here for?"

"My rugged good looks I suppose. That and I'm just a likeable guy."

The door to the room slowly opened and a woman entered. Trigger smiled shyly at the woman while Parker watched as she placed a small cylindrical object in her left pant pocket. It was most likely a key to the door.

"How do you do today Ms. Annabelle?" Trigger asked.

"Fine Trigger." She answered.

Parker knew her face. Not only was she the woman who knocked him on his rear prior to his current situation, but also something about her seemed familiar.

"Do you mind leaving us alone for a moment?" She asked.

"Of course not." Trigger said as he slowly exited the room. "Just, don't let your guard down with this one."

Once Trigger had shut the door, she slowly approached the bars and gazed at the man behind them.

"You look nice without a blunt instrument in your hands, Ms. Annabelle." Parker said.

"Who are you?" She asked. "Are you another Pirate? Or an exile?"

"An exiled pirate, you got me."

"You're not in a position to make jokes."

"It's a defense mechanism, it's what I do."

Eva didn't seem to be entertained by the Parker Wallace charm. Though there was something about him.

"What were you doing in the city?" She asked.

"Same reason as anyone else I guess." He responded. "Just trying to get by. What's a nice girl like you doing here? I mean, you're much better dressed than any of these other pirate women. Your clothes are cleaner for sure. You don't smell like a trash heap. You've obviously got access to clean water."

"I'm here for purposes beyond your understanding."

"You're from inside the walls, aren't you? You live in Dublin?"

"How could you guess that?"

"People on the outside of those walls don't have much. With these pirates everywhere, supplies to keep the body odor away is hard to come by. If someone looking as you do came walking through any of these cities, you'd be robbed and left to rot in a matter of minutes."

"You'd be surprised. I can handle myself."

"Which is why you're able to walk around here freely. Meaning you're somewhat important at least. We all know that Feng is Roland's little puppy, but he's not exactly trustworthy, is he? So, you must be here as an emissary for Roland. Now I ask again, what's a nice girl like you doing here?"

She looked Parker in the eyes with surprised curiosity. Not only was he very observant, but he practically knew exactly what her purpose was. Though she wasn't going to let him know that.

"Like I said, you wouldn't understand." She replied.

"Explain it to me." Parker said. "I've got some time."

"Your time is rather limited. Captain Steel will be here soon."

"That's cute." Parker said laughing. "Steel doesn't concern me in the slightest."

"You've eluded him for a long time, which makes him extremely anxious to see you Mr. Wallace."

"You do know who I am." Parker said with a hint of pride.

"Tell me, why do you risk coming into the cities when you know how dangerous it is?" Eva asked. "You know they're actively searching for you and yet you continue to sneak into the lions' den as it were. What do you hope to accomplish?" Eva asked stepping closer to the bars once again and placing her hands just above Parkers'.

"It's called survival. Something a puppet for Roland wouldn't understand."

"Survival means killing innocent people?"

"I've never killed anyone, and since when is a pirate considered innocent? They kill all the time. That doesn't seem to bother you much."

"I was told you're a threat to our way of life inside the walls."

"Servitude under a dictatorship isn't a way of life, but I'm flattered they think I'm so dangerous. What other lies do they tell you about me?"

"You're a terrorist. King Roland speaks about your constant irritations, how you disrupt the supplies being brought into the city."

"I've only taken a little food for others that needed it more."

"You've helped criminals escape custody."

"Slaves for Roland? Yeah, I helped them escape."

"Stealing is stealing isn't it?"

"You're one to talk hanging around with these pirates. I've taken from Roland and his men, that's a fair statement, but I never killed anyone for it. If they died it was because Roland had them executed and blamed it on me. Anything I took, I've given it back to the people they stole it from in the first place. Unless they were murdered first, then I do tend to keep it for myself or redistribute it to others. I have a selfish desire to live I suppose, but you, you're hanging around pirates who kill and take just because they can even if they have more than enough."

"That's not who I am."

"But that's who they are, and you're here to serve their leader who is far worse than them. How do you think Roland came to power? He was a soldier first." Parker said sliding his right hand down the bars. "People like Roland, they will kill for power and have people killed in order to keep it. Live under his rule, in his city and you can have whatever he wants you to have so long as you give him twice as much back. People in the coastal villages can't afford to give up what they don't have, so I fight and steal for them, not just myself."

"What you're doing is the fastest way to get yourself killed then."

"Well I can take care of myself better than you think. Besides, what makes you care so much?"

Parker quickly stuck his hand in his pocket and stepped away from the bars.

"I didn't say I cared. I'm just trying to understand what you're after."

"Freedom for starters. Not having to look over my shoulders for a scrap of bread. Being able to sleep at night without a constant worry that someone is about to attack me or my friends would also be nice."

"Your militia is going to fall. You must realize that by now."

"My militia? Wow they really lay it on thick, don't they? I don't have a militia."

"You're alone?" She asked somewhat unconvinced.

"Of course I am. What kind of evil propaganda is that vulture spewing?"

"He says you're a terrorist leader, that you have pockets of military soldiers hitting our outposts."

"What outposts? I'm just one guy out here. I don't have an army. What I do have is compassion for the less fortunate. Something Roland clearly lacks."

"Why does he perceive you as such a threat?"

"That's a good question. I don't know how I ended up on Roland's most wanted list, but trust me, I'm not the guy he says I am."

Eva looked intently into Parkers' eyes to see his sincerity. She didn't know why, but she somehow knew he was telling the truth.

"One last thing I need to ask." She said whispering. "You said a name before."

"Eva?"

"How did you know that name?" She asked quietly.

"I honestly don't know."

"Tell me the truth." She demanded yet still keeping her voice down.

"I am telling the truth. I don't know how I knew that name. It just came to me when I saw you."

Eva stepped back and stared into Parkers' eyes trying to understand why he seemed familiar to her.

"What is it?" He asked.

"There is something very familiar about you." She answered.

"Maybe we knew each other in a past life?"

"I doubt it. You don't seem the type that I'd associate myself with."

"You're really trying to hurt my feelings." Parker said with sarcasm.

Suddenly the door to the room opened once again and Trigger stepped through.

"Sorry to interrupt Annabelle, but your time is up." Trigger said. "I have to prep him for the captains' arrival."

"I understand." Eva responded. "I'm leaving now."

Eva glanced at Parker once more and then exited the room. Parker watched as Trigger carried a familiar bag and placed it on the table.

"That's my stuff." Parker said.

"Aye it is."

"Well this has been fun." Parker said reaching into his pocket. "I think it's time I get going."

"Might be a good idea."

Parker pulled the key Eva had kept in her pocket and used it to unlock the cell door.

"Where'd you get that you crafty bugger?" Trigger

asked walking toward Parker.

"It's magic." Parker said extending his hand to him. "Thanks Trigger, always a pleasure."

"Anytime Mr. Wallace." Trigger responded shaking Parkers' hand.

"I think you should seriously disappear this time. Isn't this the second time I've slipped away under your watch?"

"Third actually, there was the time with the wagon, and you slipped out of the back, then the time before that when I tripped with another guard chasing you out of the city."

"Oh yeah. Well, this time they might kill you. I appreciate everything you've done for me in the past, but.... you need to get out of here as quietly and quickly as possible. There's a town just south of Bray, they have need of some supplies. I left a bag just outside of the city, you'll know where. It's full of canned goods, maybe a few old shirts and stuff. Take it to them and tell them I sent you. They'll keep you hidden for a while."

"I owe you Parker."

"We're good. You've helped me plenty."

"You be careful out there. It's starting to get a bit too dangerous even for you."

"Stay safe."

Parker shook Triggers' hand again and grabbed his gear off the table.

"Hey Trigger, one more thing." Parker said. "Who would know about the people being taken out of here. What's the story there?"

"I'm not sure. That Annabelle might know a thing or two. She claims to have been sent by Roland to oversee a project that Feng is in charge of. Not many details floating through the air around here I'm afraid."

"Thanks again." Parker said as the two men exited the holding area and went their separate ways.

An escort remained beside Eva as they walked toward the rooftop door while a guard unlocked it. Once the door was open, Eva entered alone as the guard closed the door and locked it again. On the roof, there was a small shack-like structure that held a small mattress that fit a twin bed. It had no blankets and no pillows. Eva hadn't been used to so little accommodations for quite some time, but this was a sacrifice she was willing to make for now. She stepped over to the ledge of the roof and peeked over to see the four-story drop below.

Looking out toward the city she could see it wasn't that big. There were few buildings scattered across the landscape, all of them had been retaken by nature as the vines and grass hadn't been cleared away in decades. Far off into the distance, she could see the walls of Dublin standing high. It seemed small from being so far away, but she knew in person that the city was massive in size.

"Be careful." Parker said stepping out the shadows. "That's a long way down."

"How did you get out?" Eva asked shocked.

Parker stepped forward and held an empty hand up in front of her face.

"That is my little secret." He said as he magically revealed the cylinder key he had picked from her pocket.

"Give me that!" She said reaching for Parkers' hands. "That's Feng's key!"

"When I'm done with it." He said making the key disappear once again with a slight of hand movement.

"If he finds out you have that he'll change all the locking codes. It'll be useless to you."

Parker began walking toward the ledge of the building and looked over the side.

"Sometimes things just get misplaced. I'm sure it'll turn up again eventually."

"How do you know I won't tell him you have it?"

"Something tells me he didn't even know you had it. This key unlocks quite a bit of stuff. I'm pretty sure it doesn't belong to you."

"I can call the guard right now."

Parker held his hands up playfully and smiled but made no attempt to stop her from shouting for help.

"You are unbearable." Eva said.

"If Feng found out that I got his key from you, I can't imagine he'd be very happy."

Eva quickly began to search Parkers' pockets for the key.

"Watch it, I'm ticklish!" He said laughing.

"You're going to get us both killed." She responded.

"Now why would they kill you?"

Eva pushed Parker away from her and stepped back toward the ledge of the building.

"You're not really with them, are you?" He asked.

"What are you talking about?"

"You don't hide it very well. You're going under a false name because you don't trust them. They bring you up here and they lock the door behind you because they don't trust you. What's the deal with you? Why are you even here? Wouldn't an emissary for Roland be taken better care of?"

"There are bigger things at stake here than you realize."

"You're a prisoner, aren't you?"

"Don't be ridiculous."

"Maybe even Feng doesn't know why you're here, but I'm not an idiot. I know something's up, so what is it? Why do they lock you up at night?"

"Please, just don't…"

"I can help you, if you'll let me."

"Why would you want to help me? You don't even know me."

"I don't know. There's something about you that I like." He said.

"I wonder what that could be?"

"No, I'm serious. You seem like you need help and that's the kind of guy I am."

Eva remained silent for a moment.

"It's not that simple." She said. "I am from Dublin, and Roland sent me here to check into a project he's set up. Feng and his band of pirates have been supplying it, but he doesn't completely trust them. I wasn't exactly announced before my arrival."

"What project?"

"Even I don't know. It's a huge secret, but Roland sent me to verify its progress."

"So, you're like some kind of VIP or something?"

"Not exactly. Roland was also sending some of his elite enforcers a couple of days after me, to make sure that I did as I was told."

"Steel?"

"Yes. Among others."

"Then he's not just here for me."

"He wasn't supposed to be here until tomorrow, but your recent capture prompted his early arrival. Feng has been heading the project, but Roland is starting to think Feng is plotting against him. Feng is ambitious to say the least."

"If you can't trust a pirate, who can you trust?"

"This isn't a joke."

"Why would Roland need Feng in the first place? Doesn't he have enough zealots for that?"

"Because despite your disgust for Feng, he's good at what he does. He's discreet, and with him on the outside Roland doesn't have to sully his own reputation to acquire supplies."

"Wow, people on the inside of the walls really have no clue what goes on out here?"

"Are you kidding me? Roland keeps them all in the dark. No one asks questions."

"Yeah, well fear keeps people in control."

"Fear? You've never been inside the walls of Dublin,

have you?"

"Of course not, but I do know how Roland treats his people."

"I don't think that you do…" Eva started but was interrupted by a noise down below. Parker and Eva both looked over the ledge to see captain Steel arrive with a small group of soldiers.

Captain Steel was a large muscular man with close-cropped hair and a deep baritone voice.

"Where's Feng?" Steel asked one of the guards.

"He's in his quarters captain Steel." The guard responded.

"And the prisoner?"

"He…. escaped sir." The guard answered unnervingly.

"What? When?"

"We discovered his cell was empty only a while ago."

"Then why isn't this place locked down?" Steel yelled.

"We're searching sir. We have limited people in this area."

Steel was very annoyed as he turned to his own men.

"Cover the exits and stand watch." He ordered. "Parkers' already long gone by now but stay alert. If he does happen to show up, put an arrow through his eye. I've got to meet with Feng."

Parker and Eva moved away from the ledge.

"He really doesn't like you." Eva said softly.

"Yeah, no kidding." Parker responded. "I think I'll make my way out now."

"Wait a minute. I can't just let you leave."

"I'm not giving you a choice. The best thing for you to do is keep quiet and trust that I'll come back."

"Trust…?"

Parker smiled and was about to walk away until he

caught a glimpse of a shiny object hanging around Eva's neck. It was a necklace with a golden chain, and a diamond in the center.

"Polaris?" He asked staring at the diamond.

"What?"

"It says Polaris on the back of your necklace. Where did you get that?"

"I've had it my entire life. When I was given to my mother, this was all I had with me."

"Given?"

"It sounds silly, but my mother told me she was walking through the forest one morning to go to the lake to fetch water. She found me lying in a wicker basket and all I had with me was this necklace. There was a note that said it was a gift and that I should keep it with me always."

"That doesn't sound silly to me. We're more alike than you think."

"What do you mean?"

"I'm an orphan too. My 'parents' found me in the woods as well."

Eva stepped away from Parker and looked over the edge of the rooftop. She was overwhelmed with confusion. The man standing beside her was meant to be a prisoner. Parker Wallace was a huge threat to King Roland's empire, why she wasn't certain anymore, but each time his name was brought up a long list of crimes followed. However, something about him was so familiar.

It wasn't just her feelings either, to him, she worked for an enemy capable of sending him to his death, but something about her made him feel as if she were trustworthy. He longed to hold her in his arms and never let go. It was as if she were a friend he hadn't seen in years and they were finally reunited. He walked over to her and put his hand on her shoulder. Her hand slowly met with his and she turned to look him in the eyes.

"Why do I feel like I know you?" She whispered.

"I'm not sure." He answered. "I feel the same."

"Why do I feel so close to you? We've only just met. This doesn't make sense."

Eva turned away to gaze at the small city surrounding them.

"Truthfully, why you?" Parker asked. "What are you doing here?"

She started to turn to back to look him in the eyes but looked away from him instead.

"There's something I have to do." She answered. "My reasons are my own. You should go before they find you."

"You could come with me."

"I can't leave, not now."

"Why not?"

"I can't explain right now, but you have to go. I just hope you know what you're doing."

"Kind of, sometimes I just wing it." Parker said as he walked to the side of the roof and grabbed his backpack he had left there. He moved to the edge of the building and pulled out a rope with a grapple on the end of it. He spun the rope and tossed it to latch on to a telephone pole across the street.

"I'll see you again." He said to Eva before swinging away to the building on the other side. Eva watched as he retrieved his grapple and disappeared out of sight. The small number of guards below never even knew he was there.

CHAPTER FIFTEEN

Parker traveled for nearly two days before reaching his destination. He had made record time as he barely stopped for more than thirty minutes at a time, only breaking to nap or eat. He also took a few detours on the route home just to throw off anybody that might be following him. Parker was extremely good at covering his tracks. He finally arrived at a clearing near the end of a forest and at the edge of a large cliff and pulled a flashlight out of his backpack flipping it on and off twice in the direction of a large empty field. In the darkness, he saw a bright flash of light blinking back at him. He walked toward the area where the flash had come from and approached a large tree stump. After knocking on the top of the stump twice, it opened to reveal a hole in the ground and a man holding a flashlight in Parkers' face forcing him to cover his eyes.

"What's the password?" The man asked.

"We don't have a password Dale." Parker answered.

"We do now." Dale responded. "So, what is it?"

"I'm gonna punch you if you don't get that light out of my eyes and let me in." Parker replied.

"You may enter Sir."

Parker entered the hole and closed the tree stump that served as a hatch. He gave the guard a flick on the head and a playful pat on the back before continuing. There were several tunnels underground, each one led to a metal hatch door. Inside each door was a series of rooms large enough for a family. It had taken Parker and his brother a long time to dig out all the dirt and rocks to tunnel through and forge a home for themselves.

It was well hidden inside the cliff and gave them a sense of security, but the more they searched the cities for their own survival, the more people they found in need of shelter. It became easier to make more tunnels for everyone to live in as their numbers increased. They even managed to install vents to allow airflow throughout the living quarters for every family. Putting the village underground was a logical idea considering its location.

It wasn't perfect, but it was home. A hidden home inside the cliff. It was one of the safest places in Ireland where Roland and his army, or the pirates, or even the Ash demons for that matter, wouldn't even think to look. He walked up to one of the metal doors and slowly opened it to sneak inside. He entered the living area to find a six-foot-tall African man sitting in a rocking chair in the corner, all the while whittling a small piece of wood.

"Trying to sneak in?" The man asked with a Nigerian accent.

"What are you doing here?" Parker asked.

"Isaac needed a chair repaired. I just finished a bit ago and started working on this." Ox answered holding up a piece of wood as it started to take the shape of a dog. "Plus, I tend to worry about people when they decide to take off by themselves with no one to watch their back."

"I know, I know. You're starting to sound like Isaac."

Oscar Lawson, or Ox, was Parkers' closest friend. They had met over ten years ago. He had survived for a few years on his own but eventually he had slipped up and was about to be killed by a group of Ash demons that had been tracking him. Parker and his brother Isaac happened to be nearby and were able to save him. They brought him to live with them in the underground community. Ox had even helped them dig most of the tunnels to fit more people and handcrafted most of the furniture they had himself. Since his rescue, he vowed to follow Parker into any fight. His reasons for leaving his home country were difficult to talk about. Ox rarely spoke of his past, but he did reference a wife and a daughter on a few occasions. Parker never was given the full story of what had happened, but he did know that Ox sought revenge and nearly ended up dead himself if he and his brother hadn't intervened.

"You were supposed to wait for me." Ox said. "I could have used some time away. I was bored."

"The important thing is, you had some time to yourself and I made it home just fine."

"Uh-huh. What happened?"

"Nothing."

"Something always happens when you go off on your own. Do you need stitches or any kind of medical attention?"

Parker sighed as he tossed his backpack onto the floor and sat in another rocking chair directly across from Ox.

"I got caught by Feng, knocked out by a girl, who I plan on seeing again soon, and Steel is extremely unhappy to see I escaped, yet again."

"Ha! Sounds like an ordinary trip for you then."

"However, it wasn't all for nothing." Parker said reaching into his boot and pulling out the cylindrical key he stole from Eva. He then tossed it over to Ox. "Take a look at what I lifted."

"This is a digital key for electric locks. Where did you get this?" Ox asked as he examined the item.

"Took it from the girl I mentioned. I thought you might be able to do something with it."

"It's old. Hard to believe it survived all these years."

"Can you make a mimic from that?"

"It might take some time to download it to another copy, but first I have to find an identical cylinder to copy it to or else we can't use it."

"Do we have any in the supply room?"

"There should be a few lying around. I'm sure we've picked up one or two somewhere."

"Great. Do it as quick as you can, I can only imagine how much trouble it's caused since it went missing. As soon as you're done, I'm headed back out."

"Did you plan on sleeping at all? Like ever again?"

"While I'm waiting for you to copy that key."

"I'll get right on it." Ox said as he placed his wooden project in his pocket and exited the room.

Parker let his eyes close and before he knew it, he was fast asleep. He had been up since two o'clock the previous morning as he barely slept the whole trip home. The most sleep he'd gotten in the past couple of days was the hour of unconsciousness he experienced when Eva had knocked him out. Suddenly Isaac entered the room and kicked Parkers' relaxed legs, forcing him awake.

"Hey!" Parker said. "Nice to see you too"

"Quiet." Isaac said with a Scottish accent. "Agatha is still sleeping."

"A gentle nudge might be more ideal next time then."

"Rough trip?"

"Not too bad compared to some."
Isaac stood in front of a shelf and rested his arm on it.

"How'd the search go?" Isaac asked. "Any good supplies?"

"Just some basics, not enough to brag about." Parker answered.

Judging by the tone in Isaacs' voice and the fact that he wouldn't look Parker in the eye, it was obvious that his brother was troubled.

"If you're going to lecture me, get on with it so I can get some sleep." Parker insisted.

"Why would I lecture?" Isaac asked. "It's not as though you're going to listen to me anyway."

"You preach the same thing all the time. I really don't need to hear this right now."

"You've got to be mad going into the cities alone."

"Here we go." Parker said standing up in defeat.

"Don't you know how dangerous it's getting out there?"

"Of course I do. You know I can take care of myself Isaac. Dad taught us how to keep a low profile."

"He taught us well enough, but it doesn't mean you

can't make mistakes. You've got to learn that going out on your own is too risky. What if something happened to you?"

"Look at me. I'm fine."

"How many times have you almost gotten caught in the past two months?"

Silence covered the room for a moment as Isaac stared at Parker in disappointment.

"I'm a little fuzzy on the details…" Parker said hesitantly.

"Four times." Isaac interrupted. "Ox said you've had to fight to get away at least four times."

"Uh…well."

"Well what?"

"Five if you count recent events."

"Come on, Wally."

"Why don't you come with me next time? Ox is great to have around in a fight, but it's not the same without you. It would be just like old times."

"I have too many responsibilities now. I have a wife to care for and a community that looks to my leadership. I can't go out there risking my neck anymore."

"We'll watch each other's back like we used to. You know you miss it."

"No Wally."

Parker hated it when Isaac called him Wally. It was a nickname he had endured their entire childhood. Isaac used to tease him with it until it just became a bad habit. Parker understood from the time he was a boy that he had been found abandoned and even still carried his own last name of Wallace, but it made no difference. Isaac was his brother, blood relation or not.

"I just want you to be more careful." Isaac said. "Stop trying to do everything on your own, I may not go with you, but Ox and some of the others can."

"I'm not like you Isaac. I'm not afraid of a fight and I don't need babysitters watching my back. I move faster when I'm on my own."

"I'm not afraid of a fight, but I'm also not out there looking for one."

"I'm not exactly looking for them, I just find them."

"We have the ability to grow our own food here, and with the generators and solar panels we've salvaged, we have plenty of power. Why do you need to get out at all?"

"Isaac, there are other people out there that don't have what we have, and we can't support them all here. I do what I can to help."

"Wally…" Isaac began.

"I can't just sit around and do nothing. I have this need for…, things aren't exactly easy around here, but we're doing okay. If I have the ability to help other people, I'm going to."

"I don't disagree with your intentions, but you've got to play it safer. You have no obligation to push yourself so hard. No one asks you to go out there days at a time and put yourself in harms' way like that."

"They don't have to ask Isaac. It's just who I am."

"You've always been this way. You've made it your own personal mission to help others by putting yourself at risk. Why do you do it? What goes on in your head that makes you want to be the hero to everyone?"

Parker didn't know the answer to that. He had always been that way for as long as he could remember. He had an instinct to help others and he had skills and knowledge that he couldn't explain. It was these things that made him realize that if he had the chance to help others then he had a responsibility to do so.

Agatha, Isaac's wife of three years entered the room with a blanket wrapped around her. Parker grabbed his backpack and headed for the exit.

"Hey Parker." Agatha said calmly.

"Hey." He said as he reached for the door.

"It doesn't have to be your burden all the time

Wally." Isaac said as Parker stopped to listen. "The world is a rough place, and I hate to break it to you, but you aren't going to change it. Sometimes you just have to look out for yourself."

"It's not about me." Parker said as he turned away and exited the room. Isaac walked over to Agatha and kissed her on the forehead.

"I'm sorry if we woke you."

"You can't stop him." She said. "He believes in his heart that he can help somehow. Your parents couldn't keep him out of trouble either."

"I know, I was there for most of that trouble." Isaac said.

"Which doesn't help the situation much, you gave it up, and he didn't. You can't force him to stay, and you can't make him take backup. He obviously doesn't want to put other people at risk."

"I know, I just worry." He said sitting in the nearest chair. "He's out there every day and night and I...." Isaac sighed; the words escaped his tongue. "He pushes too hard. I don't want anything to happen to him. The world seems more dangerous now than it ever was."

"You know he gets his stubborn side from you." She said as she sat down on his lap and rested her head against his. "You were just as bad, if not worse when I first met you."

"Inherited trait from my father. If only he and mother were alive today, perhaps things would be different. You and Wally are the only family I have now. You two are the ones I care about the most."

Agatha moved her head to give Isaac a kiss. A few silent moments passed before the two of them fell asleep in the chair, relaxed and safe in each other's arms. Parker however was wide-awake once again as he walked down the corridor to his room. It wasn't large, just enough room for a bed and some walking around space. At the far end of the room was a large curtain. Parker pulled it aside to reveal an opening in the cave wall that was his window.

From there he could see the ocean stretching out into the distance. The sky was getting brighter mean the Sun was hinting at its slow, but inevitable arrival. The clouds were pink and scattered throughout the sky like someone had taken a brush and painted them on a light blue and yellow canvas. It was at that moment that Parker felt a sense of peace.

He knew deep down that his excursions were useless. Sure, he helped a few people scattered around the coast and further inland, but if people like Feng and Roland existed, his endeavors would continue. He longed for a day when the people could be set free and live like normal once again. Between Roland, pirates, and Ash demons, there wasn't much he could do. He knew Isaac was right, and if he wanted to affect any real change, Parker would have to do something big. He wasn't sure if recruiting people and taking the fight to Roland was the right thing to do, but the thought had crossed his mind numerous times.

Parker scoffed at the thought of him leading an army. Brushing off the idea, He decided to lie down on his bed for a few minutes before Ox came knocking with that key. Eva had hinted at some big project, and Parker was always ready to throw a monkey wrench into Roland's operation. Maybe this time, he could uncover something to take the dictator down a few notches. He shut his eyes and quickly fell asleep. He was about to be in for another long trip.

CHAPTER SIXTEEN

Two days later, Parker and Ox stood in front of a large steel door on the outside of a huge compound. Two sentries that had been posted there lay on the ground unconscious. Adding insult to injury, Parker and Ox also stole the sentries worn down leather jackets to be more inconspicuous, but Ox was a tall muscular gentleman, so neither jacket would fit him. After trying on the jacket, Ox groaned in protest and simply removed it and tossed it, covering the unconscious sentry's face. The compound had been there for a few decades, long before Parker was even born. The location itself wasn't far from where Parker had been locked up just a few nights ago. He and Ox had been there before but had never gotten inside. The outer walls were too high and were covered with razor wire preventing them from climbing over.

There had been many wars in the country since what some people called the fall of civilized life. Later, when Roland had taken over, Feng and his men moved in to secure the territory for themselves with his permission of course. Parker had known that Feng was allowed to operate in exchange for his services.

Parker took the copied key he had gotten from Ox and placed it in a small circular hole in the door.

"Let's try this out." He said looking at Ox.

Little green lights on the outside of the gate began to flicker indicating there was an electronic locking device reading the data on the key. They could hear the tumblers inside the door clanging loudly and retracting. Finally, the door slid into a slot on the right side, allowing the two to enter.

"See, I knew I could do it." Ox said patting Parker on the back.

"You're the best digital locksmith I know." Parker replied.

"I'm the only digital locksmith you know."

"That's why you're the best."

Parker and Ox entered a large courtyard. There were no patrolling guards in the area, and everything seemed to be quiet.

"Are you sure you want to do this?" Ox asked. "It's broad daylight."

"Seems like a decent challenge to me." Parker answered. "They don't expect us during the day, let alone inside one of their most secure compounds."

"Sometimes I think you are crazy."

"And other times?"

"Crazy, you are always crazy."

"No arguments here." Parker said in agreement.

"What is the plan?"

"We should split up and keep a low profile." Parker answered as he gave Ox the duplicated key. "I'd rather not draw too much attention on this trip."

"Bag and collect?"

"Exactly."

"Where would you like me to go?"

"I think the mess hall would be a good place to start, but if you just so happen to find an armory…"

"You want me to take some of their weapons?"

"Only what you can carry. Food first, and then if you have room for some decent equipment afterward then go ahead. Sabotage the rest."

"What are you going to do?"

"I need to find Eva, the woman I took the key from."

"Before you go diving headfirst into something like usual, are you absolutely sure you can trust that woman?"

"Of course not, but Ox, you just have to follow your gut sometimes."

"My gut I trust. It's yours I worry about."

"Relax, I got this." Parker said as he started moving away to the opposite end of the courtyard.

"I'll save you a seat." Ox said quietly.

"Not if I get there first." Parker replied.

Parker watched as Ox went on his way and then he himself proceeded to a door not far from where he was standing. After a few minutes of cautiously searching the building, he moved onto the next one, which was connected via a catwalk on the second floor. It was there he spotted Eva in the center of an outdoor connecting bridge with Feng. Parker ducked behind the wall so he could eavesdrop on the conversation.

"Annabelle?" Feng said. "What prompted you to join me on my stroll through the facility?"

"I wanted to speak to you on a delicate matter." She replied.

"How delicate?"

"One that should be discussed in private."

"There is no one here Annabelle. This is as private as it gets around here."

"I was sent here to check the status of the project. We were supposed to leave three hours ago. What is the holdup?"

"We had a bit of trouble with the transport. Captain Steel is aware of the issue."

"Well I'm not captain Steel. My point is, I need to be kept informed of what goes on around here."

"You are not in charge." Feng said stopping in place and pointing at Eva. "This is my part of the world, while you are here, you answer to me."

"I answer to King Roland regardless of where I am, it's him who sent me here."

"King Roland trusts my judgement. I have been his ally for some time now. You are the one he doesn't trust."

"What makes you say that?"

"You arrived unannounced, but I was given specific instructions to keep an eye on you, just in case. Why would an emissary of King Roland need such supervision?"

"You pry where you shouldn't." Eva said firmly. "Your curiosity is without merit. Have you given thought that perhaps he simply wants me to be kept safe? I think you misinterpreted his instructions."

"Or he doesn't trust you?"

"Why wouldn't he? Why don't you fill me in on my reputation around here?"

"If you want information, I suggest you get it from your own people. Captain Steel can decide how much use you are to us."

Feng began his walk again and stopped a few feet ahead of Eva.

"While we are discussing the subject of trust." Feng began. "It does make me curious about our little mishap a few nights ago."

"To what mishap are you referring to?"

"We had Parker Wallace, a known enemy to King Roland, safely locked away in a cell."

"I was the one who caught him if you remember correctly."

"Yes, and yet you were the last one to speak to him before he vanished."

"If you're implying that I had anything to do with his escape…"

"Not at all." Feng interrupted. "I'm just curious as to what you wanted to speak to him about."

"King Roland and his army have been trying to track down Parker for years. He's been sabotaging weapons and killing soldiers left and right for who knows how long. I wanted to meet him up close and personal. The man behind the rumor as it were."

"He is a very efficient adversary." Feng said as he stepped toward Eva and brushed his hand against her cheek.

"Why would you be so fascinated by a criminal?" He asked.

"Because despite all the stories I've heard, he doesn't

seem like a terrorist leader to me." She answered pushing Feng's hand away. "He seems like he's just another survivor trying to get by outside the walls of Dublin. Though I don't doubt the stories that are told about him stealing supplies. That much is very true, but he's not a killer."

"There's more to him than what stories you've been told. If you haven't been trusted with that information either, then that's where this conversation ends. You have a part to play Annabelle. Don't go digging where you shouldn't. Do your job and go back to your pampered city of morons. Oh and one other thing. You wouldn't happen to know anything about my key going missing?"

"Of course not."

"Hmm."

Feng turned and continued his path to the next building, leaving Eva standing alone on the bridge. Once Feng was out of sight, Eva turned to go the other way and found Parker leaning against the railing.

"Have a nice walk?" He asked with a smile.

"Are you crazy? It isn't smart for you to be here now." Eva said walking toward him.

"I had to return this." Parker said tossing the stolen key to her.

"Steel and his men are all over the place. Since you escaped, they've been doubling up on the security around here."

"It definitely isn't working. Where is this transport you mentioned?"

"Did you not hear what I just said?"

"There's something going on behind closed doors, you seem interested so, let me help you figure this out. I like mysteries. Plus if it upsets Roland, then I gotta get involved."

"You don't understand. You can't get involved right now. You shouldn't even be here."

"Look, you're on the inside. We could help each other…"

"This is so much bigger than you think it is." She interrupted. "The only way you could help me right now is by letting me turn you in."

"If I let you turn me in, they'll kill me."

"Which is why you should run instead, or else I'll have no choice."

"Come with me."

"Don't ask me to do that. I can't."

"I can tell you don't belong here. I can protect you if you'll let me. You can't possibly want to live under Roland's thumb anymore."

"Please understand that you don't know everything that is going on here. You don't know what's at stake."

"Just talk to me."

"Please just go." She begged. "I have my reasons."

Parker was annoyed and knew he needed to do something. Nothing he was saying could convince her to join him. He would have to find another way. Instead he decided to take her advice. Maybe a better plan wasn't such a bad idea. Now was the time to get out and come back later. Maybe when it was a bit safer again.

"Fine, you win." He said defeated. "I'll leave when I find my friend."

"You brought someone here with you?"

"Yes. Just keep people distracted for us. As soon as I get to him, we'll be gone and out of your way."

Eva thought hard for a moment. She wasn't the best at spontaneous planning, but an opportunity had presented itself to her. Maybe there was a way Parker and his friend could help after all, but it wasn't going to be pretty, not for them anyway.

"Where is your friend?" She asked as she pulled a pulse gun from a holster on her hip and pointed it at Parkers' head. "If I'm going to find out what's going on, I have to do it my way. I can't waste this chance."

"What are you doing?"

"I'm sorry, but you're going to have to run."

"Are you insane?" Parker asked with his hands in the air.

"Last chance, run." She said as she charged the gun, preparing it to fire. "Guards! There's an intruder!"

Parker knocked the gun from her hand. In retaliation Eva kicked Parker in the stomach and pushed him over the railing of the bridge. Gravity took over as he fell to the ground below. A large pile of bushes managed to break his fall and absorbed some of the impact. Parker looked up toward the bridge to see Eva peeking down at him, and then several guards appeared beside her and began shooting their pulse rifles at him. Parker darted away as quickly as he could as a series of small green discharges from the guns crashed into the ground behind him, sending dirt and debris into the air. Finally, he was out of sight and the shooting stopped.

"He wasn't alone. Check everywhere!" Eva shouted.

Ox stood in the armory holding one of the many pulse rifles as he placed a small round device over the charging mechanism of the weapon. He pushed a small red button on the side of the device and the gun let out a small electronic hiss, which informed Ox that the weapon was now useless. There hadn't been that many guns to work with. The guards roaming around the compound were using most of them, but Ox still sabotaged a good portion of the reserve weapons. He picked up his backpack and started for the door cautiously, however as soon as he opened it to exit, he was greeted by weapons fire from a group of men in the hallway outside. Ox avoided the blasts rushing toward him as he jumped back into the armory and pulled his weapon from his side holster.

Ox's pulse gun was modeled after an old-fashioned revolver, and it certainly packed a punch. As one of the enemy guards tried to rush into the room, he was greeted with a quick burst from Ox's revolver and was knocked off his feet and slid back into the hallway with the others.

"I can't feel my chest!" The guard shouted as one of the others pulled him to the side.

Captain Steel, and another of Roland's personal guard, captain Lao entered the hall during the gunfight and kept themselves behind cover. Eva appeared on the other side of the hall, keeping herself out of harm's way as well.

Where Steel was a tall, muscular man, Lao was much shorter at 5 feet, 7 inches, and of Korean descent. Both men had made a name for themselves as King Roland's elite, but they were both extremely competitive with one another. Steel was Roland's main enforcer, and it was he that was charged with the capture and execution of Parker Wallace. A job that over the past few years had proven to be more difficult than anyone would have thought. Lao on the other hand was an experienced martial artist, and marksman, as well as second in command to Roland himself. Both men alone were dangerous, and even though they weren't the closest of friends, when they worked together, they were nearly unstoppable.

Ox had managed to hold his own against the oncoming force but wondered to himself where Parker was. The room was full of rifles that he could have used. Had he known what was going to happen he wouldn't have disabled them all. He still had his equipment, but compared to his adversaries, he wasn't going to last long. Ox could see Steel and Lao as he peeked out from cover and suddenly knew his chances of getting out unharmed sank even lower. Ox had never gone up against Steel or Lao before himself, but Parker had managed to slip passed them once before and returned home with a broken arm to show for it. When Ox had asked the best way to deal with Steel and Lao in the future, Parkers' only reply was "Run."

Steel pulled a sword from a sheath he had on his back and motioned for the men to get back. Eva knew immediately that they were planning on killing Ox and felt the need to intervene.

"Don't kill him!" She shouted.

Steel glanced at Eva as she made her way through the gun blasts to stand beside him.

"What are you doing here?" Steel asked.

"We need him alive." Eva said ignoring his question.

"What purpose would he serve?" Steel asked.

"Bait." Eva replied. "He's one of Parkers' allies."

Steel looked toward Lao and nodded his head. Lao then took a position at the end of the hall and lined himself with the door to the armory.

"Cease fire!" Steel shouted.

The men around them stopped firing. Ox took advantage of the moment to get his bearings. He didn't know what they were planning, but he had to be ready. He replaced his revolver in its holster and pulled a secondary weapon from his backpack, a pulse rifle modeled after an 1873 Winchester, but much smaller and more of a smooth design. Lao watched Steel carefully and waited. He reached into a small pouch that he carried on his belt and pulled out a little round plastic puck device. He placed his thumb over a small red button on the side of the puck and held it tight in his fist.

Ox readied the rifle and aimed it out the door into the hallway where he could see Lao at the opposite end. Steel nodded once again toward Lao and no sooner had he given the motion; Lao thrust himself forward toward the armory. He had a good thirty feet to cover in the tight corridor. Ox began firing shots at Lao who managed to dodge them with great agility. Lao ducked and weaved, running along the side of the wall and flipping himself upside down as each blast of the rifle rushed past him. He then performed a no-handed cartwheel as another blast nearly hit his feet. After a few more backward flips, and a forward roll Lao was just outside the armory doorway.

Ox and Lao glared at each other as they made eye contact. Just as Lao performed one last front flip into the room, he pressed the little red button on the plastic puck and threw it to the floor between Ox's feet. Not even a second later, a rippling blast erupted from the puck, and Ox could feel his legs go numb as he fell to the floor. A pain that felt like pins and needles stabbing him in the legs overwhelmed him until suddenly he felt nothing. As if he didn't have legs at all. He continued to hold the rifle and tried to aim it at Lao as quickly as he could, but Lao just reached out and grabbed the weapon by the barrel and pulled it from Ox's hands. Lao turned the weapon back on Ox and fired at both of his arms leaving him completely paralyzed.

A swarm of soldiers rushed into the room as Lao exited and returned to Steels' side. Eva was amazed at Lao's abilities, and even a little frightened. Ox was not able to stand on his own and had to be carried out of the armory by four men.

"Not bad." Steel said to Lao.

Ox was carried to Steel who looked him over as if he were inspecting the man.

"What do you suppose we should do with him?" Steel asked.

"He's a tough one." Lao replied. "Take him to the train."

"Yes sir." A guard spoke.

"Now back to you." Steel said as he turned to face Eva. "You want to tell me what you're doing all the way out here?"

"King Roland sent me." Eva said slightly nervously. "I was only trying to prove myself as his aid."

"Were you now? I guess we'll see."

Steel and Lao turned to exit the room leaving Eva standing in the long corridor alone. She had to be more careful or her plan would come unraveled way too soon.

CHAPTER SEVENTEEN

Parker hid behind a stone column as two sentries rushed by him. He had lost Eva in his attempt to hide from the guards. He didn't know what was going on in her head, or whose side she was on, but he needed to find her and Ox before something really bad happened. After hearing what sounded like a fight only moments ago, he figured he was too late already. He rushed through a small corridor leading down a flight of stairs and entered a room that looked almost like an old subway station. He started down the steps slowly until he finally heard voices coming from below. He stuck to the shadows as much as possible and peeked around a corner to see Steel, Lao, Eva, and Feng standing on the platform overlooking the train tracks. There were also two guards holding Ox up by the arms. His hands and feet were bound in chains as they dragged him toward the platform.

"I don't believe it is necessary to take him to the mine." Feng said. "Parker will undoubtedly return for his friend. What do you suppose will happen when he finds out where you've taken him?"

"Feng is right." Lao agreed. "He'll try to track us."

"I don't think so." Eva began. "Parker has proven his intelligence is above average, but he has yet to discover anything that has been going on within these walls. He couldn't have been here long, and he left in such a hurry that most likely he won't be back again any time soon until he has a plan of action. By then, his friend will already be gone."

"My concern is how did he get as far as he did this time?" Feng asked.

"It's easy if you have one of these." Eva replied as she pulled the fake key from Ox's pocket and then while holding the real key in her other hand, she reached into Feng's pocket as if she were retrieving it from him.

"What is that?" Steel asked.

"It seems Parkers' escape wasn't exactly unforeseen." Eva answered.

"What are you talking about?" Feng asked.

"During Parkers' fight with your men, you managed to disappear while he subdued all of them." Eva said.

"I'm not much of a fighter, he could have killed me." Feng protested.

"So, you ran like a coward?" Lao asked.

"No, he didn't run." Eva corrected. "He gave Parker the key to make a copy and get into the base. After he left, I went in and took Parker down myself. That's the only reason he was captured."

"Why would he help Parker?" Steel asked.

"Feng has his owns malicious, greedy, reasons for playing both sides. Whatever his goals are, he has no loyalty to King Roland. He must have been colluding with Parker for years now."

"What are you trying to do?" Feng asked. "I've been nothing but loyal to Roland…"

Steel stretched out his arm and grabbed Feng by the throat and squeezed tight.

"Feng and Parker have been working closely together all this time." Eva continued. "It's no surprise he's been able to evade you for as long as he has. Not to mention all of his 'miraculous' escapes." Eva said hoping she wouldn't get caught in her lie.

"You can't believe her." Feng struggled to say, his throat being crushed by the force of Steels' hand. "I wouldn't side with Parker. Annabelle is trying to turn you against me!"

"Annabelle?" Steel asked. "Whose Annabelle?"

Eva knew that she would be exposed this way at some point, so she had to choose her words carefully.

"I gave him a false name." Eva responded. "I knew I couldn't trust him."

Steel brushed off Eva's response and turned his

attention back to Feng. The distant sound of an approaching train caught Feng's attention and Steel slowly moved him to the edge of the platform.

"Don't do this!" Feng begged.

Eva tried extremely hard to maintain her composure. She watched with a sickening feeling deep in the pit of her stomach as Steel was the only thing keeping Feng from falling backwards.

Parker watched as the two forces were turned on each other. Eva was obviously working an angle, one that he hadn't seen coming. He wondered if it was something she had planned before he picked her pocket, or after.

"You betrayed us Feng." Steel said as he kept his feet planted firmly on the edge of the platform. The lights from the train could be seen in the tunnel to their right and were getting closer by the second.

"She is lying!" Feng said. "I've got a good thing going with Roland. Why would I jeopardize that? She has her own agenda. She's playing all of you for fools!"

"That isn't true." Eva falsely corrected. "I have nothing to gain by turning you in."

The front of the train became visible and moved slowly closer. It was an old solar-powered train consisting of the control car and one passenger carriage. The train may have consisted of more passenger carriages at one point, but from the look of its condition the rest of it was more than likely destroyed or used as scrap metal. The sweat poured down from Feng's forehead as he was inches from death.

"Eva has shown to be a faithful soldier to King Roland." Steel said. "He obviously trusts her more than you. Looks like you've been replaced Feng."

"Please don't!" Feng begged.

Steel quickly pulled Feng forward and released his throat.

"I'll leave it up to King Roland to decide your fate." Steel said glaring at him.

"I have done nothing...." Feng began to speak but

just before he could finish his words Lao stepped forward and jammed his foot into Feng's chest sending him flying backwards on to the tracks below. After a short scream, Feng disappeared beneath the train. Steel grabbed Lao by the arm and pulled him away.

"What do you think you're doing?" He shouted angrily.

"He was a traitor." Lao answered as he grabbed Steels' hand and shoved it away.

"His fate wasn't for you to decide!"

"We are both under orders to eliminate any threats against King Roland. I acted under his authority. As you should have."

"We don't kill people in cold blood!" Steel shouted.

"When don't we?"

Parker was surprised to hear this coming from one of Roland's own guards, even more so captain Steel himself. Eva tried not to allow the disgust to show on her face as Steel approached her and placed his hand on her shoulder. She was fighting back the urge to vomit as the guilt of what she had just done played with her stomach. She may not have pushed him to the tracks, but she knew it was her fault none the less. Feng had been a loyal partner to Roland. She had no intention of him being killed, but it was no time to show signs of weakness. She still had a role to play.

"You want to be very clear as to why you are here." Steel said calmly.

"I wish to serve my King further." Eva lied. "I'm just trying to earn my place. I assure you, I'm here under Roland's instructions."

Steel looked into Eva's eyes and she looked into his. This man had an incredible poker face. She couldn't help but think that any second, he would grab her by the throat and possibly snap her neck. Eva was suddenly startled and jumped at the sound of the train doors opening. Two men stepped onto the platform and took Ox by the arms, escorting him on board.

"Where are you taking him?" Eva asked.

"Why don't you both come along?" Lao responded. "Perhaps it's time you two were filled in on our special operations. Feng won't be joining us after all, and we'll see how strong you both are in your services to King Roland."

"You doubt my loyalty?" Steel asked.

"If you are loyal, then this will just be a minor inconvenience of your time." Lao replied.

Parker watched as Steel, Eva, and Lao entered the train, leaving the other two guards on the platform. The train began to move forward to the exit of the tunnel, opposite of where it had entered. Ox was on board, which meant that if Parker wanted to save him, he needed to be as well. The train moved closer to the tunnel as Parker rushed down the stairs.

"No time for finesse." He said to himself.

Both guards turned after hearing the loud footsteps approaching behind them. Parker ducked as one guard swung his gun at Parkers' head. He quickly slammed his fist into his knee, bending it in the wrong direction. Parker then grabbed the guards' neck, holding him as the other guard pulled back his arm preparing for a tough punch. With his free hand, Parker diverted the guards' throw and kicked him in the back of the head, knocking him to the ground. He slammed his fist into the first guards' head and allowed him to fall to the floor, and then slammed his foot into both guards' faces, knocking them out instantly.

Once both men were down, Parker raced to catch up with the train. He could almost reach the railing on the back end. In a matter of seconds, he would run out of platform, and then reaching the railing would be near impossible as the train began to pick up speed. He pushed himself as hard as he could and leaped forward. His hand grabbed the railing as his feet dangled underneath him. Finally, he pulled himself up.

Once the train was out of the tunnel and Parker could

see daylight, he climbed onto the roof. As long as they didn't come across any other tunnels, he could safely ride on top of the train the entire trip. He thought about jumping inside with the element of surprise and getting Ox out of there right away but decided against it. From the looks of it, Ox wasn't able to stand under his own strength and Parker couldn't carry a man of his size out on his own, especially while under pursuit, but also, he had some questions to ask Eva. Questions he wasn't sure he wanted to hear the answers to.

After the train was about a mile away from the compound, the track began to curve back toward the other direction. Parker watched closely ahead, keeping an eye out to make sure nothing would jump out and knock him off the roof while getting an idea of how to get back from wherever they were headed. The train crossed a fifty-foot long bridge that led from one side of a cliff to another. A river flowed beneath the bridge and Parker was compelled to look over the side at the three hundred-foot drop. After they crossed the bridge the only thing left to view was the countryside. The tracks followed the coast, and Parker couldn't help but glance out toward the ocean as often as he could.

The ride lasted a few hours before they reached their destination and stopped inside the cave of a large mountain where the tracks dead ended into what appeared to be a train station. Parker lay flat on his stomach as Steel, Lao, and the two sentries exited the train with Ox being dragged along with them. It seemed that the feeling had returned to his legs only a little. He still couldn't walk on his own, but it wouldn't be long before he was his normal self again. Parker watched as Eva exited the train as well and followed behind them. Once they were all out of sight, he dropped down and kept a safe distance back.

Just before continuing his pursuit, he spotted something of interest on the far end of the station. Two motorcycles were parked side by side. They were in amazingly good condition considering the age. Parker had found pieces of one in ruined city some years ago. The ones he had just laid eyes upon were probably some of the last ever built. They dated back to just after the world stopped using gasoline as the main source of fuel. These were solar powered with a battery that could last up to four days. Technology truly was amazing at the time. A smile formed on Parkers' face.

"I'm definitely stealing one of these." He said quietly to himself.

After following them out of the station and deeper into the cave, he saw them stop in front of a large steel door. Lao pulled a digital key from his pocket and held it out to Eva.

"This is only meant for King Roland's most trusted soldiers. Lao said. "What you see in here doesn't leave this place."

"I understand." She said taking the key.

"Roland has big plans for you now. Don't disappoint me."

Steel was cautious to trust Lao, he knew that this mine housed a major project, but he never knew what. Lao was a trusted agent for Roland, but Steel was one of his personal guard. He wondered why this place had been such a big secret even from him. Eva placed the key into the door and opened it. After they all entered, Parker slowly and carefully followed behind barely catching the large door before it closed.

He traveled down a flight of stairs and entered a large room where he saw Eva and the others standing at the edge of a metal catwalk.

"Here we are." Lao spoke.

Eva looked over the railing into the fiery pit of smoke. The catwalks lead to a winding metal staircase that descended deeper into the cave about five floors. Along the rocky walls of the cave, there were people of all ages. Young, middle-aged, and elder, slamming pickaxes and shovels into the rocky interior.

"You have children here?" She asked."

"We do indeed." Lao answered. "Though, not the one you're searching for."

Just like that, the words pierced Eva's heart and she could feel her stomach turn to knots. Her eyes were drawn to see Lao staring at her with a smirk on his face.

"You belong to us." Lao said softly with a firm grip on her shoulder. "Prove your worth and maybe you will find who you're looking for."

Eva swallowed hard as she turned her attention back to the people being used as slaves all around her.

"These people don't look like criminals." Steel said.

"They are all peasants." Lao said with disgust. "Useless people living in disgust and wasting away into nothing. Roland put them to good use."

Eva was shocked. She looked to Steel to see that he also was seeing this for the first time. However, nothing could have prepared either of them for what they were about to see next.

A young boy, around the age of seventeen suddenly dropped his pickaxe. The sharp object fell to the deep bottom with a loud crashing sound. Then, out of nowhere, an Ash demon jumped to the boy's side and growled in anger.

"Oh my." Eva said silently to herself.

"I'm sorry!" The boy shouted in fear.

The demon pulled a whip from his side and then began to strike the boy repeatedly. Red marks appeared on the boys back as the demon showed no mercy. Another demon at the bottom of the pit picked up the pickaxe and then began to climb the rocky wall with great agility and speed. Once he reached the boys' location, the Ash demon pulled the boy sharply to his feet and shoved the handle of the axe into his hand. He pulled the boy's face close to his and snarled as if to say, "Don't drop it again."

Steel gripped the railing tight whitening his

knuckles.

"What is this?" He asked.

"This is how Roland plans to secure his legacy." Lao answered. "There is something of great value buried in here. Finding it is very important to Dublin's future."

Lao and the others began walking down the stairs as Parker slowly moved toward the railing. His face filled with an expression of rage that he couldn't control. His fists clenched and his heart pounded in his ears. The heat from inside the cave caused him to sweat. The environment was horrible. Screams and cries could be heard along with cracks of the whips by the demons. Eva fought back tears as she saw the pain and suffering of the people around her. She looked at every face and did not find the one she sought. Lao was right, her plan was for nothing, and soon she would pay for her mistake. Her only hope now was indeed Parker.

Once they were halfway toward the bottom, the two sentries tossed Ox onto an outcropping of the cave interior where a demon stood.

"Fresh meat." Lao said with a smile.

The demon nodded and handed Ox a pickaxe, which he tossed to the ground in defiance. The demon shoved his fist into Ox's stomach and then forced the axe into his hand once again. Ox acted as though he was about to perform the rebellious gesture again, but he looked up and saw a young girl standing next to the demon and decided against it. The girl was no older than thirteen, her little face covered in dirt. The demon pointed at the rocky wall and pulled Ox toward it like he was a weightless doll.

Lao and the sentries continued down the stairs. Steel moved toward Eva and placed his hand on her shoulder.

"This is wrong." She whispered.

"Easy." Steel whispered back to her.

"What purpose could this possibly serve?"

"King Roland orders that anyone able to work must do so." Lao answered. "It was Feng's job to find them have them transported here. They are all criminals and thieves."

"How do you figure that?" Steel asked. "That boy looks harmless."

"Anyone outside the walls of Dublin are criminals. They steal the air we breathe; they're very existence is a disgrace to our city. They have no lives, so we're giving them one."

"They're people." Eva said.

"They are less than people." Lao responded. "It will be your job to make sure we have plenty to work this mine."

"My job?"

"You get to take Feng's place. Not as a leader, only to continue the work he started here. We will find his proper successor later."

"Roland says the Ash are evil." Steel said. "Why are we working with them?"

"Mutual gain. We have something they want, and our King has made a deal. The city stays at peace as long as the Ash is on our side."

Steel walked away knowing full well if he hung around any longer, he'd do something he'd regret.

"We need to meet with the leader of the Ash. If you wish to join you can." Lao said to Eva.

Eva looked at Ox, who raised his eyes to meet hers. A single tear rolled down her cheek, and Ox turned away in anger.

"I think I need some air." She said wiping the tears from her face.

She then proceeded back up the staircase as fast as she could, trying not to look weak. It was more difficult then she thought. Lao watched her as she continued out of sight. He let out a slight grin knowing that she was distraught by what she had witnessed. He was even more curious about Steels' position on what he'd seen. Only time would tell where their loyalties were. Which Lao felt he already knew.

Parker watched as Eva raced toward the top of the

211

stairs and rushed out of the cave ahead of her. He stood with his back to the mine entrance and waited for Eva to go by him. She didn't even notice as she ran past him toward the train.

Parker quickly followed behind her and watched closely. Her emotions finally got the best of her and she fell to her knees and cried. She leaned forward and cupped her face in her hands. Parker slowly approached behind her. Her crying was uncontrollable as she struggled just to catch her breath. Parkers' questions were answered. He knelt beside her and put his arms around her shoulders. Eva didn't even act surprised to learn he was there. She allowed herself to fall into his arms as he tried his best to comfort her.

"I'm so sorry." She cried. "I didn't know it was this bad."

"We're not going to let them get away with this." He responded.

Parker knew for sure, that Eva's intentions weren't wrong. Ox was used as bait, which Parker hated, but he understood now. If she had handed Parker over to them, he'd be dead. Ox, on the other hand, wouldn't be executed on sight and could be used as a worker. He still didn't know what was motivating Eva or how much she had known all along, but something was driving her forward. She obviously had an idea they were taking people, but not for such cruelty, and she certainly didn't know the Ash were involved. When the time came, she would need to explain herself. Parker slowly moved her away from him as she began to compose herself.

"If we're going to do anything about this, you have to let me help you." He said.

"What do we do?" She asked.

"Go back inside. Get me the layout. See if you can buy me enough time."

"Enough time to do what?"

"Ox needs his strength back. Tonight, we'll go in and

get these people out. When the Sun comes up first thing tomorrow morning, we'll steal the train and be long gone before they can catch up."

"What about the Ash demons?"

He stood up and felt her hand reaching for his.

"Get me a count on how many of them there are."

"And then what?" She asked.

"Then I'm going to kill them all."

CHAPTER EIGHTEEN

Ox hit the ground hard as he was shoved into the tight room with all the other people who were forced to work the mine. The spaces were close, and people could barely move without bumping into someone else. Ox stood in front of the cell doors as two demons poked him in the back with long pointed spears.

"Watch it!" He said as he moved away from the bars. He sat on the only spot on the ground he could find that was available. His long legs had no choice but to lie across an older man in front of him.

"Forgive me friend." He said quietly, but the man slept soundly from exhaustion. The other men and women around him quickly lay down to rest, with no concern of anything else around them.

"You'll learn to sleep wherever you can." A young female voice said to him. "You'll need the energy."

Ox stared into the eyes of the young girl. He had worked beside her for the last few hours. Though neither one had spoken to the other, Ox felt obliged to listen to her words of advice. He was new to the current situation, whereas the dirt and scratches on her face and hands were an indication that she had been there for some time.

"Do they have any water around here?" Ox asked.

"They give us water and bread twice a day." She answered. "Sometimes they mix in some milk and scraps of meat to help us keep our strength up. Those days they make us work longer though."

"I must have missed the dinner bell."

The girl reached to her side and picked up a small brown sack full of water. It was an old fashioned Bota bag, made of leather and lined with resin to keep the liquids from leaking out. Ox took a couple of small sips and handed it back to her, nodding his head graciously.

"They usually give us something to carry it in." She

said. "It's best to save what you get until you finish for the day. If you need to drink, do it sparingly. You could also use some to clean yourself, but after a couple of weeks, you'll realize it doesn't matter. It's better to stink then to die of thirst."

She placed the sack on the ground beside her but continued to hold it tightly in her hand to ensure no one else took it from her. Ox looked around, and then back to the girl who was staring blankly at the ground.

"Why do you not rest like the others?" Ox asked.

"I have a hard time sleeping." She responded.

"Do you not get tired?"

"I always feel tired, I just hate dreaming."

"Do you have many nightmares?"

"Not nightmares. My dreams are usually nice."

"Why do you hate them?"

"Because I wake up."

Ox could see her eyes, cold and comfortless, without hope. It was no way for a child of her age to feel.

"What is your name?" He asked.

"Grace." She answered.

"How long have you been here?"

Grace was silent a moment.

"I don't know." She answered. "I've lost track, but it's been a long time."

"My name is Oscar, but my friends call me Ox." He said to change the subject.

"Why do they call you Ox?"

"Perhaps it's the smell." He joked.

The young girl almost had a smile on her face.

"A young girl such as you shouldn't hold back such a nice smile."

"Nothing to smile about here." She said. "You had better get some rest before tomorrow."

After a few moments in silence, the snores of the people around them could be heard. Ox moved a little closer to Grace so that he could continue the conversation more quietly.

"If you don't mind me asking, what do you dig for?" He asked.

"Something the Ash want I guess." Grace answered.

"Do you have any idea what it is?"

"No."

"How do you know if you find it?"

"Anything that gets dug up, they collect it. So far nobody has found anything of value to them."

Ox continued to survey the room to see even more children, All of them older than Grace. Some of them were sleeping, and some were sitting in the corner, their knees against their chests, crying in silence, and praying for the nightmare to end.

"Grace." He said leaning toward her. "This will be the last night you stay in this place."

"Why would you say such a thing?" She asked as if she were offended at the words.

"Because it is true." He continued. "I have a friend on the outside. He is very resourceful and very stubborn, which makes him extremely dangerous to the people holding you here. He knows that I am missing, but I feel it deep inside my heart that he is not far away. He will get us all out of here, or I will do it myself."

"Your friend may be very brave, but he doesn't have a chance of getting us out of here. Demons aren't to be trifled with."

"I see in your eyes that you have lost hope, but I'm telling you that now is the time to have it again."

"I gave up on hope." She spoke softly.

"Never give up on hope. This too shall pass child. Do not fear Ash demons either. My friend and I have killed many in our time together."

"Who is your friend?" She asked.

"His name is Parker Wallace."

"Parker Wallace?" Grace asked as if she were familiar with the name.

"Yes." Ox said.

"I've heard his name before. The soldiers who come to deal with the demons have cursed and shouted about him. Each time they utter hostel words amongst themselves, the name Parker Wallace echoes throughout these walls."

"He has caused them great misfortune in the past. This is absolutely true."

"You fight with him?"

"Many times, but also alongside him." Ox said sarcastically. "He saved my life years ago, and I have been by his side ever since."

"Parker Wallace and the Ox Man. It's you."

Grace stood up and began to move slowly around the room, leaving Ox sitting curiously on the floor. She began to whisper in the ears of some of the others. Then those people began to whisper to other people. Ox could hear them mention his name as well as Parkers' and continue. Suddenly the people were up on their feet and began to scramble and communicate with one another quietly. Grace reached for Ox's hand and led him toward the wall on the other side of the room.

"This is important." She said. "I'm sorry I lied to you."

People gathered around behind them, blocking them from view from the cell doors. Another group of people began to quietly move rocks away from the wall and placed them on the ground.

"We think this is what they are searching for." Grace said pointing to the wall.

Ox was stunned at what his eyes had been introduced to. It was a metal hatch that had been rusted shut, with a circular handle that had to be turned to open it. He could barely see it in the darkroom, but there was just enough light shining inside to make out the letters engraved on the hatch.

"PLUTO ONE."

Eva sat in a chair across from Steel as he poured her a cup of tea. It turned out they had places to rest deep within the mine itself. Lao didn't protest when Eva asked for a place to stay for a while. She had told him she needed time to process the day's events. Steel even agreed with her. The room was large and seemed to be an underground bunker built specifically for when Roland's soldiers visited to check on the mine. Lao had already gone to his own personal bunk leaving Steel and Eva to fend for themselves. Eva had been sent in by Parker to gather more information about the mine. Steel had been silent since they had first arrived. Both were trying to gather their thoughts on the situation at hand.

"It tastes a little bitter." Steel said handing her a cup.

"It's all right." She said. "Thank you for this. It's been a long time since I've had real tea."

Steel sat down in a chair across from her. Eva had found out everything she needed to and was killing time before she was ready to return to Parker. She was having a hard time figuring out Steels' emotional state. He was quiet and difficult to read.

"I'm afraid I need to confess something." She said.

"What would that be?" Steel asked leaning back in the chair.

"I don't feel entirely comfortable with the situation around here."

"I'm not exactly surprised. You don't hide your feelings that well."

"Doesn't it disturb you that we're working so closely with Ash demons? These creatures are sworn enemies to humanity."

"That's what they tell us."

"It has to make you wonder, what could King Roland possibly have to offer the Ash demons that they would need our help at all?"

"I've been working for Roland for several years. His methods of persuasion are unscrupulous to say the least. You're better off not digging too deep."

"Why do you work for him?" She asked.

"As if I had a choice." He answered.

"You're saying you don't?"

"My father was the personal guard to King Roland's predecessor Aiden. He passed a few months after Roland's ascension, and I inherited his place."

"Is that what you wanted?"

"It didn't matter what I wanted. It was what I trained my entire childhood for."

"So, considering recent events, you will continue to work for him is that it? You don't care about what's going on around here? Roland speaks ill of the Ash demons in front of his kingdom yet hides his dealings with them in the shadows."

"What do you expect me to do about it?" Steel stood and tossed his cup aside.

"Roland has been lying about everything. Doesn't that change anything? Are you really so naïve that you didn't see it all this time?"

"What are you doing?" Steel asked. "What kind of trouble have you been trying to stir up? This whole act you're putting on, like I can't see through it. Lao undoubtably suspects you of something, and here you are trying to play me?"

"That isn't what's happening." Eva responded slightly worried. "I'm trying to find my place same as you."

"I already found my place. I think you should worry about yourself. Stop acting like you know me and don't ever call me naïve again."

"What will you do then? Ash demons enslaving men, women, and children to do their dirty work. Roland allows it, so where does it end? How long before Dublin is crawling with Ash while you stand guard and do nothing?"

"You don't go up against a man as powerful as Roland and get away with it. I've seen how he treats his enemies. It isn't pretty."

"We can't just ignore this. People in the city need to know about this place."

"You need to keep quiet. I'm tolerating your mouth for now, but Lao won't. Keep talking the way you are, and you'll be seeing Feng sooner than you'd like."

Eva sipped her tea quietly instead of speaking another word. Steel stormed out of the room to his bunk down the hall. He was visibly conflicted and confused, that much Eva was sure of. She finished her cup of tea and exited the room. Steel wasn't exactly what she had thought. His family was kept in high regard, which some people, like Lao couldn't understand. She knew he had trained his whole life to be his father's successor, but after learning of the latest atrocity, Eva had hoped that perhaps she could find an ally in Steel.

Lao on the other hand was not on Eva's side, that she was sure of. She had heard plenty of stories of his rise through the ranks to Roland's side. Lao was a trained soldier but had a knack for stealth and agility. For many years, he served side by side with Roland in the military. When the previous King entrusted his thrown to Roland, Lao was quickly promoted to his second in command.

After a couple more hours had passed Eva made her way to the exit of the mine where the train was located. She searched to find Parker and was quickly pulled to the shadows by an unseen force.

"Shhh." Parker said silently.

He uncovered his hand from her mouth and pointed to a soldier that had walked to the front of the train. The soldier took a quick look around and then turned back. He had been patrolling back and forth since the sun went down. Parker and Eva made their way behind the train as quietly as possible. She watched Parker as he focused his attention around the corner.

"Is it safe?" She asked.

"Not yet." He whispered. "Wait until he goes back inside."

Parker waited and relaxed as the soldier began his walk back toward the entrance to the mine. Once the soldier was gone Eva quickly relayed all the information she had gathered.

"From what I was able to see, there are thirty Ash demons on the inside. There are only four soldiers, including Steel and Lao, and two guards that came with us from Feng's compound."

"Let's go." Parker said as he reached for Eva's hand and walked toward the entrance.

"The demons shouldn't be patrolling." She said. "With the prisoners locked away, they wouldn't need more than a couple of guards to watch the mine."

"Your point is?" He asked.

"You don't need me to go in there with you."

"I might need you for a distraction."

"A distraction?"

"Or a hostage, whichever works at the time."

"What are you talking about?"

"They don't know you're on my side. I could use you if I get caught."

"Great plan." Eva said, obviously unpleased.

"Isn't it though?" Parker responded sarcastically.

"Wait."

"What?" He asked.

"What about Steel?"

"What about him?"

"He hasn't been a part of all of this. He's just as confused as we are to see this place. I can tell he isn't completely on board with it."

"That guy has had a target planted on my back for a while now. He's the least of my concerns."

"We could use him."

"Forget it. Let's go."

The two of them walked across the catwalk overlooking the deep pit. Parker peeked over the side to see the sentry that had patrolled outside moving along on the second floor of the winding staircase. Parker motioned for Eva to keep moving. They continued down the stairs until suddenly an Ash demon began ascending along the cave wall. Eva noticed him first and stopped abruptly. The creature climbed with remarkable speed. The sentry below watched as well, although he didn't seem surprised to witness such an incredible sight of agility. Eva quickly motioned Parker to stop.

"You need to hide." She whispered.

"Where?" He asked.

There was no way he could stay out of sight. He was completely exposed.

"Do something." She whispered.

Eva peeked her head over the railing to see the demon appear just beside her. She gasped as its eyes locked on to hers and growled. She took a step back and looked behind her to see Parker had vanished. She turned her attention back to the demon, which continued to stare at her, unflinchingly.

"Just stretching my legs." She said as she attempted to hide the fear in her voice. "That a problem?"

The demon tilted its head, snorted, and began his ascent once more. Eva exhaled sharply and looked around for Parker.

"Parker?" She whispered. "Where are you?"

"Shhh."

The sound came from below her. She peaked her head over the railing to see Parker hanging just underneath.

"What are you...?" She began to ask but stopped when she saw that the sentry had begun to walk up the stairs once again, making his way back to the mine entrance.

Parker held on as tight as he could, he was a good twelve feet from the next level. If he dropped down, the noise would almost certainly alert the guard below him. He wasn't going to be able to pull himself up either. It was everything he could do to just not let go.

The guard finally made his way up the level just under Parker. He watched and waited for the guard to get closer and then he dropped down behind him. The guard immediately turned around to see Parker, but before he could even shout or pull his weapon, Parker shoved his hand over his mouth and slammed his fist into the guards' face. He quickly dispatched the sentry and picked him up, carrying him over his shoulder. Eva quickly caught up with Parker and continued down the stairs.

"Nice work." She said.

"It's what I do." He responded.

Eva moved first, making sure no more guards or demons were lurking about. Parker found a small hole dug into the rocky wall and shoved the unconscious guard inside and then moved over to Eva's location.

"The holding cell is down that corridor." Eva said pointing to a narrow passageway to the right of the stairs. "The prisoners will be in there with two ash demons watching the door."

"Okay. Get back to the train and wait for us there. Stay alert because I don't know where that demon went."

"What do I do if he's near the train?"

"Take him out quietly."

"You want me to take out a demon? Do you not realize how big those things are?"

"Well aware."

"You're kidding."

"Of course I am." Parker smiled. "Just get to the train, if the demon is there, act natural. He shouldn't even bother you."

"Please be careful."

"Always."

Parker watched as Eva quickly made her way back up the stairs. He continued down the narrow corridor until he saw the barred doors that held the prisoners. Two ash demons stood leaning against the wall just outside the door. Parker quietly pulled the dagger from his side and moved cautiously toward them. He stuck to the shadows in the corridor, but once he was exposed by the light, he would have only a matter of seconds to take both demons down without making too much noise.

He finally reached the end of the shadows and waited for the right moment. He quickly darted across the ground with his dagger at the ready. The demons both spotted him and pulled their swords. Parker deflected every strike against him as he slammed his dagger into the head of one demon, killing it instantly and then quickly grabbed its sword and shoved it into the other demons' chest. Both went down with ease turning to ashes as they fell. Parker retrieved his dagger and wiped the ash-covered blade off on his pant leg. He returned it to its sheath and grabbed the keys that had fallen to the ground after the fight.

"All right people, you're free to go." Parker said as he unlocked the door and opened it. He stood with the door wide open and then peaked into the darkness of the cell, unable to see anything inside.

"You're free to go." He repeated as he waited for the people to exit but no one came out. Parker reached for his backpack and pulled out a flashlight. He shined the light into the cell to see over a dozen people standing with their backs against the far wall. Each of them stared at him without making a sound, nor moving toward the exit.

"What's your problem, let's move." He said shining the light at one of the prisoners.

"Parker?" Ox's voice called from the darkness.

"Ox? Where are you?" Parker said entering the door.

"Over here."

Parker shined the light around the room and made his way to the far wall where the people had gathered around Ox.

"I came to get these people out of here, we need to go." Parker said.

"We can't leave yet." Ox spoke.

"Are you out of your mind?"

"There is something you need to see."

"We don't have time."

"You have to make time. This is what these people have been digging for."

Ox grabbed the light from Parkers' hand and shined it on the hatch door.

"They uncovered this about six months ago when someone had the idea to dig a hole to escape, but they couldn't get passed this."

"What is it?"

"I think it's a door."

"A door to what?"

"I don't know, but whatever it is, it's what the Ash demons are after. They are certain of it."

"If you found this six months ago, why didn't you just show it to them?" Parker asked one of the diggers.

"If they had what they were looking for, what reason would they need us?" Grace asked.

"We had finally been able to turn the handle and I was about to open it when we heard you outside the cell." Ox said.

"Keep a watch on the door." Parker told one of the diggers.

He shined the light on the hatch and handed it to Ox to hold. Parker turned the handle on the door causing it to squeak as it twisted. He gritted his teeth at the sound as he continued to slowly turn it. The sound of the hatch clanging echoed through the room as Parker lifted the hatch open. Ox held the door up to make sure it wouldn't drop on Parkers' head as he handed him back the light to look inside. Parker shined the light and saw a ladder across the roof of the interior.

"There's a ladder, but it's across the ceiling." Parker said.

"Why?" Ox asked.

"Maybe it's upside down. You want to take a look inside?"

"Nah, I'm good out here."

"Are you sure?"

"All yours."

"Fine."

Parker climbed into the hatch. The ladder was bolted to the wall over his head and he made his way along the wall underneath it until finally, he couldn't go any farther. He shined the light downward to see a hallway leading to a small set of stairs to a large door at the bottom. Doors were scattered along the wall on one side.

"There's a hallway leading down to a door." Parker said as he handed the light to Ox and reached into his backpack for a rope. "Tie this end to something."

Ox gave the light back to Parker and walked to the opposite end of the room and tied the end of the rope around the bars of the door.

"You sure you don't want to go down the deep dark hole?" Parker asked.

"You got it covered." Ox answered.

"Fine." He said again.

Parker took the other end of the rope and tossed it down the small corridor.

"All right listen." He said looking at Ox. "There's a train just outside the entrance. Get these people on it. Eva is waiting for you."

"Eva?" Ox asked shocked. "It's her fault that…."

"Ox? I need you to trust me."

"I do not trust her."

"Noted, but she's got our best way out of here." Ox nodded his head.

"Get to the train." Parker continued as he removed his shotgun and gave it to Ox. While it wouldn't work to paralyze an Ash demon, the power from any impact would certainly knock them off their feet.

"If you're not being chased, wait ten minutes and I'll be right behind you." Parker said to Ox.

"If we are being chased?" Ox asked.

"Then just leave."

"Parker…"

"You get these people out of here. I'll find my own way if I have to."

They both nodded to each other in understanding.

"I'll save you a seat." Parker said as he descended out of sight.

"Not if I get there first." Ox replied.

Ox held the gun tightly and moved to the door. He signaled the people behind him that it was clear, and the group quietly followed. After a couple of moments, Parker continued his descent into the dark hallway. The room was at a slant, making it difficult for him to keep his balance, but the rope was helping. Getting down to the rooms below was proving to be more difficult than he had initially thought.

He shined the light along the wall. The interior looked far different than any structure he had ever seen. He checked each room as he passed by them. There was nothing inside but old bunk beds with worn down covers and pillows laying on the floor. Spiders and other insects had made it their home. It made him even more curious as to what the place really was. As he was about halfway down the hallway, he saw a large engraving along the wall.

"United States of America." He read. "What in the world is this thing?"

He slowly made his way to the door below him and went inside. There were shattered windows at the front of the room, broken into pieces by the rocks on the other side. There were three metal chairs bolted to the floor. Placed in front of each chair was a large computer terminal with no signs of power. In front of the middle chair was a large steering wheel. It was then Parker understood where he was.

"It's an airship."

He shined the light around the room, amazed at where he was standing. He had seen relics of old airplanes and helicopters before. The ones Parker had seen hadn't been used in years. Even as amazing as they may have been, they were nowhere near as advanced as the one he currently occupied. Parker could only assume that the ship had crashed over a hundred years ago. Given the angle, it had gone down nose first. He wasn't quite sure how big the ship was but judging by the size of the room he was in; he could only surmise that it was massive in scale. When it crashed it must have buried itself deep into the mountain. The structural integrity was incredible. The ship had seen better days, but it was surprisingly intact.

He focused his light on an object lying on the other side of the computer terminal. He held tightly to the rope and stepped down the inclined cockpit to get a better view.

"What the...?" He asked in shock as he inspected some skeletal remains of a body lying in front of him.

Perhaps it had been there since the ship had crashed. All that remained were its bones, pieces of the clothing it had been wearing, and a dagger sticking out of its torso. However, it wasn't the skeletal remains that startled Parker, but the fact that the remains were unlike anything he had ever seen. The body itself was normal, but there were two heads connected at the shoulder. Parker shined his light across from the figure in front of him and spotted another on the other side. He thought it could be the killer of the unique person before him.

"I guess this thing scared you too." Parker said, mostly to himself.

WARRIOR FROM AVALON

Parker was puzzled by the double-headed humanoid lying in front of him. The ship was identified as a U.S. aircraft, but the body struck Parker as alien. He didn't know if he was quite ready for that revelation. As he studied the bodies around him, Parker noticed that the normal skeleton was holding something in its hand. He slowly made his way to it and grimaced as he pulled the fingers back to retrieve the object. As he attempted to open the ring finger on the hand, suddenly it popped off.

"Whoops…." He groaned. "Sorry about that."

Finally, Parker picked up the object and shined his light on it to get a better view. It was a small purple orb, no bigger than an apple.

"Why would you hold on so tight to this?" He asked.

"Perhaps he wanted to protect it." A woman spoke in the darkness.

Parker quickly drew his sidearm and pointed it at the source. Nimue held up her hands as if to show that she was unarmed. He watched as she slowly moved across the floor. Her bare feet stood flat along the angled surface, but she made no indications that she was struggling to keep her balance. Parker on the other hand, held the orb tightly in his left hand and his pulse gun in the other, all the while struggling to maintain his own balance without the assistance of his rope. At the same time, her body glowed as if she were made of light. Not only that, but Parker was amazed at her beauty and grace. Something about her made him feel nostalgic.

"Who are you?" He asked.

"I'm a friend." She answered.

"How did you get in here?"

"Right now, that isn't important."

Parker noticed something was off about her appearance. She was fully transparent allowing him to see through her body like a projection.

"Wait a minute, you're like a hologram." He said as

he moved closer and waved his gun through her torso. "I've heard about those. An Artificial Intelligence program made from a beam of light or something. You're a three-dimensional image. That makes sense."

"Please listen to me Parker." She said. "We do not have much time."

"A very smart three-dimensional image?"

"I'm your friend, not a hologram. You must trust me. That orb you hold in your hand…."

"This thing?" He asked holding it up for her to see.

"It is what Hades has been seeking."

"Hades, who is Hades?"

Parker took the orb and placed it into his backpack and holstered his sidearm. He looked Nimue in the eyes and couldn't help but feel there was something familiar about her. It was as if he knew her. In one quick motion, Nimue's hand shined a bright light and she moved it as if to place it on his cheek.

"What's happening here?" He asked. "What are you doing?"

"This is much bigger than a corrupt King and his lust for power." She began. "Your fight for survival all of these years was your subconscious desire to put your training to use. You've been compelled to help others because deep down, it's who you are. It's time you embraced your true purpose and continue in the war against Hades. He is out there somewhere. It's time to get back into the fight."

"I don't understand what you're talking about."

"Just listen to me. Hades has found a loophole to establish his presence on earth. King Roland is nothing more than a puppet in a grander scheme. You have to stop them."

"What do you expect me to do?"

"In time Parker. Right now, all you need to know is that this mission is more important than you could ever imagine. That is why we are granting you a gift to aid you on your journey. It's important that you remember."

"Remember what?"

All the light in Nimue's hand slowly transferred to just her fingertips as she jammed them into Parkers' left temple.

"Everything."

Parker shouted in pain as he was suddenly overwhelmed with bright flashes of light. Images of things he had seen before but couldn't remember. He saw himself on a bridge in the rain, trying to help a woman out of a car. Then he was on an island fighting another man with a sword. Next, he was in a fiery room with a giant monster holding him by the throat. The pain was so sharp he couldn't help but drop to his knees and almost slid down the slanted floor. It was the most unbearable pain he had ever felt.

After a few more seconds, the pain went away as quickly as it had begun. Parker stood up as best he could, trying to catch his breath. Everything seemed to be going back to normal. He looked around the room to find Nimue had vanished into thin air. He still had no explanation for what had just happened, but he knew for sure it was time for him to go. Ox and Eva would be leaving without him. He shined his light around the room one last time before making his way out of the ship.

CHAPTER NINETEEN

Ox led the group of people away from the top of the circular stairs and out to the exit of the mine. No ash demons or soldiers had been encountered along the way. Grace held tightly to Ox's hand as the early morning sunlight started peeking in through the tunnel entrance. Her and the others shielded their eyes at first as it had been some time since any of them had seen true daylight.

"We have to hurry." Grace said. "The demons will be looking for us to work in a matter of minutes."

"We're almost to the train." Ox assured her.

Ox looked out to see the train just a few feet away and stepped out. He felt a sudden pull at his hand that held his weapon. It wasn't Grace, but Eva standing beside him. She had waited on the outside of the door for them to arrive. Ox almost instinctively put the gun to her head but didn't.

"Shhh." She said with her finger over her lips.

She pointed around the corner, signaling Ox to take a look. He cautiously moved his head to see and spotted an Ash demon. It was the same one that had passed Eva and Parker on the stairs. It had been pacing in front of the train since earlier.

"What is it doing?" He asked.

"I don't know." Eva responded.

"He's waiting for me." A voice spoke from behind the group.

Lao rushed out of the mine entrance and attacked, along with several ash demons. Steel stood at the entrance, unsure of what he was going to do next.

Ox fired several shots hitting a few demons in the process. The blast wave knocked them off their feet for a moment, which is what Ox had intended to do, but it wasn't enough. They were being quickly overtaken. Ox wrestled one demon to the ground and quickly took its sword. Eva pulled a dagger from her boot as Lao approached her with a smile on his face.

"Looks like the secret is out." Lao said to Eva.

The other people rushed toward the train as demons began beating them with whips and chains, knocking them down and dragging some away.

Grace rushed to the train as fast as she could but was quickly knocked to the ground by one of the demons. The creature stood over her holding two short swords, spinning them in its hands as if to intimidate her. The demon was about to slam the blades down on top of her, but she quickly lifted her foot and kicked it between the legs. The demons' eyes widened as it dropped the blades, both landing on opposite sides of Grace. The demon dropped to its knees and held itself, groaning in pain.

"Whatever works." She said as she returned to her feet.

Suddenly another demon approached her holding a long chain. Grace quickly picked up the two swords and turned to the demon ready to defend herself. The demon smiled a slimly grin and scoffed. Grace then began to spin the swords in her hands with great speed. She took a martial arts stance and smiled back at the demon, which was now staring at her curiously.

"Now I have weapons." She said firmly. "I'm not going back in there."

Steel stood back, his mind filled with anger, but he knew he couldn't just do nothing. He had no love for any of the people around him, but they were still people. Steel pulled his sword from its sheath and made his way into the fight. Ox turned to see Steel about to slash him with his sword. Eva could see them over Lao's shoulder. She felt a deep wave of disappointment wash over her. Steel was obviously more emotionally cold then she thought.

Two demons entered the holding cell where the miners were kept. One demon spotted the rope leading to the hatch door and rushed over to it. It shouted to the other to look inside. As the two of them poked their heads into the hatch, Parker grabbed them both by their necks and pulled them into the ship. The demons screamed as gravity did its job. Parker quickly grabbed the rope and pulled himself out of the hatch.

"Thanks for the lift boys." He said

He rushed out of the cell and made his way to the circular stairs. Demons had covered the area. Parker stopped in his tracks, but it was already too late. Once they spotted him, he began to count them in his head as he slowly moved back to the narrow corridor. There were a dozen demons' glaring at him angrily.

"Hello, what's all this then?" Parker asked as the Demons slowly moved toward him with their swords ready. Parker unsheathed his long sword and stood ready to defend himself.

"First come, first serve." He said.

Three demons ran for him swinging wildly, but Parker guarded against them with great ease and dispatched them with little effort. Then more demons rushed toward him shouting battle cries. Parker rolled forward and jammed the tip of his sword into one demons' belly, killing the creature instantly. He returned to his feet just in time to deflect another demons' blade from slashing him across the arm.

"I'm getting better at this." He said as he pulled out his dagger.

Demon after demon charged at him, but each one met with a quick demise. Parker made his way up the stairs, easily taking down any demons that crossed his path. Finally, he made it to the exit and spotted Ox clashing swords with Steel. He then saw Eva going up against Lao. Parker could see Lao toying with her, allowing her to think she stood a chance. Parker ran over to help, catching Lao by surprise.

"Parker!" She shouted.

"Get the train started! He shouted. "Go!"

Lao swung his sword around in his hand. Parker griped his sword tightly, anticipating the attack.

"Why am I not surprised to find you here?" Lao asked.

Parker defended against Lao's swift attacks as Eva ran toward the train. She spotted a demon beating a young man with a whip and jammed her dagger into the back of its head as she passed by. The young man quickly jumped up and ran to the train. Eva then spotted Grace fighting off the demon that was attacking her with a chain. Grace was surprisingly holding her own very well as she slashed at the demon until finally, it fell over turning to ash, dropping the chain to the ground.

"I need your help!" Eva shouted to Grace.

Six demons began to circle around her. Grace was already exhausted but used every ounce of her strength and rushed over and jumped in front of Eva ready to defend her. One by one the demons began to attack, but Grace fought them off with speed and coordination. Eva watched Grace's back even fending off a few of the attackers herself. Once the demons had been dealt with, Eva waved the people toward the train. In no time flat, the miners were making their way on board. Eva glanced over to see Ox still in a fight with Steel.

"Make sure we got everyone." Eva said to Grace.

"I can help you." Grace replied.

"Do as I say."

Grace nodded, somewhat frustrated while Eva ran to help Ox, but did as she was told. Ox was not a weak man by any means but was still having a difficult time with Steel. Ox gave him a swift kick in the stomach knocking him back a few steps. Eva pulled Ox aside just as Steel was about to compose himself.

"You have to stop this!" She shouted as she threw her hands up to Steel.

"Get out of my way!" Steel shouted back.

"This isn't right Steel! You have to let these people go."

"I could care less about these people. This man and his friend have been my headache for far too long." He said swinging his sword once again, but Ox guarded against his attack.

"I know what Roland has forced you to do." Eva said once again placing herself between the two men, trying to convince Steel to give up. "I know how much it hurts you to be betrayed by him."

"You know nothing!" He swung his sword at her however, his swing was lacking strength. It was as if he didn't really want to hurt her and she had plenty of time to dodge.

"We can fight him together. Just help us."

Steels' sword clashed with Ox's one last time, but even Ox noticed a change in Steels' power and finally they pushed each other away. Eva rushed in between them one last time.

"You have a choice now." She said. "This is your chance to make the right one."

After a moment's hesitation, Steel lowered his sword. He glared at Ox and slowly took one step forward.

"This doesn't change anything between us." Steel spoke calmly. "If I see you again, we'll finish what we've started."

"We aren't the bad guys here." Ox said to Steel. "You've chosen the wrong side."

"I'm on my own side." Steel responded. "And I still don't like you."

Slowly but surely the ash demons were losing the battle. Grace had managed to get most of the people on the train while Ox and Eva helped pull along a couple of stragglers. Lao continued his attacks against Parker, who was doing the best he could to defend himself. Lao was an

WARRIOR FROM AVALON

experienced opponent to say the least. Eva stuck her head out of the train to see the two continuing their fight.

"Parker, come on!" She shouted.

Lao kicked Parker in the chest knocking him to the ground.

"Just go!" He yelled back.

"No, Please!"

"Ox, get them out of here!" He shouted as he shoved his foot into Lao's stomach forcing him away and returned to his feet.

Ox moved to the front of the train and began pushing random buttons until he felt movement. Slowly the train began to move forward. Lao diverted his attention to the escaping prisoners and made one final kick knocking Parker to the ground yet again. Lao ran for the train and grabbed onto the rails as it slowly moved out of the cave. Parker began to get up, but an Ash demon grabbed him and forced him to the ground again. He punched it several times in the face to no avail. Suddenly the demon was lifted into the air. Parker looked up to see Steel standing over him holding the demon over his own head. He quickly got to his feet and turned to watch Steel bring the demon down breaking its back over his knee. Steel then pulled out a dagger and jammed it into the demons' head turning it to ashes at his feet.

Parker knew Steel was tough, but he couldn't help but feel a cold chill at the sight. Both men locked eyes. There was no respect between the two, no friendship. It was then that Steel tossed a digital key to Parker.

"I'll kill you if I ever see you again." Steel said.

"Fair enough." Parker replied as he ran for the nearest motorcycle.

He had to do his absolute best to catch up to that train. He used the key Steel had just given him and listened to the roar of the engine. He had never driven any kind of vehicle before, so his first attempt at going forward ended in the bike accelerating and stopping suddenly.

"Cheesy peaches!"

Steel rolled his eyes as Parker fumbled with the brake and the accelerator. Finally, and with an extremely embarrassed look on his face, Parker made his way out of the cave and sped off to catch up to the others.

"This is the guy that evaded me for so long?" Steel asked himself as he shook his head. "He doesn't need me to kill him. He'll do it himself eventually."

Even though he had gotten a slow start, Parker could see the train not too far ahead of him. It hadn't picked up enough speed just yet so Parker pushed the bike as fast as he could in an effort to catch up.

On the train, Lao had managed to climb onto the roof and was slowly making his way toward the other side. Eva turned around to see Parker on his bike behind them.

"Slow down!" She shouted to Ox.

Ox turned to see Parker and then reached for the controls. Just then Lao appeared through an open window on the side of the train kicking Ox in the process. Ox was knocked to the floor but quickly recovered. The two men began fighting each other as Eva and Grace ran to the back of the train to help Parker. Each time Ox reached for the control's Lao would kick his hand away. Several of the men on board would often try to interfere with the fight, but Lao was extremely gifted in hand to hand combat. He was easily capable of fending off multiple enemies at once. Ox was holding his own as best as he could, but it was no use, he wasn't as adept in martial arts as he would like to be and needed Parkers' assistance.

Parker accelerated the bike to the point he was just a few feet away from the side of the train. Eva stretched out her hand waiting for him to be within reach when Lao spotted them and rushed to the back to stop Parker from boarding. He kicked Eva's hand away, but Grace immediately jumped on Lao's back and dug her fingernails into his neck. Lao spun wildly trying to knock her off of him. In his sporadic movement, Eva was knocked over the railing. She quickly reached out and caught the bars and held on tight as her feet dragged along the tracks. Ox grabbed Lao and dragged him back inside the interior of the train with Grace still clinging tight on his back.

Parker raced as fast as he could to stay beside the train so he could get to Eva and pull her to safety, but he knew he wasn't going to be able to reach her without pulling the bike onto the tracks. He held down the accelerator and slowly worked himself into a standing position on the seat of the bike. The machine wobbled as he tried maintaining his balance. He could feel the bike was about to fall over. It was now or never, and with one final move he leaped toward the side of the train with an outstretched hand and grabbed hold of Eva's leg. He held on tight as he was dragged along behind the train.

"What are you doing?" She screamed.

"I missed the bars!" He shouted back.

Parker reached up and pulled himself to the railing and grabbed on. Eva couldn't hold on any longer and the extra weight Parker added onto her was too much. Her hand released the railing, but Parkers' quick reflexes caught her just in time, and within a matter of seconds they both managed to get onto the train.

Inside, Lao was quickly gaining the upper hand. He reached behind him and grabbed Grace by the shoulders and pulled her over his head tossing her to the floor. He then performed a spinning kick to Ox's face, knocking him down. Lao turned to see Grace, still trying to focus after being thrown so hard. He reached his arm back and swung to hit her in the face but out of nowhere, Parkers' hand caught Lao's fist before it could connect with Grace. He kicked Lao in the stomach knocking him off balance.

"Really?" Parker asked. "You're just gonna go after a little girl like that? What a shame. How about you and I have a go at it?"

WARRIOR FROM AVALON

Parker tossed his backpack to the side of the carriage and rushed at Lao as everyone around them scattered to get out of the way. He was able to deflect every attack Lao could throw at him. The small space inside the train wasn't convenient for either man. The two of them were at a disadvantage in terms of techniques in such a confined space. Lao grabbed at Parkers' neck who immediately head-butted him. For the first couple of minutes, neither of them was able to inflict any kind of serious pain.

Parker realized that he was getting nowhere. He had to get Lao into an open space. The problem with that idea was that Lao was just as skilled, if not better. Lao continued to rush at Parker, performing several close quarter maneuvers that Parker was easily able to avoid. He knew his pressure points and guarded himself intelligently. Lao was becoming more and more frustrated.

Parker stood in the doorway from one carriage to the other. Ox, Eva, Grace, and the rest of the people were standing behind him in the second carriage. Ahead of him was Lao and behind him were the controls to the train. He suddenly had an idea. All he had to do was get Lao away from the others. That was the true goal. Ox would be able to lead them all to safety. If Parker could defeat Lao, which he was unsure he could do, he would be able to meet up with them later, but at the very least by them time to get away. He quickly scanned the wall behind him and saw the switch that would decouple the two carriages. He slammed his elbow into it fast and felt the pull of the train. Lao was no moron and quickly rushed away to jump to the other carriage. If Lao could get to the people then Parker would have no choice but to follow, but Parker was one step ahead. With one quick effort Parker grabbed Lao's belt pulled him onto his back.

"Ox!" Parker shouted. "I'll save you seat!"

"Parker no!" Eva shouted as she attempted to run to him.

Ox nodded in understanding and pulled Eva away from the doorway. Parker ran to the front of the train, dragging Lao's flailing body behind him. He reached his hand out for the controls and shoved the lever forward causing the carriage to reach its maximum speed. He turned to see the carriage behind him as it began to drift away, slowing down rapidly. Ox would allow the carriage to go as far as it could take them before ditching it.

Lao kicked Parker in the face, forcing him to let go. He quickly moved away from Parker, but it was too late. He couldn't get to the other carriage and he surely couldn't jump at the current speed without causing serious injury. He turned to face Parker, who had a smile across his face even as he spit blood from his mouth and wiped at a cut on his lip. Parker turned back to the controls and used the force of his weight to break the lever from the terminal. He held it out to Lao and then dropped it on the floor.

"Looks like you missed your stop." Parker said with a smile.

"Very clever." Lao said. "You may have saved their lives for now, but I'll catch up to them eventually. You on the other hand, I can deal with now!"

"Bring it on short stack!" Parker shouted as Lao raced forward to attack.

CHAPTER TWENTY

Parker and Sang stood in a narrow hallway. The walls were so close together that the two men had no choice but to turn sideways to move through it. There was nothing in the room at all, only an entrance and an exit.

"What is the purpose of this?" Parker asked squeezing through the hall following Sang.

Sang didn't respond right away. He stopped halfway through the hallway and turned his body to face Parker. Suddenly Sang lifted his fist to Parkers' mouth busting his lip on impact. Parker reached for his mouth but then saw Sang swinging his other hand for another strike. Parker quickly deflected it as fast as possible and then took a few steps back out of Sang's reach.

"This passage is the most difficult to maneuver in." Sang said. "If you can fight in here and hold your own against me, then out in the open where there is plenty of room you should be undefeatable in combat."

"You could have just said that before." Parker said as he gave Sang a powerful uppercut to the chin.

Sang and Parker attacked each other with quick jabs and kicks using what little room they had to gather strength for each strike. Sang swung at Parkers' head, but Parker ducked down and quickly slammed his fist into Sang's knee. Sang placed both of his hands on Parkers' back and cartwheeled himself over his shoulders to the other side pushing Parker to the floor in the process. Parker scooted himself across the floor as Sang tried to stomp down on him with his feet.

He quickly kicked Sang in the face and then in his chest. The impact was so hard that Sang went backward while Parker scooted across the floor further. He quickly returned to a standing position to see Sang already charging at him. Punches were being thrown, left and right, but the two men were able to deflect each other's attacks with great ease. It was a few moments later that Sang backed away with a smile on his face.

"Not too bad." He said as he gently clapped his hands together.

Parker smiled and let down his defenses. Sang seized the opportunity and rushed toward Parker and placed both of his elbows against the sides of the wall as he raised both legs into the air to shove them into Parkers' chest, but Parker leaned backward forcing Sang's attack to fall short of his target. As soon as Sang's legs dropped back down to the ground Parker shoved his shoulder into Sang's body knocking him from the air and down to the floor. Parker cautiously went to help Sang off the floor in case the fighting was meant to continue. Sang laughed as he allowed Parker to help him to his feet.

"I thought I had you there." Sang laughed. "Good job. Never let your enemy get the upper hand."

"You're a sneaky one Sang." Parker replied.

"I am impressed."

"You taught me pretty good." Parker replied as Sang slammed his forehead into Parkers' A rough headache overtook him as he fell backwards. Parker watched Sang stand over him and then stretched out his hand to help him up.

"You still need some work."

Parker stood in front of Lao on the train as it raced along the tracks. He had a sudden and terrible headache that he couldn't explain. He hadn't been hit that hard yet, but he felt as though he had just been head-butted. He was remembering something that had never happened. A man named Sang fighting with him in a narrow corridor. He remembered it as if it were recent. Parker wondered if this was something that Nimue had been talking about. It was only then he ever remembered her name.

WARRIOR FROM AVALON

Lao rushed toward him throwing punches wildly as if he were an animal fighting for a scrap of meat. Parker deflected every attack with precision and careful timing, and it was only a matter of seconds before Lao was on his back a few feet away while Parker looked at his hands with great confusion.

"Where did that come from?" Parker said to himself.

He was remembering techniques he had never learned before. He had always been a great fighter, even better than most, but never that great. Lao was one of the deadliest combatants he had ever faced and now Parker was able to read his every move like Lao was calling them out to him.

"You think you can make a fool out of me?" Lao asked angrily.

"I think I already have." Parker answered.

"That was a rhetorical question!" Lao shouted as he threw another string of punches toward Parker.

Parker dodged the attacks without even throwing a single punch and ended the series of hits by sweeping his leg underneath Lao's, tripping him so that he fell onto his back yet again.

"It's pretty easy actually." Parker said with a smirk.

Lao flung his legs into the air and pushed off the ground with his hands launching himself to his feet. He swung at Parker faster and harder, but Parker countered every attack with little effort. Finally, Parker grabbed Lao by the back of the neck and dragged him toward the door at the back of the train. The tracks moved fiercely behind them with great speed. Lao tried to fight him off, but Parker was the stronger fighter this time.

"This is where you get off!" Parker said as he shoved Lao out.

Parker watched as Lao rolled along the track unconscious from the impact. He couldn't believe how easily he was able to defend himself. His confidence had grown instantly. He still couldn't understand the memory or the skills he had acquired afterwards, but he was extremely thankful that it kicked in when it did.

The train jerked as it sped along the tracks. The carriage shook and Parkers' swelled head was quickly popped like a balloon when he realized he was still gaining speed. The train groaned as the wheels underneath grinded against the metal. The carriage rocked back and forth knocking Parker off his feet. He pulled himself up as fast as he could and looked out of the window to see the cliff outside. He gazed straight ahead and saw the bridge ahead of him.

"Maybe this wasn't such a great idea!" He said to himself.

The train began to lift itself up on one side tilting the carriage knocking Parker to the floor once again. The entire carriage crashed down on its side sliding closer and faster to the edge of a cliff off to the side. Glass rained down from shattered windows while Parker tried to cover his face to protect himself from the sharp debris. He could see the edge of the cliff approaching ahead. He crawled away from the front of the carriage as fast as he could and grabbed on to one of the seat legs that was bolted to the floor.

The carriage began to slow as it scrubbed along the ground. Parker shut his eyes and expected the worst. Fear engulfed him, but it wasn't the fear of death. He was afraid for Ox and the others. The last thought on his mind was a prayer that they would make it home safe.

A couple of hours had passed when Parker woke to find himself still inside the train. His surroundings were a blur at first, but it wasn't long until his vision returned. The train had rolled down the cliff and was hanging at an inclined angle. Parker had slid to the back of the train while he had been unconscious. It was a miracle that he hadn't fallen out. He could feel the carriage rocking gently back and forth as if the slightest shift of weight caused it to stir.

He had a pain on the left side of his forehead and saw blood as he pulled his hand away. He started to raise himself off the floor but felt a quick and terrible pain at his right leg. A large shard of glass had penetrated above his knee and was bleeding profusely. He immediately reached for his backpack only to find it missing. He knew right away that he had left it in the other carriage with Ox and the others. He gently raised himself up and grabbed at the piece of glass in his leg.

"Just pull hard." He said to himself as he gripped the top of the glass as tight as he could between his fingers.

"One, two…." He started. "…Oh forget it."

He pulled as hard and as fast as he could until the shard was free from his leg. He groaned and grunted at the pain. After a moment passed, he tossed the shard of glass out of the carriage. He then ripped the sleeve from his shirt and tied it tightly around the wound on his leg. He took another couple of minutes to compose himself and then tried to stand up slowly. The incline of the train made it difficult to stand so he reached for the seats and anything he could to steady himself as he made his way up the inside of the carriage. He was almost to the top when suddenly the train began to slide further down the cliff's slope. Parker was knocked off balance and slid all the way back to his starting position.

The extra weight caused the carriage to slide even faster. Parker gritted his teeth and ignored the pain in his leg as best he could. He stood up and ran up the incline as the carriage moved even faster over the edge. As he reached the end, he dove through the broken front window landing on the slanted cliffside. It was still too steep as he began to slide down as well. He could see the train go over the edge just ahead of him. With one last effort he reached out and grabbed the edge of the cliff as he looked down just in time to see the train slam hard into the rocky waters below. He gripped the rocky surface tight as he began to pull himself up, but his left hand slipped, and he dangled off the edge. He let out a small scream as he saw the trains wreckage beneath him. Quickly he reached his hand back up and pulled himself onto the sloped surface.

Slowly but surely, he crawled his way up the slanted ground, gripping and digging his hands into the rocks and dirt as he made the climb. He let out a small sigh of relief when he finally reached level ground. After he was safely at the top, he took a few minutes to catch his breath.

"That could have gone better." He said sarcastically as he flipped over onto his back and sighed in relief.

Noon had arrived as Isaac entered the living area of his underground home. It had been a few days since Parker and Ox had left to head back into the city. He didn't like being kept in the dark and was more worried than ever. He walked over to the shelf against the wall and stared at several wood carvings that Isaacs' father had made over the years before he had passed on. He had whittled a small deer, a bear, and even a wolf. Amongst the wooden animals was a digital picture. The picture was in an old plastic case that displayed a four-second looped image of Frank, a fourteen-year old Isaac, and an eight-year old Parker. Long before, when the device was more commonly used, a person could capture small videos and photos, but the device Isaac had was slightly damaged, so the image he would look at was the last the camera ever took. The battery was easily rechargeable if you had a connection to some form of power and the proper charging cable.

The picture was a digital image of the three of them standing side by side. Frank would reach over to dust dirt from Isaacs' shoulder. Isaac would look over at Parker and point his finger at his chest. As Parker looked down, Isaac flipped Parkers' nose. Frank would smile and the picture would replay again. Isaac picked up the device and smiled as the thoughts of that day played over in his mind.

It was twenty-two years ago. A deer walked out of the large, forested area until it came upon a stream and began to drink. The wind blew softly against its fur, but little did the deer know that it was being watched. The string of the bow whispered with a creaking noise as it was gently pulled back. The arrow's point was aimed steadily and with a soft exhale of air, the string was released, and the arrow soared straight into the deer's broadside. An eight-year old Parker Wallace looked on as his arrow had hit the target with great precision.
"Well done boy." Frank said in his thick Scottish accent. "Your first deer at that."
The three of them walked over to the fallen animal and Parker watched with tear-filled eyes as Isaac pulled the arrow from the deer's lifeless body. Frank looked up to see the hurt in Parkers' eyes and went over to console him.
"What's wrong?" Frank asked.
"I killed it." Parker replied. "I've never killed anything before."
"It's all right son. It's part of nature. You want to eat, don't you?"
"Yes, but did I have to kill that one?"
"Would you have rather killed a different one?"
"I don't know."
"It's all right to feel a bit bad for them, but it's how we survive. We don't kill for the sport of it. We only kill what we are going to eat."
"He didn't feel anything Wally." Isaac said as he overly exaggerated the simulation of the kill. "You probably made its heart explode."
Parkers' face grew sadder.

"You're not helping Isaac." Frank said with a chuckle. "It's okay to feel sad for it Parker, but we need the meat. We'll give thanks for it at our blessing for dinner."

It was an hour later the three of them had arrived home. Lora was hanging up clothes on a wire just outside of their small cottage. Parker and Isaac both ran to hug her upon their return. Frank arrived moments after, dropping the deer from his shoulder and gave Lora a gentle kiss on the head.

"How did it go?" Lora asked.

"He got his first deer, on his first shot no less." Frank answered. "Never seen anything like it."

"Well done Parker! You did that all by yourself."

"Aye, he's got a natural talent for a bow and arrow. Now all we have to do is take a few scraps into town for trade and we'll be eating well for the next week or so."

"One minute." Lora said as she ran into the cottage and then returned holding a small camera. The device was extremely old considering its condition, but its power cell lasted a very long time.

"Time to update our memories." Lora said holding up the camera.

"All right boys, stand up straight." Frank said as he reached over and dusted off Isaac's shoulder.

"You have something on your shirt Wally." Isaac said as Parker looked down only to have his nosed flicked.

The four of them laughed as the camera made a click, indicating that it captured the moment.

"That's a keeper." Lora said smiling.

His mothers' words echoed in his head as Isaac returned the picture to the shelf. There was a sudden knock at his door, and he moved over to open it only to find one of the other men who lived in the underground home standing on the other side.

"You need to see this." The man said.

Isaac followed him as they ran toward the community entrance. He climbed the ladder to peek out and see what was going on. Ox had exited the forest with over nearly a dozen people following behind him. Not nearly as many as they started out with during their escape just a couple of days ago. Isaac opened the hatch and climbed out to greet Ox.

"What's going on?" Isaac asked. "Where have you been?"

"These people need our help." Ox replied. "Take them inside. They need rest and food."

"Where's Parker?"

"He stayed behind to buy us time to escape."

"You shouldn't have brought them here in broad daylight."

"I covered my tracks as usual. I had to get these people to safety as quick as possible, I can explain more later."

Isaac looked at the faces of the men and women lining up before him. He nodded his head in understanding as one by one the people were helped inside by other residents of the underground community.

"We don't have space ready for this many people." Isaac said quietly.

"We can work that out." Ox said. "We did have more, but most of them had villages not far from our route back. There were half a dozen young ones among them that were taken in by others. The rest of them just need some time before they journey back to their own homes, but for now we have to protect them."

"What happened to my brother?"

"He can take care of himself. He'll be along soon. I'm sure of it." Ox said pulling the Orb out of Parkers' backpack. Ox had fortunately grabbed it before they left. Eva's eyes lit up at the sight of the orb being held in Ox's hand. It was beautiful, and it glowed a purple glow before turning a solid color.

"What is that?" Isaac asked.

"I'm not sure, but I found it in Parkers' backpack." Ox answered. "He must have found this inside the mine we rescued these people from. Roland had them digging for this."

"Roland is forcing slaves to dig in mines now?"

"Using Ash demons as slave masters."

"That's not possible. Ash demons don't serve humans."

"Tell that to the ones we killed." Grace interrupted.

"It's true." Eva said. "I saw it with my own eyes."

"Grace, you should go inside with the others." Ox said.

"I just spent too much of my life inside a cave. You're not forcing me to go into another one."

"This one is safe child." Ox said.

"I don't care. I'm not going in there." Grace said as she ran off into the woods.

"I'll go get her." Eva said.

"No, I'll go." Ox corrected. "Isaac, take this inside and hide it. We can't let Roland or anyone else get their hands on this until we can figure out what it is."

"Or why it's so important to them." Isaac said nodding in agreement.

Ox watched as Isaac and Eva entered the underground and closed the hatch behind them. He then walked into the woods to find Grace sitting on a fallen log.

"We shouldn't be outside right now." Ox said. "I promise you'll be safer inside."

"I'm just not ready yet." She said.

"Okay." Ox said sitting down on the ground beside her. "Then the two of us will sit here until you are ready. Why don't you at least rest your eyes? I will keep a lookout."

"You don't mind sitting with me?"

"Not at all. The fresh air is good for us."

Grace leaned against Ox's arm and her eyes began to close due to her being so exhausted. It was the first time she had been able to rest so comfortably. Ox stayed alert as he looked around the forest and just let his mind wander a bit while he waited. He looked down at Grace and smiled.

"Dream those good dreams child." He said. "There is nothing to be afraid of now."

CHAPTER TWENTY-ONE

"Please, tell me how he managed to slip through your fingers this time." Roland said as he paced the floor in front of Steel. Roland was a man in his late seventies with white hair and stood nearly six feet tall. His eyes were incredibly unique with a dark color to them. He walked with a limp and carried a cane in his right hand. The room in which he stood was large and consisted of marble floors and large columns that held up the ceiling. There were numerous leather chairs and a desk where Roland would sit. These items were easily obtainable for a man in his position.

"I'm finished." Steel said keeping his eyes focused on the floor.

Roland glared at Steel in frustration.

"You care to run that by me again?"

"I refuse to continue my services under your rule." Steel explained.

He had given it a lot of thought. Maybe it was the stupidest idea he ever had, but confronting Roland in person was the only thing he felt was right. Roland wasn't taking it very well.

"Have you forgotten all that I've done for you?" Roland asked. "I gave you purpose, and I gave you title. If not for me, you'd have been cast outside the walls to fend for yourself years ago."

"I haven't forgotten, but with every order I follow I seem to lose another piece of my soul. I've served you for years without doubting your orders, no matter how cruel they seemed because I trusted you. My father trusted you, and I never questioned you because of that, but in light of recent events, I can't help but wonder what more atrocities you'd have me commit based on a lie. With Ash demons involved, I will serve you no longer. I have nothing left to offer, so you may as well kill me and be done with it."

WARRIOR FROM AVALON

Lao approached from behind Steel wrapping his own hand in a bandage. He had many cuts and bruises after being thrown from the train just hours earlier but was still fully capable of making the journey back to the compound. From there it was only a few hours or so to Dublin. Steel had arrived first but made no effort to hide the fact that he let Eva and the others escape. Lao couldn't help but smile as Steel was his strongest competitor. Seeing him lose everything made Lao's day that much better.

"What do you think?" Roland asked. "Does Steel deserve a swift death for his betrayal?"

"He did serve you proudly all this time, but who knew he had a conscience." Lao said. "Should I just slit his throat and be done with it?"

"It doesn't matter anymore." Steel replied. "The things I did in your name, had I known I was a tool for the devil, I'd have killed you myself given the chance."

Roland was angry but smiled an evil smile as he sat in the chair behind his desk. Lao stood behind Steel with his hand on the hilt of his sword, ready to unsheathe it at the slightest indication of violence, or if his King ordered Steels' execution.

"Like father like son." Roland said.

Steels' eyes moved away from the floor to glare at Roland behind the desk.

"Your father had a change of heart as well." Roland continued. "He learned the truth early on. I guess he was much smarter than you, which is why I had to kill him myself."

Steel quickly stepped forward only to have the blade of Lao's sword gently touching his neck. Steel was unable to move forward without losing his head in the process.

"It breaks my heart to lose such a talented drone." Roland said. "Unfortunately, you leave me no choice captain."

"Better make it quick." Steel warned. "I won't make it easy."

"No, no. I'm not going to have you killed. After all you did for me, I can't just let you die. No, I think exile will suit you better."

"You think that will save you?"

"Trust me, it's much more fun this way." Roland said with a smile. "You get to spend the rest of your days alone, fighting for your own survival, knowing that you did horrible things in service to me, the man who murdered your father with his bare hands."

Steels' anger grew at the words he was hearing. He clenched his fists until his knuckles popped at the strain.

"Kick me out of the city, fine." Steel said. "I'll find my way back in before too long. You won't see it coming."

"Too easy." Roland replied. "Have him sent somewhere far away. Make him work for it."

"I know just the place." Lao said.

"There is no place far enough!" Steel said.

Lao moved the blade from Steels' throat and quickly slammed the hilt of his sword into the back of Steels' head as hard as he could. Steel fell to the ground as he was knocked out from the impact. Lao opened the door and called in two sentries to retrieve their former captain.

"Lock him in a carriage." Lao said. "I'll be along with more instructions shortly."

"Yes sir!"

The doors slammed hard and silence engulfed the room.

"Easy come, easy go." Roland said jokingly. "What of the airship those slaves managed to uncover before their escape?"

"There was nothing." Lao explained. "The orb was not where you thought it would be. We can only determine that Parker found it first."

Roland used his cane and slapped a small glass vase off his desk, shattering it into tiny pieces on the floor.

"We need to deal with him fast." Roland said. "He's a bigger pest than I thought he'd be."

"He caught me off guard." Lao said. "He's only one man, I'm sure I can…"

"He's more than that." Roland interrupted. "I have plans that stretch even farther beyond this simple kingdom. Plans that keep being put on hold because of that boys' interference. Parker stays on the watch list for immediate execution but bring the other one here to me alive."

"With all due respect, do you think it is wise to choose him as your successor? I would be greatly honored to take your place."

"You have been a great asset all these years captain Lao. You would make a great host, but it must be of my bloodline. I can't just take whomever I wish. Besides, you are more valuable to me as my second. In the coming years, I'm going to need you by my side."

"Then I will continue as instructed my King. What of the woman?"

"Eva." Roland said with a smile. "Did you do as instructed?"

"I did."

"Once she has served her purpose, we'll deal with her. Get back out there and find that orb."

"As you wish." Lao said as he bowed his head and exited the room.

Parker wandered through the woods, taking all the side paths that he remembered from the numerous traveling he had done. He was hurt, but he was going out of his way to ensure he wasn't being followed. He could have easily gone directly home, but he wasn't about to lead anyone that could be following him there. He felt paranoid for some reason. He could hear nothing behind him and there was no one around him, but he sensed that someone was following him. He made his way to a small lake and rested a moment on a stump. He took the bloody wrapping from his leg and set it beside him. He checked the wound to see that it was better already.

"Wasn't as bad as I thought." He said to himself.

Suddenly his reflexes kicked in and with a swift move he pulled the dagger from his belt and spun around to hold the blade to the throat of the person he thought had been following him. Nimue stood with the blade near her throat but showed no sign of fear as she wasn't physically there anyway. Again, she had appeared only in her spirit form, standing fully transparent in front of Parker.

"You are good." She said with a smile. "I don't know how you even knew I was here."

"What did you do to me?" He asked returning the dagger to his belt.

"What are you talking about?"

"The images in my head, back at the ship, you did something to my mind. I'm hallucinating or something."

"Those aren't hallucinations. I unlocked the dormant memories in your brain. They're not meant to harm you but help you. The headaches will subside."

"I never did those things." He said as he sat down again on the stump.

"Not in this life you didn't."

"What does that mean?"

"You've been around a lot longer than you think. You are remembering events from your past life."

"They're scrambled, they don't make any sense." Nimue sat down in front of Parker.

"You're first life ended over three hundred years ago. After your bridge accident, I had you sent to the Island of Avalon to begin your training for when you would return here in this time."

"You know that sounds crazy right?"

"It's the truth." She assured him. "You volunteered to come here and fight."

"That doesn't sound like something I'd do."

"It's exactly something you would do. You did in fact."

"Come back to life to scavenge for food and hide from Ash demons." Parker chuckled. "I wouldn't have made that choice."

"Why do you fight then?" Nimue asked. "What purpose drives you? No one asked you to take on this role of protector. You could have lived this life however you wanted. Safe and secure in your underground community. Quietly so that you don't draw attention to yourself. So what makes Parker Wallace fight?"

"I do it because…." The words were lost in Parkers' head.

"You can't escape your own heart." Nimue responded. "No matter what life you live, you're still the same person that you've always been. You sought purpose in both lives you lived, and this is your opportunity to do something greater than you could have ever dreamed."

"You sent me back here to fight Roland?"

"Roland is nothing. Hades is your true enemy."

"Hades?"

"Hades, the god of the Underworld, is the real threat to this world."

"Why do I feel like we've had this conversation before?"

"Because we have. You were reborn on Earth for this very reason…"

The memories began to return to Parker as Nimue told his story. He could see it clearly in his head as if it had happened yesterday. His arrival on the island of Avalon all the way to his fight with Hades and his journey to the Underworld. He could see it all, but still had a little trouble understanding.

"I set him free?" He asked.

"Yes, and he holds the key to the gates of Elysium."

Parkers' memory flashed of all the people he saw in the Underworld, frozen like statues. The people that were being brutally punished that he couldn't help.

"The captured souls." He said as if he were having a revelation.

"Precisely."

"It's still a little fuzzy, but I can remember them."

"It will all come back to you in time."

"Why can't I remember everything? Why is it all so sporadic?"

"You've lived two lives now. You can't erase those memories. To hit you with them all at once would be too overwhelming. Your mind would shatter."

"Yeah, we don't want that." He said standing up. "So where is Hades now?"

"I'm not sure just yet."

"Aren't you are supposed to know these things?" Parker asked. "How can I help you if I don't even know where to start? The world is a big place."

"Hades is keeping himself hidden. I don't know how, or what he's waiting for, but you'll never find him just by looking."

"So, what can I do? Why did you even bring me back? If the gods still exist, why can't they fight their own battles?"

"We have been involved in this war since before you were born. Zeus will not allow any of the other Olympians to attack his brother."

Nimue could see Parker was showing signs of frustration.

"Long ago I saw an image of the future." Nimue said. "It wasn't a god that stood in victory over Hades. It was you." Parker was silent as Nimue continued. "I was taken prisoner by three psychics known as the Ancients. They had always known power, even when I was a child, fighting them proved difficult. Thankfully, I was quickly rescued by my friend and mentor, Merlin, but before our escape I had caught a glimpse of things that have yet to pass. You were there Parker. An ordinary man at war with a god, and there were other people with you. Not one of them was afraid to fight beside you or even die for you. You are going to inspire so many people. They will be with you in the ultimate battle to end this war and save our people. So many will join you to fight together in ultimate triumph, and you were standing tall at the head of the army. This image filled me with a hope I had thought I'd lost."

Nimue reached her hand out as if to place it on his shoulder though it hovered just slightly above him.

"You are our ultimate weapon against Hades." She continued. "The last chance the world has rests on your shoulders."

"That's how you saw me?"

"Yes."

"What happens next?"

"I don't know." She said dropping her hand. "The future isn't certain, but all I know is that you are more important than you could ever realize."

Parker nodded his head in understanding.

"Well then, what's my first move?" He asked. "What should I do?"

"You must get to Eva." Nimue answered. "Her safety is of the utmost importance."

"Eva? What does she have to do with any of this?"

"Everything. You and she have a strong connection. She was at your side on Avalon."

"Wait, I can remember that." Parker said with a surprised smile. "That's why we feel so close to each other now."

"I'm not sure how just yet, but Eva has a key role in all of this. You have to protect her and the orb."

"Eva should be with Ox. They have the orb with them. I imagine they are with my brother Isaac by now."

"She needs you Parker. Even she doesn't yet know how much."

Nimue began to walk toward the lake as she prepared to leave.

"I have a question before you go." He said.

"What is it?"

"Why do you appear this way? I'm always able to see through you. I mean literally."

"We all have a part to play, but because of the law set forth by Zeus I can no longer bring my physical form to Earth, not without drastic consequences."

"That still doesn't make sense. Why create a law that basically prevents you from helping us at all. It's like you've got both hands tied behind your back."

"I have rules to follow. It's as simple as that."

"Okay then. Since Zeus has left his brothers mess for us to clean up, I guess I need to get moving if I plan to catch up to the others."

"God speed Parker Wallace." Nimue said as she watched him walk behind the trees in the distance. A small grin appeared on her face as he faded from her sight, though her focus on Parker was quickly broken as Ares appeared beside her in his spirit form.

"For someone who holds the world on his shoulders, he doesn't look like much." Ares said with a smirk. "Of all the mortals we've used in the past, you'd think we could have done much better than this one, right?"

"We didn't choose this one, fate did." Nimue said walking away from Ares. "I'd appreciate you not spying on me when I use the viewing machine."

"Fate may have misled you I'm afraid."

As she stepped away, the images of the woods she was just in faded away leaving a large flat stone slab. The stone slab sat between two large stone pillars that were spinning rapidly, but then slowly came to stop as she moved further from it. The controls to the viewing machine were on a metal pedestal that lowered once Nimue had finished.

The viewing machine was Nimue's bridge to Earth. Since she could no longer physically travel there, it was her way of interacting with Parker and the others. By using the machine, not only did it project a holographic image on the stone slab in front of her, but her consciousness would leave her body and go where she wanted leaving her physical form to remain in place.

By other means of magic and science, she could transfer power or objects via the machines consol. The machine itself was used by the other Olympians at times in the past to keep watch over mankind, but they would also use it to appear before man as a spirit form for other means. Many of which were of a selfish nature. Nimue was the only one who bothered to use the machine at all anymore. The others had left their desires to see the world due to the command of Zeus, but Nimue had a purpose.

Ares quickly caught up to her as the two of them casually strolled into the halls of Mount Olympus. The large hall was mostly white but shimmered with golden light as if the marble floors and walls were laced with gold from within. A bright red carpet led them from the entrance to a large set of double doors at the end of the hall. After stepping away from the viewing machine and returning their full consciousness to Olympus, they both stood in full physical form.

"What is it about this man that makes you stare at him as you do?" Ares asked.

"What are you talking about?" Nimue asked back.

"It certainly isn't his looks, but I'd give up every weapon in my armory to have you look at me like that."

"No, you wouldn't, everyone knows you love that armory."

"That is true, I have every weapon imaginable. Well, almost."

"Don't you have something better to do than follow me around?"

"I just wanted to see what all the fuss was about with this guy. He is a great fighter to be sure, but I ask again. What makes him so special?"

"I like his eyes." Nimue said as she continued moving while the double doors opened by themselves. Ares didn't follow behind her but could feel her annoyance with him as she left his side.

"That which is done in the dark will be exposed in the light." He said silently to himself. "I'll find out what I need to know soon enough."

CHAPTER TWENTY-TWO

Ox walked toward the entrance to the underground community with Grace by his side. He had sat in the forest for a couple of hours whittling a piece of wood while waiting for Grace to wake up. She had not slept that well in a long time. Ox lifted the fake tree stump to reveal the passage underground for Grace to enter.

"If you need time, I have plenty." He said.

"It's all right." She responded with a change of heart. "I trust you."

Ox smiled as he climbed down into the hatch and then assisted her as she followed behind him. Dale stood to the side as Ox greeted him with a handshake before escorting Grace further into the tunnels. Grace looked at the tubes and wiring on the ceiling of the tunnel with lights scattered along to illuminate the way.

"Where does the light come from?" She asked.

"We have several generators that power the entire community." Ox answered. "We have been here for many years. We have a garden to grow food as well."

"That's amazing."

"It took a lot of work. There were numerous trial and error methods to make everything go smoothly. It took a long time to get this place in the shape it is today, but we did it."

"Are there a lot of families here?"

"There are over a couple dozen people at least."

"Any kids my age?"

"Not really, I'm sorry."

"That's okay."

"Parker and his brother started this place together with the hope that people would have families here. His brother is mostly in charge."

"Like King Roland?"

"Not even close. Every person that enters this place is free to come and go as they please. We offer jobs here to help sustain our lives for the better. The only cost of living here is to contribute to the betterment of the community."

Ox and Grace approached a large steel door and entered it to reveal a large underground dining room. The ceiling was high, and the table was long, built big enough to sit at least thirty people. The table stretched from one side of the room to the other.

"That is a big table." Grace said with wide eyes.

"Each person normally eats in their own accommodations, but at least once a week we gather here to share each other's company."

"Does everyone have a place to sit?"

"We make it work. Often some will serve others first, and then when it is time for them to eat, they will be served by the people who they served. We come together here to give thanks to God for all we have been given. In the world we live in, it is a blessing to have this."

"This is wonderful."

"Oh, you want to know what the best part is?"

"What's that?"

Ox kneeled beside Grace to whisper in her ear.

"Every family brings food to share." He said patting himself on the belly. "So we eat like pigs."

Grace let out the biggest smile Ox had seen on her face yet. They continued their way through the dining area, and for a brief moment Ox remembered his daughter. It was a tough thing to be reminded of, but Ox's attention was immediately caught by Agatha as she placed a pitcher of water onto the table. There were other women and men from the underground community setting up the table as well. Each person placed down either a basket of fruit or a pitcher of water or even homemade wine.

"It looks as if they are preparing for a feast as we speak!" Ox said with a smile on his face.

265

"We are actually." Agatha said with excitement. "Isaac wanted to throw a small celebration for our guests. To give thanks for their freedom, and to serve them properly before they depart. Should they choose not to stay. We felt it was the least we could do."

"That is a great idea. Would you like any help?"

"Not at this time, but we should be seating everyone shortly. The guests will be served first."

Ox nodded his head and continued to the other side of the dining area. After proceeding through the doors ahead of them, they began to descend further into the tunnels.

"How far down does it go?" Grace asked.

"It goes down a long way." He answered. "As more people come in, we dig even deeper."

"Is it secure? What about air?"

"Relax child." Ox said with a laugh. "We encountered numerous problems while living underground, but we have made adjustments and additions to ensure that it is totally safe. So do not worry yourself."

After a little bit more of a hike, they finally reached the doors to Ox's home. He opened the door allowing Grace to enter first. Ox pressed a switch to turn on the lights. His room was a decent size. He had a table and a couple of chairs in one area, a large bed on the opposite side, and along the far wall he had a curtain hanging up. Grace walked over to the curtain and opened it to reveal a beautiful view of the ocean.

"Sometimes I can stare out of that window for hours." Ox said. "The world is an ugly place, but it's good to appreciate what beauty you can find."

"I haven't seen anything so beautiful in so long." Grace said staring out of the makeshift window. "Could I find a place here?"

"You do not want to go home?"

"I don't…I'm not." Grace couldn't find the words.

"It is okay child. Take your time."

Grace walked over to one of the chairs and sat down. Ox took a seat in the chair across from her.

"These chairs are nice." She said changing the subject.

"I made every piece of furniture in this room myself." Ox said with a smile.

"Really?"

"Of course! That big table that we passed in the dining room, I made that as well. Though that one took a little help."

Grace was beginning to smile more and more with Ox around. Ox could only imagine the horrors this brave young girl had witnessed, and he would do as much as he could to help her recover.

"My father died trying to save me." Grace said randomly while fighting back tears. "We had a small wooden house by the beach near Millisle."

"You do not have to talk about this now." Ox said.

"They attacked at night, demons and soldiers." She continued ignoring his words. "My mother was killed when they first set fire to our cabin. We were outside bringing in the fishing nets, and when they grabbed me, my Father fought back. He was a great fighter, and he taught me a lot, but we were caught off guard."

"You are a very brave young girl Grace." Ox assured her.

"I froze. I could have fought back, but I was too scared."

"You did nothing wrong. Your Father wished to keep you safe, and he gave his life trying to defend you, but he taught you well and you have survived this long under extreme oppression."

"I wish I could have saved him."

"I understand your feelings child, but it has made you much stronger. I did not know your father, but I know he would be very proud of you today."

Grace launched herself from her chair and leaped into Ox's arms hugging him with tears pouring down her face.

"It is okay." Ox said softly. "You have a place here now."

The room fell silent as Ox held Grace in his arms. She felt as if her emotions were being released all at once and cried the hardest cry in a long time. Ox didn't speak another word for the time being. He could feel her little arms squeezing around his neck as tight as she could, he simply patted her on the back and shed a tear of his own.

It wasn't long until Isaac opened the doors to the dining hall and began to escort what was left of the miners to their chairs. The large table held the small dozens of people as they each took their seats. No sooner had they sat down they waited anxiously for the meal to begin. One older gentleman began to reach for a basket holding a bunch of steaming hot potatoes, but his hand was quickly slapped away by another older lady sitting next to him.

"Don't go grabbing stuff you old pig!" She ordered silently. "It's impolite."

"I ain't got time for manners woman." He replied. "We haven't seen this much food in years."

"We're guests here. You're gonna get us thrown out on the first full day."

"I'll keep this as brief as possible." Isaac said with a smile as he stood at the head of the table. "I know you're all still tired and you've had little to eat. None of us here can imagine what you've been through out there, but now you are here with us."

Isaac reached down and grabbed a cup of water that had been placed in front of him.

"I'd like to toast to your liberation." He said raising his cup. "For those of you who choose to return to your families, we wish you safe travels. We will give you enough supplies for your journey home. For those of you who wish to stay here, it'll take some time to get your spaces ready, but you can live here as our family. We welcome you with open arms."

Many of the miners were smiling and a few were even wiping tears from their eyes, having not seen such kindness in many years. Everyone took a sip from their cups as Isaac, Agatha, and the others began to serve the people their plates. The miners were ecstatic at the sight of a plate of chicken breasts, grapes, and potatoes being placed before them. Eva sat at the far end of the table next to an empty chair that was meant for Grace. She looked around the room at all the people and at her own plate. She maintained a blank stare on her face as Agatha touched her hand to her shoulder.

"Enjoy your meal." Agatha said with a smile.

Meanwhile outside, just above ground where the fake tree stump hid the hatch entrance, Dale paced around, having been asked by Isaac to keep his eyes out for Parker. He watched as the sun began to set in the distance beyond the cliff. He turned and began to pace away from the cliff as an arrow flew out of nowhere and entered his forehead, killing him instantly.

Several soldiers exited the forest, each with bows ready to take down anything that crossed their path. Lao followed closely behind them, holding a small device in his hand. It had a small screen that displayed a map of the area. A white dot indicated his position, while a red dot blinked on the screen. He smiled as he saw the white dot overtake the blinking red.

"They are below us." Lao said smiling. "Find the entrance."

It wasn't long until one solider lifted the stump over the hatch and dropped in a smoke bomb.

"Go!" Lao shouted.

The soldiers quickly put on gasmasks as they entered the tunnels below and began shooting arrows into the heads of anyone they came across or just simply cut them down with a sword. One by one, the guards of the underground community were taken out until they finally reached the door to the dining hall. Lao placed his ear against the door and could hear people talking and laughing.

"Time to ring the dinner bell." He said softly.

The doors to the dining room blasted open with quick intensity, followed immediately by Lao and his soldiers. Any man that drew a weapon was quickly taken out by Lao's forces. One soldier aimed an arrow at Isaac and was ready to release the bowstring before Lao grabbed it and stopped him.

"Wait!" Lao ordered as he approached Isaac. "I know this one."

The community and the miners were all pulled away from the table and shoved against the wall.

"You look just like your father." Lao said to Isaac.

"What do you want?" Isaac asked.

"I want to join in the celebration!" Lao answered drawing everyone's attention to the table. "Look at this! Where do you find all of this? Do you grow these yourselves?"

"Take whatever you want, just leave these people in peace."

"I think I'll do just that." Lao said waving a soldier over to him. "Search the bunker, find their garden, and bag up everything. Leave nothing behind."

"Yes sir."

The soldier did as he was told, taking a few of the other soldiers along with him. Lao searched the faces and spotted Eva against the wall among the others.

"Oh, look who it is!" He said pointing her out. "You forgot to say goodbye before."

A soldier grabbed Eva by the arm and pulled her to her feet. The soldier forced her over to Lao who immediately slapped her in the face. Isaac started to move over to attack Lao but was stopped by one of his men.

"We've got a lot to discuss." Lao said angrily to Eva.

Just outside the dining room a little further down the tunnel, Ox and Grace walked side by side on their way to the feast. Grace was feeling better, and she was excited to sit down for a large meal. Ox had talked it up quite a bit and they were a little disappointed they were late to the party, but they had good reason. Ox's smile quickly disappeared as he saw a soldier rushing down the tunnel, his bow already aimed.

"Look out!" Ox said as he pushed Grace out of the way of the incoming arrow. The arrow grazed Ox's arm, as it flew passed. He quickly rushed toward the soldier before he could retrieve another arrow from his quiver. Using his size to his advantage, Ox punched the soldier in the face, and then lifted him up slamming his head into the ceiling of the tunnel, rendering him unconscious. Another soldier began to rush down the tunnel toward them, but Ox had already pulled a dagger from his belt and threw it into the approaching enemies' shoulder. He quickly rushed over and punched the man hard in the head knocking him out instantly.

"What's happening?" Grace said.

"I'm not sure, go back to my quarters and wait for me." Ox answered.

"Ox no!"

"Do as I say child!" He said. "I will be back for you!"

Ox watched as Grace hesitantly retreated down the tunnel. He proceeded to the outer door of the dining room, slowly turning the handle, and cracking the door to peek inside. He could clearly see Lao standing before Eva and Isaac. His soldiers surrounded the room with their bows ready to fire at the slightest protest.

"Any word on Wallace?" Lao asked a soldier.

"We're still searching Sir." A soldier replied. "It looks like he didn't make it back yet."

"What of the artifact?"

"Also unknown Sir."

"Perhaps someone else could tell us where to find it." He said to Eva.

"I don't know what you're talking about." Eva responded.

"Come now, you know exactly what I'm talking about." He said with a smile. "It's the very reason we sent you here."

Isaac, Agatha, and many of the others were shocked to hear Lao's words. Even Ox was caught by surprise as he stayed hidden behind the door.

"Don't." Eva whispered.

"How do you all think I could possibly find this place so easily?" Lao said as he held up the tracking monitor he had used to find the signal. "That's right." Lao continued as he pulled a small blinking device from Eva's pocket. "This little device led us right to you."

"We welcomed you into our home." Agatha said to Eva.

Eva was at a loss for words.

"Tell me they planted that on you." Isaac said.

"I'm sorry." Eva said sincerely. "He gave me no choice. They only want the orb."

Lao then tossed both the tracker and the small blinking device to the ground as he glared into Eva's eyes.

"Now, Eva." He said quietly. "Where is the artifact? You were supposed to have it ready when I got here."

"I don't know." She said shaking her head. "It isn't here."

It was then a soldier entered the opposite door of the dining room holding the orb in his hand.

"No." Ox said to himself.

"Then what's this?" Lao said as the soldier handed him the artifact.

"All right, you've got what you wanted." Isaac said. "Please just take it and go. We don't want more trouble."

"It's not that simple." Lao said. "I've been ordered to bring you back with me."

"Then so be it. I'll go willingly, just leave this place in peace."

"No!" Agatha shouted as she ran to Isaac.

One of Lao's soldiers grabbed Agatha by the hair, pulling her backwards and shoved her to the ground.

"Take your hands off of her!" Isaac shouted.

Lao then punched Isaac in the face, knocking him to the ground as well.

"I give the orders around here." Lao said.

"You have the artifact!" Eva proclaimed. "Please, there is no need for this!"

"I am not a man without mercy." Lao said turning back to Eva.

He nodded his head to his men who immediately placed their bows over their shoulders and then each drew their own pulse powered sidearm's.

"Shoot them all in the head." Lao ordered.

"No!" Isaac shouted.

His words were lost to the others screams as one by one Lao and his men shot everyone in the head rendering each of them unconscious in an instant. Ox watched in horror from the other side of the door, frantically trying to come up with an idea to help that wouldn't get everyone killed. Isaac jumped to his feet to protect his wife, but Lao quickly turned and fired the pulse gun into both of his legs, forcing him to fall to the ground yet again.

"You monster!" Isaac said dragging himself toward Agatha.

"Lao!" Eva shouted. "You said you didn't want to hurt anyone. You only wanted the orb. You've got it!"

Eva looked at all the people she had tried to help free only to realize that it was her fault that this was happening to them now. She felt the wave of guilt wash over her. Lao looked around the room and then grabbed a piece of chicken from a plate on the table.

"This is quite a place here, but really, it isn't safe outside the walls of Dublin. People need to understand that Roland provides safety and security. How can we allow people to struggle so hard out here? It isn't humane." He said as he took a big bite of meat.

Two soldiers grabbed Isaac and began dragging him out of the room, but before they could exit completely Lao shouted an order to halt.

"Let's leave a clear message for Parker, should he return." Lao stated. "Burn everything."

"You said you had mercy." Eva shouted.

"I didn't lie." Lao said in his defense. "They are all unconscious. They won't feel a thing."

"No!" Ox shouted as he barged into the room.

He quickly took out the first soldier he came across grabbing his pulse gun and using the soldier as a human shield. Lao's men fired at him as he was forced back to the doors of the dining area. Eva took cover under the table as Lao grabbed a bow and arrow from one of his men. One soldier grabbed Eva from under the table and dragged her to the exit along with Isaac.

"Agatha!" Isaac shouted.

Lao smiled as he wrapped a cloth around the tip of his arrow and dipped it into a bottle of a strong smelling substance he had pulled from his pouch. Another of his men lit the cloth with a flame and with a quick aim, the flaming arrow was released into the table. Ox fired back as the human shield he'd been hiding behind fell to the ground unable to take any more hits for his captor.

Lao and four of his men began dousing the room with a flammable liquid they had brought with them, soaking the floor all over. They tossed bottles of the substance all over shattering them to pieces. As Ox was about to dart over to Agatha and pull her to safety a large flame burst between them, forcing Ox to retreat to the door he had entered through.

"Burn it all!" Lao shouted.

"What about the people sir?" A soldier asked.

"What of them?" He replied coldly.

Ox shouted at the words. He had no way to move around the room as the fire spread far too quickly. Grace entered through the doors behind him shouting his name as she saw the flames building in front of him.

"Ox!"

Tears filled his eyes as he made several attempts to reach into the fire to pull anyone he could to safety, but it was no use. He couldn't reach anyone through the flames intense heat. He again made several attempts to reach through to grab Agatha's arm. He stood as close as he could. His arm began to burn as the flame violently kissed his wrist all the way up to his elbow.

"Ox please!" Grace shouted again.

The flames were getting higher and spreading even faster. Grace didn't have a choice. She ran to Ox and pulled at his shirt as hard she could until he could no longer ignore her. They quickly exited the room and slammed the door behind them. Ox let out a loud roaring scream of anger knowing that on the other side of that door, his friends and family were burning to death. He was full of rage, unable to control his outburst. He slammed his fists against the door, scaring Grace to the point she had no choice but to back away. Ox dropped to his knees, his fists still banging on the door which began to burn from the heat within.

"Please." Grace said with tears filling her eyes. "We have to get out of here."

Ox took a step back as smoke began to seep through the cracks. He wiped the sweat and tears from his face and stood to his feet. Grace was with him, and he needed to keep her safe. He turned quickly and grabbed her hand as they raced back to his room. Once inside he ran to the curtain and jerked it from the wall completely. He reached down and lifted Grace to the window.

"Hug the cliff as best you can." Ox said. "I am right behind you."

Ox ran around the room grabbing a small hatchet from the corner, and a dagger on a shelf. It was all he had left after his capture before since they took his weapons. He quickly exited the room behind Grace. They stood on a ledge just outside. As they made their way as far over as they could Ox looked up to see the top of the cliff. It was going to be a bit of a climb, but Ox was strong and would surely be able to do it.

"I need you to do something." He said as he tucked the hatchet into his belt. "I want you to climb onto my back and wrap your arms around my shoulders."

"Are you crazy?" She asked looking down at the rocky waters below.

"We have to get to the top. If you hold on tight, I will get us there."

"You promise you won't fall?"

"I promise you; I will not fall." He said with determination.

Grace nodded her head and reached up to grab Ox's shoulders. He bent down as much as he could while still hugging up to the wall. Once Grace was holding on tightly, he began his ascent up the rocky cliffside. It was the hardest climb he had ever had to make. As he progressed further, Grace could see the smoke emerging from his room down below. The fire had spread through the entire bunker. She shut her eyes tight as she held on to Ox. He was pouring sweat as he inched higher and higher. The climb felt as if it was taking forever. His arm burned with every stretch, but he was strong. He was not about to give up. The top of the cliff was within reach, and they were only seconds away before they would be standing on a flat surface.

"I will not fall."

CHAPTER TWENTY-THREE

Parker rushed out of the forest only to find smoke and flames rushing up from where the hatch was once hidden.

"Oh God no!" He said looking into the entrance to the underground tunnels.

He dropped to his knees putting his hands on his head in confusion. He could feel the tears beginning to fill his eyes, completely lost in what to do. It was then he could see in the darkness ahead of him two figures approaching him. Their images made blurry by the flames. Parker had no weapons on him, having lost everything back at the train. He was still ready for a fight, but then he felt a slight bit of relief to see Ox and Grace moving closer to him.

"Ox!" He said as he ran to his friend.

Ox immediately dropped to his knees, partly in exhaustion, but more in sorrow. Parker began to slow his steps as he was only a few feet away from them.

"What happened?" Parker asked, praying in the back of his mind for an answer he knew he wasn't going to get.

"I am so sorry my friend." Ox cried. "I tried."

"My brother?"

"They took him, along with Eva." Grace answered.

"Agatha?"

"I tried to get to her, but I couldn't!" Ox continued to say revealing the burns on his arm to Parker.

Parker dropped to his knees in front of Ox and hugged his friend as the two of them cried at the loss of their family.

"I'm sorry Ox." Parker cried. "I wasn't here."

Grace watched, filled with sadness as the two men cried together. She walked to their side and placed her hands on both of their shoulders. After a few moments passed, Parker stood and looked around, uncertain of what to do next.

"Where did they take Isaac?" Parker asked.

"We are not sure." Ox answered as he stood to his feet. "It was Lao that came."

"How is that even possible? I took every alternate trail I could to keep people from finding this place. How could he even get here before me?"

"Because he had help. Your friend led them right to us."

"Eva? She wouldn't do that."

"She did!" Ox shouted. "We trusted her, and she brought them right to our home. She betrayed us and every death is on her head!"

"No, why would she?" Parker asked himself in confusion.

"I don't know what her reason was, but it's true. She had a tracker on her that Lao followed. She was not who you thought she was."

"There has to be another explanation." Parker said shaking his head.

It was truly unbearable. Isaac and Eva had been taken, his sister-in-law was dead, and a great number of people Parker called family were gone in one night.

"We have to assume they went back to Dublin." Ox said.

"You think they took Isaac there?" Parker asked.

"They must have. Parker, they took the purple orb from your backpack."

"Oh crap." Parker said in shock.

"What is it?" Grace asked.

"I'm not sure exactly. We have to go after them. We have to get them both and the orb back."

"Didn't you hear what I said?" Ox asked with a hint of anger. "Eva was manipulating you this whole time."

"I heard you Ox, but we still need her."

"What could we possibly need her for? Unless we plan to make her answer for all that she has done here. Every person we lost tonight is because of her."

"There has to be more to this. Eva wouldn't do…"

"She did do this!" Ox inturppted. "She brought the tracker! It was not planted on her!"

"I can't accept that Ox. I can't believe that she did this for her own personal gain."

"Why can't you? You've known this woman a few days."

"It's hard to explain right now, but you have to trust me. There's more to it then you realize."

Ox thought for a moment and nodded his head. He knew Parker well enough that he wouldn't act without a good reason. He trusted his friend without hesitation.

"What do we do?" Ox asked.

"We need to make our way to Dublin as soon as possible."

"It is about a two and a half days trip if we want to stay hidden."

"How do we get inside when we get there?" Grace asked.

"Excuse me, you aren't going." Parker said.

"I can help."

"You're just a kid. We'll drop you off somewhere safe along the way."

"I can fight too."

"That's not happening." Parker said firmly.

"She did fight off a couple of demons back at the train all by herself." Ox said. "She is not helpless."

"It's not a good idea." Parker said. "What is she? Ten?"

"I'm thirteen, I think." Grace said almost in tears. "I don't have anywhere else to go. I want to stay with you guys."

Parker could see the look on both Grace and Ox's faces. Who was he to make decisions for them?

"All right, I guess you're not gonna give me much choice, are you?" Parker asked.

"Before we go, we should get a couple of hours rest." Ox said. "We can make for the old shack."

"We need to go after them now. We can't wait around too long."

"Parker, they took Isaac and Eva for a reason. They probably need them alive. We need time to plan, and you need time to rest. We will go to the shack and wait a couple of hours."

"All right, I get it." Parker said.

Ox walked over to Parker and placed his hand on his shoulder.

"We need to take the time to mourn." Ox said. "You need a clear head for what we are about to face."

Parker agreed with Ox. He was angry, he was confused and little more than a wreck as he stood at the graveyard of what was once his home. The journey ahead was going to be rough, and he couldn't help but wonder what Eva's intentions were. He wouldn't know for sure until he could find her again, but for the time being, he needed to think of a way to get her and his brother back from Lao as well as find out what was going on. Parker walked close to the edge of the cliff and looked out toward the sea. He kneeled and bowed his head, saying a prayer for those he had lost.

Isaac leaned his head against the barred windows of the wagon Lao and his men were using to transport him in. He was still feeling the numb tingle in his legs as he had to pull himself with his arms to make any kind of movements, which also proved difficult as his wrists were tied together in restraint. Eva sat on the other side of the confined space, her hands also tied together, as well as her ankles. She had no desire to be close to Isaac, keeping herself out of arms reach of him. Isaac was angry, and Eva knew that she was the last person that could calm him down. Outside of the carriage, Eva could see Lao and his men, escorting their mobile prison on their own horses. It was too quiet. The only sound that could be heard was the footsteps of the horses as they slowly walked on the road.

"Isaac, I'm so sorry." Eva said, going against her better judgment.

She was being weighed down with guilt from what had happened. She kept telling herself that it wasn't her fault. She had no idea what Lao would do, but inside her own mind, she struggled with the thought. Did she really not know what Lao would do or was she so desperate that she ignored her own conscience.

"I didn't mean for any of this to happen." Eva said fighting back tears.

"Don't speak to me!" Isaac shouted as he turned his attention to Eva. "They may have killed them, but you led them directly to us!"

Eva flinched at his words and turned her attention away as tears began to flow down her cheeks.

"You don't understand…" Eva began.

"There is no understanding!" Isaac interrupted. "You can't excuse yourself from what you've done! My wife! My family! They are all dead because of you!"

The words pierced Eva's heart as if they were knives. She turned her head shamefully away from Isaac, who also turned his attention to the view outside the bars. Lao could hear the entire conversation from outside. He couldn't help but smile at the turn of events. Soon, they would be back in Dublin, and the real show would begin.

Ox and Grace sat on the floor of the old shack in the woods. It was just a small shelter Isaac and Parker had used before they began the underground community. Over the years they would store supplies there that they could use in an emergency, but also get some rest should they be too tired to travel home. It was tucked away in a heavily secluded area, so it was extremely hard to find for anyone who didn't already know where it was. Parker sat on the edge of a small cot located in the bedroom of the small shack. He hadn't even tried to lay down to sleep. He knew he needed to rest, but so much had happened and his mind wouldn't let him relax.

He looked up from the floor to see ghostly images walking around him. He watched as people moved passed him carrying pocketbooks and cell phones. Suddenly he saw himself sitting at a table with a half-eaten sandwich sitting on a plate in front of him.

He found himself staring at dozens of people in the food court of the outlet mall he worked security for a long ago. Parker could see teenage girls taking selfies and making kiss faces to their cameras. He watched people enjoying their meal, all the while looking at their cell phones, barely conversing with the person across from them. Just as quickly as it all appeared around him, they began to fade away, becoming ghostly images once again. He surveyed the room only to find himself sitting on the cot again with nothing but a wood floor and broken windows surrounding him.

"What do you dream about?" Eva asked Parker.

Parker stood alongside Eva on the Avalon beach overlooking the ocean. He had several cuts on his face from training with Sang and Arthur just hours ago.

"What do you mean?" He asked her in return.

"Before all of this." She replied. "Before you came here, and after this is all over."

Parker thought for a moment as he looked out to the sky above the water. It was a beautiful day and as he glanced back at Eva, he felt his heart skip a beat. She was absolutely breathtaking.

"Family." He answered. "I used to dream about having a family."

Eva was invested in his words. She smiled as the wind blew her hair in her face and she brushed her bangs out of her eyes. Parker reached down and picked up a seashell and gave a hard toss into the water.

"People always talk about the next big thing." He continued. "I want a new car, or a new house. That stuff is nice and all, but family was always more important to me."

"Why?" Eva asked still smiling.

"Because I never truly had one."

Eva reached out for Parkers' hand and squeezed it tight. The two of them began walking along the shore as she gently hugged his arm.

"Sounds good to me." She said.

"Parker?" Ox said knocking as he entered the room and snapping Parker back from his newfound memory. He stood up and dusted off the back of his jeans. He wasn't sure how long he'd been sitting there to tell the truth, but it felt like a while. His thoughts were all over the place. Eva was the most prominent. The woman from these memories he had and the person he just recently met seemed both one and the same, but also incredibly different. Who was she to him before? Who is she now?

"How are we looking on supplies?" Parker asked pushing Eva to the back of his mind.

"We do not have much." Ox answered.

"Guess I took a little more than I left."

"Were you able to get any sleep?"

"I got enough. What do we have?"

Ox pulled a slightly torn backpack with a broken strap from his shoulder and placed it on the floor in front of him.

"We have six throwing knives, a couple of flashlights, a half-empty first aid kit, one empty canteen which we can fill at the lake nearby, and a few cans of food with no labels."

"What about Isaacs' bow?"

Ox grabbed the backpack and led Parker to the front room of the shack. He lifted a couple of floorboards to reveal a compound bow and quiver with nine arrows inside.

"It's basically the only real weapon we have." Ox said picking up the bow and handing it to Parker.

"It'll have to do." Parker said as he pulled back the bowstring.

"I know how to use one of those." Grace said pointing at the bow.

"Not this time kid." Parker responded.

Ox grabbed three of the knives from the backpack and handed them to Grace. She looked up at him curiously as she placed them in her pockets.

"If you are traveling with us you need to be able to protect yourself." Ox said. "You are only to use them in an emergency."

"I understand." Grace said nodding her head.

"It's time to get moving." Parker said as he placed the quiver over his shoulder.

The three of them headed out of the shack and made their way into the forested area toward the road that would lead them to Dublin. Though nature had taken over most of the world, some roads managed to remain intact. Most were overtaken by grass and trees had grown for so long the roots had broken through the roadways beside them. Parker and the others walked a few miles and came to what used to be a roundabout. There were a few houses and old businesses that still stood but were so run down they weren't fit for living in or much else. There were also several older vehicles scattered about in the parking lots and some even left in the streets.

WARRIOR FROM AVALON

None of the vehicles had wheels. Cars had become much more technologically advanced before everything went bad. There wasn't a need for gas as most cars had been adapted to solar and electric energy. They would often have a system in place where they could even drive themselves. Cars didn't exactly fly, as advanced as they were, but powerful magnets were placed in the undercarriage of all vehicles, and other magnets were buried under the roads themselves, causing the vehicles to hover as the magnets repelled each other. The vehicles were propelled forward using a thruster type adaptation.

Even the roads were more digitized. There was no longer a need for red lights or hanging indicators. If a car was supposed to stop so others could pass by going a different direction, a barrier would rise out of the road forcing the vehicle to a complete stop. It also had a repelling field so that cars wouldn't crash into it at high speeds. Once it was the other cars turn to pass, the barrier would lower back down and raise itself up on the other side. It wasn't a perfect system, but accidents had decreased significantly.

The roads could also display letters to inform drivers of an accident ahead or road work. They flashed quickly to inform the driver in a decent amount of time to prepare for the inconvenience. At that point in time, it was just how life was. Parker had been born way too far after it to really see its benefits. Now it was as if it were all dead and useless. Not a single car was in working condition. Not that they wanted to draw that kind of attention. Ox walked to a sign at one end of the roundabout.

"R 420." He read. "This is the right way. Let's get back into the wooded area and keep going North West."

"Why don't we just stay on the road?" Grace asked. "Wouldn't it be faster to just go straight and not take chances getting lost?"

"We need to keep behind the buildings and stay within the trees to keep out of sight." Parker answered. "Roland still has plenty of pirates and soldiers that would rob us and kill us if they catch us out on the streets."

"If we push hard enough, we can get to Dublin by tomorrow evening." Ox spoke.

Ox and Grace began walking ahead of Parker. He let them get a few paces ahead and did a quick look back to make sure they weren't being followed. Once he was certain there was no one around he caught up to the other two. After a couple of hours hiking through the woods, they decided to take a break. Ox passed Grace the old canteen they had salvaged from the shack. They had managed to make a quick stop and fill it full of water before the trip. Then there was a howl in the distance that immediately caught their attention.

"What was that?" Grace asked.

"Cheesy peaches." Parker muttered to himself.

"Was that a wolf?" Ox asked.

"Wolves, plural."

"Weren't they extinct in Ireland?" Grace asked.

"Not since the late 2200s." Parker answered. "Something about genetic recreation and animal activists bringing them back to the area. I read a book about it when I was younger."

"Well I never saw one." Grace whispered.

"We've had our fair share of encounters." Ox said softly.

Parker pulled the bow from his shoulder as they heard another howl getting closer. Ox pulled one of the throwing knives from his belt and gripped it tight.

"They're just wild dogs, right?" Grace asked. "How much trouble could they be?" Parker squinted to see a wolf in the bushes just a few feet ahead of them.

"Lots." He said as he pulled an arrow from his quiver and drew back the bowstring. "Especially when their hungry."

Parker took a deep breath and waited for his moment. The wolf was snarling its teeth, ready to attack at any sudden moves. It was growling and licking its lips as if it were already tasting the flesh of the three people before it. Parker aimed his arrow, still holding his breath. Slowly the wolf was inching forward from the bush, saliva dripping from its mouth. Parker exhaled as he set the arrow free from his bow.

CHAPTER TWENTY-FOUR

The arrow flew fast as it missed its mark and bounced off a nearby tree, missing the target completely.

"You need to work on your aim a bit." Lucas said as he paced behind Parker.

"That's putting it mildly." Parker said.

The two men stood in an open field just behind Lucas' cabin. There were large man-sized dummy targets scattered along the field at different distances. Some already had holes in them from where Lucas himself would practice. Parker was aiming at a target Lucas had set up over seventy yards away.

"There are many factors in archery. You have to consider the environment around you. Is there wind, is the target moving, how far away is it. You've got to quickly consider all of these things before you even draw the bowstring."

Parker grabbed another arrow from a table sitting in front of him.

"What kind of bow did you use before?" Parker asked.

"I was familiar with every bow you could think of in my time period." Lucas answered. "Since my arrival here time progressed, and I was granted every bow in existence to practice with. So far anyway."

"Which one is your favorite?"

"I really like the one you're using now. The recurve bow, but I do like how the compound bow is a bit more tactical."

"I'd take a good old-fashioned crossbow. That'll do some damage."

"That's too easy. The real skill is in a longbow."

Lucas grabbed the bow from Parkers' hand and picked up an arrow from the table. He pulled the bowstring back and fired at a target more than ninety yards in front of them. The arrow found its place directly between where the eyes would be on the target dummy.

"Don't lean back, and don't lean forward." Lucas said. "Keep your feet shoulder length apart, and rotate your elbow so that it bends sideways, not to the ground."

Lucas grabbed another arrow from the table and drew back the bowstring. Parker watched as Lucas released the arrow, and once again, the arrow hit its mark between the eyes of the same dummy, splitting the arrow that had been shot there only a moment ago in half.

"That my friend is called a Robin Hood." Lucas said with a grin.

"You're kidding me." Parker said in surprise. "I didn't think that was really possible. How did you do that?"

"Most archers have a one in three thousand chance of hitting that mark, but I've had a few hundred years to practice."

Lucas returned the bow back to Parker, who gripped it tightly in his hand. He grabbed another arrow from the table and pulled the string back.

"Don't grip it so tight." Lucas instructed. "Relax your fingers on the bow, and when you pull back the string, breathe in. You should exhale as you release the arrow."

Parker did as instructed. He relaxed as much as he possibly could and pulled the string back yet again. He took a deep breath as he focused hard on his target. The wind gently caressed his cheek and with a long exhale, he released the arrow into the air.

The wolf fell dead to the ground as the arrow hit directly between its eyes. Parker quickly grabbed another arrow from his quiver and drew back the bowstring to prepare for another to appear. Sure enough, four more wolves darted out of the bushes and trees, snarling, and barking as they rushed toward him and the others. In rapid succession, Parker shot each wolf in a matter of seconds, each arrow making headshot after headshot. Ox and Grace looked in amazement at the speed and accuracy Parker had displayed. Parker looked around to see all the wolves lying dead around him.

"How in the world?" He asked, stunned at his own skill.

"These creatures will go extinct again with you around my friend." Ox said as he stood to his feet. "I didn't think you used a bow in a while, have you been practicing again?"

"Sure." Parker said still surprised. "I think we should get moving. We only have a couple of hours until sunrise."

Parker approached each wolf and retrieved the arrows he had used to dispatch them. He felt bad for killing them, but in the current situation, it was the only option. After they had gathered what little gear they had, the three of them began making their trek through the forest again.

It was a long trip before the three of them reached the outer walls of Dublin. They would stop every so often to rest, but none of them got more than a couple of hours sleep at a time. At this point, the afternoon Sun was slowly peeking out above the trees in the distance. They stood in awe as the walls stretched into the sky before them.

"Well that's high." Parker stated the obvious.

"How are we supposed to get inside that?" Grace asked.

"We can't go around." Ox answered. "This wall must stretch around the entire city."

"Well we're not going over either." Parker answered.

The wall stood at two hundred feet and stretched from side to side, too far for Parker to even guess its circumference.

"Where do you think the entrance is?" Parker asked.

"With all of the roads to enter the city, I imagine we could go either way and find one, but it's not like they're going to just let us walk right in." Ox answered.

"We have to get in somehow." Parker said. "I guess we'll improvise as usual."

It didn't take them too long to walk around as the three of them had to duck behind some trees once they reached an entrance into the city. There were at least six sentries posted at a gate standing at about fifty feet tall. Parker watched as a horse and buggy pulled up to the gate and one sentry pushed up on a lever that electronically lifted the gate. Once the driver had pulled inside, the sentry pulled the lever back down and the gate closed.

"They have power." Ox said. "They must be using the cities old power station."

The sentry who had opened the gate returned to the other five and stood guard once again.

"Do we take them out?" Grace asked.
Parker and Ox both looked at Grace and shook their heads.

"Easy there tough gal." Parker said. "If we take them down, somebody is sure to notice. If they have power, they may have ways of communicating between outposts. I'm almost sure this isn't the only entrance that has guards."

"What do we do then?" Grace asked.

"I'm still working on it."

Parker and the others moved in closely but quietly so they could assess the situation more thoroughly. They watched as the sentries were all talking amongst themselves, but there was no way they wouldn't notice the three of them trying to slip passed them. Parker was racking his brain at an idea to get through. He could easily take each of them out with his arrows. He had enough but didn't want to kill them. Just as the thought entered his mind, one sentry reached for a radio attached to his shoulder. The radio was loud enough that Parker could hear voices speaking clearly through it.

"Entry point one, all clear." It broadcasted loudly.

Each of the other gates stated their status one right after another. Finally, the guard in front of Parker stated his situation.

"Entry point eight, all clear." He said.

Parker and the others listened and waited while they tried to come up with a plan. The radio had gone through eighteen entry points before it went silent again. After about thirty minutes passed the check-in began again.

"Entry point eight, all clear." The sentry repeated.

Parker and Ox ducked back down behind some bushes where Grace had been patiently waiting.

"Okay, these guys check-in with each other about every thirty minutes or so." Parker said. "If we take them out, all of the other guards are going to know something is up. We aren't going to have enough time before someone catches on."

"Could we wait for the next round, let them clear it and then move in?" Grace asked.

"No." Ox answered. "Even if we did, after we're inside, there will still be no one to answer the next call. It could cause an alarm within the city. That could cause a lockdown and then we'd do what?"

"We have to get through that gate, without alerting anyone." Parker said.

"Do we wait for another wagon to come through, or find some disguises?" Ox asked.

"That could be a long wait." Parker answered. "We may not have that kind of time."

"I could act like I'm in trouble and lure them away." Grace said.

"I don't think that would work either. These guys don't look too stupid."

"Well, why don't we just knock them out and take the radio with us?"

Parker and Ox looked at Grace curiously, then to each other.

"Why not?" Ox asked. "That would make the most sense."

"All right then." Parker agreed. "That could work. You might be useful after all kid."

It was a few minutes later Grace watched from a safe place while Ox and Parker had managed to sneak a little closer. From her viewpoint, she was able to see all six guards. Parker and Ox stayed hidden behind some shrubbery. It felt like forever, but they knew they had to wait for the next round of check-ins before they could attack. Parker had estimated about thirty minutes had passed when the voice on the radio came through again.

"Get ready." Parker whispered to Ox.

The two of them waited patiently for their gate to clear. Entry point seven cleared and the guard with the radio did his mandatory check-in.

"Entry point eight, all clear." The guard said.

Parker and Ox rushed out silently and quickly as they dispatched the first two guards in the front. Parker reached out and grabbed Ox's hand and the two men clotheslined a third guard. The last three guards were still trying to collect their thoughts as the attack completely came out of nowhere. Ox managed to punch two of the other guards in the face rendering them unconscious easily. Parker grabbed the guard holding the radio, ripping the device from his shoulder, and flipping him forward onto his back. He then kicked the man sharply in the head, knocking him out. With all six guards down, Grace ran to catch up from the forested area she had been hiding in.

"We need something to tie them up." Parker told Ox as he began dragging the unconscious guards to the wooded area out of sight.

After a few moments passed, all six guards were placed around the base of a large tree. Each guard's hands were zip-tied to the guard next to him. Ox had even found some cloth to place in each guard's mouth, so as they regained consciousness, they wouldn't be able to cry out for help. One guard had already begun to open his eyes as Parker placed the wadded cloth into his mouth.

"I feel a little bad about this." Parker said sincerely. "Your boss is a jerk though, so maybe not that much."

Parker stood up, turned down the volume on the radio and placed it in his back pocket. Afterward, he quickly joined Ox and Grace at the large gate. Ox lifted the lever allowing the gate to rise. Parker and Grace ran under and entered the city. Ox had decided to leave the gate open as he caught up to the others.

"We may need to get out quickly." Ox said patting Parker on the back. "Let's just remember which gate we came in."

"Good thinking."

"Oh, what about our weapons?" Grace said. "Your bow and arrows are going to stand out."

"She's right." Ox said.

"All right." Parker said. "Only carry what we can conceal."

Parker removed the quiver from his shoulder and tossed it into the bushes beside them. He took the bow and reluctantly did the same with it.

The three of them began to walk a long path which had large stone walls on either side. An opening could be seen straight ahead, which led directly into the city. As they came to the end of the stone path, Parker, Ox, and Grace couldn't believe the sight before them. From their view, a large stone palace could be seen in the long distance ahead. It seemed so big that it was certainly located in the direct center of the city. On either side were towering buildings, neither reached the heights of the palace itself, but both were connected via catwalks and bridges.

All around them were people walking along the city sidewalks. Buildings were placed all around, and some of them were at least ten to twenty stories high. The roads were in working condition as Parker watched multiple hovering cars pass by them. A large digital barrier stopped a couple of the hover cars from driving through an intersection. Another barrier on the side lowered so more cars could pass instead.

Parker was speechless. He hadn't seen a city so massive still thriving as the one before him. He looked to the left at a restaurant where people were sitting at an outside dining area, enjoying meals that he hadn't seen since his past life. Everything looked so normal, like they had traveled back in time to a period before ash demons, and pirates. It was an amazing sight.

"I had no idea that Dublin was so…" Ox began to say.

"Advanced?" Parker asked.

"Uh…yeah." Grace said.

"Parker, this doesn't look like a city enslaved."

"Yeah, I know. Appearances can be deceiving."

"How is this possible?" Grace asked.

"Roland must have ensured his city was in prime shape. People don't ask questions when they have no reason to."

As the three of them began to walk further into the city, Grace noticed a poster attached to a wall just outside of a small building. The poster had a 3D picture of Parkers' face, spinning around slowly. Words were written just above his head.

"Wanted?" Grace said as she pointed the poster out to Parker and Ox.

Parker looked at the image of his face spinning in circles and ripped the wanted poster from the wall.

"Wanted," Parker began to read, "For acts of terrorism against the city of Dublin, disrupting supply lines entering the city, the murder of innocent citizens, kidnapping, robbery, arson, and conspiring against the King?"

"That's quite a list." Ox said.

"It's a scare tactic." Parker replied. "As long as the people are afraid of me, they won't question him. I'm a scapegoat to his crimes. Aside from the supply lines stuff. I did that."

"Uh, guys." Grace said getting their attention.

Parker and Ox looked to see Grace pointing at several posters that were scattered around the busy city streets.

"I think it's safe to say, you're going to be popular around here." Grace said.

"Cheesy peaches, that's bad." Parker said. "People are going to spot me in no time flat."

"I think I have an idea." Ox said as he pointed to a clothing store.

Ox and Grace entered the store leaving Parker standing in an alley to the side. Ox searched the racks looking at all the fashionable suits and shirts displayed. He even spotted a couple of mannequins wearing dark blue hoodies and sunglasses.

"This might work." Ox said as he reached for the hoody on the mannequin.

"Excuse me, what are you doing?" A voice asked. Ox turned around and spotted a young woman staring at him.

"I would like to trade for this." Ox said nervously.

"That's the display apparel. The items for trade are right over there."

"Of course, I'm sorry." Ox said clearing his throat. "I did not see it."

WARRIOR FROM AVALON

The female employee rolled her eyes and walked away as Ox walked over to the shelf and picked up the blue hoody. He raised his eyes to see Grace had vanished.

"Grace?" He called out.

Ox began to search the store frantically, only to spot Grace sitting on a small bench with her old shoes tossed to the side. She placed a pair of boots on her feet and smiled when she looked up at Ox.

"Don't disappear like that please." Ox said softly as he approached her.

"What do you think?" She asked holding her foot out to show off her new boots.

"I think they look great. We need to go."

"How are we going to pay for these?"

"Pay?"

Grace then pointed to a sign on top of the shelf where she had picked up her boots.

"300 credits?" Ox read. "This is a city of thieves."

Ox looked around and saw a sign that said Employee's only and through a small window an exit sign.

He grabbed Grace by the hand and the two slowly made their way to the back. As he passed by a rack of large brown trench coats, he looked around and pulled it from the hanger. He and Grace then snuck out of the building through the back entrance and met with Parker in the alley. Ox tossed the hoody to Parker who immediately put it on, zipping up the front, and pulling the hood over his head.

"What is that for?" Parker asked as he saw Ox putting on the trench coat.

"I have never found a jacket my size anywhere in our travels." Ox said. "Do not deny me this."

"Fair enough." Parker said nodding his head.

"That was a really cool place." Grace said impressed. "I'd steal from there again."

WARRIOR FROM AVALON

"I can't believe Roland has this whole city working." Ox said. "It's like the outside world has no affect here."

"A place of this size would have attracted the Ash demons long ago." Parker replied. "Roland really does have a deal with them."

The three of them made their way back to the city sidewalks.

"We need to assume that Isaac and Eva are in there somewhere." Parker said pointing to the large palace in the distance. "We just need to find a way in."

It was then the radio began to speak in Parkers' back pocket. They stepped off to the side to remain incognito. Ox and Grace provided cover while Parker ducked down a bit and waited for gate seven to say all clear.

"Entry point eight, all clear." He said in a slightly gruff voice.

"Do you think that worked?" Grace asked.

Parker shrugged his shoulders as there was silence on the other end of the radio for a moment, then finally they heard Entry point nine give the all-clear. The three of them exhaled in relief.

"Let's go." Parker said returning the radio to his pocket.

Just as they began to walk again, speakers all over the city began to play loud music which caused everyone around to stop in their tracks. The music sounded like trumpets as if they were announcing something important. Parker watched as people everywhere began to stop what they were doing immediately.

"Attention all citizens of Dublin!" A female voice said over the speakers. "King Roland has announced an immediate gathering at the palace square. All citizens are required to attend. Please make your way to the palace square. Thank you all and many blessings."

299

Suddenly everyone around began walking toward the palace. Parker, Ox, and Grace joined in with the crowd that surrounded them.

"What's going on?" Grace asked.

"I have no idea, but let's just go with them." Parker answered. "They make for good cover."

People all over made their way to the center of the city. Shop owners exited and locked their doors while other people in the larger buildings also left in single file. It was highly organized as if they had done this gathering many times before. It was going to be a bit of a long walk, so Parker and the others just did what everyone else was doing to blend in. Once they reached the palace square, Parker and the others would need to find a way to get inside.

CHAPTER TWENTY-FIVE

Isaac had finally gotten the feeling back in his legs, making it easier for him to walk as Lao and a few guards escorted him and Eva down the palace hallway. Both still had their hands restrained as the guards guided them by the arms. They arrived at a large door and Lao stopped them before they could enter.

"Consider yourselves lucky." Lao said as he reached out to open the door. "He still has use for you."

They all entered the room where they could see Roland standing behind his desk holding the purple orb in his hand. The orb was glowing bright but quickly dimmed as he placed it in a box on his desk.

"At last." Roland said.

Eva was shoved into a chair sitting at the side of the room, while Isaac was forced right in front of Roland just on the other side of his desk.

"We finally meet in person."

"This moment isn't as great for me, as it is for you apparently." Isaac said.

"Just give it time my boy. This day will go down in history. You should feel honored to play such an important part of it."

"Do you not understand the pain you've caused me? The people I've lost over the years because of you."

"I do understand it completely. You have experienced great loss in your days, haven't you?"

"Yet you talk about it so calmly, like you have no remorse."

"You're right because I couldn't care less." Roland said with a smile as he circled his desk.

Roland quickly opened a set of double doors behind his desk revealing the beauty of the city to his prisoners. He motioned for Isaac to come closer but stopped him before he could set foot on the balcony just outside.

"I have worked hard to make this city what it is." Roland said. "It took a great number of sacrifices. Not from me of course, but it did take a great portion of my time. Go ahead, take a listen."

Roland closed his eyes as the voices of the people from the palace square could be heard cheering his name.

"These people have no knowledge of the crimes against humanity that you do on a daily basis." Isaac said. "If they did, they wouldn't cheer for you as they do."

"Which is why I have your brother to thank for that." Roland replied. "I commit the crimes, but your brother takes the credit. These people don't ask questions. Why would they? I give them everything they could possibly want, and in exchange they give me what I need."

"Slaves." Eva said.

"More or less." He replied. "They will do whatever it takes to protect a King that brings them comfort. I provide for them, and so they serve me without hesitation."

"You are a disgrace!" She shouted. "You use people, and you exploit weaknesses and force them to serve you. Just like you did with Steel. Just like you did with me! If these people knew the truth, they'd fear you and run!"

"Would they?" Roland asked. "You are right actually. If they knew the truth about me, they would flee in terror. However, many of these people grew up here, safe, and secure behind these walls. They know nothing of the outside except what I tell them. The truth is what I say it is. That's how it's been and that's how it will be."

Roland walked over to Eva and grabbed her by the jaw squeezing hard.

"I could kill you right in front of any of them, and they would cheer!" He said as he released her mouth. "I could simply tell them what an awful person you are. A follower of Parker Wallace, the man who haunts the outer world. Humanity at its best. They believe everything you tell them. It's quite incredible really."

"Then why don't you?" She asked in anger. "Just do it then! Toss me over the side and tell them how evil I am."

"Tempting, but I'll have to pass for now." Roland answered as he looked at a clock he had on the wall and made his way for the balcony. "We shall continue this conversation, but first I need to address my sheep. Oops, I meant subjects. So confusing I know." Roland said jokingly.

He then stepped through the doors and rested his hands on the balcony railing. The people below cheered and clapped at his presence. Down below, blending in with the others, Parker, Ox, and Grace watched as the people around them showed nothing but love for their King. Roland pulled a small microphone from the side and placed it on the railing in front of him. His voice boomed over the loudspeakers below.

"My loyal citizens!" He began. "Today is a glorious day!"

The people below continued to cheer until he began to speak again.

"Not only, do we live in the greatest city in the world, but we are doing the impossible. We have shown that we can survive on a cruel and hateful planet. Not only are we stronger than ever, but we are united!"

More cheers erupted at his words.

"I am happy to report, that once again my most trusted soldiers have destroyed yet another of our enemy's strongholds." He continued. "They quickly uncovered a plot against this city where the evil terrorist leader Parker Wallace, had been using Ash demons to enslave people and use them against us."

"It was Parker who saved us!" Grace shouted, but it was no use. The roar of the crowed concealed her words. Parker placed his hand on her shoulder and shook his head as if to tell her not to draw attention.

"For years now, this evil madman has tried day after day to destroy our city from the outside." Roland said. "His army making multiple attempts to breach our walls and enslave all of you, and yet again we have pushed them back!"

The crowd cheered and clapped at the lies they were being fed. Isaac and Eva shook their heads in confusion. Isaac suddenly tried to run out to the balcony and scream the truth to the people, but Lao quickly grabbed him and held him back forcefully.

"I am happy to say however, that soon we will have the means to fight this monster." Roland began again. "We are planning at this very moment, a way to rid ourselves of this terrorist threat once and for all. Soon it will be a reality."

Parker, Ox, and Grace couldn't believe their ears. This was why Parker was seen as such a threat, but for what purpose. He had certainly been a problem for Roland and his soldiers, but to the point of being a terrorist against the city seemed to be a huge stretch. The people around them were eating it up like candy. Every lie Roland spoke they took it as truth. Why wouldn't they? He was their leader. They had no idea he was stealing from people outside of the wall to provide for them, and they certainly wouldn't question the man that kept them safe and their bellies full. Parker couldn't wait for the opportunity to expose Roland for the evil monster he truly was.

"I also have some other unfortunate news to share with you dear citizens." Roland said as if he were wiping a tear from his eye. "I'm afraid that during our last skirmish with Parker Wallace, one of our most trusted captains was lost. Captain Steel was brutally murdered by Parker himself and his body burned just outside our city walls in a direct display of true horror."

Parker was shocked by the reactions of the people around him. They were simply ignorant of the truth. Was

WARRIOR FROM AVALON

Steel dead though? Did Roland have him executed and Parker blamed for it?

"Parker will be brought to justice." Roland continued. "We will track him down, along with his closest allies and we will bring him to face judgment before you all!"

The crowd clapped and praised Roland as they looked up to him with joyful cries.

"Now for my final words before I release you all to return to your glorious day." Roland said. "We have all known for some time now that my leadership was coming to an end. I'm afraid that day is coming soon."
Once again, the crowd began to protest with sadness.

"It is time that I pass my title on to someone else." He continued. "I have selected a successor to take my place as your King, just as I was chosen for you so long ago. He will lead you into a much more prosperous world and finish what I started. His name is Isaac!"

Isaac stared at Roland in confusion. Standing in the crowd below, Parker and Ox were also puzzled by the statement.

"King Isaac will continue my legacy, and I expect his rule will be just as appreciated as mine was. He will protect you just as I have. Under his guidance, I can tell you that this city will continue to thrive gloriously. I thank you all for my time with you. This is truly the greatest city of all because it has such wonderful people to populate it. Long live the King!"

"Long live King Roland!" The crowd shouted. "Long live King Isaac!"

"What just happened? Parker asked Ox.

It was then the radio began to speak once again in Parkers' pocket. He had also unfortunately forgotten to turn the volume back down.

"Crap!" He said as he reached for the dial.

305

Parker kneeled to hide in the crowd as he brought the radio to his ear. In his failed effort to be discrete a citizen standing nearby took notice. He could hear the soldiers on the radio clearing each gate. Parker looked at the citizen and shook his head.

"It's not what you think." Parker said softly.

"It's him!" The citizen shouted. "He's infiltrated the city!"

"No, don't!" Grace shouted.

"Parker Wallace!" The citizen continued to shout. "Parker Wallace has infiltrated our city!"

Above them, on the balcony, Roland couldn't resist a smile.

"This is too perfect." Roland said. "Grab them! Bring them to me!"

Soldiers appeared as the crowd scattered to get away from Parker and the others. No more than fifteen soldiers circled around them, each pointing long spears at them as well as pulse guns, giving them nowhere to run.

Only a minute or so later, Parker, Ox, and Grace had any weapons they were carrying removed, and their hands zip-tied behind their backs. They were immediately escorted to the palace interior. The soldiers shoved Parker and the others into the room with Isaac, Eva, and Roland. Lao sent all the guards away except for the four that had already been there.

"What a great surprise indeed." Roland said with a smile. "I couldn't have expected you'd be here this soon. This is too good. Parker Wallace finally here, in my presence. How did you like my speech?"

"You okay Isaac?" Parker asked ignoring Roland.

"Agatha?" Isaac asked, knowing the answer but hoped for something different.

"I know, I'm sorry." Parker said with tearful eyes.

"Where were you?" Isaac asked with a hint of anger.

306

"What?"

"Oh, don't be mad at him Isaac." Roland said. "He was only trying to save people from me. People like Eva here."

Roland walked over to Eva and pulled her hand restraints forcing her to stand.

"Eva was so brave." Roland said. "She really did impress me by her infiltration into Feng's compound. At first, I wanted to kill her for it, but I thought why not?"

"Let go of me." Eva shouted.

"I set her loose just for you. She's an amazing tracker and she was supposed to find you Parker, but it seems she tried developing a brain after I let her leave the city. My beautiful little decoy sent to distract you and figure out where all of you were hiding. I guess she thought she could outwit me, falsely exposing Feng as a traitor, but it didn't quite go your way did it little one? Feng was getting a bit too ambitious for his own good so no big loss there, but Eva, so conniving, that was a surprise even to me."

"You really did it?" Parker asked. "You led them to us?"

"It isn't her fault." Roland spoke. "She had the best of intentions until Lao was able to get her back on track. Didn't you Eva? Bring her in."

Lao stepped to the door and opened it allowing a young girl, no older than ten, with dark black hair and bright blue eyes to enter. Roland grabbed a dagger from his belt and cut Eva's restraints setting her free. She looked to Roland and then quickly ran over to the young girl.

"Annie!" Eva said as she hugged her. "Are you okay?"

Annie said nothing. Eva held her close. As she was about to make her way to the door Lao closed it once again.

"Not so fast." Lao whispered.

"Let us go." Eve demanded. "I did what you wanted me to do."

"Don't worry. You and your sister will be free to leave…" Roland said. "Once our business here is finished. Isaac here is about to ascend to the throne."

"You're dumber than you look if you think I'll do anything for you." Isaac responded. "I'm not falling for your tricks."

"None of you truly know the scope of what I've done. You've all been a part of this little game of mine for a while now, but I've been pulling the strings since before any of you were even a thought. In your case Mr. Wallace, that'd be both times you were born."

"Excuse me?" Parker asked.

"Tell me Isaac, do you remember that day twenty-two years ago?" Roland asked. "How about you Parker? Don't tell me you haven't thought about vengeance. Roland himself told me the whole story."

"What?"

Twenty-two years before Parker and Isaac stood in the same room as Roland, they were just outside the small cottage with their parents Frank, and Lora. Two young boys whose only worry was the deer Parker had killed hours before and keeping their hands clean before supper.

"Time to update our memories." Lora said holding up the camera.

"All right boys, stand up straight." Frank said as he reached over and dusted off Isaac's shoulder.

"You have something on your shirt Wally." Isaac said as Parker looked down only to have his nosed flicked. The four of them laughed as the camera made a click, indicating that it captured the moment.

"That's a keeper." Lora said smiling.

Then the sound of horses could be heard not too far away. Frank's smile disappeared in an instant. He grabbed the device from Lora and gave it to Isaac.

"Isaac, take your brother and head into the forest." Frank ordered. "Don't come back until after dark, or until I come to get you myself."

Isaac looked at his Father and Mother curiously.

"Go now boys!" Frank shouted.

Isaac grabbed Parker and their supplies and headed into the forest as they were told. Just as they were out of sight, Isaac stopped and turned back.

"What are you doing?" Parker asked. "Dad said to go."

"Something's wrong." Isaac answered.

From the bushes where they were hiding Isaac could see his parents and four soldiers on horses riding up to their cottage. As they arrived, only one man got down from his horse and walked toward Frank and Lora. Isaac couldn't hear their conversation, but he watched curiously.

"I've told you time and time again." Frank said sternly. "We don't want your help and we're not moving to your city."

"I only came to offer aid to her Frank, not you." The man said.

"She is my wife Roland. She doesn't belong to you and she never will."

Roland removed the helmet from his head and tossed it to the ground.

"We are meant to be together Lora." Roland said. "I am a high-ranking officer to the King. I could provide for you far better than he ever could. The city is safe and it's where you belong!"

"We were only together once Roland." Lora said. "It was a mistake."

"You don't mean that. Think about it! The city is the only form of civilized life left on this entire planet. Out here you'll live like a peasant, scraping for food in filth. You'll have nothing!"

"She made her decision!" Frank shouted. "Now I'd like you to kindly get off my land."

"Your land?" Roland laughed. "This land belongs to King Aiden!"

"Then tell your precious King Aiden to come move me himself." Frank said as he shoved Roland away.

"Stand down men!" Roland shouted as his men began to dismount from their horses. "You best not test me, or you'll soon regret it."

"Leave this place, now. You've no claim to it or anyone or anything here."

"Very well. I'll leave once she brings me our son." Lora's eyes widened.

"That's right!" Roland continued. "I know Isaac is mine Lora! We all lived in the same village before. It was when King Aiden recruited me, you and I were together that day! When I left for training and returned, that's when I learned that you had run away with Frank, to settle down out on your own. It wasn't long after I heard you were with child. I know that he is mine!"

"Frank is his Father!" Lora shouted.

"I think its past time you left!" Frank shouted. "All of you."

Roland breathed harder and harder as Frank continued to shove him back toward the horses. The rage built up deep inside his very soul until he could no longer restrain himself. Roland unsheathed his sword and in one quick motion, he thrust it deep into Frank's chest.

Lora screamed as she ran to catch her fallen husband. Isaac could see the whole display from his hiding spot in the woods. He was shaking in anger and fear but placed his hand over Parkers' mouth to stop him from screaming. Isaac knew he had to protect his little brother above all else. He grabbed Parker and turned him away from the violent act that just happened in front of them.

"Frank!" Lora shouted. "What have you done?"

"You love him so much?" Roland said as he grabbed her by the neck and strangled her with his bare hands until finally, he snapped her neck. "You'd choose him over me? Then you can join him!"

"Captain!" A guard shouted as he removed his helmet. A much younger Lao dismounted from his horse and rushed to the fallen body of Lora. Lao reached down and checked her neck for a pulse.

Roland snapped out of his blood rage and held up his own hands in disbelief at what he'd just done. He quickly turned to his men and mounted his horse.

"Put them in the cottage and burn it!" Roland ordered.

Lao and the other soldiers stood in silence for a moment. Roland could see their confusion and restraint.

"Your commanding officer issued a direct order!" Roland shouted. "Burn it!"

Lao nodded his head as he and the others did as they were told. Isaac and Parker watched in horror as the soldiers lit their home on fire and then vanished into the woods where they came from. Isaac was full of rage and anger. He vowed that one day he'd find Roland and kill him with his own hands. However, things hadn't gone the way Isaac had hoped. Years passed as he and Parker repeatedly disrupted Roland's activities once he had ascended to the position of King. They thought they had been annoying him to be sure, but it wasn't enough for Isaac.

Not long after he met Agatha, whom he told the entire story of his parent's murder. She had convinced him that revenge wasn't the way. Agatha had instilled a goodness in Isaac that he thought he had lost. It took time, but eventually, he forgot about his vendetta and settled down with her and focused more on his family and growing his own community. It was Agatha's death that brought all the pain and rage back into Isaacs' very soul.

CHAPTER TWENTY-SIX

Roland stood before Isaac and Parker, reminding them both of the day he had destroyed what their lives could have been.

"You're not my father." Isaac said in protest.

"Frank raised you, but it was Roland who gave you life." Roland said.

Parker watched curiously as Roland walked to his desk and opened the top drawer. He pulled out a small dagger, made completely of bone with a spiked handle. Roland held it tightly in his hand as he walked back toward Isaac.

"I am the one who orchestrated your parent's murder." Roland said proudly. "I sent Eva to find your little underground community, and it was I who ordered Lao to kill everyone there. Especially your wife Agatha."

"Don't you dare say her name!" Isaac screamed.

"Isaac, don't." Parker pleaded.

"Lao told me she begged to be sparred, that she showed every sign of pathetic weakness. Just like your parents did that day."

Isaac's rage was growing beyond his control. The four guards around them began to move toward him until Lao held out his arm for them to stand down.

"She was holding you back from your true destiny Isaac." Roland continued as he cut the restraints around Isaacs' wrists. "I had to get you motivated somehow." Roland placed the dagger in Isaac's hand.

"Isaac, he's baiting you!" Parker shouted.

"It's time to get the revenge that had been denied to you for so long." Roland said as he stretched out his hands, making himself an open target for Isaac. "Embrace your destiny and kill me."

Isaac held the dagger tightly in his hand. He looked to Parker who was shaking his head. Isaac gripped the handle as tight as possible and shoved the dagger deep into the chest of Roland with as much force as he could.

"NO!" Parker shouted.

As Isaac removed the dagger from Roland's chest, Roland himself smiled. Suddenly black smoke burst from the wound and circled around him and Isaac. The lights in the room flickered on and off with intensity. The smoke was so strong it was knocking objects off the walls and the desk.

"What's happening!" Ox shouted.

"I don't know!" Parker replied.

Isaac watched as the smoke seemed to have a mind of its own. He yelled as the smoke entered his open mouth until finally it was gone, and the room fell silent.

"Isaac?" Parker asked. "Isaac talk to me!"

Isaac took a deep breath and exhaled. He opened his eyes to reveal them to be a darker color than they once were.

"Isaac has left the premises." He said with a smile and his accent completely gone.

Lao stepped toward Isaac and kneeled before him.

"How are you feeling my King?" Lao asked.

"Like a whole new me." Isaac answered.

"Isaac, what's wrong with you?" Parker asked. Isaac stepped toward Parker and stared him in the face.

"Come on Parker, don't you recognize me yet?" He asked. "Look passed this image of your dear beloved brother, and straight into my eyes. Think hard."

It was the eyes that Parker found familiar. He saw them before as if it were from an old dream he once had. Or maybe it was more of a nightmare. Parker had a sudden memory flash of himself fighting a monster in a burning room. He could see clearly, the eyes beneath the flames. As he stared into Isaac's eyes, he could see those same dark colors yet again.

WARRIOR FROM AVALON

"When I heard that you were alive and well, here and now, I couldn't resist but to make you the most hated person in the country." Isaac said. "It wasn't part of my plan, but it fit so perfectly I couldn't help myself. Fate really did bring us together. It's just fortunate for me that I realized it before you. I should thank you for setting me free all that time ago. You remember, don't you?"

"It can't be." Parker said with a shocking realization.

"That's right boy. Now you see the real me."

"Roland wasn't working for you. You've been him the whole time?"

"Only since his first day on the throne. Before that, I was King Aiden and before him King Gazorith, and so on and so forth. You think I'd begin a kingdom, and then leave it for a human to rule? You're all so greedy and angry. Zeus should have listened to me a long time ago."

"Hades."

"What are we missing?" Ox asked Eva.

"I don't know." She responded as she pulled Annie as close to the door as she could.

"How are you here?" Parker asked.

"It's simple really." Isaac/Hades said. "When this all began, I started a fight to reclaim this world for myself. You were all flawed and inferior, but Zeus wanted us to leave this world in your uncapable hands. I for one couldn't stand it! All I could do was sit in the Underworld and watch as you all destroyed this planet as well as each other, and then the humans would die and pass on to heaven, the Elysian Fields, or my little corner of the Underworld. It sickened me to my very core. Why should you all have the privilege to live in eternal bliss, after all the chaos you create? So, I decided that if I wanted things back the way they were, all of you would need to be destroyed instead."

"Not as easy as you thought, was it?"

"I'll admit, I was surprised your kind could put up such a good fight. I realized that if I wanted to claim this world as my own, I would need to wipe out every last one of you, but even in death you are granted access to paradise, so I had to put a stop to that as well."

Isaac/Hades paced the floor in front of them as he continued. "It was Arthur who nearly bested me. We fought a great battle, and I nearly killed him in the process. He recovered unfortunately. He even made a deal with Zeus, the hypocrite, to imprison me on that forsaken island and destroyed my physical body, but little did he know, I had already made a deal of my own."

"What deal?"

"Arthurs' father, Uther, gave me his very soul and promised me the right to inhabit his bloodline."

"Isaac is a descendent of Arthur?" Parker asked.

"Indeed he is, as was his father Roland, his father Aiden, and Gazorith before him. That's the link to them all."

"This isn't happening."

"When you and I fought before, you set me free from that place, albeit painfully so. I knew long ago I wasn't going back to the Underworld. Thank the Ancients for that tidbit of information. I managed to find my way back to earth and have passed from body to body for well over one hundred years, building my kingdom, all thanks to this."

Isaac/Hades held up the dagger, covered with blood from Isaacs' hand. He set it on the desk to reveal four tiny, pointed spikes across the handle, which Isaac had poked into his hand during his rage.

"This is called the Gae Bulg." Isaac/Hades said. "It was made from the bones of Coinchenn, a sea monster from ancient times. By squeezing his blood onto this, Isaac made the same vow his ancestors did and surrendered his body to me."

"Unknowingly!" Parker said with scorn. "Bring him back."

"I think I'll cruise around in this for now. My vessel was starting to show its age after all, but this one should last me until the final hour."

"Final hour?" Parker asked.

"When that time comes, I will use the orbs power and let this world be torn from existence, and only my survival will be certain. Then I will remake the Earth to suit my purpose."

"You're insane."

"Too bad none of you will be around to see its greatness."

Isaac/Hades nodded to Lao who immediately unsheathed his sword and made his way in front of Parker.

"It still troubles me that you managed to show up yet again." Isaac/Hades said.

"What can I say, I'm persistent." Parker responded.

"When we fought before, I could have sworn I left you for dead, yet here you are. This time, I'll make certain you don't trouble me again."

Two of Lao's guards grabbed Parker by the arms and held him in place. Without hesitation, Lao took his sword and shoved it straight into the center of Parkers' stomach.

"No!" Ox shouted as he struggled to get free from one of the other guards.

Eva and Grace cried in fear and watched in horror at what was happening in front of them. Eva turned Annie's face away and was confused to see her sister was showing no emotion whatsoever.

"Where is all that annoying talk now?" Lao asked.

The pain was overwhelming as Parker dropped to his knees. He struggled to stay upright as he strained to pull free from his restraints. Lao kneeled in front of Parker and grabbed the handle of his sword, but instead of removing it, he pushed it in further in until the blade was sticking out of Parkers' back.

"Please stop this!" Eva shouted.

Tears began to run down Ox's face as he struggled to get free forcing one guard holding Parker to go assist the one holding Ox.

Parker looked down to see the sword in his stomach and could feel the urge to pass out. He was losing blood and knew he didn't have much time. Parker raised his eyes to see Lao kneeling in front of him with an evil smile across his face. With as much strength as he could muster, Parker forced his head forward slamming it into Lao's forehead knocking him to the floor. Parker then maneuvered his hands upwards behind his back, connecting the zip ties holding his wrists together with the blade of the sword sticking out of his back. The zip-ties snapped at the blade and Parker was free.

He was quick to his feet and painfully pulled the sword from his own stomach and turned around slashing the guard beside him in the leg and kicked him to the floor. The two guards holding Ox were distracted enough that Ox managed to head-butt one and jammed his foot into the others knee, knocking them both down. Parker rushed over and cut the zip ties from both Ox and Grace.

"Go!" Ox shouted to Grace as she darted for the door leading out of the room.

In the meantime, Isaac/Hades had ran behind his desk and pulled a sword from a sheath, ready for a fight. Lao was to his feet and charging at Parker, but Parker quickly put him back down with a punch to the face and a kick to the stomach. Isaac/Hades ran toward Parker with his sword ready to attack. Parker defended as best as he could against the strong attacks.

"You will not be the end of me!" Isaac/Hades said angrily.

"Maybe not today, but it is coming!" Parker responded as he shoved Isaac/Hades into the desk knocking him over. Parker was about to stab Isaac/Hades but stopped when he threw his hand into the air in defense.

"Strike me down, and big brother goes with me." He said to Parker.

Lao was just about to stand to his feet, but Parker turned around, took the sword and shoved it into Lao's leg so hard that it went straight through and into the floor trapping him in place.

"Down boy." Parker said as he pointed at Lao.

"We need to go now!" Ox shouted as he led the others into the hall.

Parker raced to catch up with them. Everyone fought their way through the interior of the palace, dispatching any guards that managed to find them on their way out. Parker was getting weaker by the minute, so Ox elected to put Parkers' arm around him and help him get out of the palace as he put pressure on his own stomach. Grace rushed ahead with Eva and Annie, finding a hovercar passing by. Grace stepped out in front of the car forcing it to a stop. Ox quickly pulled the driver from the seat and Grace jumped in behind the wheel. The others followed with Ox in the front passenger seat and Parker, Eva, and Annie hopped into the back of the car.

"I can't reach the pedals!" Grace said as she saw soldiers rushing out of the palace in pursuit.

Ox shoved his foot over to the drivers' side pressing down on the accelerator hard. The hovercar rushed forward quickly as Grace attempted to steer, crashing into signs on the sidewalks. The car jerked around as the magnetic field pushed the car away from other cars on the road. The car spun in circles as everyone inside held on. Finally, Grace managed to get her bearings and she steered toward the city gate they had entered from.

"Watch the barrier!" Eva shouted.

WARRIOR FROM AVALON

Grace steered the car around the barrier. Other cars honked as they rushed in front of them.

"I can see the gate!" Grace shouted.

Eva had placed her hands on Parkers' wound in an attempt to stop the bleeding.

"Annie, see if you can find something to cover his wound."

Annie did nothing. Eva turned to look at her to see she was still unresponsive.

"Annie!" Eva shouted. "I know you're scared, but we need to help him!"

"What's wrong with her?" Ox asked.

"I don't know." Eva responded. "She's completely out of it. She may be in shock."

"Take this!" Ox said as he tore off the bottom half of his trench coat.

Eva took the piece of cloth and pressed it hard against Parkers' stomach.

"Are you okay?" Parker asked softly, struggling to keep his eyes open.

"I'm okay." She answered. "I'm so sorry. He threatened to kill her, but I didn't know that...I didn't understand what was happening. I made a huge mistake."

"You could have told me."

"I thought I was doing the right thing. I should have.... I wish I could..."

Suddenly Eva was interrupted with a sharp pain in her back. She gasped as she reached behind her at the stabbing pain and found a dagger stuck into her back just out of her reach. As she turned to face Annie, she could see her sister's hands covered in blood. Parkers' eyes widened as Eva fell over on top of him. Annie's eyes met with his as she smiled.

"EVA!" Parker shouted.

Annie opened the back door and jumped from the car just before they passed through the city gate and down the road leading away from Dublin. In the distance behind them, Isaac/Hades stood on his balcony overlooking the city. He watched as the car sped toward the city gates. He stretched out his hand and could feel Eva's life-force leaving her.

"You're mine now." Isaac/Hades said with a smile.

Parker struggled as he removed the dagger from Eva's back. Ox set the car on cruise control and turned himself around in the front passenger seat to see what was happening behind him. Parker used the torn cloth and pressed it against Eva's back.

"What happened?" Eva asked confused.

"It's going to be okay!" Parker said.

The back seat was covered in blood, both from Parker and Eva.

"That doesn't look good." Ox said softly.

"What do we do?" Parker asked.

"Breathe my friend, you are no condition to panic."

"I have to save her." Parker said as his eyes struggled to stay open.

"Breathe Parker!"

It was no use. Parker fell over unconscious. Ox grabbed him and pulled him to the floor in the back and pressed his hand against Parkers' wound. With his other hand he placed his fingers on Eva's neck, checking for a pulse. Grace looked over to Ox as he removed his fingers and matched her gaze, slowly shaking his head. Eva was gone. Once they had traveled far enough away, Ox told Grace to drive the hovercar into a wooded area. The car immediately dropped to the ground as the forest had no repelling magnets to hold it up. The car slid through the trees until its momentum had slowed and rested against a large bush. Ox pulled Eva and Parker from the back seat of the car and placed them both on the ground not far away.

Parker had lost a lot of blood already and his face had grown pale.

"What do we do?" Grace asked in a panic. "What do we do?"

"I do not know." Ox answered.

Grace kneeled beside Eva and brushed the hair from her face.

"They had her sister?" Grace asked. "She did this."

"We need to get them somewhere safer."

Ox helped Grace place Eva on her shoulders. Eva was easy for Grace to carry, but she still needed Ox's help picking her up. Ox lifted Parker and placed him over his own shoulder. The two of them carried the others further into the woods as fast as possible. It wasn't far until they found themselves near a small lake and placed their friends down just a few feet from the water. Ox sat next to Parker and continued to check the wound on his stomach to find that the bleeding had somehow stopped.

"That is the strangest thing I've ever seen." Ox said.

He curiously turned Parker onto his side to check the exit wound on his back only to find that it had disappeared entirely.

"What is happening?" He asked looking at his fallen friend with great confusion. "I saw the blade go straight through."

Ox wasn't too sure of what was going on. Things had taken a strange turn from just a simple tyrant ruling over the city of Dublin to whatever that was back there. He couldn't make sense of the conversation between Isaac and Parker. Why did Isaac turn on them? What did it all mean? Parker knew more than he had let on. Ox never lost his trust in him, but what was he hiding?

The more he looked at Parkers' wound, the more questions he had. How was it even possible that he was healing so fast? Ox and Grace knew they had to watch over their fallen allies. Unfortunately Eva was already gone, and Parkers' life was seemingly hanging on by a thread. The two of them would have to wait to get the answers they needed. What they didn't know was that they had stumbled upon something much bigger than they had anticipated. Little did they know, their journey was just getting started.

Nimue stepped away from the screen as tears filled her eyes. Having watched the entire moment play out before her with no possible way she could help, was almost too much to bear. She could see Parker lying on the ground across from Eva's lifeless body. She stepped away from the viewing machine and left the room through the only door, but instead of entering the halls of Olympus, she found herself in the living area of her private home deep beneath a lake.

Nimue's house was round both inside and out and the colors were a teal mixed with dark green. There were no corners anywhere and a massive window adorned the wall with a clear view of fish swimming around just outside. Her furniture was dark blue with white bookcases on each end. In the center of the room was a medium sized round table with a large glass bowl sitting on top of it. She stood over it for a moment and placed both of her hands on opposite ends of the bowl. Slowly she submerged her face into water inside.

An image flashed into her mind. She saw Dublin in ruins. Isaac stood atop a massive pile of skeletal remains. He held a large orb in his hand that emitted the brightest light. In his other hand he held Parker by the back of his head, his face beaten and bloody. Isaac smiled an evil smile and smashed Parker in the face with the orb knocking him unconscious. Parker fell down the mountain of skeletons and landed at the bottom, his eyes drained of life. Isaac's body began to disintegrate leaving only a bright light. Once the light had cleared, Hades stood in its place in full grotesque form, massive in size. His smile full of sharp teeth and fangs. He held the orb in his hand, but now it is like a marble due to Hades enormous size.

"And then there was darkness upon the earth!" Hades said with a smile.

Nimue stepped away from the contents of the bowl and gasped for air as she fell to her knees. Her features were pale at the sight she had just seen, and she struggled to catch her breath, but not from the submersion. It was more from the shock of what may be to come. She gathered her thoughts and stood to her feet. The vision the Ancients had showed her, the one she had seen long ago had taken a turn for the worse. This new vision suggested they will lose the war, but she was determined that it would not happen that way. Parker was still her best hope at fixing the future, but it was going to be much more difficult than she had originally thought. She would not let Hades win no matter the cost.

"Until my dying breath."

To be continued in
WARRIOR FROM AVALON
BEYOND THE LOST SOULS

SNEAK PEEK

The city of Dublin was lit up beautifully as the sun had gone down for the evening. Most of the citizens had finished their daily activities and returned to the safety of their homes. Hades himself sat at a small square table in a medium sized dining area just outside of his palace. He had several guards standing at a distance around him as protection, not that he needed it. Lao himself limped as he made his way to a seat across from him. Hades used a knife to cut off a small piece of steak he had sitting on a plate in front of him.

"My King." Lao said.

"How is the leg captain?" Hades asked.

"Very well, I'm ready to return to work."

"That's good, but I need you rested and in fighting shape. Give your leg time to heal."

"Understood Sir. How is the new vessel working out?"

"The taste buds are slightly off." Hades said taking another bite. "Colors look a bit different as well. Nothing I can't get adjusted to. What's the report from the outer walls?"

"The search team found no bodies. There was no trace of the large man or the little girl either."

"And Parker?"

"Nothing."

"Well, they had to have taken the bodies somewhere. That wound you inflicted on him was fatal. He couldn't have survived it in any case."

"What about the other two?"

"What about them?"

"They are still out there. I could order another team...."

"That won't be necessary." Hades interrupted. "I have Isaacs' memories. Ox would be the one to fear, but he knows little enough to be a threat. Without Parker to lead him around, he'll probably go back to scavenging again. Now that Eva has been taken care of as well, I feel we can move along with my plans unhindered. Even now I can feel her presence in the Underworld. The other two are not an issue. I won't waste manpower on their capture. Unless they happen to show up again, forget them. We have bigger matters to attend to."

"With all due respect, the man they call Ox is a tough individual. The girl may be of no threat, but he could still be a problem."

"Are you doubting me Lao?" Hades asked glaring as he cut another piece of his steak.

"No sir. Say no more. Forgive me for overstepping." Lao said as he bowed his head and stood up.

"It's okay to remain vigilant just to be certain, but I've dealt with the main issues. We may have a lot of work to do, but your job now is to keep this palace secure and wait for further instructions."

"Absolutely my King." Lao said bowing his head once again. "What of Eva's sister?"

"The control I had over her worked like a charm, but now that she's served her purpose, I have no need of her. She'll regain her will back eventually without my influence."

"What shall I do?"

"Turn her loose outside the city, feed her to the dogs, use your imagination captain." Hades said continuing his meal with no real interest in the conversation.

"As you wish." Lao said.

Lao walked away from the table and made his way from the patio and into a courtyard area not far from there. Soldiers were standing at attention, going through the usual drills before heading off to their assigned patrols. It was just another night in Dublin, but now there was something else. A lingering feeling Lao had deep within himself. He hadn't expected to feel the emotions he had buried inside. His mind continued to replay the events that happened in his Kings office just the night before. He could hear the words of his master echoing in his head.

"You were all flawed and inferior, but Zeus wanted us to leave this world in your hands. I for one couldn't stand it!"

Lao had never questioned Hades intentions, but he had never fully heard the extent of his master's plan. The news of the earth coming to an end wasn't much of a surprise to him, but with his master's anger toward humanity, Lao wondered if his survival even mattered. Was he helping Hades to secure a place in the new world, or was he helping Hades to eradicate all mankind? Including him? He brushed off his thoughts. Surely in the aftermath of Hades' victory, there would be a place for him at his side. Lao glance up to one corner of the courtyard ahead of him. Annie stood motionless with a blank stare on her face. He walked over to her and kneeled down.

"Hello little one." Lao said.

Annie simply looked up at Lao, her tiny hands still covered in her own sisters' blood.

"Are you hungry?" Lao asked.

ABOUT THE AUTHOR

Henry Michael Kincaid is an up and coming American Christian author from the North Georgia Mountains. Since he was a child, writing and storytelling has been a great passion of his. His love for narrative driven video games and movies has sparked his imagination for years. Space epics and historical myths are some of his greatest interests to say the least. As a writer his dream is to create worlds rich with creativity that reach deep within the imagination of the readers, so that they can see the pages come to life in their own minds. His novels include the

WARRIOR FROM AVALON series, and with many more to come. In his spare time he enjoys being with his family, and his dogs. He also loves to travel, write, read, and immersing himself in anything that has a strong narrative.

AUTHORS NOTE

The story of Parker Wallace has been replaying over and over inside my mind for well over twenty years. It was in one of my English Literature classes that I was told the story of King Arthur and his Knights of the round of table. After the introduction of the legend himself I began researching everything I could on my own time. King Arthur was called the once and future King. While the return of King Arthur was my inspiration for the story, I ended up putting that idea aside to focus on characters of my own creation. I wanted to write about the myths and legends but put my own spin on it. The more I wrote, the more my own characters took a front seat in the story I wanted to tell. It has taken a lot of time and patience, writing, and reading, and writing more. This started out as a fun little project of my own but has grown into something beyond what I ever thought it could be. The story I want to tell has gone from one single short story to what may span over a series of books. I hope anyone who reads this enjoys it as much as I enjoyed writing it. There is so much more to come, and I can't wait to share this journey with you all.

THIS SERIES IS DEDICATED TO THE MEMORIES OF

My Father Henry Edward Kincaid
and my Grandparents
Maynard Wallace Kincaid, Doris Inez Hicks, J.L. Hicks, and Lorine Kincaid.
We love and miss you always.

SPECIAL THANKS

    I want to thank God for blessing me with this opportunity. Many times while writing this story I refused to believe it was my imagination alone it was coming from. Without God I don't think I would have the ability to put this together. I could only describe this as a creative gift that I'm being allowed to share. It is because of my faith and trust in him that I knew this is what I wanted to do. I also want to thank my wonderful wife Breelle Kincaid for her encouraging words and her motivation for me to follow my dream of becoming an author. Without her support, I never would have challenged myself to pursue this after over twenty years of waiting. There have also been several people who have encouraged me on this journey to bring my vision to fruition. Whether it was reading my early drafts or listening to me babel on with ideas, they have been a part of this in their own way. I want to thank each of them all as well.

My Mother Linda Kincaid
and the following awesome people.
Doug and Susan Williams
Auston, Michelle, Tony, and Sandra Davenport
Austin and Whitney Roberson
Lisha Martin
Kizzy Goodwin
Alisha Selvidge
Jeff Moyle
Tracie Cook

Thank you all for the support you've given me over the years, and I can't wait to share what comes next.

WARRIOR FROM AVALON

For more information and to stay updated on future novels in the WARRIOR FROM AVALON series, sign up for our newsletter at
www.warriorfromavalon.com